GRAVEMAIDENS

GRAVEMAIDENS

KELLY COON

DELACORTE PRESS

All rights reserved. Published in the United States by Delacorte Press,
an imprint of Random House Children's Books,
a division of Penguin Random House LLC, New York.

Delacorte Press is a registered trademark and the colophon is a trademark
of Penguin Random House LLC.

Visit us on the web! GetUnderlined.com

Educators and librarians, for a variety of teaching tools,
visit us at RHTeachersLibrarians.com

Library of Congress Cataloging-in-Publication Data is available upon request.
ISBN 978-0-525-64782-9 (hc) | ISBN 978-0-525-64785-0 (lib. bdg.) |
ISBN 978-0-525-64783-6 (ebook)

The text of this book is set in 11.5-point Adobe Jenson Pro Light.
Interior design by Ken Crossland
Jacket art and design by Sammy Yuen
Jacket art used under license from Shutterstock

Printed in the United States of America
10 9 8 7 6 5 4 3 2 1
First Edition

For my mom, who took me to the library.

For Matt, who took my breath away.

The Boatman's Refrain

The river is wide
The river is deep
I take their souls to earn my keep

The end of day
Is the start of night
I bathe in horror, bask in fright

Three queens of beauty
Maidens fair
I'll hide their souls within my lair

For the river is wide
The river is deep
I take their souls to earn my keep

CHAPTER 1

TODAY, THREE GIRLS would be doomed to die an honored, royal death.

A coil of dread wound itself around my guts at the thought, but I took a deep breath and focused on the little boy standing in front of me. Getting wrapped up in Palace rituals wasn't part of my duties, but healing a child *was*.

Especially when his cure meant food for my family.

"Open your mouth and say 'Ahhh' as if the Boatman were chasing you." I held his face, which was covered in crumbs. Probably the remnants of a thick slice of warm honeycake. My stomach rumbled, imagining the treat he'd likely enjoyed. Beneath the mess, his tawny cheeks were unusually pale.

"*Ahhhhhh!*" the boy screamed.

Smiling slightly, his innocence a welcome relief from my dark thoughts, I stuck the end of a spoon into his mouth to hold down his tongue, angling his head to the morning sunlight to see inside. Behind me, his mother hovered, smoothing her violet tunic and patting her hair, which was fastened into two neat buns above her ears. When she fidgeted, the gold chains looped around her forehead shimmered in the light streaming in from the window.

Despite the circumstances, it was nice to see that the mothers who had all the wealth in the city were no different from the mothers in my neighborhood who had none. When it came to their sick children, their hands twisted nervously in the same way.

The boy's throat was blistered white. I smoothed my hands over his bare back and touched my lips to his forehead to check for fever—an old healer's trick, since lips are more sensitive than hands. He was slightly warm but not worryingly so. The glands in his neck were swollen, as they should be with an infection, but this child would be able to fight it off. His muscles were strong, his reflexes good, his eyes clear. Unlike the children of my neighbors, he was undoubtedly fed daily with the freshest fruits and vegetables, the finest fish and meats. I swallowed my hurt at the inequity.

But it wasn't this child's fault.

"You're going to be just fine." I ruffled his silky hair.

"I am?" He popped his thumb in his mouth and sucked furiously, then withdrew it when his mother looked sideways at him with eyes outlined by thick strokes of kohl. "Are you sure?"

"Of course I'm sure!" I took his chin in my palm. "Why do you ask?"

"Because the Boatman comes when you're really sick." His lip trembled, and the thumb went back into his mouth.

I took his other hand in mine. "I'm sorry if I scared you when I mentioned the Boatman. The truth is, he's not so scary at all. He's a helper to the gods. Did you know that?"

The lie rolled effortlessly off my tongue.

He shook his head.

"It's true. The Boatman is just a man who lived long ago." I looked around the common room for something to add a note of truth to my tale. A carved-wood sicklesword, one that was, no doubt, modeled after his guardsman father's, sat atop a braided rug next to an emerald-colored floor cushion. "The Boatman used to be a *guardsman*. But now he's a helper. When you die, you pay the coin for your passage and the Boatman scoops you up, puts you into his rickety boat, and paddles you off to the Netherworld, where there are endless parties and games and honeycake forever and ever."

I squatted down to his eye level. "But he only comes if you're very, very sick—*which you are not*—or very, very old—*which you are not*, although you do *look* much older than you are with these big, strong muscles." I squeezed his little arm.

He giggled around the thumb in his mouth. Then his eyes grew serious. "Will Ummum be there in the Netherworld when I go?" He looked at his mother, who ran her clean, carefully tended fingernails down her arm. From the direction of the sleeping quarters, an infant wailed.

"Yes. Before you go with the Boatman as an old, old, old man"—the smile flickered again—"she will be there waiting for you with the biggest honeycake of all."

My throat constricted as I finished the story, but I forced the sorrow away with every bit of my strength.

I stood and turned to his mother. "Do you have any garlic?"

"Let me check with the servant." She called into the other room. "Hala?"

A girl my sister's age—maybe fifteen years—appeared in the doorway, holding the squalling infant in her arms. She was the child of one of my neighbors. Women of my stature often sent their unmarried daughters to be servants in other people's households to earn coins or food. "My lady?" she said, her eyes on her bare feet.

"Where is the garlic?"

"It's in the bin near the door. Shall I fetch it for you?"

"Why do you suppose I asked for it?" The woman crossed her arms over her chest. Hala dipped her head, her cheeks blazing, and retreated with the infant.

I took a breath, forcing myself to put on the mask of civility I wore daily when dealing with the ill and their families. "To help ease his throat and take away the infection, mix six crushed cloves in a flagon of warm water and bid him gargle with it."

She nodded her agreement. "He won't like it, but if it will help, we will do it."

"Yes, and it will have to be twice a day for three days. By

the end of the third day, if his symptoms persist, send for me again and I will bring a stronger tincture."

"Okay. Thank you, A-zu." She turned, as if to go.

"Oh, no, my lady. I am no great A-zu. My abum is the best healer in the city." *No matter what anyone thinks anymore.* "I am merely his apprentice."

"Well, then why didn't he come himself? Why did he send you?" She looked me up and down.

Why didn't I keep silent?

I stared at my dirty toes, encased in sandals that were two years too small. There was no easy way to answer her question. When my mother had passed away a moon ago, he'd lost his will to tend to himself, let alone anyone else. Not only had I taken on the tasks of running the household and caring for my sister, but I'd also been visiting his patients all over the city. As his healer's apprentice, it was my duty. Plus, we had to get paid.

"He was called away for an emergency, my lady, but I'd be happy to send him when he is back if you need him."

I was making a promise I might not be able to keep, but the coins were already in her hand. If she opted not to pay me, there was nothing I could do, and I had to take care of my family.

She blew out an exasperated breath, then looked back at her little boy, who was squatting on the rug, playing with the sicklesword. "Fine," she murmured. "Take this and be gone."

She dropped six shekels into my hand, pulling away

quickly, as if I were the one with an illness. I stuffed them into my healing satchel before she could change her mind.

"Thank you, noblewoman. I appreciate your generosity." I nodded once to the boy and then to Hala, who'd come back with the garlic and the red-faced baby. Right before I closed the door, the woman snatched the garlic from Hala's hand and yelled at her for not moving faster. I cringed, thinking of my own sister taking a scolding like that, as I headed quickly toward the marketplace. Thankfully, with the healing practice, I hadn't yet needed to subject her to a wealthy woman's whims. I shook my head at poor Hala's fate.

Such was life for those born low and for those like us, cast into poverty after the biggest regrets of our lives.

At least now I had the means to buy grain and could be out of the marketplace before three perfectly healthy girls were called upon to lie in the cold embrace of a dead ruler.

░ ░ ░ ░ ░

The Libbu, the marketplace that wrapped around the base of the Palace, pulsed as people from all walks of life streamed in and out of the main gates, buying, selling, and trading. Gold and crimson flags snapped in the breeze atop the merchants' stalls as sellers called out their wares: hand-woven linens, pots of spices, gleaming fish caught fresh from the Garadun and its tributaries that very morning. Young boys carried flapping ducks by their feet. Others tugged roped rams in from the farms. The aroma of sweet simmering spices—cinnamon, cardamom, cloves—filled my mouth with water as I walked through the gate.

It always felt distinctly alive in the Libbu, despite the fact that we were all supposed to be mourning Lugal Marus's impending death. As the ruler of our city-state, he was due the respect of our grief, and most believed he was due three Sacred Maidens in the Netherworld.

The ritual was supposed to be an honor.

But I knew better.

For a healer's apprentice like me, who knew the rigid terror that accompanies death for many people, it was not a day to be joyous. Three young women were going to *die*. They'd step onto the Boatman's skiff and shove off toward the Netherworld.

I shuddered, though the sun warmed the skin of my exposed shoulders. Those poor girls. They were likely thinking only about living in the Palace, basking in the riches and glory it had to offer. But when the lugal passed, they'd enter the tomb with him as queens, never to emerge on this side of life again.

No thought of those they left behind.

What made the town crier's impending announcement bearable was the knowledge that no one who lived near me in the huts along the wall would be selected, even though the choices were supposed to be based on beauty alone. For the past several generations, the daughters of the rich were always chosen, because their fathers could fill the Palace coffers with silver in exchange for the honor.

I took a deep breath and tried to focus on my mission: purchase food for my family, then get back home before the crowd thickened in the Libbu for the celebrations that would begin after the Maidens were selected.

A jeweler held necklaces of lapis lazuli and topaz under my nose as I drifted by his booth. I turned away, not being able to afford something so grand, and was nearly knocked off my feet by my closest friend in the city.

"There you are!" Iltani grabbed me in a fierce hug, and held me at arm's length. "Let's grab some barley and dates and head out to the fields to see that gorgeous farm boy of yours, Kammani. Get into some trouble. You can run off with him while I distract one of his field hands." Iltani raised her eyebrows and linked her arm through mine as we dodged a man holding a bleating goat over his shoulders.

Heat colored my cheeks as I turned toward her. "He's not *my gorgeous farm boy.*"

"Oh, please do not deny it. You're nearly betrothed." As we walked by a stall brimming with ripe fruit, Iltani plucked a green grape from a basket and popped it into her mouth, much to the merchant's annoyance. "And besides, you should be grateful he's still even considering it, since people like this one"—she nodded to the merchant woman, who was staring slack-jawed at us—"want nothing to do with you, despite your abum being the BEST HEALER IN ALU!"

"Iltani, be quiet!"

As I pulled her away, she eyeballed the merchant brazenly, as if daring the woman to say anything about her theft or her ill-timed comment. The woman didn't. Despite being born into a low social status, Iltani could get away with murder, because she looked more innocent than she was. Bronze freckles, like clay flicked across clean linen, lay across her small, upturned nose. Twin dimples appeared in her cheeks when she grinned, as she was doing now.

"Honestly," I told her, "you don't understand the wealthy like I do. You could be whipped for stealing. Or worse!" We wound our way through the crowd, sidestepping requests to purchase goods I could no longer afford.

"Well, if I were as lovely as Nanaea, I wouldn't have to steal, now, would I?"

"She's here?" My heart leapt. I hadn't woken my sister to say goodbye this morning before I'd left on my rounds. She'd been snuggled in our pallet, one arm flung across her face, the other curled against her chest. I'd pushed her damp, ebony hair off her cheek, considering it, but after the way she'd whimpered in her slumber the previous night, I'd let her sleep.

And then I saw her. She and two of her friends—new ones, since her old friends from the wealthy class wanted nothing to do with us after we'd been cast down—skipped along, trying on gauzy scarves and copper bracelets under the merchants' watchful eyes. It reminded me of how we used to play together, running in and out of the freshly cleaned quilts drying on lines stretched from home to home, draped in our mother's heavy jewels. I thought longingly of those days, free from worry. From heartache. I didn't care about the wealth they'd stripped from us when we lost our status, although our previous lives had been easier, for certain. Now I only wanted a day I didn't spend shackled by responsibility.

Nanaea, younger than I by only a year, didn't seem to be bothered by any of it in the least, except at night, when the nightmares overtook her. By day, she was still as free as a child. A child trying to live as though she still had the status we once did, wrapping scarves around her shoulders we couldn't afford to buy, trying bracelets on her arms she'd never wear in this lifetime again.

"Of course Nanaea is here. Do you think she'd miss the selection of the Sacred Maidens for anything?" Iltani brushed her hair off her forehead, leaving a smudge of dirt. I wiped it off with the back of my hand, doing my best to ignore the flippant way she'd talked about the announcement. No thought as to the terror those girls would experience when they were ensconced inside the black tomb with a dead body, forced to drink poison or be run through with sicklesswords. But I didn't blame her. It was a tradition almost everyone considered an honor.

Everyone but me.

I shoved away my somber thoughts as the stout town crier huffed by, a trumpet made from a tree root for amplifying his voice wedged under his arm.

The Sacred Maiden announcement? So soon?

I had to hurry. I turned toward another stall and, out of the corner of my eye, spotted a boy in the town crier's wake, wearing a stark white tunic with a clay tablet on his hip. A page. The young boy turned his face to the sun, and the breath caught in my lungs.

My brother.

"Kasha!"

He'd been taken from our home to live in the Palace after my father had failed to heal the lugal's son, who'd fallen from a Palace balcony and died.

It was fair punishment, everyone had said. A son for a son.

But it didn't *feel* fair. It felt like theft, a crime we couldn't do anything about. And although we hadn't been completely restricted from seeing him, as the years had passed, his responsibilities in the Palace, or a diminishing desire, kept him away from us more and more. I missed that little face. I waved to him, trying to get his attention, but he moved through the crowd after the crier, his shoulders thrown back as if he hadn't been stolen from his family and forced to fall asleep each night without anyone to sing to him. I quickly inspected a basket overflowing with lentils before my emotions took hold.

"Are you all right?" Iltani waved a gnat away from her forehead and squinted in Kasha's direction. "He didn't hear you, I think."

"I'm fine." I swallowed thickly. "I just need to be about my business and get back home. I don't want to be here when they call the Sacred Maidens."

11

"Well, good luck pulling Nanaea away from this crowd." She raised her eyebrows, then looked over my shoulder. Her smile widened into a grin I knew meant trouble. "Gods of the skies, my friend. Look who's here." She nudged me, and I turned.

Dagan, Farmer's Son, stood thirty handsbreadths away in his family's stall, bartering with a man over a barrel of wheat. He spotted us over the man's shoulder and sent me a brilliant smile. Over the past several years, I'd watched him transform from a scrawny child with ragged black hair to a thick-chested boy who was nearly a man.

I offered him a quick smile, then turned away, my cheeks flushing.

Iltani tugged me back around. "You can't avoid him forever, and why would you even want to? No one else of his stature is going to ask for your hand, and besides, look at him! You could build an entire Palace using the stacked bricks of his abdomen alone." Iltani plucked a stem of yellow chamomile from a cask full of water next to the lentils and tucked it behind her ear.

He was bare to the belt. Sweat clung like honey to the hard clay of his chest. I blushed furiously and forced my eyes elsewhere. The problem wasn't that I didn't care about him, because I certainly did. We'd played together in his barley fields since we were children, tying the grasses into chains and pulling each other around like mules at the plow. His mother had been friends with my abum growing up. Our eventual match was all but guaranteed.

And despite us losing our status, he—one of the wealthiest men in the city because of all the land his family owned—still courted me. I was supposed to feel grateful for the favor. Even Iltani said so.

But I couldn't *focus* on him. I had one mission and one mission only: care for my family. Today, that meant buying food for them and then getting back to the hut to help my abum make preparations for his patients, assuming he could gather himself enough to minister to them. Nanaea stood nearby at a merchant's stall with her two friends, giggling as the man made a dog perform tricks for her.

"Kammani," Dagan called, pushing his hair out of his eyes. "You can't pretend you didn't see me. I know that lovely face of yours all too well."

A smile tugged at the corners of my lips. I couldn't help it.

Iltani elbowed me in the rib cage. "Let's go over there. He has food to sell, does he not?"

"K!" Dagan called. "Come over to me. I've hardly seen you at all this past moon!" He reached up and tied his black hair into a knot with a leather cord.

At my nickname, I turned toward him and caught Iltani's smirk. "Why are you making that face?"

"Oh, I don't know. That blush along your cheekbones is telling me that you've been thinking of Dagan in a way that is not altogether wholesome."

I sighed. "Gods of the skies, Iltani. Silence yourself. Let's just go see what he wants." I did readily admit that seeing him wouldn't be the *worst* thing that could happen to me today, and Iltani was right. He *was* selling grain. I tucked a wayward strand of hair behind my ear and tried to smooth my worn tunic as we maneuvered to his stall.

He was stowing shekels in a bag on his hip as we reached him, and his eyes lit up like dawn when they met mine. His dark lashes accentuated the amber eyes I knew so well.

He nodded to me, then reached across the stall and took my hand. "Good day to you, Healer's Daughter." He brushed full lips across my knuckles, his beard, just beginning to thicken, tickling my hand.

"Such formality. What's the occasion?" I smiled, mustering all my resolve to pry my eyes away from his light brown skin and thick shoulders, corded and rippled from working long days at the farm.

"Can't even a bumbling fool like me have some manners in front of a beautiful woman? Two of them?" He nodded at Iltani but grinned at me.

"I award you three points for your efforts at flirtation," Iltani saluted. "Now serve us beauties some food. We're starved."

Dagan laughed, and my attention fell to the barrels of barley at his elbow, my stomach rumbling in response. I was about to ask for a fair price on them when Nanaea joined us, the copper from three glittering bracelets on her arm winking in the sun.

Where in the name of Enlil did she get those?

"Hello, Dagan." She flashed him a brilliant smile.

Iltani kicked me in the ankle.

"Nanaea, we're busy here, as you can plainly see." It wasn't that I was *jealous* of her stealing Dagan's attention, but her loveliness was beyond compare. Her hair, eyelashes, and brows were full and shiny, her teeth perfectly straight. Her cheekbones were high, like my father's, and her skin was tinged rose under her copper glow. Men practically broke their necks to stare after her as she went down the street, her hips and breasts curved in a way that made them long for her. I adjusted my healing satchel over my rather straight shape in response.

"Oh! I didn't mean to interrupt, Sister."

But the twinkle in her eye made me strongly suspicious that she did. She leaned across his stall, and her tunic draped open, exposing ample cleavage.

"Ahhh, Nanaea. How are you this fine morning?" Dagan studiously avoided looking down her tunic, staring into a basket of emmer wheat as if the mysteries of life could be found within.

"I'm fine, as always. Thank you for asking." She shot him a grin, smoothing a shiny curl away from her face. It didn't matter that she was dressed in rags. Her beauty needed no adornment.

"Nanaea was just leaving. Weren't you, Nanaea?" Iltani stared hard at my sister.

She blinked, wide-eyed, back at Iltani. "What did I do?"

"Don't play innocent with me," Iltani began, but I interrupted her. I didn't need any of this back-and-forth. I needed food, and I needed it now. My stomach ached with emptiness, and I was certain Nanaea was starving, too. She hadn't had anything to eat since yesterday afternoon, unless she'd gotten a free meal somewhere.

Dagan, busying his hands, scooped a flagon into a bucket of water, then tipped back his head and drank deeply. I watched his throat move with every swallow, wondering what it would feel like to lay my lips there. Heat rose to my cheeks.

He finished the last of the water and offered the cup to me. I shook my head.

"Are you so afraid to drink after me?" He smirked. "You've eaten mud right out of my hand before, so don't think of yourself too highly."

I smiled, remembering the day he was talking about. He'd dared me to taste the mud on the banks of the Garadun, and after I'd done it, I'd shoved a whole handful into his mouth. We'd both had grit stuck between our teeth for the rest of the day. "I'm not afraid of you. You know that."

His wide smile softened a bit. "It seems as if you are. You've stayed away almost this whole moon." He searched my eyes, his hurt showing plainly.

But how could I explain my absence? That the honor of our presumed betrothal felt a little like he was granting me a favor I hadn't really asked for? That my abum kept me so busy these days I was barely sleeping? That the reminder of those lazy days of just enjoying a basket of figs under the shade of a palm tree with him was like a knife in the gut when the weight of the world was crushing me?

I was spared the difficulty of an answer by a wealthy woman shoving past us to order some emmer, paying no mind that I was there to do the same. Filling a small linen bag with the grain, Dagan handed it to the woman, who dropped a whole mina into his outstretched palm. She turned and strode away but not before looking down her nose at us. I ignored the slight, but Nanaea's face fell. I squeezed her hand as my stomach growled loudly again.

"Dagan, can you give us a fair price on the barley?"

"Yes," Iltani piped up. "And add in a small—very small—sack of emmer, some honey, and maybe some of the watercress? You could toss in a few honeycakes as well." She grinned widely enough to show all her teeth. "For the privilege of serving us." She produced three shekels. Far too little for what she was asking.

Dagan scratched his beard, round eyes going back and forth between Iltani and me. "Of course, but you don't have to *buy* it. Don't be silly. My family is happy to give it to you."

I bristled. "Because we are lowly? And can't take care of our own?" My response came out sharper than I intended, the rich woman's disdain like a nettle under my skin.

Dagan stilled. "No. That's not what I meant."

"Well, what *did* you mean?"

"You are my—my"—he placed a hand over his heart, his face growing earnest—"my friend. And you *have* been forever. I just don't understand why you're upset with me. I'm trying to help."

"I know that. And I'm not upset with you." I sighed heavily.

17

"I'm . . . tired, I think." And as soon as I said it, the enormity of my exhaustion hit me like a fist. I wasn't just tired. I was *weary*. Too weary even for this conversation. "Dagan, I must apologize, but I have to go about my day. I need to check on my abum. Come, Iltani. Let's move on before the crowd thickens for the Sacred Maidens." I dipped my head away from the hurt in his eyes to find Nanaea studying me quizzically. I knew Dagan's intentions were pure. I didn't need her silent accusations. Nevertheless, it wasn't his job to support me or my family, even if he wanted to help.

Nanaea shook her head, her long curls springing out in every direction. Her hair was as black as my father's. I'd taken on more of my mother's coloring, with warmer brunette hair and golden-brown eyes.

"Who cares if someone gives you a gift? Isn't it nice not to have to toil away day after day for a change? Get back to a little bit of normalcy?" Nanaea asked.

"Is that how you got those bracelets? Someone *gave* them to you? What do you think the merchant will want in return, Sister? Nothing is free."

She knotted her brow in annoyance, then turned away.

She was so naïve sometimes. Then again, she hadn't been the one to instantly have to grow up when hearing my mother's last words.

Suddenly, the town crier's horn pierced through the Palace Libbu. Heads turned toward the sound. Faces all around me grew excited as babble grew in fervor. Merchants quickly closed up shop, dropping draperies across their stalls and sealing things up tight.

"It's time, Sister!" Nanaea squealed, grabbing my arm. Her two friends ran off and got lost in the crowd. "The Sacred Maidens are going to be chosen!"

I rubbed my aching eyes and sighed heavily.

Iltani nudged me. "At least it will be entertaining."

"Iltani's right. Come on. Have some fun for once in your life. We never get to do anything like this anymore! Don't you remember the beauty of our old life? How fun it used to be to attend festivities?" Nanaea bounced up and down, biting her lip. "The dancers will be there, and maybe even the fire throwers!"

"Fine." I couldn't take this away from her after everything else she'd lost.

"Well, not before you get this." Dagan scooped some barley into a bag, twisted it closed, and shoved it into my healing satchel before I could refuse. Iltani sent me a look that tamped down any argument.

He sealed his barrels of grain and stepped out from the stall. He wore freshly cut sandals and a crisp jade-colored tunic. He tied his money purse onto the belt at his waist, right next to a long, sharp dagger encrusted with emeralds at the hilt. No one would dare steal from him.

"I'll accompany you ladies if you don't mind a stinking donkey like me trailing after." He grinned, his teeth flashing white against his black beard.

"We shall be glad to have you join us," Nanaea murmured,

then she stumbled, *a bit too conveniently*, and Dagan offered his arm. She slipped her hand through his proffered elbow, wrapping her fingers around his muscle.

I let myself turn to stone.

"Sister?" she asked, tossing her hair over her shoulder and smiling back at me. "I think I will watch the bear perform after the announcement, if I may. He's so cute!"

"Do whatever you want, Nanaea. I'm not your mother."

Iltani sucked in her breath.

"I shouldn't have said that," I muttered immediately. But the words had been spoken, the pain inflicted.

Nanaea's eyes clouded over briefly at my words, but she turned away from me toward the crowds ahead of us. Dagan patted her hand, casting one long look over his shoulder at me.

Iltani linked her arm through mine and gave it a supportive squeeze. As Nanaea and Dagan walked away, his back rippling with strength, her shapely hips swinging, I thought that if anyone didn't know them, they might think that *she* was the sister on the verge of being betrothed.

And despite being a healer's apprentice, I didn't have a remedy for the ill feeling in my gut that accompanied the thought.

CHAPTER 2

THE CROWD SWELLED as we navigated around throngs of people, some arrayed in rags, some in jewels, to the center of the Libbu, where all official announcements—news of wars, festivals to come, and trade deals to keep the bands of mercenaries away—were made. Jingling their tambourines, a dance troupe in orange tunics shimmied for shekels in front of the pleasure house, where women draped in sheer fabrics peeked from the second-floor windows.

A gray donkey lumbered beside us, its back bowed with the burden of barrels marked with the crescent-moon insignia of Assata's Tavern, the hub for gossip and news in Alu. Assata and Irra, the owners, were friends of those of us along the wall. They always welcomed my father happily when he visited if someone traded him a bubbly sikaru or two for stitching up a cut.

I often went with him, and the smells of the place—old wood, spilled wine, cinnamon from Assata's cookies—brought me back to being six years old, seated on my father's knee, with Nanaea occupying the other. I remembered the joy I'd felt with my cheek against his chest as my sister and I laughed at his stories. We'd had our first drink of sweet sikaru from his cup, and he'd promised to continue to treat us to more as long as *we* promised not to tell my mother. Nanaea and I still drank the brew with extra honey and a pinch of cloves as he'd taught us, although we could rarely afford the treat these days. I shoved down the memory and wondered where he was. Probably slumped over a little table in the tavern, drunk out of his head.

Guardsmen in silver breastplates and greaves, impenetrable leather covers that strapped around their calves and forearms, carried maces and sickleswords, daggers and whips, to keep the crowds streaming through the Libbu gates in line. A scuffle broke out near the pleasure house, and one man landed a punch to another man's jaw before a guardsman backhanded them both to the ground. I winced, thinking of the broken teeth.

We followed a family with three girls arrayed in rainbow tunics and clattering beads, likely hoping for their names to be called, to stand near the cedar platform. White silks as big as sails stretched from beam to beam, providing shade to the town crier. My brother, Kasha, stood at the corner of the platform, chin up, eyes wary, poised to do the town crier's bidding, it seemed. He looked so much older. So *official.* My chest swelled with the barest twinge of pride.

Behind the platform, the Palace loomed large and golden, shimmering in the afternoon sun. Smoke rose from the blue temple at the very top of the four-tiered structure, a sign that someone inside was praying.

In a flurry of dust, a caravan of guardsmen and horses paraded down the road that led from the Palace's large central doorway. A luxurious sedan chair covered in flowy white drapery and golden tassels swayed as eight sweating men bore it slowly to the platform. A girl's somber face peeked out from around the curtains and then immediately retreated. It was Nin Arwia, the lugal's daughter and heir to the throne since her younger brother, the malku my father had failed to heal, had perished.

I'd met the nin once, just a few moons before we'd been cast out. We'd spent the afternoon together as my father healed a friend of hers. She'd been a quizzical, cunning girl, as curious about healing as I'd been about Palace life. But after her brother died and we were forced out of our home, watching our furniture and bedding and clothing and jewels taken in chests to the Palace for redistribution, I never talked with her again.

The nin's sedan chair came to rest in front of the platform, the men beneath breathing heavily from the weight they bore. Guardsmen swarmed around it as the curtains were shoved aside and a man leapt gracefully down, his broad silver breastplate with a carving of Enlil, our winged god, reflecting the sun. He had to be Ensi Uruku, the man in charge during the lugal's illness. His spiked mace swayed on his belt as he ascended the stairs to his sumptuous viewing box, perched high above the platform.

Then the nin disembarked from the sedan chair, looking as delicate as a reed growing on the banks of the river. Her knee-length black hair flowed after her like a banner. As she took in the crowd, she dipped her head, carefully steadying her headdress with one hand. Round pendants of lapis lazuli hung from her ears, and her slender neck was draped with copper necklaces encrusted with jewels, just one of which, I was certain, could have fed my family for an entire moon.

Once she was seated next to Ensi Uruku, the town crier, his big belly straining the fabric of his tunic, attempted to gain control of the crowd with outstretched hands.

Behind him, Kasha, a smug look on his face and scrubbed as clean as I'd ever seen him, shifted the tablet in his arms and came to attention.

I caught Nanaea's eye, nodded toward Kasha, then straightened my shoulders, pulling my features into a look of haughtiness. She snickered and elbowed me softly in the ribs.

Nanaea never held a grudge for very long, and her laughter quelled the nerves in my stomach at the thought of what was about to transpire. I looked around for my abum, then shook my head. He wouldn't have come, not with this many people around to point and whisper at the healer who'd failed the lugal.

When the crowd quieted, the town crier raised the trumpet to project his words to everyone in the Libbu.

"Women and men of Alu, I come to you today to honor a sacred tradition that has been passed down from generation to generation," the crier bellowed, his bushy eyebrows knit across a wide, flat forehead.

Dread wiped the smile from my face as excited murmuring spread across the crowd like wildfire.

The town crier held up his meaty hands. "*Silence!*" Behind him, two startled birds took flight from one of the cedar beams. "I am here at the behest of Ensi Uruku, Lugal Marus's second in command, and Nin Arwia, the lugal's daughter."

From their viewing box, the nin and the ensi stood briefly and raised a hand. Ensi Uruku leaned down and whispered something in her ear, and the wavery smile fell from her face. I leaned to the left, trying to get a better view past the heads of people in front of me as fear gripped my belly. The town crier held out a hand to Kasha. Struggling with the weight of the tablet, my brother handed it to him, then stepped back into place, his chin held high.

"Per Nin Arwia's wishes, and upon her advice, it is my duty to announce the selections for Lugal Marus's three Sacred Maidens. These girls will have the privilege of accompanying the lugal to the afterlife if he should pass. There, these Sacred Maidens will have the great honor of serving him for eternity. Before they go with the lugal, they will move into the Palace to prepare for their final journey."

Cheers and chanting broke out around me. Many women

held their hands up to the sky, praising Enlil with zealous fervor, while others danced, their faces masks of holy gratitude. Nanaea, lit up like a torch in the temple, joined elbows with her friends, who'd managed to find us. The excitement was enough to knock her sideways for at least the next moon.

The horror of it was making my hands shake.

From the platform, the crier raised the tablet with the inscribed names and squinted at the script. The crowd quieted down to whispers and shifting. Everyone wanted to hear. Iltani squeezed my hand with the strength of three men.

"Dear Enlil," I whispered.

"Yes, Enlil. Be merciful," Iltani said. "May the nin have selected girls who have no hope for a better life on this side of the Netherworld." She clutched my hand in hers. On the other side of her, Nanaea held clasped hands to her mouth in prayer.

They *wanted* to be selected.

"No, Iltani." I expected my sister to want the favor, but Iltani had some sense about her. "You don't understand. This isn't some honor." I lowered my voice when a wealthy woman who'd been shouting Enlil's praises looked at me aghast. "Whoever is chosen must cross the river with the Boatman. They'll be sacrificed for some stupid tradition and leave their families behind." An ache welled in my chest at the thought, and I swallowed hard.

She shrugged. "The good news for *you*, then, is that we'll likely be passed over. No one wants a societal castoff, or a dirty little rat like me. Besides, I'd rather have a couple of rich girls chosen for the sole purpose of getting them out of my hair."

"Iltani!" I couldn't believe she could *joke* at a time like this.

"What?" She grinned, and nodded toward the front, where the town crier was raising the trumpet to his mouth.

"And now, ladies and gentlemen of Alu. The names of Lugal Marus's Sacred Maidens!"

The crowd screamed and yelled and sang and danced. One woman near the very front threw herself at the town crier's feet in religious fervor and had to be dragged away by the guardsmen. He silenced the crowd again, and around me voices calmed, hands stilled, breaths slowed. He paused, waiting silently, his eyes taking in the crowd. Reveling in his moment of glory. Every eye in the place was fixed on his mouth, awaiting the words he'd utter next.

My own blood felt as if it were going to bubble up and burst from my skin.

And then the crier's voice cracked the silence in half. "The first Sacred Maiden is—Simti, Fishmonger's Daughter!"

My mouth dropped open in shock. She was *one of ours*! She did her washing along the river on the same day I did. I'd chatted with her many times. The crowd of my neighbors exploded into celebration while the nobility muttered.

Nanaea gasped in awe. "Can you believe it?" she squealed.

"No," I answered breathlessly.

Simti stood near the back of the crowd in a homespun

tunic that could barely conceal her womanly curves. Her eyes were a rich umber, her skin a burnished brown. Her black plaited hair fell to her shoulders. She looked frightened but pleased as she straightened her tunic and walked steadily to the platform to stand next to the town crier. A woman from the Palace court placed a flower crown on her head and golden beaded necklaces about her neck. A smile broke across her face as she waved to the crowd, and I understood their choice. She truly was beautiful. Extraordinarily so. I was still sure there wouldn't be another girl chosen from against the wall, although in my opinion, Nanaea's beauty outshone even Simti's.

Simti took a step to the side as the town crier opened his mouth wide again, this time not even using the trumpet to assist his booming voice. "The second Sacred Maiden is— Huna, Merchant's Daughter!"

Next to us, a group of wealthy women rejoiced, hugging each other, tears streaming from their eyes. A loud cheer came from a group of merchants near the back of the crowd, no doubt celebrating their success.

Huna, a girl with a bulbous nose and frizzy sable hair chopped below her shoulders strode purposefully to the front, a look of pleased shock on her sallow face as she passed through the crowd to stand next to Simti.

Iltani snorted. "Oh gods, she's a real beauty. I'll bet the Palace only chose her because her father is the richest merchant in the city."

"Is that one of the girls you wanted dead?"

"No, but she'll do." Iltani grinned.

She was absolutely terrible when she wanted to be. But her eyes followed Huna as she lowered her head to be draped in necklaces, and the wistful expression in them told me she wanted—at least with some small part of her—to have the honor herself.

"Let's hope they continue this trend of selecting the wealthy." Dagan walked behind Iltani, to come stand by me.

Nanaea's eyes followed his every move. "You're only saying that because you're rich, Dagan, and that isn't fair. Every girl should be eligible for the honor." She stuck her hand on her hip.

Dagan met my eyes behind her back, his lips compressed. He shook his head. "I never understood it, myself. We can't know for certain *what* lies beyond the grave." He shrugged. "It could be honor. But it could be emptiness. Or horror. We won't know until we cross the river ourselves."

Wealthy or not, it appeared he was on *my* side.

But he was the only one. In the crowd around me, eyes were clenched tightly in prayer, hopeful smiles plastered across faces. Girls clasped hands with one another in a circle, heads bowed, foreheads pressed together. Fathers danced their daughters around in circles while mothers sang into the air, praising Enlil for whatever was to come.

I strained forward, trying to see past others jostling for a good view themselves. Nudging around a man with a little girl on his shoulders, I managed to get a quick look at the platform. Simti and Huna, beaming, stood shoulder to shoulder, stooping from time to time to toss roses to the crowd from a dwindling pile at their feet. My little brother walked forward to hand a fresh basket of flowers to Simti, and when he looked up, his eyes landed on mine.

"Kasha!" I held up a hand, but he looked away, his cheeks reddening.

My stomach clenched.

That flush on his cheeks wasn't from embarrassment that I'd shouted his name.

It was the look he'd worn when my mother found out he'd traded one of her necklaces for a poorly carved toy catapult in the Libbu.

It was *guilt*.

He *knew* something.

The crier held his hand up one more time to quiet the chanting of the crowd. "Fine ladies and gentlemen of Alu. There is one more girl who will have the distinct honor of joining the lugal in the afterlife, should he pass." The crowd hushed as every face turned toward his booming voice like flowers into the sun. Without thinking, I reached for Dagan's hand and clenched it with all my might.

"The third and final Sacred Maiden is—Nanaea, Healer's Daughter!"

A collective gasp rose from the crowd as hundreds of faces turned to look at Nanaea. She stood, transfixed by shock.

But I—I couldn't breathe.

I felt like a fish at the end of a spear, gasping for air. This was a mistake. It *had* to be a mistake. The crowd swam in front of me, wailing and stomping, some in celebration, some howling in rage, their faces transformed by fury that our disgraced family had been given the honor. My knees gave out, and all of a sudden, I was being held up by a pair of strong arms. Dagan pressed his lips to my ear and said something, but I couldn't hear it. I couldn't understand.

The only thing I could see was my little sister, with her bouncing curls and blooming cheeks, turning to me, her face radiant with joy. She tugged me away from Dagan and pressed me to her warm chest, and I clung to her as if I were drowning in a raging river and she was the only one who could swim. Too soon, she untangled herself from my desperate embrace and floated to the platform to join the two other Sacred Maidens. Someone placed a flower crown atop her head and draped a long necklace around her fair neck. She stood on the platform, shining like a star in the heavens, blowing kisses to the cheering crowd.

When I found my voice, I could not contain it. "*Nanaea!*" I screamed, choking on her name.

But others screamed for her louder.

On the platform, she preened like a bird, twirling as if she were already a queen. She was vibrant. Glowing. Blossoming like a rose in the sun. In her mind, this was her chance for glory, and my neighbors in the crowd weren't helping. They drew near her like little moths to a flame, chanting her name and grasping her outstretched hands. For the briefest of moments, I allowed myself to admire how freely she could give in to her passions. She accepted moments of beauty when they came.

But I always saw the logic of things. And what Nanaea didn't realize was that, although she might end up a queen in the Netherworld, she'd have to cross to the other side in the arms of the Boatman first.

And there was nothing I could do to stop it.

CHAPTER 3

I SANK TO my knees, the feet of rejoicers kicking up sand around me.

"Kammani!" Dagan's strong arms pulled me from the ground and against the warmth of his body. I turned to stone as his round, bright eyes searched mine. "It will be all right, sweet. Nanaea will be all right. She *wants* to go—" He grasped for any words that might comfort me, even though he knew just as well as I did that nothing would really calm me. Not now.

It would not be all right. Nothing was all right. She was *my sister*. We'd shared a bed since she was born, both of us breathing as one as we drifted to sleep, her head tucked into the crook of my arm. We'd sat at my ummum's feet while she'd spun the pottery wheel, each taking a turn dipping our hands into the cool, gritty water. But since Kasha had been taken, our ummum had passed, and our abum had begun drowning her memory with the sikaru, Nanaea was the only person in my family I really had left.

And now the Palace wanted to take her away from me, too.

Iltani rubbed my back, scowling at Dagan. "This isn't the time, you clot. Clearly, the honor is not so wonderful for K! Her sister is going to *die*. And Kammani's already lost so much!"

My head swam with unshed tears. How was I going to explain this to Abum?

"I know." Dagan's voice rumbled against my ear. "I'm sorry. I wish the lugal hadn't gotten sick. Then none of this would even be happening."

"Well, no one can turn back time, so there's no use thinking that way. If Lugal Marus is going to die, then Nanaea is going with him unless we flee the city." Iltani dipped her head low and was chatting with Dagan about the possibilities of getting out—whom we could bribe, how much it would cost—when something she had said dinged in my brain.

I pushed away from Dagan's embrace. "What did you say, Iltani?"

"I said, I think that surely we could get a guardsman to work with us."

"No! Before that."

"I have no idea."

"You said, 'If Lugal Marus is going to die.'"

"Yes. What of it?"

"Well, what if he lives?" I pushed my hair back from my

34

eyes, looking wildly around the Libbu. The crowds were celebrating, heading toward the festivities near the gates, where musicians were already performing with songs and harps and tambourines. Nanaea and the other two Sacred Maidens, their eyes alight with the honor, were being carried on their cushions by the guardsmen. As Nanaea rocked unsteadily overhead, she threw back her head and laughed. Then her eyes landed on mine and she blew me a kiss.

Her naïveté sealed my decision.

"Are you all right?" Iltani grabbed my hands, my sorrow reflected in her soft eyes.

"Yes. Yes, I am. Because I know a way to prevent Nanaea from becoming a Sacred Maiden altogether." I rubbed my hands down the sides of my tunic. "I have to go. I have to go to Assata's."

"What are you talking about? For sikaru?" Dagan's voice was even. Calm. But there was no time for calm.

"No! Not for sikaru. Because *my abum* is probably there, drinking his life away. I have to get him. I have to tell him what's happened and make him go to the Palace." I turned toward Assata's Tavern.

"Kammani! Wait! Your abum is in no condition to go anywhere if he's been at Assata's." Dagan gently tugged at my hand. "And besides, he can't walk into the Palace and start making requests to save his daughter after everything that happened with the malku." He shrugged apologetically.

I wriggled my hand free of his and pointed to my temple. "My abum is brilliant. He is the greatest healer this city has ever seen. Even if we have been cast out, he could heal the lugal—"

"—but that doesn't matter, because nobody would let your abum near him!" Iltani tried to pull me into a hug, but I shook her off, hope surging through me despite her fears.

"I have to go. There's no time to lose."

"Are you even listening to me?"

"No, I'm not."

I took off for the tavern, and within moments, Iltani was at my side, rolling her eyes, disagreeing with me thoroughly, but as loyal as she could possibly be. I glanced back when Dagan didn't join us. He stood five steps behind, hands on hips, skepticism written all over his handsome face. Boisterous revelers streamed around him like schools of fish around a river stone.

"They won't listen to him anymore, my sweet. I'm telling you," he said. "Iltani is right. And—"

I cut him off with a hand. "Dagan?"

He lifted those amber eyes to mine.

"What kind of sister would I be if I didn't try?"

※ ※ ※ ※ ※

As we stepped over the threshold, entering the cool, shadowy interior of Assata's Tavern, Dagan's arm brushed against mine. The heat from his body seeped into my fingers, and I flushed from chest to cheek, chiding myself for such a foolish reaction when I desperately needed to find my abum.

36

Assata was one of the rare shop owners in the Palace Libbu to allow poor customers to drink her sikaru. I suspected it was because of her own humble beginnings, although she never liked to speak of her birth in Kemet, outside Alu. Her noble husband, Irra, had bought her the tavern, and she'd made it blossom into the busiest spot in the city, filled with people day and night.

I eased myself through groups of both rich and poor women and men, to a table near the back, where my father had been sitting day after day since my ummum had died. His stool was there, as were three empty tankards and a bowl with bits of braised lentils coating the bottom, but my father was missing.

Iltani edged past a man wobbly on his feet from sikaru. Behind us, a group roared with laughter as another man fell off his stool in a complete stupor. Assata's and Irra's guffaws were the loudest of the lot. Though different physically—Assata was little, wiry and strong, while Irra was round-cheeked with a big belly and a beard voluminous enough to swallow her whole—they could both shake the roof off the tavern with their laughter.

"Three sikarus, Assata!" Dagan called above the din of the crowd.

"I'll be over there directly, Farmer's Son!" Assata wiped down the bar, still chuckling to herself, then grabbed three tankards from the shelf behind her.

"I don't have coins to pay for a drink," I said quietly. "I barely have the shekels to cover the taxes." Plus, aside from the sack of barley, I hadn't gotten any food for the evening meal. And I'd probably need several rounds of tinnuru bread, as well, to help Abum soak up the sikaru.

"It's my treat. For both of you."

I clasped my hands together. "I don't need your charity."

"I know that." His eyes tightened at the corners.

"Oh, relax." Iltani snorted. "After the morning we've had, you need it."

One will not hurt. I am not my abum, after all.

We sat on the stools around the table, Dagan situating himself across from me, his knees grazing mine.

The sikaru would definitely calm my nerves, but besides the effect that too much of it had on my abum, accepting the gift bothered me because it was pushing me closer to an acceptance of the betrothal. Like I needed him to take care of me, when I had everything under control.

His mother already considered me a daughter of sorts, having a house full of sons but never a girl of her own. And I'd seen the way Dagan had been looking at me for the past year. His eyes landing softly on mine while we walked to fetch water. Or his hand lingering on my arm when assisting me into his cart. As for how I felt . . . my insides squirmed.

Sitting across from me, so easy in his own skin, he was certainly the most attractive man in Alu, and I'd never find anyone as kind, or as *willing*, as Iltani repeatedly reminded me, but I was already drowning in other responsibilities. The last thing I needed was a marriage and children while also trying to prevent my sister from skipping happily to her death and my father from drinking himself to his. Never mind the fact that I wanted to be a healer—and a great one, at that— more than anything in the world.

"Do you think she's seen your abum?" Iltani asked, pulling me from my thoughts.

"This is probably his mess." I nodded to the tankards at the table, which were promptly swept away by one of Assata's barmaids. "Do you think he'd go a day without sikaru? And she feels sorry for him and lets him run a tab, which is probably fifty minas at this point."

"It's a full talent and thirty more minas on top of that," Assata intoned as she clunked a tankard of sikaru in front of each of us, her cheeks flushed red under her warm brown skin. "And it doesn't need to be repaid anytime soon." She nodded toward my cup, sweeping a black braid away from her forehead with her forearm. "I added honey and cloves to yours."

"You remembered."

She winked. "Of course I did."

"Has he been here?" I took a sip of the sweet, bubbly concoction. It slid crisply down my throat.

"He has indeed. Damn near cleaned me out of the duck. He had three full bowls and then asked for some figs for dessert!"

"That sounds delicious. When you get one for me, fill it to the brim, if you'd be so kind." Dagan patted his flat belly, and my eyes wandered to the taut muscles of his abdomen. Heat crept into my face and I looked away, pushing all other thoughts aside so I could concentrate on the real reason I'd come.

"Do you know where he's gone? I need him to present himself to the lugal. I'm not sure if you've heard."

"Nanaea's been chosen. Yes, I heard." Assata stood, her serving tray on one hip, eyes soft on mine. "She's so beautiful—and so is that other girl. I'm not surprised, to be honest."

I nodded, my eyes falling to my hands. "But I need to find my father so he can go heal the lugal and stop this."

Assata raised her eyebrow at the comment. "Why would you want to do that?"

I sighed. She didn't understand. Nobody did. "Never mind. I just want to know where he is."

"He left out the back door and hasn't returned." Her lips pursed as she studied me. "You need some of this duck," she declared, changing the subject with practiced ease. "You look thin."

"It'd be my honor to treat you," Dagan offered.

Iltani kicked me under the table before I could protest.

"Fine." I sighed, my stomach aching with emptiness. Even if I wanted to refuse, I wasn't sure my body would allow it. "My thanks."

"Kammani," Dagan said. "I know you are searching for a solution here, but you know as well as I that your abum can't walk into the Palace and tell the lugal he can heal him." He looked pointedly at Assata. "Don't you agree?"

"Is that your plan, Kammani? Trying to heal the lugal? It's a noble one, because Enlil knows he's been better than my old ruler in Kemet." Assata shifted her serving tray to her other hip.

"Yes, Assata. If I can get him to heal the lugal, then Nanaea will stay with me." I swallowed roughly, fiddling with my cask of sikaru.

"Well, your abum *is* the best healer in the entire city. Everyone knows that, even if they've forgotten temporarily."

"Everyone but the Palace," Dagan said. "If they believed it, they would have sent for him already." He shrugged an apology. "Besides, the Palace *has* their own healer. Wouldn't he have tried everything by now?"

"He has a point." Iltani slurped her sikaru noisily.

I nudged her elbow so it slipped off the table. Mead spilled down the front of her tunic, and she laughed, spewing more from her mouth.

"Their A-zu is probably worthless, considering the lugal is dying," I muttered. "And my abum tries things that others do not! Even with the little malku." I lowered my voice. "He was as good as dead the second he hit the ground, yet my abum did everything he could to heal him for three days. There was nothing else he could have done."

"Sure, but people don't believe that. They think he failed," Dagan said, his tone apologizing for his words.

"Which is a *lie!*" I slammed my hand on the table, sloshing the sikaru from our cups and drawing curious glances from those around me.

Dagan reached across to touch me, thought better of it, and withdrew his hand into his lap. We sat, each of us lost in our own thoughts, sipping our sikarus, trying to work some way out of this mess. Assata left to tend to another table, then came back, lifting our tankards, wiping the spills from the heavy wood.

Dagan brightened and reached across the table. My hand disappeared inside his. "Kammani! Why don't *you* go?"

Iltani, Assata, and I all looked each other.

"Me?"

"Yes! Who else? Aside from your abum, you're the best healer in the entire city, and you haven't been tainted with failure as he has, either."

Oh. But I have. He just doesn't know. "Although your faith in me is sweet—"

"—and warranted," Dagan added, and pursed his lips. He knew what I was about to say.

"I'm not the best person for this job." I swallowed thickly. "I couldn't . . . risk it."

Under the table, Iltani squeezed my hand.

He blew his breath out. He knew he wouldn't win. We'd spent many turns of the sundial on his farm arguing over things, so he knew I was tenacious when my mind was set.

Then a thought occurred to me as Iltani waved to one of Assata's tavern maids for a refill, and I sat up just a little bit straighter.

"Assata—can you call for a messenger?"

"I suppose, but why?"

"If my abum can't walk into the Palace and tell them about all the people he has healed since the malku died, then a messenger could just spread the word in the Palace about his triumphs. How he, Shalim the great A-zu, may have made a costly mistake in the past, but he is incredibly skilled *now*. He's healed all of these hundreds of people *since*. Then maybe Ensi Uruku and Nin Arwia would hear the gossip and they'd call him in to help."

Iltani groaned. "This is an even worse plan than the one before. I love you, Kammani, but you are unmoored."

Dagan rubbed his chin. "I disagree. We know he personally wouldn't be believed, but if others were spreading the word about the people he's healed in the last few years, then the Palace may come to their own conclusions and call him back." Dagan nodded, sipping from his tankard. "It's smart. It plays to their arrogance."

Assata snapped her fingers just as Iltani opened her mouth to argue. "If that's your decision, then it appears we have the right person for the job, Kammani girl."

I turned as a boy with black curls, wearing a crisp white tunic and a self-sure grin, weaved around men twice his size.

"Kasha." My chest swelled with love for this boy. Although he'd failed to warn me about Nanaea's being chosen and had stayed away from our home of late, I couldn't help but forgive him. He was my brother.

I enveloped him in a hug, and a heady scent of incense

wafted from his clothing. Cloves, something smoky, and earth. I held him for just a little longer than he liked, and he wiggled out of my embrace.

"Aren't you supposed to be with the town crier? Will you be punished?" I held him at arm's length.

"No." He shrugged. "He gave me some time to myself. I thought I might come in here to see Abum, but he already left."

My heart squeezed as I took in his deep brown eyes and noble nose, the precise image of my abum stamped upon this little face.

"And what is this smell?" I demanded. "You're scented like the perfumer's stall."

"Sit, sit!" Dagan patted the stool next to him.

A bit of arrogance crept into Kasha's eyes as he lifted his chin and sat carefully next to Dagan. "I was bringing the Sacred Maidens their scents, Sister. They were given spices to wear before returning home to pack up their belongings. I had to run and fetch the bottles." He blushed, his skin flaming red. "I spilled some."

"Speaking of the Maidens," I began, "why didn't you stop by our hut to warn me that Nanaea would be chosen? Do you not find it terrible?"

"Because you'd have that scowl on your face, as you do now," Kasha answered, squirming under my gaze. "I knew how you'd feel."

I was certain he did. Nanaea was, after all, his sister, too. And he'd lost more than I. "It's going to be okay, Brother. I have a solution."

My words tumbled from my mouth as I explained his task while Assata flitted away to fetch us bowls of duck. She brought them back in no time, clanking the meals down in front of us. The meat, glistening in a sauce with braised lentils and topped with watercress, steamed into our midst, and we all dove in. I nearly swooned with the richness of the first bite and had to stop myself from devouring it like a wild animal. I hadn't had a meal like that in far too long.

Around bites, I prompted Kasha, who'd taken to chatting with Dagan about one of his little brothers at the farm. "So, what do you think?"

Kasha's eyes grew wary. "I suppose I can try," he mumbled, licking the last bites of duck off his spoon.

"Try? What do you mean, 'try'?" I wiped my mouth on a scrap of linen and folded it neatly next to my bowl.

"No one is going to listen to me, Sister." He settled the spoon carefully back in its bowl, then raised his eyes to mine. "Nobody does."

My heart ached for him then. But I couldn't let it get in my way. Emotions were terrible in that they kept you from what you needed to do most. "Maybe I didn't explain myself well. You don't have to convince anyone of anything. You kind of 'spread the word' about Abum and let them decide to call him on their own."

"No, *you* don't understand. It's meddling with business that doesn't include me. And that kind of thing can get a person whipped. Trust me." His eyes grew wary.

My heart thumped. *Has he learned that personally?* I

swallowed. "Yes, but my darling boy, can't you find a way to do it sneakily? You're one of the best talkers I know! You can do this!"

"Yes, but Kammani, the lugal is going to pass to the Netherworld. There's nothing I can do that will stop it. Besides. If Abum goes there and fails to heal him, he'll be put to death this time. There wouldn't be a third chance." Kasha swallowed thickly. I reached across the table and squeezed his hand.

His words hit me like a brick. I *couldn't* lose my abum. My mentor. The only parent I had left. Not after everything else that I'd lost. I tried to calm myself as I stroked Kasha's fingers. But there was no way my abum couldn't heal the lugal. He was too good. The malku situation had been an accident. And besides, wasn't Nanaea's life worth the risk?

I softened my tone, sensing my little brother's unease, and took both his hands in mine. "Kasha, we have to do *something*. We can't let Nanaea go to her grave without trying. You're smart, and the only one who lives at the Palace. Can't you try?"

Kasha shook his head. "The matter is done, Sister. I'm not going to put myself at risk when Nanaea herself wants the honor."

How was I going to convince this boy? This boy trying to be a man. He didn't have the foresight to realize that this was the only way to save Nanaea. Why wouldn't he see that I needed him to do this for us? Tears pricked my eyes, and I gritted my teeth. "Kasha, please. After everything that's happened, we are still family. That's what Ummum always said. We stick together no matter what. Why can't you *see* that?"

"Kammani, hey," Dagan chimed in, stroking my arm gently. "Ease up. Let him go."

"What?" I asked.

And then I looked down at my hands joined with my brother's across the table. I was squeezing his so tightly I could feel the little bones inside. My knuckles were white. I immediately let go but couldn't stop my hands from trembling.

"Sister! What's wrong with you?" Kasha winced, rubbing his fingers.

I stood, knocking over my stool. "I don't know." My head swam, and suddenly everything was too loud. "I'm so sorry." I reached for him, but he pulled away.

"Kammani, let's go. Let's get out of here and get some fresh air, okay?" Iltani's cool hands guided me from the table, and I found myself stumbling toward the door under her arm. Dagan stood, ready to follow me outside. Next to him, Assata placed a hand on his arm and shook her head. Panicked, I pushed myself away from Iltani and out of the dimness of Assata's tavern into the bright sunshine before the tears overtook me.

I stumbled to a bench beneath an olive tree and wilted onto it, my face in my hands.

Promise me—no more tears. Just—strength. You're the only one who can help.

The voice of my dead mother rang in my ears. I had to stay strong for Nanaea and take care of her. As the oldest, it was my responsibility. And besides, even if it weren't, I was the only one left who could.

Taking deep breaths, I forced back my choking tears as Iltani eased herself down beside me. When I looked up, I was collected, although the tears were thick in my throat. I stared across the expanse of the Libbu, where festivities were in full swing. Nanaea, Simti, and the other Maiden were dancing on the platform, surrounded by fire throwers and jugglers. A crowd danced at their feet.

"Kammani, I think your plans are a mess, but I am your friend and I will help you figure something else out."

"*I* will think of something else. It is not your burden to bear." I reached a hand over and squeezed hers. "I thank you for the offer, though."

"Well, you don't *have* to do it alone, you know. I'm here if you need me." She plucked a branch from the olive tree and stripped it of its leaves. "Kasha will come around. He's already been through so much, so he knows how bad it will feel to lose her." She smiled sadly. "And even if he doesn't, I'm willing to help you." A group of noisy young men already in their cups walked by, crowing at us both.

I turned away. "And I appreciate it. I do. But I'm fine. I'm going to go to the hut and think of what to do." There was a part of me that wanted to just pack my bags and flee the city with Nanaea—my mother had often told me stories of cities along the river filled with happiness, ruled by gracious lugals and sarratums who ensured equality. But Nanaea would put up a fight if I tried. She'd been practically glowing when she was selected.

"I can join you. I'm headed that way, of course." Her little mud-brick hut was four down from mine.

A twinge shot up my arms, and I glanced down at the white knuckles of my clenched fists. My nails were cutting into my palms. I let go and shook them out. "I'm going to go alone, if you don't mind. I'd appreciate your thanking Dagan for the sikaru and duck for me, though." In my current state, it would be better for me to cool down by myself. Collect my thoughts. Figure something else out so I didn't try to squeeze the life from the next person who opposed me.

"Don't do this. Don't shut me out. It's heartless, my friend," she grumbled as I stood. Nanaea danced on the other side of the Libbu, lost in her glory, completely unaware of the burden I bore. I brushed sand off my frayed tunic but didn't know why I bothered. It was drab, fraying, and nearly a year too short. Who cared if it was covered in dirt?

"I'm not heartless." I pinched the bridge of my nose, then dropped my hand. "I'm tired."

"And sad, but you won't let yourself grieve."

"Maybe," I said, looking deeply into her eyes. "But who has time to think about the past when my sister's future is at stake?"

With that, I walked down the pathway toward my hut to find my drunken father and a reason to keep holding on.

CHAPTER 4

THE CURVING, DUSTY alleys in the poor section along the wall eventually dwindled to the dirt path that led to my home. Reed ropes, stretched taut from one roof to another, held clean tunics, scarves, and coverlets as they dried in the sun. Children ran from hut to hut chasing squawking chickens while mothers a few years older than I called out of doorways for so-and-so to get back home.

My neighbors smiled or nodded as I passed. Some raised a hand in greeting. Most of the people standing with babies on hips, loitering in doorways, shelling beans around cook-fires, chatting, eating, breathing . . . living . . . had welcomed us into their neighborhood with open arms. They'd brought my mother business, scraping up coins for one of her lopsided clay casks. Watched Nanaea when my mother was occupied. Cobbled together meager meals after she'd passed.

Helped us.

I pictured myself as one of these women shooing their children from the fires. Would I ever be content that way? Heavy with child? Tending to the cookpot while Dagan threshed the wheat and penned the sheep?

That vision wasn't clear to me, even though everyone else could see it plainly. Even Abum, in one of his coherent moments, had mentioned that he'd like to settle the betrothal one day soon so he wouldn't have to worry about me.

As if he worried about anyone but himself these days.

But what about what *I* wanted? I kicked a stone and sent it skittering off through the sand into the reeds along the massive wall that surrounded the city. If I could picture my future exactly as I wished, I'd be a healer, living alone or with a man who understood I didn't want a brood of children to take care of. Or, worse, babies who died or girls who were put to death on a whim. Not I. I'd take care of all the people of Alu instead. I'd work throughout the city setting broken legs, healing breathing ailments, and tearing the sick right out of the Boatman's arms.

As I splashed water on my face and hands from the cistern at the door, a forlorn melody sung in my father's wavery baritone filled my ears.

Drunk out of his head, yet again.

I wearily removed my sandals and stepped inside. "Abum?" I blinked into the dimness.

He was seated on the floor on a pile of dirty linens, his hands covered in blood, crooning a lullaby.

"Abum!"

Rushing over to him, I knelt at his side. A copper dagger coated in congealed blood lay on a braided rug nearby. I knocked the knife away and grabbed his wrists. He continued to sing.

"She is fair, she is fair, she is lovely and fair—"

"Abum! What have you done? Where are you hurt?" I grabbed a clean linen from his healing table and dipped it into a pot of cool water on the floor, then wrung it out and wiped his hands and wrists to find the source of the bleeding. His left palm was gashed quite deeply from thumb to little finger. He'd need stitches, an astringent, and a pain tonic, too.

"What happened?" I growled as I took another fresh linen and wrapped it around the wound, knotting it neatly. It would have to do until I could blacken a needle and find some thread.

"There was a boil on the palm, and it had to be lanced."

"A boil?"

"Yes. A nasty one." His eyes rolled back into his head. "It had to be done, Ku-aya. I don't need your scolding now. You hear me?" His words were slurred. His eyes were slits. And he'd called me by my mother's name.

"You're a mess." I stood and rummaged through the pots and tonics on his healing table. I knew for a fact there was no boil. He was hallucinating or delusional or something. Maybe he'd gotten into the poppy. "And I need you to be sober. You have to go and present yourself to the lugal. He needs healing." I picked up a tonic, uncorked the bottle, and sniffed. Myrrh.

Perfect to ward off infection. I placed it in my healing satchel at my waist and looked for the feverfew leaves, which would help with the pain but wouldn't addle his mind any further. Now to find the needle. I poked around the various pots. My father mumbled.

"Did you hear me? Lugal Marus is dying, and you're the only one who knows enough to heal him." *Where is that needle?*

"She is fair, she is fair, she is lovely and fair—"

"Silence yourself!" I cried. "Where is the stitching needle? I know you were out at the coppersmith's today with his son. Did you take it there with you?" I took off my healing satchel and set it on the ground, rummaging through the contents.

Do I have it?

Nothing.

"Abum. Where is that needle?"

He mumbled something incoherent about the sleeping quarters and lay down on his side as I ran past the frayed curtain and searched everywhere. I threw dirty linens from the basket near the window. Pulled the quilts off everyone's pallets. Checked under the rugs and on top of the table.

Nothing. No needle.

Anger bubbled in my gut. I breathed deeply and went back out to the common room, then squatted in front of my father.

"I need to stitch you, so you can get cleaned up and present yourself to the lugal in the morning. Do you think you can do that for me?"

At that, he opened his eyes and a spark of lucidity crept into them. "Lugal?"

"Yes!" I clutched at his coherence with all my might. "Nanaea has been summoned as one of the Sacred Maidens. If Lugal Marus passes, she'll go with him. She'll die! You have to go and heal him!"

He pushed himself up to sitting, scratching his beard with his good hand. "Sacred Maiden? Nanaea?" His eyes grew puzzled.

"Yes. They're going to kill her if you can't heal Lugal Marus. Will you present yourself to him on the morrow? To try to save her?"

"*Marus?*" he suddenly shouted. He attempted to stand, swinging wildly, and knocked over a cooking vessel, which shattered on our hard-packed floor. He seethed, his face misaligned by old anger.

"Abum!" I scooted away from him, holding my tinctures to my chest. This wasn't him. He had always been kind. Gentle. I bit my lip as he raged, taking punches at imaginary enemies, cursing Marus's name, and weeping for Kasha. But he soon gave up. He plopped down heavily, muttering to himself. After a while, a slow, lazy smile spilled crookedly across his face and his eyes slipped back into their delirium, drowning in the forgetfulness of free drink.

"She is fair, she is fair, she is lovely and fair—"

I closed my eyes. Maybe my plan *was* naïve. If my abum couldn't even pull himself together for a few moments, what hope did I have that he could climb up from the depths of his sadness long enough to remedy the lugal? And if he failed, he'd die and everything would be infinitely worse!

I swallowed, unclenched my fists, and willed despair not to settle inside my bones.

After several moments, my father slumped against the wall, fell heavily to his side, and lapsed into the deep sleep of the stupidly drunk.

Behind him, pressed between his back and the wall, was a small leather sack. I recognized it immediately as his stitching kit.

"You aggravating man." I tugged it out and pulled on the drawstrings to open it. Nestled inside was the bone needle and a tangle of threads.

I took the needle to a candle and held it over the flame to sterilize it. Then I dipped the threads in the myrrh to clean them and threaded the needle with a steady hand.

My father flipped to his back in his sleep, and his left hand flopped carelessly to the side, blood already seeping through the bandage. I walked over with my supplies, sat near his head, and slapped his cheeks repeatedly.

He didn't even blink.

If only I could be so blissfully unaware.

Gently, I placed his hand on my lap and began unraveling the linen. I took the myrrh and rubbed it into his laceration, hopefully healing any bad humors inside, while he whimpered my mother's name in his sleep. I may not be able to heal the wounds her death had inflicted on his mind, but I knew how to heal the wounds on a body.

When I was certain he'd settled back down, I took the needle in my hand and stitched.

❦ ❦ ❦ ❦ ❦

Hours later, when the night sky was awash with twinkling stars, Abum was resting comfortably on his pallet in our sleeping quarters, and I was beyond tired, collapsed against the wall of the common room, sipping cool water from a flagon. I was at the point of exhaustion where reality and dreams seem to unite.

After stitching his hand, I'd scrubbed our home from top to bottom, boiling clothing and linens and hanging them to dry, scrubbing every filthy cookpot, and beating out rugs. I'd arranged the contents of his healing table in groups according to use—tinctures for sores, breathing elixirs, tummy remedies—and had managed to scrounge together bits and scraps of food to go with the barley from Dagan into a semi-decent vegetable stew, which I'd forced, repeatedly, down my father's throat. After taking a little for myself, I left the rest bubbling lightly over hot coals in the yard for Nanaea when she returned home from wherever she was, and now I was contemplating the reason that Enlil, the god of our skies, would take a perfectly healthy mother from a perfectly decent man and her children.

Just as my thoughts turned grim, Kasha, his brown eyes round with excitement, burst into the common room, startling me from my thoughts.

"Kasha!" I clutched my chest. "You terrified me! You can't barge into our home without announcing your arrival. You're liable to get a blade to the throat!"

He was breathing heavily, a tablet tucked under his arm. "I couldn't help it. You have to read this. You're not going to believe it!"

"What is it?" I stood, reaching for the tablet. Maybe the Sacred Maidens were being released! Or the Palace had changed its mind about wanting impoverished girls as Sacred Maidens!

He placed it gently in my outstretched hands. "It's from Uruku and Nin Arwia, Sister. It's for Abum. Read it." His eyes were lit from within. "I ran all the way here from the Palace to give it to you the second it came from the scribe."

I quickly scanned the tablet, which was still damp from the engraving.

> *Shalim, A-zu of Alu:*
> *This is an official notification of Lugal Marus.*
> *Do not delay in reporting to the Palace with your*
> *healing remedies at first light. Instructions will be*
> *given to you upon arrival.*
> *Sacred Maiden Nanaea, Healer's Daughter, will*
> *be retrieved from your home two days hence.*

It was sealed with the insignia of the king: a lion with three ruffled roses adorning its neck.

"He's summoned Abum to heal the lugal. He can save Nanaea!" Even though I'd asked it of him, I couldn't believe that Kasha had managed to accomplish such a task so quickly. I pulled him to me fiercely, kissing the top of his curly head.

"How did you do this, you wonderful boy?" I asked, my voice trembling.

Just then, a thought flickered to life inside me: if my abum saved the lugal, he would not only save my sister, but he could also restore some of his own reputation. As hope flooded my chest, a large shape stepped into the room, blocking the light from the cookfire outside.

"I went to the Palace with him." Dagan cleared the threshold and ducked inside.

My hand fluttered to my throat. "You did?"

"I wanted to speed things up. If he only spread the word around, it might be too late for the lugal. The Palace needed to know how good your abum is, *now*. I requested an immediate emergency meeting with Nin Arwia and Ensi Uruku. We provide the grain to the Palace, so they were apt to listen to me. I could, if I wanted, withhold the harvest. Starve them."

"Oh, Dagan, what did you say?"

He laughed. "Nothing so threatening. They know it, though." He cracked his knuckles. "I spoke the truth. I said they needed to reconsider Shalim. That he's the best healer in the city. And that his daughter, Kammani, is a close second."

"You said that?"

"Of course I did. You are. You're the best healer, next to your abum. Even my ummum says so."

His mother was a practitioner of herbal medicine herself and, when necessary, could be relied on for the basics.

"Nin Arwia argued against it at first. She said she wasn't sure she could trust him. But Ensi Uruku thought maybe they could give him a chance. He called a scribe to give the order, and she stamped her approval." He shrugged. "Besides, I wanted to do everything I could to help save Nanaea."

"And I thank you. I do. For—doing that. For helping all of us. My family." My shoulders sagged in relief.

Dagan took my hands in his calloused ones, rubbing his thumbs along my palms. "Kammani, you are my family, too. You know I think of your family as my own."

"She knows it, Farmer's Son. She knows."

We all looked toward the sleeping chambers. My father stood, leaning against the doorway, his hair awry, his eyes bloodshot but a little clearer.

I handed him the tablet. He didn't look at it.

"I heard. When am I to leave?"

"At first light," I whispered.

"Then I'd better rest. Kammani, my daughter, will you pack my things?" he asked hoarsely. "Leave some pots for yourself; you'll have to see to my regular patients while I'm at the Palace."

I nodded quickly. I was doing it already anyway. "So you heard us talking about Nanaea? They're coming for her in two days. You understand what's at stake?"

"Of course I know what's at stake," he whispered, his eyes filled with such torment, the anger I'd felt toward him earlier melted away. Then he stumbled, bracing himself against the doorway. "More than you know." He disappeared into the other room. A moment later, the candle was snuffed out.

The three of us stepped out of the stuffy common room

into the freshness of the night. Kasha squatted near the cook-fire, poking at the coals with a stick. Seeing him there like a normal little boy with his family was a balm to my spirits. He'd have to return to the Palace soon, but maybe if my abum managed to heal the lugal, Kasha could come home. I dared not even think it. Hope is a wonderful, terrible thing. It can make you long for things you have no possibility of gaining.

A group of girls, Nanaea included, were shrieking and laughing around a blazing cookfire halfway down the street. She'd returned home halfway through my housekeeping, hugged me tightly, then bounded over to Simti's hut to celebrate, oblivious of my worry. Her wild curls stood in every direction as she giggled and pranced around, decked out in scarves. She pivoted her hips and rotated her belly like a snake while her friends fell over each other in laughter.

The heat from Dagan's body as he stood, transfixed by Nanaea's alluring movements, was the nudge I needed to say my goodbyes. "Well, I suppose I'll see you on the morrow." Quickly I headed toward my home.

"Kammani."

My back stayed turned.

"I'm sorry," he said gruffly.

"For what?" My shoulders felt tight. Stiff.

"For Nanaea."

I sniffed. "I don't give three figs about you gawking at my sister over there. You're free to stare at whomever you like." The words were harsh, I knew. And probably more than a little dishonest.

He laughed softly. "Oh, sweet, I wasn't looking at her. Really. I mean, I was, but more—absently. And I apologized because I'm sorry that she's been chosen."

My face flushed. "Oh. Well. Thank you."

Behind me, his presence loomed large. He took a step closer, and my whole body responded. Tingles ran up the nape of my neck.

"And I'm sorry about your ummum, too."

The ache to melt into him was overpowering. To give in to the strength of his arms for one second and be a girl again, not someone who had to bear the weight of her family on her shoulders. The need for it was so strong, I could feel my resolve giving way.

"And for your abum, who is so sad and angry, he doesn't know what to do with himself. I'm sorry you're going through all this."

It wouldn't do to encourage him. I couldn't give him the life he wanted. A family. A soft place to land. I had to stay too strong to be that for him. He rubbed his hands down my shoulders. I bit my lip. Hard.

"It isn't fair, Kammani, what's happened. Please. Will you look at me?"

I turned around to face him, but I refused to meet his eyes. He ran a thumb down my cheek. "And I'm sorry I stepped in when you didn't want me to. But I'm only trying to help you."

At that, I backed away.

"I know, Dagan, but I can *do* this. I am managing fine on my own."

He rubbed his beard. "Are you really?"

I stood up straighter. "Yes, as a matter of fact, I am."

"Good. Then I don't have to worry."

"Well, I'm glad that's settled. So if you'll excuse me, I need to go fetch Nanaea before she wakes up all of Alu." I turned and strode purposefully toward the gaggle of girls.

"Kammani?" he called behind me.

"What is it?" I turned.

"If you ever do need help, you know I'm here, right?"

"I know. I've always known."

"And I would not fail you. Ever. Not in our lifetimes." His words were almost a question. A recommitment to the betrothal offer, maybe. His eyes were filled with such hope, I had to close that door.

"Goodnight, Dagan." I softened my words with a hand over my heart.

Around mouthfuls of stew that was *supposed* to be for Nanaea, Kasha whistled long and slow, then laughed uproariously when I glared at him. "Mind your business, Brother."

Dagan pressed his hand over his heart, then turned, whistling an off-key tune, and disappeared into the fields toward the flickering lights of his home, so close and yet so far from my little hut.

CHAPTER 5

NANAEA PILED HER springy black curls atop her head and smiled at her reflection in the cracked washbasin outside the doorway. The sun, standing high in the sky, didn't seem to bother her a bit, but I was already worn down from the heat and the rounds I'd made in the morning—my own as well as my abum's, which I'd been covering since he'd left for the Palace yesterday.

After scrubbing himself behind the hut, Abum had dressed in the tunic with the fewest stains—one that would have been tossed into the beggar's bin when we used to have wealth but now was the nicest he owned. He'd combed and oiled his black hair and beard, then nervously packed and repacked his healing satchel with remedies and tinctures. His hands had shaken, and more than once I'd found him guzzling a flagon of water, probably wishing to the gods it was sikaru.

He'd pulled me aside and kissed my head, then held me

to his chest before he'd left. I'd clung to his torso, despite the morning heat. Eventually, he'd pried my arms from around his waist and told me he wouldn't fail our family—not again, not *ever* again—and that he'd be a better man and would restore my faith in him and change the minds of those who thought him less of a healer than he was.

This was his chance for redemption, and he wouldn't waste the opportunity.

Then he'd left, and I'd done everything in my power not to go straight to my pallet and weep, praying to Enlil that my abum would be able to heal the lugal, hoping he'd be received warmly.

Despite the tears thick in my throat, life had moved on, just as it always did, and pressed me into service. Earlier, a little girl seven houses down had been ailing with a fever. The mother and I had bathed the child, and I'd given her some althea seed tea to clear up the rattling cough. She'd been resting peacefully, only slightly warm and much more content, when other patients had clamored for my attention. I'd stitched a young man's arm after he'd slashed it wide open in a tavern fight, and drained an infected lesion on an old woman. Then I'd checked a young woman's belly, as she was due to deliver her child any day and the midwife was busier than ever.

"What do you think of this look?" Nanaea said, frowning into the washbasin, the sunshine casting a golden glow over her thick black curls.

"I think it's fine." I tucked a tincture for moon-blood cramps into a knapsack she'd take with her to the Palace.

The guardsmen were due to come for her this morning, and Nanaea had left all her packing to me, as if she were already a sarratum married to the lugal, with people to do her bidding.

She snorted and let her hair fall down around her shoulders. "Don't be jealous I'm to be a Sacred Maiden, Kammani." She puckered her lips and pinched her cheeks for color. "It doesn't suit you."

I sighed. "I'm not jealous, Nanaea. I'm just worried about what's going to happen to you."

"You can tell yourself that, but I think you're envious."

"I'm certainly not."

"Why are you being so mean to me, then?"

I barked a laugh, wiping the sweat from my brow with the back of my hand. "I'm not. I'm worried sick about this entire mess, and you know better than anyone that sometimes my worry comes out wrong."

"Yes, like meanness and jealousy. Just like you were jealous when you were a girl and Ummum would take me to the Libbu with her and you had to stay with Abum."

"I *wanted* to stay with Abum! I was learning how to heal. What were you doing? Learning how to spend shekels? Good use you've been making of that skill in the last four years." I folded one of her worn tunics and shoved it into her knapsack.

My stomach rumbled. I'd had barely enough food to scrape together a meal for Nanaea this morning before I'd left, and a few bits of bread to feed myself. I was going to have to barter my healing services for food again if I didn't collect the shekels half the city owed my family. Although it would only be me here for a while, since both my abum and Nanaea would be gone. The thought of staying in the hut alone—with just my memories—was impossible.

Maybe Iltani would stay over.

"You can say what you want. I know you envy me. But I want you to know that I don't blame you." She plucked a bud of yellow chamomile from a bush my ummum planted years ago, held the flower to her nose, and breathed deeply. "It is *such* an honor."

"Gods of the skies, Nanaea. Will you listen to yourself? I honestly don't understand why you think dying is an *honor*." I swatted away a horde of gnats trying to make me their morning meal.

She held a hand to her chest, her eyes wide open. "It isn't *dying*. It's stepping over into new life." She primly turned back to her reflection and piled her hair again on her head, pulling a few tendrils free around her face. She let half of it fall and pinned the front back with silver combs she'd somehow tricked someone into buying for her.

In truth, though, it wouldn't matter how she prettied herself. Nanaea had been blessed with a beauty that surpassed everyone. Even though she'd come of age just a year ago, men of all classes—even the noblest in the city—had been hounding my father at every turn for a chance at her hand. Now the Boatman's hand was the only one she'd be able to accept.

She stood, tightened the belt at her waist, and fastened a crown of yellow chamomile on her head.

"You look nice," I admitted begrudgingly.

Her face softened, and she blinked quickly. "Thank you. I mean that."

Around us, folks were going about their daily business. Shrieks and laughter floated in the air from Simti's home from time to time. Just then, Simti stepped out of her hut and waved a bright yellow shawl over her head at Nanaea, who answered with a smile and a quick wave of her own. They were both so excited to get to the Palace. I was praying with everything in me that my abum was already well on his way to healing the lugal. Surely two days would be all he'd need if he'd been welcomed with kindness.

I wondered what Abum had already done to assess the lugal's health. He'd likely listened to his chest, felt his belly, checked the lifeblood flowing through the passages in his arms. Lifted the lugal's eyelids and made certain the pupils dilated appropriately. Checked for bedsores and asked whoever had been caring for him about his fluid and food intake.

I wished my abum had sent word through Kasha of the steps he'd taken yesterday, but I hadn't seen him since the day Nanaea was chosen. I sighed, stuffing the last of Nanaea's precious few possessions into her bag. I'd hear from him soon.

"There. All set."

Nanaea looked quizzically at the knapsack I'd prepared for her. "Kammani, they aren't going to have me walking around the Palace in all these ratty clothes. I'm certain I'll be getting an entirely new wardrobe, complete with a jeweled headdress and carnelian earrings and gold necklaces. You wait. You will not even be able to recognize . . ."

The words weren't out of her mouth when we heard murmurings and then shouts coming from down the road. I pushed my hair out of my face as I jogged lightly to the pathway to see what the commotion was about. Kicking up dust as they directed four magnificent white stallions around the huts and hovels of my neighbors was a group of four guardsmen from Lugal Marus in their shining breastplates. Two of them wore leather necklaces with what appeared to be finger bones dangling down from their throats. Trophies from a past battle? I winced at the thought.

Maces hung on their belts, along with sickleswords and daggers. Their beards were cropped short, to their chins, except for one with black wavy hair, who was shaved clean. As their horses picked their way down the path, their armor and weaponry clinked and clanged like bells.

"They're here!" Nanaea squealed, racing to my side. "I had no idea they would send *four guardsmen* all the way here to pick us up. Can you believe it?"

I certainly could. They'd sent eight when we'd been cast out.

She squeezed my arm and danced around, like she had as a little girl when she'd gotten a taste of her first honeyed fig. We'd all cried with laughter at her antics. She'd whirled and shrieked and run from one end of our neighborhood to another. It hit me then how important a task my abum had taken on. She *was* just a child, still. She had no idea what she was getting into.

From Simti's hut, at the end of the dusty pathway near the wall, there was a flurry of excitement. Her mother, father, and siblings hustled out of the house and hugged one another as they stood, ready to hand Simti off to the guardsmen. But when the men reached her hut and Simti stepped out shyly, her parcels and bags tucked neatly under an arm, the guardsmen didn't even pause. Their eyes remained resolutely forward.

Right toward us.

Nanaea's smile wavered for a moment, and then it popped back brilliantly. "They must have a kind of *order* for the Sacred Maidens. Perhaps they want to pick up the most desirable first!" She squealed again and ran back down the little path that led to our hut, then disappeared inside. I followed, and she emerged a moment later with my mother's river-blue shawl draped over her elbows. The guardsmen were two huts away.

"Nanaea, no. You can't take this with you." I lightly tugged it from her arms. It was all I had left of Ummum. My father had burned my mother's things the day after she'd passed, but I'd managed to hide this before he'd cast it in the fire. If I smelled it deeply enough, I could make out the faintest scent of her skin. Nanaea sometimes wore it around the hut, but I wasn't letting it get any farther than that.

"What? Of course I'm taking it." She grabbed it and held it away from me.

"Give it back, Nanaea. You don't know what you're doing."

"I know exactly what I'm doing, Kammani. I'm taking this with me! Do you think she'd want it here in our old hut when it could be in the Palace with me?"

"In the *grave* with you, I think you mean." I made a move for the shawl, but she jumped back, out of reach. "Nanaea, give it to me, or I swear by all that is holy . . ." I didn't have time to finish. A jangling of weaponry and bridles coming to a stop gave me pause.

Nanaea stepped forward, wrapping the shawl over her elbows again as one of the four guardsmen dismounted and ambled the short distance to stand in front of our cookfire.

It was the clean-shaven one. He was taller and leaner than he'd looked astride the horse. Black curls fell to his chin. Like everyone else of the wealthy class, he lined his warm brown eyes with kohl, but against his tan skin, it served to accentuate his thick lashes.

"Kammani, Healer's Daughter?"

Nanaea stepped forward, a dazzling smile plastered across her face, no doubt struck by the man's good looks. "I think, kind sir, you mean 'Nanaea, Healer's Daughter,' and I am she." She curtsied with practiced grace, the lessons from our old life serving her well. "I'm ready to go to the Palace."

The guardsman looked back to his comrades, still on their horses. One of them handed him a small tablet. He uncertainly ran a finger over the markings, licking his lips in concentration.

Behind him, another guardsman snorted. "Can't you read it?"

"Can you?" The young guardsman tossed the tablet into the dirt, his face reddening in embarrassment. "It doesn't matter what it says anyway. Ensi Uruku said to bring 'Kammani, Healer's Daughter.'"

Nanaea stood to attention, confusion on her brow. "There must be some sort of mistake. I am Nanaea, Healer's Daughter, one of the Sacred Maidens. *She* was not chosen." She pointed at me, as if any of this was my fault.

There was no way they could have mistaken the two of us. Yes, some considered me pretty. Dagan did, and I wasn't completely immune to the eyes I often felt following me around the city, but as far as looks went, Nanaea won. Easily.

"Let's see what this says." My throat was nearly nicked by a quickly drawn sicklesword as I stooped to pick up the tablet. The young guardsman was poised to kill me.

"You have not been invited to touch the lugal's property." My hands shot into the air.

"I'm—I'm sorry," I sputtered, holding my breath lest I accidentally brush against the gleaming edge. My hands shook as I swallowed my terror.

I met his narrowed eyes above the sicklesword as his cheeks flushed. Breathing through the panic trying to claw its way out of my throat, I tried to think logically. His embarrassment was making him aggressive. I needed to boost his ego to get him to stand down. While Abum was healing powerful patients, men who'd been in the lugal's court, he often acted more deferential. He said that sometimes people needed to *feel* as if they had power, even if they were completely at your mercy.

So I stooped even lower and turned my face up beseechingly. "May I stand?" I asked.

His eyes flicked over my face. I read the indecision, but slowly he regained his confidence. "Yes," he answered, "but do not touch Lugal Marus's decree."

I stood and backed slowly away with my hands raised as he pointed the sicklesword at my breastbone. My heart fluttered like a bird trying to break free of its cage.

"Why do you want to have it?" he asked. "A girl like you?" His face was genuinely confused.

"Yes, sir, I am but a simple girl, sir. But," I added, raising my eyes to meet his for a moment before letting them fall to the ground, "I can read it. My abum is a great healer, and he taught me to read so I could understand the tablets on herbology and practical medicine. And maybe, if none of the other guardsmen can decipher it, I can try so we can sort this whole thing out so you're not facing Ensi Uruku's wrath when you return."

"Nasu. Let her read it," one of the guardsmen called. "It's better than having our heads lopped off."

The guardsman's jaw worked as he thought about it. "Fine." He let his arm fall. "Quickly."

"Yes, sir." I scurried to retrieve the tablet. I brushed the sand from its surface and trailed my finger along the etchings.

To the family of Shalim, A-zu of Alu:

    This is an official notification of Lugal Marus.

    We regret to inform you that Shalim, A-zu
of Alu, has died. Kammani, Healer's Daughter,
apprentice to Shalim, is to report to the Palace with
healing remedies at once. Instructions will be given
upon arrival.

And something snapped shut in my chest. In my brain. The weight of the words refused to take root. They drifted there, in the periphery of my consciousness, like a ghost. The tablet dropped from my hands to the ground, cracking in half on impact. The world about me ceased to be. There was just the blurry shape of the white horses stomping in the dirt, the thumps resonating as if through water.

"Kammani! What are you doing? What does it say?" Nanaea stooped to pick up one of the broken pieces, but Nasu urged her away.

"You do not have permission, girl. Do not touch the decree." He turned to me. "Kammani, Healer's Daughter. Tell us what it has said."

I heard what they were saying but could not focus on their words. My head was filled with rushing water. I was removed, floating somewhere far above, as if someone had taken my soul out of my body and sent it into the Netherworld. I was gone. I couldn't feel. I couldn't think. I couldn't do anything.

Nanaea's voice grew anguished. "Kammani! What's wrong with you! What does it say?" She angrily grabbed my shoulders. "Look at me, Sister. What has gotten into you? When am I to leave for the Palace?"

But her face was a blur.

Just then, Nasu, his sicklesword again unsheathed, stepped close. He brought the gleaming blade up and held it to my throat.

His face came into focus. The powerful reserve in his eyes. The beads of sweat trickling down his hairline. "What is the message? On threat of death, Healer's Daughter, tell me or I will do my duty."

"Go ahead and do it, if you are so brave." Part of me almost wanted him to.

He blinked, startled. "What did you say?"

"Go ahead," I whispered. One swipe of his blade and I'd be free of every single worry that had crowded my mind lately. I'd see Ummum again. Abum. And I wouldn't have to bear witness to my sister's death.

"This is your last warning."

"Kammani!" Nanaea screamed. "Tell him!"

She trembled, her hands over her mouth. Her terror snapped me back to my good judgment. I couldn't leave her or Kasha when they both so desperately needed my help. And although I knew it wouldn't make a difference if I said the words out loud, somehow it seemed as though it would.

"Abum is dead." I let the strange words roll off my tongue. For something so completely absurd, the phrase was easy to say.

"Oh no, Kammani. Oh no, Sister. No. It isn't so." Nanaea

dropped to her knees, sobs immediately racking her shoulders. I watched her, curiously. I felt nothing. Not even despair.

I looked at Nasu. "How did this happen?"

Nasu's arm slowly lowered, until his sicklesword rested at his side. He sheathed it, then spoke. "I don't know."

"Did they kill him for failing in some way? Did he . . . miss something? The lugal is still alive, isn't he?"

"Well, yes, but—"

"Then what?"

"I said I do not know." He raised his voice over Nanaea's sobs. "Did the tablet say anything else?"

Nanaea rocked back and forth, her hands in her hair. On her face. Ripping her tunic. Simti and her family ran down the street toward us, as did Iltani, her face twisted with the promise of bad news. They must have heard Nanaea's cries.

"Yes," I offered. My mouth felt numb, my hands useless at my sides. "I'm to report to the Palace in his stead."

Iltani reached me, breathless from her jog, her round, furious eyes searching my face. "Kammani. What's happened?" She took my cheeks in her warm hands. Looked back and forth between the guardsman and me and Nanaea. "What happened to her?" Her upper lip rose like a dog's on the attack.

Nasu ignored her. "And you're to take his place because—?" he questioned.

"I'm his apprentice." I laughed lightly, because nothing made sense anymore. "And I guess I'm the best option they have? I don't know."

"What happened? Tell me," Iltani begged.

"He's dead." It still didn't make sense. What could have happened to him? He was just here two days ago.

"No. Your abum?" Iltani clapped her hand over her mouth.

I nodded once, and she engulfed me in a hug. I absently patted her back as she murmured into my hair and rocked me gently back and forth. Simti, her family, and other neighbors converged on our yard to comfort a howling Nanaea. From behind Iltani's strong embrace, Nasu backed away.

"We'll be back for you in one hour." He pointed to Nanaea. "And for her and the other Maiden. Pack your things."

He mounted his mare and clicked his tongue, and the four guardsmen trotted off, weaving around the crowds that had gathered at our home to offer comfort, a handful of shekels, a basket of fruit.

These were my people. They'd give everything to help one man's family. And I'd have to leave them—the mother about to give birth, that young girl with the racking cough—to save a lugal who wanted to kill my sister and two other perfectly innocent young girls because of a tradition likely started by a man too afraid to pass into death alone.

There wasn't a choice, though. Family was family. It was a message that was my mother's constant reminder: No matter what, you take care of what's yours. No matter what, you stay strong and you take care of those closest to you. Even though we were now orphans and I was about to be completely alone, except for Kasha, who wanted little to do with me.

Even though it was now up to me—solely me—to fix

everything. Everything. I held my hands to my cheeks and focused on breathing so I didn't run down to the river and throw myself in.

A group of women held Nanaea, rocking her back and forth, singing a dirge to Enlil. They begged for grace, and their music seemed to soothe her. She hummed along in broken refrains, wiping her nose and her eyes. But beneath their dirty, shifting feet, totally forgotten, lay my mother's river-blue shawl, discarded like an old rag.

For the first time since hearing that Nanaea had been chosen, I truly felt like letting her go straight into the arms of her torturous fate. My anger surged to the surface with unrelenting force.

"*Nanaea!*" I shouted.

Iltani's arms fell from around me. "What's wrong?"

I pointed at the rumpled shawl as Nanaea brought tear-filled eyes up to meet mine. "Sister?" she asked, her lips trembling.

At the despair in her eyes, I softened my tone. Pushed down my hurt. "Pick up Ummum's shawl so it doesn't get ruined."

And at that, I turned and disappeared inside my little home, a place that used to bubble over with laughter and light, a place bereft now of any joy.

CHAPTER 6

⬥

THE THRONE ROOM, tucked into a corner of the Palace, was surprisingly cool, considering the sizzling heat of the afternoon. After a bumpy ride on horseback, during which Nanaea, Simti, and I had clutched the guardsmen we rode with in sheer terror, Nasu had taken Nanaea and Simti, dazzled out of their heads, to a courtyard, where they were met with flowers and necklaces and a parade of servants.

I was grateful the fanfare would distract her from her grief. I'd barely been able to kiss and hug her before she was swept away in a cloud of perfume and I was escorted to a small, bare room to await Nin Arwia and Ensi Uruku. I'd asked Nasu a dozen times when I'd get to see Lugal Marus to begin ministrations—time was of the essence, I'd explained—but I was left to languish until Ensi Uruku and Nin Arwia were ready to see me. Finally, after I'd chewed most of my right thumbnail down to a nub, I was led into the most magnificent room I'd ever beheld.

As a girl, I'd never have any chance to approach Lugal Marus or his ensis in his throne room. I could make no plea, I could not yet be judged, I had no say. Hence, I'd never seen such tapestries and fixtures. Torches of gold embedded with jade and lapis lazuli lit the room with a soft glow. Plush woven rugs stitched with all manner of birds, vines, gods, and goddesses lay on the sandstone floors. Frescoes covered the entire ceiling, and the throne itself was solid gold, glimmering with an unearthly sheen in the flickering light. A small pool to the right of it teemed with speckled silver fish, lazily swimming in circles in the gurgling water pouring from a small tube in the wall. The miracle of running water would have fascinated me had I not been shaking so much it was difficult to stand.

I'd been ordered to remove my sandals, so the lush carpeting tickled my toes in a startling way as, flanked by Nasu and another guardsman, I walked silently into the throne room. The other guardsman had a cough he could not silence. Was it the beginnings of a breathing plague? Or maybe a cough from the blossoms on the trees? I'd have to lay my ear to his chest and look at his throat to be certain.

But eventually, the moments fell away and the ensi, Nin, and a woman trailing behind them both, eyes fixed on her feet, entered without fanfare or guardsmen to accompany them. The woman had to be the nin's handmaiden.

As Nin Arwia settled onto her throne, she met my eyes and smiled briefly, a birthmark hovering above her lip like a crumb. The memory from my last exchange with her as a girl came rushing back. I'd accompanied my abum into the sickroom of a favored Palace servant, and the nin had been there, bathing the girl's face herself. She'd yelped and dropped the sponge when we'd entered, but my abum had reassured her that we wouldn't tell the lugal she'd placed herself in danger by coming into a sick girl's room.

While he'd tended to the girl, the nin had asked questions about what had made her so ill, and my abum bade me answer her. Before long, we were talking like old friends. But that seemed like a lifetime ago.

Does she remember me, too?

I returned a hesitant smile of my own, then looked past her to her handmaid. The woman's neck and the lower portion of her face were covered in curling, raised welts that any healer would recognize: burn scars.

And then I knew her.

She was a poor woman whose family had all burned to death in a horrible fire right after we'd been cast down. Apparently, while she had been tending to her serving duties elsewhere, her husband and three sons had gone to sleep without extinguishing their cookfire. They had all been so deeply asleep that the fire had consumed them. This woman—her name was Gudanna—had run into her burning hut again and again to pull out her children and husband, severely burning herself from the lips down in her efforts.

I remembered her plainly now. My father had treated

them all, had tried to save them but had managed to save only her. I remember the look in her eyes as he told her the news: crushing despair and even, my abum told me later, blame. She'd pounded his chest and spewed venomous insults in his face. But he hadn't held it against her, considering her grief. And those near the wall had of course tried to help her afterward, burying her dead and rebuilding her hut, but she'd disappeared, never to be seen again.

Now I knew why. It seemed Lugal Marus had offered her a position as a handmaiden to his daughter.

Ensi Uruku, seated in an opulently carved chair slightly lower than the gold throne upon which Nin Arwia sat, studied me speculatively with eyes that were a bit too close together over a nose that had clearly been broken a time or two. It turned what might have been a handsome man into someone who looked . . . misaligned.

"You the A-zu?"

"Well, no, sir, I am not an A-zu." I bowed my head. "My abum—" I almost choked on the word but forged ahead. "My abum was the greatest A-zu in all of Alu. I am his apprentice. Or was. Until he—"

"Died," Ensi Uruku finished abruptly.

Dipping my head in acknowledgment, I blinked furiously to control my sadness.

My fear.

"This is what I have read on your decree."

Would he explain what had happened to Abum? How

he'd died? A keen desperation to know settled in my chest, but it was not my place to ask. If he'd been killed for making some misstep while trying to heal the lugal, then I was in serious trouble, too. My abum could cure almost anyone, but my apprenticeship was far from complete.

I didn't even know where he was buried.

A wave of sorrow washed over me.

"But from what we hear, Kammani, you are a great healer indeed. Isn't that so, Ensi?" Nin Arwia's voice was light. Maybe even friendly. The complete opposite of what I'd thought it would be. I'd assumed she'd hate me after what happened with her brother. But she seemed kind. *Too kind?* Wariness crept up into my hairline.

"It is what we have heard, Nin Arwia." Uruku turned to me. "But what's your experience healing the sick?" he asked, leaning forward, his left leg almost imperceptibly bobbing. "Lugal Marus is deathly ill."

"From the time I was old enough to stand, I accompanied my father and worked by his side, sir." My voice wavered. "I can read, mix potions and tonics, sew wounds, lance infections, and mend bones. I'm not his equal, but I would like nothing more than to become so."

He nodded. When he didn't speak, I risked more. "If I may be so bold as to ask a question." I held my breath, praying to Enlil that the ensi would forgive me for speaking out of turn. But the question was vital to the lugal's care. "Please, go on," Nin Arwia interjected, defiantly refusing to meet Uruku's eyes when he stared at her.

"Will the Palace healer be showing me the remedies that were tried on Lugal Marus . . . before? Before my abum tended to him?" If I could eliminate the tonics both of them had concocted, I'd be better prepared to treat the lugal.

Nin Arwia spoke, the throne beneath her glimmering. "The Palace healer was called away to another city well before my abum grew ill, I'm afraid. He wasn't here to help him. So when the Farmer's Son brought your abum to our attention once again, reminding us of his skill, we thought we should try. But, ah"—she glanced at her toes—"that did not work. Now you are our last hope." She cleared her throat at the end of her speech, swallowing with some difficulty, it seemed.

Beneath my tunic, my knees shook, and I forced them still. "I shall do my very best," I repeated. "In fact, I'm quite eager to attend to him."

A ruckus behind us in the throne room took their attention from me.

A small crowd of nobles filed in, followed by a stout, wealthy man wearing a crimson tunic and heavy jewels. Accompanying him were two guardsmen with a poor woman shackled between them. Her eyes shone with an inner radiance and her cheeks glowed with passion. Her chin was set firmly. Fiercely. She stood straight, her back braced against the mutterings and jeers coming from the group of noble spectators.

Ensi Uruku's mouth turned down in displeasure. "Counselor, what is this?"

The man stepped ponderously forward to stand in front of the ensi. Chapped, meaty hands gripped a sandstone brick on which words were etched. His booming voice rang out in the throne room.

"Ensi Uruku, who is acting in Lugal Marus's stead, I ask your courtesy. We have gathered here today to give a fair trial to a commoner who has been accused of breaking a law of Alu."

Ensi Uruku squinted, then sat back heavily, crossing his arms over his breastplate. "Go on." He flicked his wrist at the man.

"Right. Commoner!" the counselor called to the woman, and the guardsmen brought her forward. The muscles in her jaw flexed, but otherwise, she looked calm for someone facing Uruku.

The counselor squinted at the brick in his hands, trailing his finger along the etchings as he read. "You are charged with speaking ill of Ensi Uruku on three separate occasions, breaking the law that states no woman may accuse a man of a crime without proof." He gestured to the crowd behind them. "We have witnesses of good repute who heard you. What say you to this accusation?"

She cleared her throat. "I do not deny speaking ill of Ensi Uruku, sir, but it was once, not thrice." She straightened her shoulders, and her face hardened.

"You realize the egregious nature of your crime, don't you, woman? Speaking out against a man with no proof at all of his wrongdoing?" Uruku said quietly from the throne.

"I don't, actually." She raised her chin in defiance.

The nobility gasped. She'd questioned a law. Aloud. Murmuring began in the midst of the crowd and spread outward. Nasu tugged me back against the wall between him and the other guardsman, as if I might be guilty by association.

Ensi Uruku gracefully stood and strode purposefully toward the woman. The counselor stepped out of his way, mopping his sweating brow with a bit of cloth.

"Well, let me inform you, Commoner," Uruku said to her. "Repeated failure to comply with the rules set forth by the Palace can mean judgment, even loss of life, whether you agree with them or not."

At that, the woman lifted heavy eyes to Nin Arwia. "But I *have* proof. I spoke ill of a man who took my daughter behind our hut to have his way with her, and I saw it with my own eyes. My accusation hardly seems worth a loss of life," she said softly, "but if I must travel to the Netherworld because of my anger at his actions, then so be it. I cannot undo what I have done." She leveled her gaze on Ensi Uruku.

My gut clenched.

"So that's your proof? Your word?" Ensi Uruku's voice was pure silk. Melted honey. Almost *warm*. But his words had the sharp edge of a sicklesword. In his mouth lay judgment. His tongue, that tiny scrap of flesh, could produce the words that would send her to her ancestors.

"I saw you leaving my daughter there behind the hut. I swear it."

He cocked his head. "But any mother would lie for a child

who took a turn in the mud with a local boy. Did anyone else see this supposed event happen?"

She cleared her throat. "It wasn't a local boy. My daughter gives her word, too."

"So the only two people who have this supposed proof are a girl who hasn't the sense to stay out of a local boy's way and a mother who is concerned about the burden of attempting to marry off a sullied daughter. But no one else saw this?" Ensi Uruku held out a hand to the counselor, who frowned, then gestured to the crowd of nobles behind him, who shook their heads. "No. No they did not because they couldn't have. But, commoner, according to the counselor, we *do* have witnesses who heard you falsely accusing me of this crime."

"Please—" she began, but he held up a finger.

"So then, we must rule."

The nobles looked at one another, murmuring, and the counselor cleared his throat. "My lord? The witnesses have yet to speak. Your ruling could be very different depending on whether she made one angry remark about you or repeatedly spread rumors. The law says we must hear from those who accuse her."

"We've heard enough." Ensi Uruku waved him away.

"But the laws must be upheld," Nin Arwia said quietly from her gold throne. She nodded to Ensi Uruku carefully, so as not to disturb her headdress, her cheeks flushing at the sudden attention from everyone in the room. "The lugal would wish it so."

Ensi Uruku brushed an imaginary fleck of dirt from his

forearm, then met her eyes coolly. "The lugal would prefer we move forward quickly so we can dismiss the healer over there"—he pointed to me and I shrank against Nasu—"to tend to his health."

Uruku nodded to the counselor. "Now. I will ask for your advice. What is the standard punishment for a crime of this nature?"

"It is, Ensi, up to the lugal to decide her fate. Some offenders have been . . . er . . . sent to their ancestors, if the crime has harmed our citizens. Some have been maimed. Some have been released, when the lugal has been gracious." He opened his mouth as if to say more, then snapped his lips closed and gestured broadly to the woman with the brick. "Nevertheless, it is now the nin's decision, with your guidance. May Selu grant you wisdom."

Uruku sighed with what appeared to be great exhaustion. "Fine. I shall consult with the lugal's daughter and decide our punishment for this woman's crimes."

His tunic flapping behind him, he walked to Nin Arwia, who was seated stiffly on her throne.

The woman dropped her eyes and stared at the lush carpeting beneath her dirty bare feet. Her knees began to tremble as Nin Arwia and Ensi Uruku deliberated heatedly, and a pang jabbed me deep in my belly. She would suffer this day. She would suffer for standing up for her daughter, who was forced against her will. The thought that Ensi Uruku and dozens of other men like him did such awful things and paid no consequences made me sick.

After a few moments more, it was done.

"Guardsmen, give her the brick," Ensi Uruku said quietly. "We offer her our mercy and hope she repents of her actions."

Nin Arwia bit her lip, her eyes tormented. Behind her, Gudanna dropped her chin to her chest, laying a hand on the nin's shoulder. My stomach turned in response. Whatever was to happen wouldn't be easy to witness. Ensi Uruku called over a burly guardsman whose eyebrows nearly met and whispered something in his ear. The guardsman nodded once, then took the brick from the judge's hand.

The woman moaned. "No, sir. Please, no."

But they dragged the woman to the center of the throne room and laid her down on her back.

"Not on the rugs, please." Ensi Uruku knitted his hands together in front of his mouth.

They pulled her to the sandstone floor as the woman squirmed beneath their strong hold, writhing and wailing in dread.

I prayed for mercy.

But it didn't come. One guardsman held the woman on her back while the big guardsman took the brick that was inscribed with her crimes and bashed the teeth from her skull with four fierce cracks. Her mouth broke apart like pottery. The crowd gasped in horror as she shrieked, cradling her face. When they yanked her to her feet, blood and broken teeth dripped from the gaping hole of her mouth. A low moan exited it. She would never speak coherently again.

"What do you want us to do with her, Ensi?" the guardsman who'd beaten her asked, breathing heavily from his efforts.

Uruku stood, averting his eyes from the wailing woman. "She has paid for her crimes. Please see to her needs and release her." He brushed his tunic off, then looked up at the nobility with hooded eyes. "We are not monsters." He strode away, summoning the two guardsmen to his side as he left.

Nin Arwia covered her mouth with the back of her hand and tentatively approached the woman, her eyes welling with tears. She knelt in front of her.

And the healer in me propelled me forward, despite Nasu's reaching out to stop me. I pressed my lips together. "Nin Arwia?" My arm shook under Nasu's hold. "May I?" I nodded toward the woman. I could surely offer a quick pain remedy. Pack her cheeks. Maybe tend to her later, after I'd seen the lugal.

"Can you help her?" Nin Arwia asked, pulling the woman to her bosom. Blood seeped onto Nin Arwia's white tunic. Gudanna approached the nin with a cloth, knelt by her side, and tried to clean her tunic, but Nin Arwia ignored her, stroking the woman's hair, her face twisted with some unreadable emotion. Not quite pity. Something else.

"Yes, my lady," I answered quickly, terrified half out of my wits.

"Then by all means."

Nasu released my arm. As much as I wanted to see the

lugal, the woman in front of me sorely needed any help I could provide. As a healer and a fellow commoner, it was my duty.

I took a deep breath and walked to the woman's side, then dropped to my knees and ran a hand along her bleeding face. She shrieked and yanked her head away from me, burying herself in the nin's skirt, delirious in her agony.

"She needs a lot of care. Can you heal her?"

"Yes, my lady, but it will take time. Maybe I should offer a quick remedy to get through the next hours so I can care for your father, and then come back to her?"

"No." The nin stroked the woman's cheek. "Do everything you can for her right now. Her punishment was not fair." She blinked rapidly. "Her crime was not egregious enough to warrant this, as earlier precedent shows, but Ensi Uruku would not listen." She met my eyes with calm reserve. "My father would want you to heal her."

She was the ruler, and I could not argue. Not when simply accusing a man could earn you a broken mouth for the rest of your life. I swallowed my disappointment, and my anxiety that the lugal was dying and my sister's life was in the balance, and there was nothing I could do about it yet.

"I'll need a clean place to tend to her, Nin Arwia." My voice trembled.

Nasu and the other guardsmen appeared at my side. "I know a place." Nasu nodded to me. "Follow us." Nasu stooped and gently wrapped the woman's arms around his neck, then scooped her up. The other guardsman ran ahead, opening doors. They headed out the north passageway, deep into the cavernous maw of the Palace.

I followed, swallowing my fear. Behind me, Nin Arwia stayed seated on the floor, watching us go. Her beautiful tunic had been ruined by the blood of this woman, despite Gudanna's attempts to wipe it clean. As I trailed after Nasu down one corridor after another, it occurred to me with hair-raising clarity that if I didn't heal Lugal Marus, Uruku would most likely marry the nin, take the throne, and be free to do whatever he wanted to any woman in Alu.

For it appeared that a ruler like him didn't feel obliged to follow the law at all, and a ruler like Nin Arwia wasn't strong enough to make him.

CHAPTER 7

THE MUTED BUSTLE of the market in the Palace Libbu outside the windows did nothing to tame the fire in my belly as Nasu escorted me, the nin, and Gudanna toward the lugal's quarters. I needed to see the lugal. Now. Too much time had already passed. Nasu walked ahead of us through the winding hallways, his hand squeezing the hilt of his sicklesword. We turned a corner, and a gust of warm air from a large window brought in the scent of blooming jasmine, a relief from the scent of blood that still filled my nose.

The woman's mouth had been a mess. Besides the handful of teeth that had already fallen out, four more had been broken in half and had needed to be removed. I'd stitched the open sockets and dabbed a topical pain remedy on the lacerations around her mouth to kill at least some of the agony. The hemp tonic I'd given her to swallow would knock her out for the night, but when she awoke— I shuddered at the thought.

The pain would be overwhelming. I'd have to get more to her on the morrow.

"We're here," said Nasu.

He stopped in front of a large mahogany door, the likes of which I'd never seen in my life. Hand-carved wood that must have cost a small fortune bore the lugal's insignia. The three blooms about the roaring lion's neck reminded me of the three Sacred Maidens ensconced somewhere in this Palace. I took a deep breath and steeled myself for whatever lay inside.

When the door creaked open into the gloomy depths of the lugal's sleeping quarters, the damp reek of rot filled my nose. The corpse of Alu's ruler lay in the center of the room on a pallet piled with crimson coverlets.

He is already dead. My hand flew to my throat as I gasped. Then the body on the bed moved.

"Abum! I'm here." Nin Arwia entered his chamber and stooped low over the lugal's pallet. He blinked at her blearily with sunken eyes

"Do you not have the stomach for this, Healer?" Nasu stared hard at me.

My mouth dry, I wiped shaky hands on my tunic and shifted my healing satchel against my hip. I could do this. I *had* to. And quickly. "I am quite all right. I was just . . . shocked by his decline."

I stepped to the window, my body shaking, then snapped the drapery open, hoping to prevent the Boatman from entering this room and stealing the lugal away before I had a chance to work on him. Light immediately filtered into his chamber.

Lugal Marus, Nin Arwia, Gudanna, Nasu, and another guardsman, who had appeared at the threshold, squinted their eyes against the change, but the breeze from the window calmed my nerves for what I had to do.

The light illuminated the severity of the lugal's illness, but I held in my shock this time. I'd give them no more reason to doubt my skills. Gray skin was pulled taut across sharp cheekbones. His hair, once wild, was oil-laden and limp against the sweat-stained pillow. His mouth was crusted with sores; his hands were covered in filth. What were his caretakers thinking?

"Lugal Marus? I'm going to check something, all right?"

When he didn't answer, I lifted the blankets covering him to find him lying in his own waste. And I knew, at once, my abum had never made it in here to see him. He would never have left him like this. Never. They hadn't even given him the chance to try. My heart sank like a stone in the river Garadun. Why had they even bothered calling him, then? To taunt him? To further humiliate him?

"We shouldn't open the draperies," Nin Arwia whispered, startling me out of my thoughts.

I took in her small frame. She'd changed her attire while I was tending to the woman with the broken mouth, and now wore a short tunic, tufted with white feathers. Her ornate headdress had been replaced by a sprig of pink blossoms tucked behind her ear. "According to whom?"

She swallowed, her eyes shining. "Whenever I was sick as a child, my ummum said to keep the draperies closed."

"Nin Arwia." I closed my eyes to keep my temper at bay. "Would she have also told you to leave your father in his own soil?"

"Everyone said not to touch him, except to give him a remedy of chamomile to calm him. That I would become sick, too. All of the court said to leave him, because he was so close to death, but I agreed when the Farmer's Son came to see me that we should at least try once more—" Her voice cracked, and she stopped speaking as tears welled in her eyes.

"Nin, I'm sorry, but I am confused. Why would you order my abum here if you weren't going to give him access to the lugal? Why would you have him *killed?*" I gestured to the pallet. "He would *never* have . . ." I let my voice trail off, because I was teetering on the edge of tears and it was *imperative* I remain in control.

Nin Arwia swiped roughly at the round droplets blazing trails down her cheeks. "His death is not on our hands at the Palace. We ordered him here because he was this city's last hope. I fought against my better judgment to even stamp the decree, for Enlil's sake. Your abum had failed us before, but I was willing to try once more to save my father's life! But he never arrived to attend him." She lifted her chin. "And when we sent guardsmen to find him, he was already dead. He'd been"—she paused, sucking in a breath, her tongue flicking out to lick her lips—"murdered. In the street." She touched my arm. "I'm—I'm sorry."

But her eyes didn't look sorry. Not sorry enough, when her words were like a fist in my gut.

"Murdered?" I whispered.

"His throat had been cut, Healer. There was nothing anyone could have done. And now?" Her chin quivered, and tears coursed down her cheeks. "My abum is going to die, too." She fell into tears then, and Gudanna pulled her close, murmuring into her hair.

Murdered? And not by the Palace? I bit my lip so I didn't cry out as Nin Arwia's shoulders shook under Gudanna's firm embrace.

"Who would murder a healer?" I whispered, my throat constricting.

Nin Arwia pulled away from her handmaiden, wiping her tears with a soft linen Gudanna produced. "I sent out an inquiry, and we questioned everyone who lived nearby, but . . . because he is . . . was . . ."

"An outcast?" My lip trembled, and I bit it again. Hard.

"No, that isn't it," she said. "We take all murders seriously in Alu," she whispered. "But with my abum so ill . . ." She gestured feebly to her father. "It made more sense to move on and bring you here as quickly as possible." She covered her eyes with her hand and wept.

I forced my own sorrow down into a box deep inside me. I had a job to do. I tried to shoo her away. Anything to get the sound of her weeping away from me. "Nin, please. Enough of that. Please, I beg you. I have work to do so your abum doesn't follow in my father's footsteps. Someone has given you terrible advice."

"Healer, you'd better watch your tongue." Gudanna's scars stretched her lower lip with each word. "How dare you speak to the nin in such a manner?"

"To whom should I speak like this, then? To you? Or to him?" I jutted a finger roughly in Nasu's direction. Anger was better than sadness. It always was. "Who left him like this? Who left him to die?" My own abum had perished alone somewhere by a knife to the throat. Bleeding out with no one to help him.

"Healer, this is a warning." Nasu's eyes flashed danger-ously.

Abruptly, I turned to the lugal. I was a healer. I could *not* be swept up with emotion when my sister's life was on the line. I swallowed with difficulty, closed my eyes, and breathed. Then I dipped my head to Nin Arwia.

"I apologize, Nin. I will remedy the situation as best as I can."

She nodded, sniffling. "Thank you, Kammani. He is all I have left. My whole family is dead. All of them. And I can help! I want to." She perked up like a flower after it is watered, and I felt, somewhere along my spine, a sense of unease.

But I nodded, remembering her sponging off her servant's face long ago. She'd have access to things more quickly than I would. "Great. Get a clean night tunic. Linens. Have the kitchen staff boil two large pots of water. Get Gudanna and him"—I pointed to the other guardsman—"to help you." I paused and checked my tone. "Please."

"Yes, Healer. I will." She scurried out of the room, Gudanna following behind, casting one sidelong glance at me full of mistrust. The other guardsman followed in her wake, but Nasu stood back against the right side of the door.

"Healer, do your work." Nasu gestured to the lugal.

"What do you think I'm trying to do?" I knew I was testing my limits, snapping at this guardsman who had just held a sicklesword to my throat, who likely had the resources and the ability to kill me without any questions asked, but I could not quell my anger. My father? Murdered? And a woman maimed for simply speaking out? What was going on in this Palace? Although I wasn't sure why I should have expected fairness. They'd wronged my family before. It appeared there was no limit to the injustice here.

But I had a job to do. Next to his bed, a small table was covered with chiseled-bone talismans. A small bird. An ox. A statue of Enlil, our god of the skies. A mother cradling a child. My father had told me that people used them to heal bad humors and ward off bad luck. Some said they could even rid a person of guilt after committing a crime. I carefully laid each figurine in a basket by the door, then draped a clean cloth across the table.

My workstation. With shaking hands, I opened my satchel and began removing tonics, salves, and creams. The jars rattled together as I breathed deeply to calm my nerves. No doubt he'd have bedsores all over his backside. The lack of care was disgusting. After unspooling rolls of clean linen and thread, I stuck my bone needle into my tunic's shoulder for easy access, took a shuddery breath, then turned to the lugal, who lay trembling. A pitiful, racking crash of breath exited his mouth.

I leaned closer to get a view of the face I'd seen only from afar. He'd been so stately, so confident and sure of himself as he stood at the center of the Palace Libbu to offer praise to Enlil for a rich harvest or to curse Alani, queen of the Netherworld, for a blight. He'd warded off the other lugals from the nearby city-states for years when they'd wanted to conquer us, and had even chosen to wed a Nin from the closest one to broker peace. She'd died, and he'd still kept the city safe. Well, most of the city.

But now? His skin was gray, his heartbeat slow and irregular. He may have harmed my family in the past, but in this chamber, he was just a patient—one I could not afford to lose.

"Sir? Lugal Marus?"

His eyes, closed tightly against the war his body waged, opened slightly.

"I'm here to heal you, sir. And I will do my very best for you. I swear it on my life."

I softly described my movements as my fingers tip-tapped over his belly, pried his lids gently open, probed along his neck, and squeezed his ribs for the telltale tug of restricted breathing. But as my hands assessed his wasted body, nothing stood out to me as an obvious cause of his illness. His symptoms—shallow breath, low fever, bluish lips, muscle twitching—were mystifying and didn't correlate with one another.

I gritted my teeth in frustration. At that point, the lugal's long, bony fingers grabbed me about my wrist, and he spasmed violently. Nasu stepped forward, his hand on the hilt of his sicklesword.

"Healer! What have you done?"

"Nothing! I've done nothing. Stand back so I can help him."

I turned the lugal over on his side while he shook, knocking off his pillows, tearing off the covers, then I grabbed a wooden spoon I'd placed on his bedside table to wedge between his teeth. As he choked, frothing at the mouth, I grabbed a bottle of corydalis to sedate his muscles, so they would stop clenching, and sprinkled some of the white powder onto my finger. When I wiped it across his lips, my finger tingled.

His hands uncurled as he slowly relaxed, his mouth dropping open and releasing the stick I'd placed there.

But then what I was dreading most happened. His eyes grew round, his chest rattled, and his breathing stopped.

"Do something, Healer!" Nasu shouted.

"Drag him to the floor!" I demanded as Nin Arwia, Gudanna, and the guardsman burst past the doorway with the supplies I'd requested. They dropped their things and flooded into his chamber.

"Abum!" Nin Arwia flung herself over his body.

"No, Nin! Move out of the way, please! There's no time!" Shoving her away, I immediately began to compress the lugal's chest with all the power in my arms, as my father had taught me. Remembering the tingling feeling in my finger, I grabbed a sheer linen cloth and placed it over his bluish lips before giving him breaths. Compressing again and again and breathing life into his body over and over, sweat poured from my brow as the muscles in my arms screamed.

"Here! Let me!" Nasu tried to push me from the lugal's side.

"No," I grunted. "You don't know what you're doing."

"But I've watched you do it now. I can help!" He roughly pulled my hands away, which were interlaced over the lugal's chest.

"Okay," I breathed, between counts. "Do as I've done!"

I sat back on my heels, panting, praying to Enlil to keep the Boatman away, and watched Nasu work, grim-faced. Determined.

After allowing Nasu one final breath into his mouth and several more moments of compressions, I placed my hand along the lugal's throat and felt his life blood pulsing. It was weak, but the steady beat was there.

"Nasu! Stop! He's breathing. Help me turn him."

We nudged the lugal gently to his side, then I grabbed a pillow from the pallet and tucked it under his head.

"Is he dead?" Nin Arwia whispered.

"No, Nin. He is alive. But he will not be for long if I do not remedy whatever healing treatment he was given prior to my entering this room. Who else besides you has been ministering to him?"

"No one that I know of."

"Have you given him any tonics or potions besides the chamomile?"

"Only the ones I've known to work. My ummum used them on me when I was younger," she whispered.

Who knew what her mother had given her? I had frustratingly little information about the healing practices in other city-states, and since our late sarratum was from one of them, she could have thought *anything* was a remedy. "He needs water."

Nodding to me, Nasu stood and poured water from the vessel at the lugal's side into a cask. I dipped the stick I'd used before into the water and dripped it repeatedly along the lugal's lips. When he swallowed reflexively, I knew it was safe to continue.

"Get a basin and hold his head to it."

Nasu's brow knotted in confusion, but he did as I'd asked, holding the basin with one hand and the lugal's head in another.

Grabbing a carafe of dried rhizome root from the table, I pulled the cork free and used a small copper scoop to tap the powder into the lugal's open mouth. He groaned and tried to spit it out. I dripped more of the water past his lips and, as expected, he swallowed.

Almost immediately, he began to retch up bile as Nasu held his head steady near the basin. Nin shrieked in horror.

"What are you doing to him!" she cried.

"Nin Arwia, I know it looks bad, but this will save him. Whatever you may have given him could be causing harm." I spoke the words with more resolve than I felt. I didn't know *what* could save him. All I knew was I could try forcing up his stomach contents to see if it helped.

After the rhizome root wore off, I stripped the lugal of his tattered clothing, bathed him thoroughly, dressed his bedsores, and changed the linens of his pallet. Nasu and the other guardsman then lifted him to rest comfortably on the fresh bedding.

His coloring didn't look any better. If possible, he looked worse. *What else can I possibly do?*

"Nin Arwia? Can you have the cooks prepare some bone broth?"

It was possible that he was also dehydrated and needed some nourishment. Who knows how regularly he'd been fed?

"Yes, yes, of course." She nodded as she wiped her tears on the sleeve of her gorgeous feathered tunic. "Of course I can. And I'll send up a tray of food for you as well."

She looked at her abum, clean on the pallet, and took a deep breath. I'd heard that sigh of relief many times before, when my father had healed someone's family member. But it was too soon for any of that. I'd yet to figure out what was ailing the king.

"Thank you for doing what you've done and will continue to do. I know that he is safe with you."

"I will try my best, Nin Arwia." That, at least, was true.

"I know that. I can tell." My admission seemed to rally her a bit. She stood straighter.

"Guardsmen? Stand outside the doorway, please, and ensure Kammani has everything she needs for the rest of the evening."

"As you wish, Nin." Nasu and the other guardsman nodded and disappeared into the hallway outside the door.

"Gudanna, come with me to secure the meals for Abum and our healer." Then she walked to me and clasped my hands in hers. "Please do not hesitate to come knock on my door should you need anything. I will be there the entirety of the evening. I'm quite worn out."

"Thank you, Nin. I will."

"Oh! I've also given you a bed inside the Sacred Maidens' chamber. I thought that if I were you"—she swallowed— "I might want the comfort of a loved one nearby."

My heart swelled at her kindness. "Nin Arwia, I thank you. Truly."

She squeezed my hands once more, then they exited, Nin Arwia's shoulders bowed under the weight of her emotions but Gudanna's straight and proud. I managed to stand confidently until they left the room.

But then I pulled up a stool next to the lugal's pallet and sank wearily onto it, my head in my hands. *Talking* to someone to discuss possible remedies would be so helpful right now. Nanaea was never much for learning about healing, but she could at least listen to my musings and perhaps give me some ideas. I made a move to stand, but the hem of my tunic was stuck beneath a leg of the stool. When I tugged it free, a purplish-blue streak appeared along the bottom of my skirt. Flipping the stool over, I discovered a velvety-blue flower petal smashed under one of the legs.

The pieces were soft like duck feathers between my fingers.

But the strangest sensation—like soft pricks from a hot needle—tingled my fingertips.

I dropped the flower to the ground and scrubbed my hand in the washbasin near the door with aleppo soap and the fresh water the guardsman had toted in.

Strange.

As I dried my hands, I searched for a vase or a wreath of fresh-cut flowers from which the petal could have come. Besides the honeysuckle tied over the doorway as a freshener, there was nothing.

Hmmm. I picked up the flower with a rag and prepared to drop it out the window.

At the last minute, though, I changed my mind and opened the rag to study the blue flower with more care. Why did it make my fingers tingle?

A conundrum.

But then I remembered that Nin Arwia had come into the chamber with a sprig of blossoms behind her ear. When she'd flung herself over her abum, she must have knocked some petals free. So it was not altogether troubling, as more disturbing things plagued my mind.

Wrapping it in a small cloth and knotting it with string, I

dropped the packet into the hearth, where it would be burned when they stoked the fires this evening. Then I dipped a rag into the cool water near the lugal's bedside table, laid it gently across his brow, and prepared myself for a long night fraught with what I could only imagine would be my terror that the lugal was dying.

And I, the new Palace Healer, had no idea how to save him.

CHAPTER 8

"THE MAIDENS' WELCOME is a tradition, Healer, and it must be attended by everyone inside the Palace."

Nasu trudged down one corridor after another to the other side of the Palace. My legs ached, following him. The sun was just peeking up over the horizon, casting the winding sandstone corridors in amber light. My head was about to explode. I'd spent the entire evening at the lugal's side, tending to his needs, fretting about my lack of expertise, and pondering the notion that someone had murdered a healer. My abum.

We were orphans.

Throughout the night, I'd focused on pushing down every single implication of that sentence, along with the stifling despair that had tried to rise when I'd chanced—in a half-asleep delirium—to utter it aloud.

Tradition would demand that I marry. And quickly. Find

someone to care for me. Secure my place in this city by being a bride. But I would not meet those demands this day.

Or any time soon.

I had too much to do.

And now, because of this Maidens' Welcome festival I was supposed to attend, my progress would be halted by my lack of rest. The thought of a sleepless day, spent in the shadow of the Maidens, made my stomach roil, although seeing Nanaea would be a welcome respite.

"Are you certain, sir, that I cannot just rest for a few turns of the dial and then see to the lugal again? Wouldn't that be better than standing around in the Libbu?" I pictured myself, flagon in hand, huddling near the courtyard wall, trying to make myself as insignificant as possible.

"You may call me Nasu, Healer."

"I thank you, Nasu. And you may call me Kammani."

He nodded once, his eyes flicking over to my face. "But the nin herself told me to fetch you so you could prepare for the festival. And now I have." We approached another heavy wooden door. Shrieks exploded from inside it as we approached the chamber I would share with the Sacred Maidens. I rubbed a hand over my face. It sounded as if my sister, Simti, and the last Maiden—Huna, the wealthy one—were inside the room. I was sure I would not have a single moment of peace before the festivities.

Simti cracked open the door, her skin glistening with some freshly applied cream, her eyes gleaming as brightly, and pulled me in before slamming the door in Nasu's face hard enough to send bits of the rough sandstone from the walls skittering down to the floor.

Our chamber was enormous and elegantly furnished. Thick crimson and white drapes hung from the two windows on the far wall, while four richly appointed pallets, covered in blankets stitched with lavender thistle flowers and trailing green vines, were tucked neatly against the wall to the right. On my left, three oversized basins were filled to the brim with steaming milk and floating red bellflowers. Nanaea and Huna were sitting in two of them, eyes closed, their hair and faces coated in what appeared to be mud. Two servant women vigorously massaged olive oil into their arms as they soaked. Nanaea groaned with pleasure.

"Isn't it amazing?" Simti grasped my hand in hers, her shiny cheeks flushed from excitement.

"That's one word for it."

She grinned, scooted toward the third basin, and dropped the linen cloth she'd been swathed in. She sank in up to her neck with a sigh of contentment.

Without opening her eyes, Nanaea said, "That's your bed over there, Sister." She pointed vaguely to the pallet closest to the door. "Your filthy tunic and old sandals are lying on the floor next to it. I told the servants to throw away the whole satchel, but they didn't listen."

"And I'm glad they didn't, Nanaea, or I'd be walking around here nude," I said, bone weary, shaken, and starving. "But I am eternally grateful to you for thinking of me."

Nanaea smiled, and the mud mask cracked. "You wouldn't

be nude. They left you several new tunics and a pair of sandals, too." She opened her eyes.

"Look over there." She gestured to a row of copper hooks hanging near my pallet, dripping milk on the servant massaging her. The woman looked at her with the placid smile of those used to attending the wealthy. Three white tunics, all stitched at the shoulder with golden zigzags, hung neatly. "I told the servants who dropped them off it's a waste for you to even have them. From what I hear, Lugal Marus is going to cross to the other side of life, and it's not like they're going to let you take those garments back home with you when you leave."

"He won't die if I can heal him fast enough. I have the tinctures to do so."

Which does me no good if I can't figure out what is wrong with him.

"Yes, so how did it go last night?" Nanaea asked, stretching back and lifting a long brown leg from the milk. The servant woman commenced massaging her foot. Nanaea sighed deeply.

I thought of the woman's face, broken apart and dripping blood onto her tunic. The decaying stench of the lugal's pocked, oozing backside. The stark misery of hearing the truth of our father's demise. *How did it go?* Not well, Nanaea. Not well at all. But I couldn't tell her. She didn't need to know the details of my abum's death. It was bad enough that she knew he was gone. Anything else would steal her joy, and I couldn't be that thief. "Oh, fairly well. I still have some remedies to try."

"Well, don't try too hard!" She sank even lower into the milk. "If his journey in this life ends soon, he will wake to a new life in the Netherworld, happy, healthy—"

"—and with us at his side," Simti finished, scrubbing her scalp with the mud.

"Yes, praise be to Enlil," Nanaea added, then sat up abruptly, splashing milk over the top of the tub. "Oh! And Kammani! We have the Maidens' Welcome festival to attend today, and it is supposed to be overflowing with dancing and tournaments and food!"

Food. My stomach grumbled, and I immediately thought of Kasha. He'd always been a hungry boy, never having enough to eat, always begging for the last scraps from our bowls. Who fed him now? Who worried for his health? I hadn't even left word where I'd gone in case he came back to our hut to look for me, although surely he'd hear the gossip in the Palace. He may not even know of our abum's death! I made a mental note to find him and tell him what was happening.

I walked to my pallet, sank down onto the coverlet, and was nearly swallowed within it. From the washtubs, Simti and Nanaea let out peals of laughter.

"What in the name of Enlil?" I struggled to sit up, then pulled up the silken bedding and discovered, to my astonishment, that the pallet had been constructed almost entirely of goose down.

"Don't worry, the same thing happened to Huna over there. Even girls with more minas than they know what to do with don't live like this." Simti reached out from the basin to grab a clean linen, dipped it into the milk, and massaged some of the mud from her face.

"Close your trap, you piece of trash," Huna growled. "Honestly, I have no idea why Ensi Uruku would select dirty rats to accompany Lugal Marus to the Netherworld. It's a disgusting choice."

"Just as I have no idea why Ensi Uruku would select such an ugly, stubborn girl," Nanaea fired back, sitting up with a splash.

"Well, at least my family will be sending me to the Netherworld with coins in my pocket so I can please the lugal with gold."

"Well, at least I will be going to the Netherworld not looking like a bloated fish."

At that, Simti and Nanaea burst into hysterical laughter.

"Nanaea, please. You're arguing about dying. Do you not see that?" I rubbed my throbbing temples, then opened my eyes to see every girl staring at me. Even the servants had stopped their massages to look at me.

I dropped my hands to my lap. "What? It is true. And yes, I've dared to utter it aloud."

Nanaea's face, damp from the bath, flushed in anger. "Sister, it is *more* than dying. I've told you this. It is stepping into a new life, a life with honor and wealth and joy. Why can't you be happy for me?"

I punched my pillow to fluff it behind my head. I did not have the energy to deal with her foolishness. She was excited about the prospect of *dying* at the hands of the leaders of this city, who'd taken everything from us, including our ummum. Because maybe if they hadn't destroyed everyone's faith in my abum, he wouldn't have been gone the night of her death, trying to heal someone else so we could get paid. He would have been home with me.

And everything would have been different.

I stifled my bleak thoughts. "Nanaea, I don't want to argue. I'm incredibly tired."

And confused.

Why is she so intent on going? Why is it so easy to consider leaving me alone?

If only my abum were here to ask! I punched down the wrenching in my gut at the thought of my abum being buried in some paupers' field or lying to rot in the midday sun. Where *was* he? Did he have the coin to pay the Boatman's passage? If not, would he get to cross the river, or was he floating somewhere, caught between the two worlds? Someone didn't just leave this life for the next and disappear. Not him. Not my abum. As I sank down into the coverlet, I pictured how he used to be before the loss of the malku had erased his smile and my mother's death had sent him into his cups. I used to make him laugh great big belly laughs when I'd say something witty. And he'd been proud of how smart I was. How I could grind the pokeroot in the mortar with such care and mix just the right amount of aloe into a salve for a burn. He'd stroke my hair and call me *Arammu*, his little love.

Tears pricked at the corners of my eyes, but I breathed in and closed the lid on that grief. I had to focus on my mission, and tears were a terrible distraction.

On the other side of our chamber, Nanaea gossiped with Simti across their tubs, and although it bothered me that she didn't see the mess of the situation she was in, I was happy that she could be pampered in a way I'd never be able to afford. Let her enjoy it just for a moment.

I leaned back and nestled carefully among the softest pillows I'd ever felt. As my eyes grew tired, I watched the girls climb from the tubs and get buffed with linens, oiled from head to toe, and brushed like horses in a stall. Then they moved to an alarmingly high pile of clothing. Huna sat on her pallet, looking over her shoulder with her nose in the air, but Simti and Nanaea pounced on the tunics with glee.

My eyelids grew heavier the longer I stared at the girls trying on various garments. They accessorized the tunics—gleaming white, olive green, royal blue—with gold belts, heavy jeweled necklaces, and carnelian and ruby bracelets, twirling and primping as they went.

I yawned widely, my body sinking into the coverlet. Sleep was an absolute necessity before seeing the lugal again. "Girls, I'm taking a nap before we head down to the festival. I must . . ."

Nanaea stared at me, a look of annoyance flitting across her features, and said something to Simti. But the walls began to blur, and their laughter faded to a soft buzz that didn't bother me greatly. The last thought I had before I let myself slide into the black abyss of unknowing was that I'd better wake up soon to see the lugal and pull myself and my sister out of this mess. My ummum and my abum, from the banks of the Netherworld, would be counting on it.

❊ ❊ ❊ ❊ ❊

The remembrance of a dream danced just beyond my grasp as my eyes cracked open into the sunlit chamber. It was something about my father as he lay cold in the grave. He was reaching out to me, his hands gray from decay, his mouth open, whispering incomprehensibly.

I squinched my eyes closed against the image and focused on the warmth of the sun's bright rays pouring through the window, the luxurious weight of my silken coverlet, the downy pillow beneath my cheek. The crushing despair would *not* settle into my bones. The ache for his smile when I looped a knot at the end of a stitch without any slack would not derail me before I was up and about my daily rounds. They would not. They *could not*. Suddenly I sat up as if I'd been struck by lightning. The lugal! The Palace! The Sacred Maidens!

As I flung the covers from my pallet in a rush, it dawned on me that the girls were gone. Nanaea's pallet was mussed, my ummum's shawl in a bunch by her pillow, but she wasn't in it. I picked the shawl up and rubbed the threadbare fabric against my cheek. Nanaea must've been sleeping with it, breathing in the scent of my ummum's skin. My heart ached at the thought, but I dropped it back down to where she'd left it and moved on. *Focus. Strength.* What time was it? The lugal had to be seen immediately. I wrapped myself in my coverlet and stumbled to the window to gauge the location of the sun.

It was midday. High noon.

I blanched. I'd slept away the entire morning and, judging by the scene below, was missing the makings of a boisterous, heavily attended Maidens' Welcome festival.

Gritting my teeth in annoyance that Nanaea hadn't bothered to stir me from my slumber, I took in the regal array stretched throughout the Libbu. Flags with the lugal's lion and blooms crest waved merrily atop the Palace walls as people dressed in their finest tunics and brightest jewels meandered below, chatting with one another over sticks of roasted meats and full tankards. Dancers in scarves with belts of coins on their hips and ribbons in their hair performed in front of a gaping group while merchants, taking advantage of the occasion, were selling their wares in tents. A tournament arena with a platform next to it, arrayed in white drapery and bursting with festoons of purple lilies and blue bellflowers, sat in the middle of the festivities.

As no one had come knocking at the door, it appeared that my presence hadn't yet been missed. And sleeping for a while had restored some of my energy.

I dropped my coverlet and walked steadily to the hooks by my bed, then pulled on one of the clean tunics and wrapped a shining white cord of silk around my head to keep my hair out of my face. A pitcher of cool water and a round of barley bread drizzled with date syrup and olive oil sat nearby, leftovers from early provisions that must have been given to the Maidens. I drank greedily, filled my stomach, and felt like a woman resurrected. I could, *would*, master the lugal's disease. Snatching the new sandals from the floor, I tied them over my feet, then picked up my healing satchel and flung it over my neck and shoulder.

Late or not, the lugal would receive my very best care. The thought of Nanaea lying next to him in a cold, dank tomb propelled me onward. As I flung open the door, a noisy group of revelers swept me into their flow.

"Excuse me!" I shouted as the crowd swallowed me up and carried me with them on their journey.

"This way!" one girl said, laughing, her copper headdress shimmering as she pointed down the corridor.

"No, thank you. The lugal needs me." Wriggling, I tried to wedge my way out of the bustle to a safe spot against the wall. But the girl linked her arm with mine and pulled me along.

"But, darling girl, don't you want to see the Sacred Maidens?"

"Well, no, actually . . ." I tried to dislodge my arm from her firm embrace.

"The Welcome festival is at hand! We're going down now to see them! Isn't it exciting?"

"No, please. Let me go—" I tried again to remove her arm,

but the crowd was loud and fast, and she was already full of sikaru. Her eyes were barely focused on my face.

"Please! Think of the dying lugal!" With one ferocious yank, I pulled myself free and fell backward into a pair of people, who fell to the floor with me.

"My apologies," I spluttered, scrambling to my feet in haste.

"It's quite all right," a soft voice answered.

"It is NOT quite all right," a sterner voice responded.

The stern voice belonged to the glaring visage of Gudanna, Nin Arwia's handmaiden.

And the soft voice was that of the princess herself. She was dressed in riches. My mouth fell open in awe at her splendor as she stood and smoothed her long gown, which was covered in red feathers from one shoulder all the way to the floor. Her bare arm was encased in glittering bracelets from wrist to elbow. On her head, a crown of woven gold adorned with three rosettes sat on her hair, which had been knotted into two puffs, one on either side of her head. Long topaz earrings dangled from her ears, while shimmering necklaces circled her regal neck.

"Don't stand there with your mouth open like a fish, Healer." Gudanna dusted off the nin's gown. "Apologize to her!"

"My deepest apologies."

Gudanna's eyes were stern, but the nin's were reserved. Possibly even soft.

"There is no harm done." The nin smiled. "Would you join us in attending the festival? It's a tradition to show the people how lovely the brides will be for my father if—" At that, her eyes filled, and she paused, clearing her throat.

"Nin, I thank you for the honor, as I'd love to go see them with you, but I must see to your abum. Nasu told me that it was important I attend, but I'd rather be about my business."

"And why didn't you care for him early this morning?" Gudanna barked. Her eyes were steely.

But there was no good answer. I couldn't tell them that after spending the night in his chambers, there was still no clear reason for his illness, despite the nin's faith in me. Or that I'd taken a rest and neglected him this morning. "I attended to him late into the night, and then other business needed my attention this morning, Nin." Heat crept up into my cheeks at the lie.

"More important than the lugal?" Gudanna placed a scarred hand upon her hip.

"No, of course not. But I would like to see him now. So if Nin Arwia could point the way? I was quite confused, coming back here earlier today."

She smiled slightly. "Maybe you're right. Perhaps we could break tradition just this once."

Gudanna stepped in. "I hate to say it, Nin Arwia, but wouldn't it look bad if Kammani, Healer's Daughter, were missing from the festivities? It's an important event! Besides, the talk of the entire morning in the Libbu has been the three beautiful girls who have come to stay at the Palace, along with another who is a healer. We should at least show her face. The noble crowd does not like the idea of a female ruler, and if you keep a curiosity such as a learned girl from their eyes for too long . . ." Her deep black eyes looked worriedly from Nin Arwia's face to mine.

I looked anxiously between Gudanna's face and the nin's. My heart rate was starting to go up beneath my breastbone. I *had to* get to the lugal. Enough time had been wasted already this morning!

"You know, Gudanna, you are right. Some are already opposing the idea of me taking my father's place if he should go, although I pray to Enlil that doesn't happen." She turned to me. "Kammani. Please attend the ceremony for a while. And then you can spend the rest of the day and evening with the lugal and I can help you with whatever you need. We both can." She nodded to Gudanna, then, like the girl before her, linked her arm through mine. "Shall we, then?"

I did my best to be courteous, but frustration welled inside until I was almost bursting. "Are you quite certain I cannot attend to him now?"

Nin Arwia nodded. "I am. Besides. He looked so much better last night when I left you with him, did he not?"

My stomach dropped, but I answered the only way I could. "Indeed, Nin. He certainly did."

But that was just the magic of a washbasin and the wonder of belief. He was certainly no better. I'd done very little to truly help him. She squeezed me to her, and the three of us headed down the corridor toward the laughter of the Libbu beyond.

We breezed into an entryway with a balcony that overlooked the bustle and merriment. When the crowd caught sight of Nin Arwia, a few of them let out a loud cheer. She lifted a hand in greeting to those who'd showed her favor, grinning and waving, her eyes shining with the recognition. But more of them remained silent, apathetic, their faces wary. Those, she didn't seem to notice.

"Gudanna, look at them all!"

Gudanna peered over the edge of the balcony, but Nin Arwia was practically throwing herself over it in her excitement.

For someone who wanted me to heal her father, this was a strange reaction to the fame that would be heightened only if he should pass to the other side.

"Kammani, all these people are here to show my family just how much we mean to them." She turned her bright eyes from the crowd back to me. "How much *my abum* means to them. And of course they want to support the queens he'll have in the Netherworld should your remedies not work. Isn't it wonderful? They love us so."

The cheer from the crowd died down, and her brow knit over her forehead as she dropped her hand and turned her pixie face to mine. She reached a small hand up and patted my cheek gently. "But I hope that your remedies work, despite how selfish it is for me to think it."

"Selfish?"

"Of course." She shrugged a dainty shoulder. "Should he

live, the Sacred Maidens would go back to their regular lives. And the honor of being a lugal's young bride in the Netherworld would be no more."

"That is the truth of it."

She smiled softly then, the crowd no longer seeming to pull her from herself. "It appears as though we might have different goals, Healer. You likely want your sister to have the glory, but I ask you to keep *my* goals in your mind as you work your remedies. Please do your best for him." She grasped my hands in hers. "All of Alu is counting on it."

"I swear it with all that is in me."

"Good. Let us go celebrate."

But as I descended the stairs in her wake, breathing in the heady scent of her jasmine oil, I realized she grossly misunderstood my motives. I wanted to keep the lugal alive for *me*, because doing so saved my sister from this so-called glory. Losing another member of my family to the Palace's terrible traditions, despite whatever riches awaited them in the Netherworld, was out of the question.

And she probably didn't love her abum as much as she said she did. For if it were my abum virtually decaying on a pallet up the stairs, I wouldn't be excitedly waving at the crowd. My focus would be on doing *anything* it took to see that he was healed, even if that meant ignoring what was required of me.

Just as I'd do anything to see my abum's face one more time on this side of the everafter.

CHAPTER 9

TWENTY HANDSBREADTHS AWAY, a bear with a ring in its nose lay dejectedly in the sand at the feet of its master, who dozed in the sun.

"I feel so sorry for the dumb beast." Iltani took a drink from her flagon, the sikaru making her eyes soft.

How she'd managed to get her hands on brew without any coins was beyond me, but Iltani had her ways.

"I feel sorry for the lugal, who lies dying while the city rejoices." I tapped my foot in the center of the Maidens' Welcome festival, with people in various states of drunkenness acting like fools all around me. There was no end to this festival in sight. A servant woman wearing a drab tunic and a hair wrap held a platter piled with crisp cucumbers, stuffed dates, sliced pomegranates, and honeycake in one hand and a teeming mug of sikaru in the other. She moved the platter for my inspection and offered me a pinch of the honeycake, which I promptly popped into my mouth. Delicious. Sweet and melting on my tongue, a treat I'd rarely eaten in the past four years. I swiped half a pomegranate and two of the dates. They were rich and sweet, stuffed with chopped nuts. My stomach almost swooned with delight.

"Compliments of the lugal," she murmured, and handed me the sikaru.

Oh, why not.

I *was* thirsty. The drink was bubbly and chilled. I sipped, which washed away some of my angst about getting in to see the lugal. The nin had bade me stay but every time I'd pestered her about whether I could be released to my duties, she'd either introduced me to someone new or gotten lost in the crowds, as she was now.

Iltani, at my side, reached out a hand for a bit of the honeycake, but the servant woman raised an eyebrow, shifted the platter out of her reach, then drifted back into the crowd.

"I suppose she is not fooled by your disguise, my friend."

She wore a royal blue tufted tunic that was too large for her frame. A dozen or so ratty necklaces hung from her neck, but her sandals were the same worn ones she'd had forever.

"Why are you wearing that anyway? Anyone can attend this festival."

"I am served better in riches than rags." Iltani raised her flagon, drained the last of her sikaru, then eyeballed my pomegranate. I tore it in half, handing her the larger section.

"See? Even *you* serve me better."

Just then, from the corner of my eye, I saw a small form

bobbing toward me. It was Kasha, his eyes wild, his curls bouncing as he jogged toward us, a worried look on his face. Behind him, the town crier huffed mightily, mopping his brow.

"Sister, I've been looking everywhere for you. I heard. I heard about Abum."

"Kasha!" I grabbed him in a stifling hug, handing my drink to Iltani. After a few moments, he squirmed away from me.

"It's true, then? He died?" His brows knotted together across his forehead.

I took his face between my hands as my eyes filled. I blinked the tears away. "Yes, Brother. On the way to the Palace. He never made it here."

He nodded, swallowing with difficulty, but did not cry. I pulled him to me once more, likely more for my sake than his. It appeared the years of being away from our family had softened the blow for him.

A servant went by with a tray full of flagons, and Iltani swiftly exchanged her empty cup for a full one.

I held Kasha out at arm's length. "Are you all right?"

He nodded, his chin set. "I never knew him too well." He shrugged, his tone light but his eyes giving away his emotion. "They took me away, and before that, he was busy." He scuffed his toes in the dirt. "But I will miss seeing him."

"As will I." My lips trembled as the words tumbled out. After collecting myself for several moments, I changed the subject to ease the discomfort for both of us. "Well, now that you're here, maybe you can tell me how to get into the Palace to see the lugal. I've been here long enough." A Palace door loomed large to my left, but it was locked, and no amount of rattling it had gotten me inside.

"Not until after the tournament, Sister." His face brightened, the bad news already forgotten.

Iltani handed me back my drink and I sipped, watching the arena fill with spectators for the tournament, in which men would showcase their speed. Their prize? A token from a Sacred Maiden—a lock of hair, a scented scarf, or a beaded necklace. Three viewing boxes, engraved with the lion and blooms, perched above the arena; there the Maidens would sit to watch the competition. Behind them, a looming catapult extended into the air like the Boatman's hand reaching up from the Netherworld.

"There you are, sleepyhead!"

Nanaea bumped into me, sloshing half my sikaru out of my cup, then twirled in her golden tunic.

"That spill is cause for dismissal from your post," Iltani said, swaying gently on her feet, a look of placid merriment on her face.

"Sorry, Sister!" Nanaea said as she spun, but she didn't look sorry at all. She looked like a queen. Blood-red hyacinths and yellow chamomile were twisted around her head in a sort of crown, while her neck, cheeks, and forehead were painted with a delicate pattern of ivy, vines, and tiny pink flowers. The vines trailed down her arms and onto her hands, too. Her lips were a deep reddish purple, as if she'd been eating berries, and her brown eyes were transformed by the addition of broad black lines above and below her full eyelashes. Only the noble could afford frankincense kohl around their eyes, which warded off infection, but now my little sister was wearing it, too. I barely recognized this woman standing before me as my Nanaea, just fifteen years.

"Yes, thank you for waking me." I wiped my wet hand down the side of my tunic. "I honestly don't believe you would let me lie there without the courtesy." She was breaking every rule of sisterhood. No matter your differences, your squabbles, you looked out for one another. You helped each other even when no one else would. *Especially* when no one else would.

Simti and Nanaea glanced at each other.

"We *did* wake you, Sister, as we were leaving."

"You did nothing of the sort."

Simti laughed. "I wish I had your ability to sleep soundly! We woke you, but you shooed us away, talking about attending to your business. You must have fallen back asleep."

"I assumed you'd be following shortly behind." Nanaea's kohl-blackened eyes stared at me unnervingly.

"Well, clearly, I did not. Why didn't you wait for me?" I hated the pleading note in my voice. The need for inclusion.

Simti tipped back her flagon. "Perhaps we should have dragged you away, because then you would have run into Dagan, who was searching everywhere for you this morning."

"Dagan was here?"

"Of course. That man will not rest until you are his wife. He's over there." She pointed to a group of men throwing knives at targets in the far corner of the Libbu. Dagan stood loosely in front of a target, a dagger held in his hand by the blade. I shielded my eyes from the sun and watched him throw. It was forceful. Solid. He hit the target with a resonating thud every time he flicked his wrist. The men around him erupted into cheers as he hit the target's center. Then, almost as if he knew I was watching, his eyes caught mine. He waved and pointed at me as if to say "Watch this" as he took two knives from sheaths at his waist. He tossed both knives behind his back, caught them by their blades, and sent them sailing into the center of the target almost effortlessly. He beamed and laughed at his trick, and I couldn't help but smile.

Beside me, Nanaea huffed. "I don't know why he continues to try to win you. You're so dismissive of him. He loves you, yet you send him away time and time again."

"Better than trying to court you, don't you think?" I asked with a sniff.

Her eyes narrowed, and she placed delicate hands on her round hips. "Too bad I'm already spoken for."

"Yes, by a man more than twice your age, likely lying in his own waste again."

At my elbow, Iltani chortled into her flagon.

Nanaea narrowed her eyes. "I'm trying to *help* you. You should be grateful Dagan is even giving you the chance at marriage, considering our status!" She pursed her lips. "If you don't watch out, you'll end up an old maiden."

"That isn't the worst thing that could happen to a person. You are *such* a child sometimes."

Nanaea sniffed. "Well, if you're going to talk to me that way, then I'm leaving. Come, Simti. We have a tournament to watch." Nanaea linked her arm through Simti's, and they glided away, a couple of guardsmen following behind as they drifted toward their boxes in the arena.

"Nanaea, I'm sorry," I called after her, but Iltani stopped me.

"Oh, leave the Gravemaidens to their own business." She leaned back and drained the rest of her flagon, then tossed the cup over her shoulder into the dirt, narrowly missing a wealthy woman's feet.

"Don't call them that."

She laughed wickedly.

"You're terrible sometimes, you know that?"

"Not as terrible as you. Besides, you love me." She grinned, and I shook my head and took another sip, noting a tingly feeling along my lips as I pulled the flagon away.

She nodded toward the crowds ahead of us. "Shall we go watch the tournament?"

I looked again longingly toward the doorway peeking into the Palace, then let my eyes trail back to the people moving into the arena. Dagan was surging ahead of us with a group of men.

Is he thinking of competing for a Maiden's token?

Despite the pull from the lugal in the Palace, I wanted to find out.

"Let's. Just for a short time. Then I'll escape and demand entrance to the lugal's chamber."

"Perfect. I'm dying to see why in the name of Enlil there's a catapult over there."

🞖 🞖 🞖 🞖 🞖

All around the arena, vendors in their finest tunics crowded in to hawk their wares. Scents of roasting ducks, freshly baked bread, and Assata's wine barrels permeated the air. A weaver handed out samples of embroidery with the Sacred Maidens' likenesses on it to the wealthy women, who oohed and aahed over her superior work. Jugglers with painted faces stood tall above the crowd on stilts, tossing lit torches back and forth to one another. Children ran in and out of the gold, jade, and crimson booths like puppies, yapping and shrieking with glee. Occasionally, a vendor would swat a backside as one ran past with his hands full of the vendor's wares.

I took another sip of my sikaru as I sat in one of the reserved seats on the platform, just a few places down from Nin Arwia, Gudanna, Uruku, and a host of other nobles. Nanaea, Simti, and Huna sat in their boxes, being fanned by servants with palm fronds. Iltani, seated with Kasha in the crowd, found my eyes amid the packed seats and stuck out her tongue.

It wasn't as if I *wanted* to be seated with the nobility. Nin Arwia had found me on the way to the arena and demanded my presence on the platform. I'd tried to excuse myself again, shoving away the urge to know whether Dagan would compete to tend to the lugal, but she'd been firm.

My eyelids and head felt heavy, the price of staying up all night. I tipped my flagon up and drained the last of the sikaru, noting the fine grit that had settled at the bottom. How different the Palace brew was from Assata's.

In the center of the arena, a group of young men—Warad, Assata's bulky son included—awaited their turn to run through a maze made from bales of hay, piles of sunbaked bricks, and merchants' stalls. The competition would not be easy. As the men maneuvered the twists and turns, they'd be dodging pitch hurled from the catapult.

It was a dangerous game, but, as the town crier had explained it, the prize of a Maiden's favor and the honor of besting every other man was worth it.

But was it really? Hot pitch could easily maim or disfigure one of these men. Absently, my thoughts wandered through the contents of my healing satchel to be sure remedies were available if someone should need it. I had aloe, and maybe some pokeroot, but no clean linens.

Guardsmen stood at the ready, a big vat of pitch at their side. I shuddered, praying to Enlil that the competitors would have quick wits and even quicker feet. Warad was the biggest worry. He was as strong as an ox, but as he hulked there on his tree-trunk legs near the starting line, anxiety stretched tightly across his thick brow, you could almost see the fate that awaited him should the guardsmen decide to be cruel. His bulk would be too much to move.

There was laughter and commotion from the far corner of the arena as someone was pushed forward from a group of young men who'd stationed themselves there.

I'd recognize those shoulders anywhere.

Dagan.

He laughed and shook his head and tried to wedge himself back into the crowd, but the town crier saw him.

"Dagan, Farmer's Son!" His bellow echoed over the arena. "Join the ranks of the young warriors already in line and hope for a token from one of these beauties."

Dagan laughed good-naturedly and waved him away. But his friends and two of his little brothers, Shep and Marduk, pushed him forward.

"Come, young man. Compete! Are you a coward?"

Now he had no choice. Dagan threw up his hands with a smile, and a cramp twisted my gut.

If he competes, will he try to win? To earn the favor of Nanaea?

Beads of sweat formed above my lip, and my stomach turned over. He walked to the starting line next to the other hopefuls and hopped lightly on the balls of his feet, scanning the crowd.

I waved a shaky hand to draw his attention, but he didn't see me.

The town crier raised his hands, and the crowd hushed to a dull murmur. "Ladies and gentlemen of Alu! I stand before you today to announce the beginning of the glorious tournament to welcome the Sacred Maidens to the Palace!" With a grand sweep of his arm, he gestured to Nanaea, Simti, and Huna. They stood, bowing their heads modestly, and the crowd went wild.

"These fine young men"—he flung his arm wide—"will compete to secure their highest prize: a token from a Maiden never before touched by a man. They're lovely, they're sweet, and they will soon be sarratums in the Netherworld!" The crowd roared their approval.

Water collected in my mouth. I really wasn't feeling well at all.

"Today these men must prove that their reflexes are sound and as quick as a lightning strike. They must fly through a maze designed to confuse. But most of all, they must avoid the guardsmen's flaming pitch!"

The guardsmen near the catapults raised their sickle-swords and spears high, playing the villains in this game, while the crowd shouted and hurled good-natured insults at them.

Flaming? I glanced nervously over at the corners of the arena and bit the inside of my cheek, stifling the urge to vomit. So *that* was what the men standing ready with barrels of water were for. To put out any fires that should start. But what if the fire hit one of the men? Hit Dagan? Hot pitch was bad enough, but if it were on fire? It would sear the skin from his bones.

At the town crier's words, several of the men drifted away from the starting line as the crowd mocked them. Cries of "Cowards!" followed them from the arena, but Dagan stayed in place. He was never one to back down from a challenge.

"So today, ladies and gentlemen, let's cheer them on. Are you ready? Let me hear it: *Are you ready?*" The crowd raised a deafening roar as the town crier's face glistened in the afternoon sun.

"Then, young men—young *warriors*—*take your marks!*"

They formed a single-file line, and Dagan jogged to the head.

"Young man. Are you ready?"

"I am." Dagan's voice was resolute. Strong.

"Then, sir, I bid you good luck. Because you are to begin in five, four, three . . ."

The crowd joined in to count Dagan down to the start. He tensed at the line, coiled like a snake about to strike. His face was acutely determined. His eyes alert. Even from where I sat, I could see the whiteness of his knuckles, the clench of his jaw. Behind him, the guardsmen reached torches up to light the pitch in the catapult.

I clasped my hands together, breathing shallowly, my head aching and swimming. "Please, Enlil, let him not be harmed," I whispered. "Not my Dagan."

❂ ❂ ❂ ❂ ❂

As quick as a fox, Dagan leapt, dove, sprinted, and dodged the pitch and subsequent fires as he easily and quickly ran through the course. His reflexes were sure, his eyes never leaving the heavens, waiting for the descent of the flames.

The crowd erupted into a frenzy when he emerged safely

from the end of the maze, his face cracked from ear to ear by a huge grin.

Then it was Warad's turn.

Things did not go as well for him. He barreled into the maze, knocking the first bales of hay completely asunder with his massive shoulders as he tried to wriggle through a particularly tight spot. And it went downhill from there. He was caught on the side of the neck with a small portion of the pitch and bellowed like a baited bear, crashing and blundering through the rest of the maze with complete disregard for the boundaries and rules.

It was obvious he wouldn't be the crowd's favorite, as he was met with boos when he crossed the finish line. I didn't think he quite cared, though, as he emerged smiling brightly, happy to have made it through.

A few more young men took their turns: one whose tunic caught on fire and had to be removed down to his loincloth while the crowd roared, and another who was nearly decapitated by a flying ball of pitch but ducked at the last minute.

And then the last young man was called.

"Sir, are you ready?"

"I am." The young man's voice rang out clear. Like a bird's. He tied his long, curly hair back with a strap of leather and tensed at the line.

The town crier led the crowd in counting him down, and like a fired arrow, he was off. He raced with incredible speed into the maze, shimmying past the corners with agility.

Surely, he'd win. He was besting even Dagan's time! The

pitch flew by him and exploded the bale next to him in crackling fire. He leapt over the flames licking at his tunic and kept on going. His head was a blur as he bounded over the barricades, scaled the piles of sandstone bricks, and dodged every ball of pitch flung at him.

Except for the last one.

Just as he rounded the corner, headed for the exit of the maze, his face exultant, knowing he'd bested Dagan's time, a ball of searing pitch hit him squarely in the middle of the back, and he fell, writhing in agony, to the ground.

"*No!*" Across from me, Iltani stood, her mouth open in horror.

But I was having trouble. My head swam, and the flagon I'd been holding clanked to the ground at my feet. Absently, I watched it roll away and down the stairs. I needed to help this boy, but my head wasn't working right.

The crowd gasped, several standing and shouting obscenities at the guardsmen. In a rush, a woman, possibly the young man's mother, leapt from the stands, calling for help from the people around her. Two of them held the young man down, and the woman took a sharp knife and scraped the pitch from her son's back while the young man mewled like a wounded animal. Iltani plugged her ears against the noise. The people loaded him into a cart and fled the field, presumably headed somewhere to treat him outside the dirt and dust of the fray.

I wanted to go. To help. But my arms were no longer moving. I lurched to stand and fell against the woman on my right.

"Girl, are you quite all right? You look ill!"

The man behind us laughed. "That's the young healer they called in for the lugal! She's drunk!"

The woman snickered, and someone shoved me up onto wobbly feet. I took two steps, and then I was falling, falling, falling onto the platform with a crash. Around me, the sky spun in a crazy circle as the feet of the rich stamped in celebration, churning dust up into my eyes. As if from underwater, the town crier announced the name of the tournament winner, and the crowd shouted his name over and over and over.

Dagan, Farmer's Son! Dagan, Farmer's Son! Dagan, Farmer's Son!

As I lay on the platform, hidden behind the feet of the celebrants, the last thought I had before the retching tore my insides in two was whether or not Dagan would claim the token he'd won.

And if he did, whether it would be Nanaea's.

CHAPTER 10

THE AFTERNOON INTO the night was bleak. I managed to attract Iltani's and Dagan's attention after the performance, and they carried me up to my chamber, where I spent the entire evening vomiting the contents of my stomach.

Dagan placed the beads Nanaea had given him around my own neck, telling me he'd taken her token only because she'd offered it first, but I was in no condition to care. Iltani sent him away when I climbed astride the stone chamber pot and wished for my own death.

In the morning, when I woke, I was alone, save a servant knitting with goat-hair thread in the corner. She informed me that the Sacred Maidens were off preparing for some sort of performance, and the "poor girl"—Iltani—had been sent away. I hadn't even had a chance to thank her. My head felt fuzzy, my hands clammy. My mouth tasted as if a cat had crawled inside it and died. After dry-retching one more time, I felt a trifle better, although shaky and worried.

What in the name of Enlil had happened to me? I didn't think I'd drunk enough sikaru to be sick from it. But apparently, I was wrong. Perhaps the Palace crafted the drink much stronger than Assata. I thought of my abum sitting forlornly, his face buried in a flagon of brew, and shame bathed me in flames. How disappointed he would be in me for allowing myself to follow in his footsteps.

Wiping beads of sweat from my brow, I got dressed and found my way to the lugal's chamber, where he lay, shallowly breathing but alive. I bathed him, gave him some broth from the kitchens, changed his linens, then left to do what I should have done from the start: say a prayer for my abum, then research a cure for the lugal.

The crisscross pattern of the reed mat dug into my knees as I knelt with a small harp before an image of our winged god, Enlil. I was in the Temple shrine, which perched at the very top of the Palace like a bright blue bird on its nest. Light filtered in through an open window. A breeze and my bout with illness made me pull a jade-colored shawl I'd found on one of the hooks near my pallet around my shoulders more snugly.

Stacked against the walls in the Temple were instruments of every kind: lyres, harps, drums, tambourines, pipes. The dome of the ceiling stretched above me, spanned by a parade of painted singers, dancers, and musicians, their robes stained the color of green olives and ripe dates. Several more reed prayer mats lay scattered across the floor like cats basking in the sunshine, waiting to be scratched.

Laying my forehead against the mat, I prayed fervently to Enlil for the soul of my abum. His face as he'd set off for the Palace just a few days ago came to mind. He'd been shaky, weak, but the set of his chin had been determined. He'd wanted to restore our family's honor. But less than a quarter of a day later, he'd been killed somewhere between our little mudbrick hut and the Palace. And by whom? For what? He didn't carry any coins in his pockets or wear jewels about his neck. He'd never be mistaken for a wealthy merchant or tradesman. Not anymore. The thoughts swirling round inside my head threatened to tear me apart, so I righted myself and took a breath while the calmness of the Temple seeped into my bones. I had to stay strong for Nanaea.

The golden ox head carved into the wooden arm of the prayer harp in my lap stared at me mournfully, as if requesting a song. There was no use. I could not make beautiful music pour out of this instrument, like the young priestesses who were seated across the Temple, strumming harps in blissful harmony, but I might be able to find a cure for Lugal Marus. The Palace library, my next destination, was down just one flight of stairs.

I set my harp against the wall with the other instruments, exited the Temple, and headed down the corridor toward the library, a cavern rumored to house tablets written in crisp cuneiform about every aspect of the city of Alu. Hopefully, I could gather more information about what could be ailing the lugal there.

"Kammani!" Nanaea burst around the corner near the library door, with Simti close behind. A guardsman followed, then stood at attention when they stopped. Nanaea's cheeks were flushed, pink blooming on her skin like roses in a garden. Her deep brown eyes were lit like torches. My ummum's shawl was tucked around her elbows.

"Kammani, you are absolutely not going to believe what I am about to tell you."

"What? What is it?"

Nanaea beamed and twirled around. "We're going to dance and sing and show off our talents! For the entire Palace court! They want us to do a special private performance. Can you believe it?"

"Yes, and, Nanaea, I know you were bursting to tell her, but now that you have, we need to go!" Simti combed her hands through her thick black curls. "The performance is a turn of the dial away, and my hair still needs to be braided."

Nanaea held out a hand beseechingly. "I thought we were wearing our hair down."

"Well, you said you wanted to wear *your* hair down, but I like *my* hair in braids."

I put my hands up. "A performance? Listen. I don't have the time. . . ."

"It doesn't matter. Nin Arwia bade me fetch you so you could get ready, too. Apparently, all of us are to be bathed and powdered and scented for the viewers' pleasure." She batted her eyes in some semblance of coquettishness.

I poked her in the arm. "Well, first, we have not even broken our fast. And second, why do I have to be there? It's not like I will be dancing or singing or whatever it is you will be doing."

"That's what we said," Simti intervened, "but the court does not care. Uruku and other prominent ensis want to see more of 'the pretty learned healer,' so you have to come, too. And this is important for us! We need to demonstrate we are fit to be Lugal Marus's sarratums. If we cannot showcase our talents well enough, we could be dismissed." Simti twisted a coil of hair around her finger. "Luckily, I can sing like a bird."

But I needed to get into the library and find something to help me heal the lugal. If I didn't determine his illness, Nanaea would be dancing for the dead instead of the living.

"I will attend the performance, but I simply cannot go and get primped, no matter what the nin has said. There's something I must do relating to the lugal beforehand."

"I know, but Nin Arwia told me to fetch you." Nanaea dropped her voice to a whisper. "She's probably too scared of Uruku to argue."

And she had every right to be.

"Fine, but I'll be along shortly. I have to go into the library first."

"Why?"

"Well—" I tried to think of something plausible. No doubt she wouldn't want to know I was going in there to find a better way to steal her dream from her. "Because I've—forgotten something in there."

She pursed her lips. "You're lying."

Blushing, I stammered something unintelligible. She could always read my face. I hadn't been able to lie to her in years. Well, except about how my abum had died, but that was absolutely necessary.

I sighed. "There's something I need to do, all right? I'll meet you at the performance afterward."

"Wait. I could come *with* you. We haven't spent any time together at all!"

"We won't have time to get ready!" Simti shrieked.

"I look lovely enough as I am," Nanaea said to Simti, hands on her round hips.

Simti rolled her eyes. "Fine. I'll meet you there." Then she turned and disappeared the other way down the corridor, leaving the guardsman confused as to which way to go. Finally, he turned and followed her.

Nanaea then turned twinkling eyes to me. "Why do you really need to go into the library? Tell me the truth."

"I can tell you, but you're not going to like it."

She frowned. "Why? What are you doing?"

"I'm looking for a better way to heal the lugal."

❖ ❖ ❖ ❖ ❖

Nanaea insisted on coming, if only to hurry me along. Since the nin had bade her fetch me, she was worried she'd be in trouble if she showed up alone.

"Let's just get this over with quickly. The performance is supposed to begin soon! And we've already wasted so much time arguing." Nanaea followed me into a cavernous library teeming with stacks of tablets of every size and shape. Tablets larger than my midsection covered the lowest recesses of the walls, while those smaller than a person's hand took up the highest nooks. Wooden tables and clay-brick benches were scattered throughout, along with an entire area dedicated to the inscribing of tablets. There were cisterns brimming with water. Feathers and other copper tools. Inks and stains in every color. Even tablet presses.

I wiped sweaty palms down the sides of my tunic. *What incredible knowledge is contained in these stacks?* I could learn everything about healing here. Or nearly everything, as many things had to be learned by doing. But the knowledge possibly contained in these tablets—the history of other A-zus' remedies, and better methods for alleviating pain—made my head spin. I could not wait to pull them all down and read over them one by one. It was disappointing that now I had just a short amount of time because of some ill-timed Maiden showcase.

"Where in Enlil's name do we start?" Nanaea tugged Ummum's shawl around her shoulders, round eyes searching the shelves. There were stacks *everywhere*. The system of organization seemed haphazard at first, but then I noticed that inscriptions were tapped in tiny letters beneath the stacks of tablets, giving the general idea of their contents.

"I'll begin over here," I said. "It looks as though there is healing history in these stacks. Maybe you can start in the rituals section over there. See if you can find anything related to his condition." I pointed at some small tablets near the back wall.

"I won't know what to look for, Sister." Nanaea grabbed a pile of the tablets, grunting with the effort, and headed for a table. "And it's likely it won't do any good anyway, right? He's nigh unto death, is he not?"

"Is that what you're hoping for?" I hoisted a heavy tablet off a shelf and wiped the dust from its surface. "That this is all for naught? Everything I'm doing?"

She sat on a bench near the table and laid out her tablets in a neat line. "You know I am." She smoothed her hair away from her face and picked up a tablet. "But it's not as easy for me as you think it is. For if my wish comes true, then you will have failed, and who knows what that means for you. I'm not as cruel as you think."

Sitting on the cool sandstone bench near her, I laid the tablet down. It crumbled along the edges. "You're not cruel. You're naïve."

"Which is likely worse to you." She met my eyes across the two tables. "I'm not a child. I know what's best for me."

"But you don't realize that what you want is not what will be delivered."

"Yes, I've heard you say it before. The Boatman." She waved her hand as if shooing away a moth.

I frowned at her ready dismissal. "Yes, him. You know the folklore as well as I. He brings people over to the other side in his skeleton arms. It is *not* something to celebrate. It would be horribly scary—"

"Death is scary. I *know* that. I was there at our ummum's side when she passed to the Netherworld, too, remember?" Her eyes flashed, but her lip trembled. "But *afterward* is what matters. *After* you cross the river. Who cares how you get there if you're greeted with new life?"

A wave of emotion swelled in my chest. "I care."

Across the room, she dragged her finger down a tablet, her chin set as my abum's used to be when he'd bicker with my ummum. But we didn't have much time.

"Listen, Nanaea, this is difficult and strange for both of us." I shrugged, my shoulders heavy with the burdens that had been forced upon me. "I want the lugal to live—"

"—and I *need* him to die," she whispered.

We sat in silence, each contemplating the other's goal, each praying to Enlil he would not hear the other's prayer. But despite my misgivings, I somewhat understood that Nanaea would feel as she did. She'd lived a life of ease, prestige, and wealth—we all had—and without any warning, all of that had been stripped away. It was hard to blame her, but sacrificing her life to have the status again didn't make any sense, either.

I breathed out through my nose, releasing the stress her words inflicted. "Can we just proceed? So I can finish and we can leave?"

She nodded once, mutely, and began to read.

Searching in earnest, I traced my fingers down the sides of tablet after tablet, looking for information about his breathing issues, foaming at the mouth, and tremors, but found, to my vexation, that the tablets weren't as organized as I'd thought. There were passages on copper smelting followed by maps of the stars. Irrigation of crops to new-moon rituals of long ago. But besides a few inscriptions on tinctures, a cure for mad-dog bites, and one strange description of resetting a broken bone, there wasn't much more about healing. Nanaea was coming up short as well, although I didn't entirely trust her to know what she was looking for, or to have the resolve to tell me if she *did* find anything. No matter, though, because time was running out.

Dejected, I decided to look in one last stack and grabbed another tablet off the top. I stopped, brushing away a cobweb from its corner. It was a poem. I read it quietly, my fingers tracing the inscription as my lips moved silently with the lyrical words.

Darling, dear to my heart,
Long is your beauty, Honeysweet,
Mistress, dear to my heart,
Far is your beauty, Honeysweet.

You have captivated me.
Let me stand, trembling, before you.
You have captured me.
Let me stand, shackled, before you.

Darling, dear to my heart,
I yearn for one caress.
Mistress, dear to my heart,
I will die for one caress.

I will seek your hand, Honeysweet.
To your father I'll go.
I will seek your love, Honeysweet.
To your mother I'll go.

Darling, dear to my heart,
My blood runs true as yours.
Mistress, dear to my heart,
My heart beats only for yours.

You have captivated me.
Let me stand, trembling, before you.
You have captured me.
Let me stand, shackled, before you.

Blood surged through my veins. Longing squeezed in my belly. Had anyone ever written such words to me? No. Never. Yes, Dagan had intentions for me. That was as clear to me as the blue waters running in the Garadun. But no one had ever written something so passionate for my eyes alone. So full of yearning and ache. But is that what it meant to be in love, anyway? Granted, I'd seen fire in my abum's eyes when he watched my mother shaping clay at the potter's wheel, and also in hers when he lovingly rubbed Kasha's head after a big belly laugh. I'd witnessed Assata wrapped in her husband Irra's arms at the back of the tavern, their lips pressed together, oblivious of everyone but each other.

I blushed at the memory.

"What is it that has your cheeks so rosy?" Nanaea leaned over my back, pressing her chin into my shoulder. The faintest scent of my ummum's skin wafted up from the shawl around her shoulders.

"Nothing." I tried slipping the tablet under another, but she grabbed it from my hands and read, her eyebrows moving farther and farther up into her hairline as her eyes scanned the lines.

I covered my face with my hands. "My biggest regret is teaching you to read."

"Why? Were you thinking about Dagan?" She smiled softly, our previous conversation melting away.

"Silence yourself. Please." But I knew my furious blushing was a beacon of truth.

She collapsed next to me on the bench, her eyes dancing. "You were! So the betrothal is coming sooner than we expect, is it? You've come to your senses about accepting his love? Have you settled the bride price?"

"Oh, stop it. Honestly." I made a swipe for the tablet and missed. "Besides, it's not as though you're completely immune to Dagan's charms."

There. I'd said it. Voiced the niggling at the back of my brain about the flirtations she'd been unabashedly sending his way.

"Sister, don't be serious. Even if I wanted Dagan, he's so smitten with you that I'd never have a chance."

"Well, he chose you for a token, did he not? After the tournament?"

She rolled her eyes. "He accepted a necklace from me rather than a lock of Huna's hair or Simti's shawl. Besides"— she pinched my arm lightly—"as I said before, I'm spoken for, unlike you."

A groan rose in my throat at her casual reference to the betrothal. "Give me that." I snatched the tablet out of her grasp. "Not that it's any of your business, but Dagan is not on my mind in that way. I don't wish to be wed and saddled with a house of boisterous children. I have quite enough to do as it is."

Nanaea dropped down onto the bench across from mine. "Oh, Sister. Is that what love is to you? A burden? I think love is bliss and happiness and joy. It is like the syrup on top of a honeycake. When Lugal Marus crosses over, he'll be returned to health and we will fall in love and live happily for eternity."

I snorted. My father awash with sikaru, drowning in his own tears after my mother died, was not bliss. The commitment of little girls to a lugal for his uses in the Netherworld once they'd been poisoned or stabbed or bashed to death with a brick was not joy.

"There's more to it than what you know, Nanaea. I have plans to be as great of an A-zu as Abum was. And a woman cannot do *everything* she wants."

She tossed her hair, some of her self-sure attitude creeping back in. "Well, I think you're wrong. You can have children and a healing practice and love and a happy life. All you'd need is a little help from time to time."

"And from whom would I get that help if you were in the Netherworld?"

At that, her eyes flitted down to the table, and she removed her hand from mine.

A coldness washed over me, because this scenario was the likely outcome. I was no closer to a cure. Because the lugal, although resting and even taking in some broth, was deteriorating in bits and pieces because of an illness that remained a mystery. Despair writhed under my breastbone like an eel.

"Sister, don't be sad. Everything will work out as it's supposed to, all right?" She stood, her deep brown eyes studying me intensely. And then she perked up.

"You know what? You could try heading over to the farm."

Absently shuffling the stacks of tablets nearest to me, I looked for a salve or a cream my eyes might have accidentally passed over. "Why would I go there?"

"Doesn't Dagan's ummum have tinctures and such?"

An image of Dagan's mother sewing a laceration on one of the hind legs of a goat flashed in my mind. "It isn't quite the same." I walked to the other side of the room and ran my finger along the stacks.

Nanaea crossed her arms over her chest. "But it's a good idea. We've found nothing in here, and you said yourself that the Palace healer was gone to another city. With Abum gone, what else are you going to do?" Her pretty eyes dimmed at the mention of our abum.

She had a point, and my heart squeezed at her trying to help me even though she believed my win would be her loss. "That's actually a very good suggestion, Sister. My thanks." I pressed a hand over my heart.

Dagan's mother might at least give me some insight. I thought of Dagan's bright smile and easy grace greeting me at the door, then shoved him from my mind.

"There you are!" Nin Arwia's voice startled me from my thoughts. She stood in the doorway, arrayed in an olive-green tunic covered at the hem in triangular gold stitching, her copper headdress slightly off-kilter.

"Your Grace. I was doing some research, and Nanaea was helping me . . ." I finished lamely, putting a tablet back on a shelf, wondering if she'd think me incompetent.

She smiled and crossed the room to link her arm through mine. "You are free to be in here. I wanted you to attend the performance to celebrate that my abum is looking a bit better! Gudanna said he was resting comfortably, so I went into the Sacred Maidens' chamber to thank you. But neither you nor Nanaea was there getting prepared." She eyeballed my hair speculatively. It was likely frizzy and covered in dust from the tablets. I cleared my throat and tried to smooth it down.

"I am prepared, Nin Arwia," Nanaea intervened. "My apologies if I caused you to feel otherwise. I'll just need to slip into a frock." She slid in beside the nin, adjusting her headdress in one quick motion. "There. Set to rights."

"Thank you, Maiden. I appreciate the touch."

My sister may have been naïve, but she was not stupid.

I patted the nin's hand. "And, Nin Arwia, my apologies. I was confirming a remedy in here, and now I'm ready to accompany you, although your abum *does* need me more. If I could just attend to him—"

Gudanna appeared at the doorway. "Lugal Marus is doing very well, Healer. Earlier today, he took some broth before falling back asleep. Nasu helped change his linens, and we've kept the drapery open as you've suggested."

"See? It's settled. We'll watch the demonstration, and then you can run off to my abum. I know he's much better in your care."

I nodded, unconvinced, but allowed myself to be led out of the cool library and into the warmth of the early morning. As we walked, Nin Arwia chattered about her new mare and her love of riding. I found myself liking her and enjoying her talk despite the fiery ball of dread that burned inside me at the thought of seeing Ensi Uruku and other courtiers salivating over my little sister.

But as was required, I followed the nin to the courtyard, deciding that my life was not in my own control any more than the lugal's death was. And hating every bit of that fact.

CHAPTER 11

✿

WE ARRIVED IN a gorgeously appointed courtyard and found a boisterous group of the Palace court milling around the benches against the sandstone wall, keeping beneath the potted palms and white canopies for shade as they sipped from flagons. Crimson climbing flowers spread from mud-brick pots to the beams of the canopies, adding a thick perfume to the air and a burst of color against the sandy beige wall.

In the center of the courtyard, a large multicolored reed mat heaped with bells, harps, tambourines, and drums waited for my sister, Simti, and Huna's performances. Musicians sat nearby, quietly strumming their lyres. Sturdy block benches made from the same sandstone as the walls surrounded the mat on three sides, giving each viewer an up-close and personal view of the girl performing.

Outside of us and a few servants, there wasn't a woman in attendance.

What kind of demonstration is this?

A few of the men were guardsmen, armored as if going to war. Sickleswords, a handful of maces, and two or three bronze socket axes and daggers hung from their sides. All the men but Uruku wore long, full beards.

Two of the men—a tall, broad-shouldered one with gray, grizzled hair and a squat, balding man with a bulbous nose—wore cloaks of hare pelts fastened to their tunics with bright silver brooches with Lugal Marus's emblem on them. Emeralds glittered in the lion's eyes. These men had to be merchants of the king. I knew Huna's father was one of them, and would bank my soul on her sire being the shorter one, wringing his meaty hands together. The squat nose on her face was a duplicate of his.

Nanaea gently nudged me and, startled, I stumbled in. Ensi Uruku stood, arms crossed, a foot tapping as if he'd been waiting for us.

Uruku's eyes crawled down the length of my body as Nin Arwia, the Sacred Maidens, and I walked toward the crowd. I quickly shifted my eyes to my feet, but the displeasure radiating from him hit me with surging force. Servants stationed around the corners of the courtyard immediately converged on the Sacred Maidens to shade their faces from the sun with shimmering white draperies.

We wound our way around the benches like a small

caravan of jeweled parcels being transported across the desert. I smoothed my hair again and attempted to wipe my hands on my white tunic. I thought better of it when I saw how dirty they were.

"You're late, girls. Very late." Ensi Uruku's back was ramrod straight.

"My apologies." Nin Arwia breezed by him, toward the benches. "There was business regarding Lugal Marus to which Kammani had to attend."

"Never mind that. You've been summoned to the courtyard this morning so we can be confident of the lugal's prize in the Netherworld."

"And where are the women who were to attend this performance?" Nin Arwia clasped her hands in front of her.

"They've been otherwise occupied, Your Grace." Ensi Uruku took in each of us in turn. Simti stared boldly at Uruku as he took in the curves of her hips. When his eyes met hers again, he grinned a small, gray-toothed smile, and she offered a mirthless half-smile in return.

Nin Arwia inclined her head. "That's fine, Ensi. These girls will make the lugal proud today. Nanaea, you'll showcase your talent first. Then Simti. Then Huna. And then we'll be on our way. Gentlemen, if you'll please seat yourselves on the benches to the left. Ladies, you may sit on the right, waiting until it is your turn."

I nodded and turned toward our seats.

"The ladies will sit with us." The Maidens and I stilled as Uruku's soft voice echoed off the walls of the courtyard. The men grinned, and one man licked his lips. Huna's father's face grew pale.

Nin Arwia turned to Uruku, squaring her shoulders. She was undoubtedly trying to figure out a way to argue with him without seeming to do so.

One man in the back grabbed his groin. "The prettiest lady can sit on my lap. Right here." Several of the men guffawed and clanked their flagons together. Ensi Uruku flicked his eyes to the man, and the oily grin melted off his face.

And then Uruku looked at *me*. He approached, one hand on the end of his mace, the other rubbing his jaw.

By my side, Simti stiffened.

"Did you mean this creature?" He reached out to touch my hair. Instinctively, I jerked away. He laughed quietly, his eyes crinkled at the edges in amusement. His breath smelled of rot.

"You're the healer, are you not?"

"Yes, Ensi."

"So . . . what's *your* talent? Are you going to tie bells onto those hips and dance? Or recite a love poem to me?"

Never. I swallowed with difficulty, my mouth as dry as a bone bleached by the sun.

I cast my eyes to my feet, so his unrelenting stare didn't unnerve me, but he gently put a hand under my chin and lifted my face to look at him. Quivering under the quiet strength of his hold, I met his eyes but could not force my chin from his grasp.

"She isn't one of the Sacred Maidens. Perhaps you've

forgotten?" Simti supplied in my stead, clasping my hand firmly in hers.

I nodded, despite the pressure of his fingertips pressing into my jaw.

Nin Arwia laid a soft hand on his arm. "I understand your request, Ensi, but the healer does not have any talents in this area. Let's proceed with those who do, shall we?"

"Well, then she can sit with me and watch the performance, can't she." It wasn't a question.

"Noble Ensi, although that would be an honor for a girl of her stature, the lugal's spirit would be most enraged if the healer who attended him were to be . . . distracted from her duties. No doubt the joy of your proximity would relieve her of her senses."

He could probably kill us all if he wanted to. None of these men would challenge him. But although his jaw clenched and unclenched, his eyes remained placid, and he didn't argue. He was either a madman or a careful executioner of control.

"Very well. Let's see their talents, then."

Clearly, he would not defy Nin Arwia. At least not when all these people were around. Huna's father looked relieved. He sat down on the benches to the left, and the rest of the men followed his lead and positioned themselves behind him.

"Nanaea, when you're ready." Nin Arwia nodded, gesturing to the center stage.

"Yes, Maiden Nanaea. I want to see," Uruku spoke softly, leaning back on his elbows.

I made a beeline for the bench, suppressing the tears that threatened to fall. Simti smiled sadly at me when I squeezed in next to her and gave me a hug strong enough to pop my eyes from their sockets.

For all her childishness, I had to give Nanaea credit. Her hands didn't shake at all as she took to the center of the court-yard and selected four bracelets with tinkling silver bells.

She slid a bracelet over each bare foot and one over each of her wrists. After tying a green silk waist scarf with even more bells around her middle, she loosened the pins from her hair. Black curls cascaded down her back like a banner. The cop-per headdress on the crown of her head shone brightly in the sunlight, and she slowly took it off and set it on a bench. As the air around us fell silent, she turned to Uruku.

"As you wish, my lord." She bowed deeply, one toe pointed to him, hands held gracefully to the left and right.

And then she danced.

For the next few moments in time, no one knew anything else but Nanaea's flashing black hair and swirling tunic. Her dancing was magic. The men were enraptured by the *ching* of the bells on her hips. The harsh crack of her hands when she clapped. Her snapped "Hah!" when she spun. The tilt of her head when she looked to the sky. Smoldering eyes flashed. Reaching fingers sought the crowd. Her feet stamped a rhythm matched only by our pulsating hearts.

After all the performances, I left her, beaming with pride, surrounded by adulating men and a sulking Huna, who'd botched her vocal performance so terribly, her father had walked out of the courtyard in haste and hadn't returned by the time Nin Arwia released me.

Exhausted from pretending I wasn't jumping out of my skin in impatience, I exited the courtyard out a side entrance to check on the lugal, with Uruku's eyes following my every move.

❂ ❂ ❂ ❂ ❂

The lugal's eyes were slits. Lips cracked and dried. Cheeks sunk into his face as if the Boatman had already claimed his soul and discarded his shell of a body for the worms.

But when I wiped a cool, damp linen down the side of his face, he stirred.

"Lugal Marus?"

His hand rose from his side and hovered listlessly above his coverlet, and I took it, squeezing with tenderness. His bony fingers curled weakly around mine, and my heart ached.

He'd stolen so much from my family, but something about the size of his hand and the warmth of the blood still coursing beneath his skin filled me with compassion. My father had died alone. I wouldn't let this man do the same, especially when my sister's fate was tied to his.

Awhile later, after I'd bathed him and trickled broth down his throat, I left the Palace to seek answers in Dagan's home. Dusk approached rapidly. Trekking quickly through the fields of barley and emmer, spurred by the need for answers, I trailed my hands along their tickly tops. Crickets stopped their chirring when I drew near and picked up where they'd left off as I moved away.

Against my wishes, my breaths got faster, my hands sweatier, the closer I drew to the farm. Dancing torches from its perimeter and candles from within radiated a warm welcome. Hopefully, answers were in there, too. At the front door, I stopped and smoothed back my hair before banging my hand against the side panel. Within moments, the front door was cautiously opened.

Dagan, holding a candle and wearing a watchful expression, broke into a surprised smile when he saw it was me. "Kammani!"

His younger brothers Shep and Marduk stood at his elbow.

"Welcome to our humble abode," said Shep. "The big man has been pining for you." He grinned, showing two pointed incisors that made him look like a dog itching for a fight.

"Get out of here," Dagan said, shoving them both down the corridor. Shep laughed, grabbing Marduk's shaggy head under his arm, and they went back from whence they'd come.

I smiled, watching them go, and Dagan gingerly placed the candle in a sconce on a table next to us, then took my hands in his. His eyes grew soft as he studied my face. He smelled like earth. And the sweetness of home. I was struck by a memory of the two of us sitting by one of his outbuildings a year or so past. After relentless work in the fields, Dagan had stopped to wipe his brow with the inside of an arm. His torso, heaving from the heft of the mattock, had been bare to the belt.

His eyes had crinkled with a smile as he'd tossed the mattock into a bin and plopped down next to me, and he'd thrown a sweaty arm around my shoulder as we'd talked about my day. His. We'd ended our conversation in fits of laughter as he'd impersonated the snorting pigs in the pen behind us. I'd felt safe and secure there by his side. Protected from the evil of the world. The day, despite his sweat and the heat and the stink of the pigs, had been perfect.

"I've missed you," he said, and like that, I found myself pulled into Dagan's firm embrace in the darkness of the front corridor. He was warm. He felt like safety. When I pulled away to look into his eyes, the candle radiated warm light on his noble features.

He tucked my hair behind my ears. "I've been worried sick ever since you fell ill at the Maidens' Welcome festival. The guardsmen always say you must be busy when I inquire at the gates. Are you all right?"

"I'm fine, of course. I've just never had the Palace brew. It struck me the wrong way." I blushed, wondering if he saw me differently after being so ill. The dimness of the entryway was a relief; at least he couldn't see my embarrassment.

"Enlil be praised." He rubbed a thumb down my cheek. I pressed my face into his warm, calloused hand. "How are things with the lugal?" he asked. "Are your methods working?"

I shook my head, and his hand fell away. "No, and it's so frustrating. I'm trying everything my abum taught me, but the lugal wastes away day after day. It's why I'm here. I was hoping your ummum might be able to guide me." And all at once, tears threatened to choke me. My eyes welled, but swallowing profusely in the dim light, I forced them back.

"Kammani," he whispered hoarsely.

Not trusting myself to speak, I buried my face once more in his chest. It felt right, being held there, like a boat moored in a raging storm. For a moment, I let myself drift in his embrace. Secure. Safe. His blood thumped under his skin as the scent of him enveloped me. He rubbed my back, and after a few moments, the air subtly shifted. My heart rate and breathing increased. His chest against my cheek felt warmer. More alive. I lifted my face to say something—not even sure what it was—but before words formed themselves on my tongue, he brought his lips down gently to mine.

For a moment, a fraction of a breath, there was nothing else but his warm mouth. His strong hands on my back, pulling me to him. Closer, and closer still.

But then I broke away, my lips zinging from his kiss. The shock set my head spinning. "Dagan." I faltered, my breath leaving my body. *What am I thinking?*

"I'm sorry. Forgive me. I've taken liberties—" He rubbed his beard. Clenched his hands into fists.

"I'm . . . just not . . . here for you. For *that*. I'm . . . I'm . . . always here for you, you see." My head was woozy, and my tongue would not properly form any words that made any sense at all. *But what can I even say?* My breath was stuck in my throat.

"It's . . . I understand . . . I don't—" He sucked in a big breath and blew it out, then ran a hand through his hair.

I stepped back, pressing a fist to my mouth, which was *on fire*, then bumped into a table. I couldn't do this. Promise him the betrothal he wanted. My ummum's and abum's deaths and the threat of my sister's had carved out most of my heart. There was nothing left to give. I took another step away, around the table, and pressed myself against the wall, willing myself to melt into the floor. "Dagan, I'm sorry. You probably think that I am ready to accept your hand. But there's so much on my shoulders—"

"It's okay. It's my fault, please. You're under a lot of stress. Say no more."

"It's just that—I don't know. There's so much for me to do! The lugal is dying and my sister needs me and—"

His face was filled with agony. "Say no more, sweet. This was all my fault."

My hands found themselves in my hair and tugged at the curls. *What am I doing?* I breathed deeply, and my heart calmed as Dagan stood on the other side of the hallway, his hands fumbling around, not quite knowing what to do. My nerves settled as I focused again on my mission. *Heal the lugal. Save Nanaea.* "Will you please get your ummum for me? It's why I'm here."

"Yes!" He practically leapt at the chance to be useful. "Yes. My ummum. I can get her. I'm so, so sorry. I didn't mean to—"

I pressed my lips together, closing my eyes against the awkwardness.

"Yes. I'm going to. Go. There." He pointed down the hallway and retreated into the shadows.

When he left, I held my hand to my forehead in disbelief. What in the world was going on in my head? Kissing Dagan? Giving him hope of marriage when there was none? I couldn't live a life at the farm, with him toiling throughout the day and coming in to eat a freshly prepared meal after tossing one of a half-dozen children into the air. Or, a worse fate: struggling to bring a child into the world, only to have it die and take me with it into the arms of the Boatman.

Except . . . he'd felt so warm. My lips still *tasted* like him. If anyone would be able to persuade me to marry, it would be him. I knew he loved me. Could I love him in the same way?

My thoughts were interrupted by a woman clearing her throat.

"Kammani?" Shiptu, Dagan's mother, asked softly from another corridor, the opposite side of the entryway from which Dagan had exited.

I tugged at the waist of my tunic. Had she seen?

"Shiptu." I angled my face to the ground to avoid her gaze. "I don't know what happened—" I started, but stumbled. Why was I explaining myself? Why did I feel the need?

"You need my help?" she asked quietly.

I looked up to judge her tone. Warm amber eyes, the same shade as Dagan's, met mine. Soft wrinkles fanned along the corners. A thousand smiles and as many worries had etched lines into her forehead. As a mother to five boys, she had every right to those lines. But her eyes were shining. A small smile played at her mouth.

"Shiptu, I'm sorry. It's not what you think."

"And what do I think?"

"That we're in love. That the betrothal has happened. It isn't like that at all."

"It isn't? From the way your hands gripped his shoulders as he kissed you, I would have sworn—"

My insides squirmed, and my sandaled feet became very important all of a sudden. I studied my wriggling toes.

She laughed, a full-throated sound that belied her small frame. "Kammani, come with me. I didn't mean to embarrass you."

Brushing past me out the front door, she walked to an outbuilding near the pigpen. After placing the torch she'd been carrying in a holder, she squeaked the wooden door open.

Blinking in the dim light inside, I waited for my eyes to adjust. I could walk across the storage shed—one of many on their farm—in three strides. Clay bins of various sizes teetered against the wall to my left, with more on shelves above. Against the far wall, beneath the rectangular window, eight large pots of grains and legumes sat squat and proud, casks weathered by many years of hands hauling them from farm to market. Dried herbs lay on shelves carved into the mudbrick wall above the grains, and various spools of goat-hair, woolen, and linen threads were propped in the corner, ready for weaving. The earthy smell of hide still clung to the grayish wool. A shelf to my right held pots full of tinctures and remedies, clean linens, and various knives and lancing tools. She'd been doing more healing and mending at the farm than I'd thought.

"Before you tell me why you came here, why don't you tell me why you aren't going to marry my son?" She propped herself against a table. "If it's because you can't afford the dowry, we can work something out."

Again, heat crept into my face. "That's not it. And, for starters, he hasn't asked. Not officially."

"Because he knows what you'll say. He's no fool. What man of his stature would want to be turned down by you?"

At the reminder that I should be grateful for his love, my anger flared. "Because we were cast out?"

"Partly," she countered, leaning back, her arms crossed against her thin chest. "And I mean nothing by that. It's how life works. But also partly because if he actually heard you tell him no, he'd have to understand that he must pursue another young woman for his bride. And trust me when I say there are plenty who would *love* the honor of being my son's wife."

Bile rose in my throat at the thought of Dagan wrapping his arms around another girl. Even if I didn't want to be his bride, I didn't want anyone else to be. I could admit that.

"I can see that the idea leaves you angry. Have you thought why that might be?"

"Shiptu, I can't. That's all I can say. Not right now." But my answer made me feel empty inside. Like I'd felt when I'd read that stupid poem.

She crossed her legs at the ankles. "It's your life, child. But I hope you realize you may regret the decision not to speak up and accept love when it's right under your nose. Trust me on that."

Across the small room, her eyes were hooded. She was clearly hiding some personal sorrow I didn't know anything about.

Does Dagan know?

"It's a difficult decision, Shiptu."

"Decision, you say." She raised an eyebrow. "What luxury is in that word."

"What do you mean?"

"The other young women in this city will be bartered for and traded like pigs. Yet you have been given the distinct honor of *choice* because your abum never agreed to Dagan's requests without your consent. And you have a good man, an honorable one who *loves* you, but you shy away." She shook her head. "You have untold wealth in your satchel, yet it remains unspent."

My cheeks flamed. "I'll think about his offer. I truly will." *As I have done, repeatedly.*

"Please do." She stood, slapped her hands against her thighs, and moved on to the business at hand. "Now. Tell me all about your problem."

So I did. I told her about the lugal's symptoms. That he'd lost his breath and foamed at the mouth. That he'd vomited and shaken terribly. I told her every remedy I'd tried and how he kept getting worse.

She listened intently as I talked, her eyes roving to her little shelf full of tinctures and cures.

When I stopped, she pulled a stool out from under a table. "Give me a hand." I held mine out to steady her as she stepped onto it and reached up to the top shelf, which was almost to the ceiling. Dust and cobwebs lined the bottles and jars. She searched through the contents, pulling corks and sniffing. Her eyes lit up when she stumbled upon a small pot with a tiny black X painted on it and a scrawled note beneath. She grabbed it, then carefully stepped down.

She pressed the jar into my hand, her expression somber. "I know what's wrong. Or at least I can guess."

I looked down at the little bottle and uncorked the top.

"Be careful with that, Kammani. Close it."

I cautiously pushed the cork back down. "Why? What is it?"

She looked past me as if ensuring that no one else could hear, even though we were alone in this outbuilding in the middle of a field.

"I think—I couldn't swear to it, of course—but if I had to guess, I'd say he's being poisoned."

My eyes flew open in surprise. "What? Poisoned?" I'd never dealt with an intentional poisoning before. I'd helped children vomit after getting into poisonous berries and helped a woman recover from eating spoiled meat, but never had I cured someone who was actively being poisoned. Still, as soon as she said it, it made sense. Maybe.

She moistened her lips. "I'm not exactly certain, I mean. Fairly so. His symptoms sound a lot like what happened to the pigs when they got into some monkshood."

I'd heard of monkshood before. My father had told me about it and had called it by its other name: wolfsbane. He'd told me they were plants that were poisonous, but I knew nothing about them.

"They don't grow around here, do they?"

"No," she admitted. "But I did get some seeds from traders and planted them near a tributary." She swallowed guiltily. "I had no idea they were poisonous. I saw the pretty flowers and thought—why not? But when the boys took the pigs to the water to give them a drink, the pigs went into the state you described after eating the petals."

"So what did you do?"

She pointed to the jar with the X on it. "I gave them that. It's a tincture an old friend once gave me. An antidote of sorts. And—it worked, which is how I knew that they'd been poisoned."

"How so?"

She blew out a big breath. "Because if they hadn't been poisoned, the antidote would have killed them. It works only if there is monkshood or another poison in the system, I believe. I gave it once to a young field hand who'd eaten the beans of a poisonous plant after his love married another; and he survived, but I tried it last summer on a goat that fell ill with some sort of sickness, and the tincture killed the poor thing. And quickly." She nodded to the bottle.

I held the antidote with shaking fingers and scanned the instructions.

Administer 2 to 3 drops under the tongue in case of poisoning by nightshade, monkshood, or hemlock. Emergency use only.

170

"In emergencies, huh? Like the 'Nanaea will die if the lugal dies' kind of emergencies?" My sister's lovely face swam in front of my vision, her eyes round and pleading. She needed me.

Shiptu smiled without any mirth. "Yes. Emergencies like that."

"How much do I give? It says two to three drops . . ."

She blew the air out of her lungs and put her hands on her hips. "But for a man his size? I'd say four drops, perhaps. Give him that and see if it helps. Better too little than too much, you know?"

Yes. I knew.

"Now go." She shooed me out the door before her, and she stepped into the chill of the evening with the bottle and a dilemma: Give him the antidote or not. How could I guarantee it would work? And if it didn't work—if he *wasn't* being poisoned—I'd be killing him myself and sending my sister to her death that much faster.

"Thanks, Shiptu. For this"—I held up the tincture—"and the advice. I'll study the lugal to see if it's the cause, and if so . . ." I shook the bottle.

"Of course. Now get on. And keep to the roads."

"I will!" I called over my retreating back. She slammed the door to the outbuilding and clanked the locking mechanism into place. I took three steps down the road and something occurred to me.

"Shiptu!" I called.

"Yes?" she answered, her arms around her body for warmth.

"What did the flowers look like? The monkshood?"

"They were blue. Kind of a bluish purple. With a sort of cap that comes down over the top."

A chill went down my spine. The flower in the lugal's bedroom I'd thrown into the fire. It hadn't come from the nin's flowers in her hair. I cursed myself for my idiocy. I might need to show it to prove what was happening to the lugal! But now it was gone.

"Thanks, Shiptu!" I cried, then took off at a full sprint.

Although I still wasn't absolutely convinced, I knew I had little choice in the matter. I'd either have to give him the antidote and trust that he was being poisoned, or allow him to die without trying at all. My first job was to dose him and wait. Then I had to convince Nin Arwia to believe me, and catch whoever was trying to kill the lugal before they succeeded.

CHAPTER 12

THERE WERE TWO guardsmen at the lugal's door. One had an unkempt black beard and brows that almost touched. It was the same guardsman who'd bashed in the teeth of that poor woman. He was slouched against the doorway, arms crossed, hands tucked into his armpits, eyes closed in a sort of anxious slumber.

The other was Nasu, who, resolute and placid as always, nodded calmly as I jogged to the doorway, my hand hiding the vial behind my back. He kept his eyes on mine as I caught my breath.

"I need in, Nasu. I need to see him."

"He's resting. Please calm yourself before you enter."

The other guardsman, who'd been asleep, snorted and roused himself, nearly falling off the stool. Nasu flicked his eyes once at the man and then back to me, a hint of annoyance the only emotion that crossed his face.

Smoothing my hair and straightening my tunic with the hand not holding the tincture, I nodded. "I'm calm and ready to cure him." *Enlil help me, I hope I can cure him.*

"She's got something behind her back, Nasu."

The other man roughly grabbed my arm and held my hand out for Nasu's inspection.

Nasu warily eyed the bottle, the large painted X giving him pause. "What is it?"

I swallowed. I wasn't dumb enough to tell him that the lugal was probably being poisoned and this antidote could be his only hope of life. The gods only knew if *Nasu* was the one doing it. It could be anyone! Studying his warm brown eyes and the set of his chin, I knew he looked earnest enough, but one never knew the thoughts of a man.

My ummum taught me that.

I covered the "X" with my thumb, hiding my nerves with seeming impatience. "It's a cure, not that it is any of your business. Nin Arwia has given me full access to Lugal Marus and trusts my judgment." *Ill-advised or not.* "Now, please, open the door."

When he didn't move, I jerked away from the big guardsman and reached around his frame for the door handle.

"She's an arrogant rat and should be dealt with as such." He unsheathed his sicklesword.

Nasu's nostrils flared briefly. "Lamusa, stand down. Kammani, go attend to the lugal while Lamusa and I chat. Go." He stepped back, and I scurried under his arm with a sigh of relief. Lamusa puffed out his chest, and with one swift move,

Nasu unsheathed his own sicklesword and brought it up under Lamusa's throat.

"Don't harm him, Nasu. I've enough to do," I muttered as I pushed into the muggy stench of the lugal's chambers.

In three steps, I was at his side where he lay, bathed in sweat, his skin pallid. Spittle dribbled down his chin and onto his neck, so I wiped his face with a bit of linen cloth. It came away tinged in blue.

My hands shook. Shiptu had said that the flowers that had poisoned the pigs were blue and the little petals I'd found under the stool's leg were blue, too.

I stared at the blue streak across the cloth, and then at the deathly pallor of the lugal. It was all the confirmation I needed. Someone was trying to assassinate him.

Prying his mouth open, I applied four drops of the antidote under his tongue, where it would be best absorbed. The squeak of the door brought my eyes up to see the nin standing in the darkness of the doorway, the light from the torches in the hallway silhouetting her from behind. I could barely see her face.

"Kammani?"

I froze in place, my hand poised over the lugal's mouth, the bottle with the X as clear as day in my hand.

"Hello, Nin." I stood smoothly to attention, tucking the bottle behind my back.

"What is that?"

"What's what?" I licked my lips. Terror filled me to my core. If this didn't work, if the antidote was going to kill the lugal instead of heal him, then all the Palace's fury would rain down on me, because the nin herself had witnessed me kill her abum.

"Behind your back." She stepped into the lugal's chambers, closing the door softly behind her, wary. Confused.

I had to tread carefully here. I couldn't explain what I'd done until I was certain he was going to be okay, but I knew that the nin was smart. She'd know if I invented a complete falsehood. And she could certainly read, so I had to keep the bottle's label hidden.

"Oh, Nin." I dropped my eyes, sank to the stool next to the lugal's bed, and covered my face in my hands. But secretly, I was monitoring the lugal. Watching for a change in him. Enhanced color. Less labored breathing. "I've administered a dosage of a remedy that will help him but may make him vomit all over himself again. I was afraid you would think I was harming him again, like you did before."

Her shoulders lost some of their rigidity, and she came around to the side of the pallet near me and perched on the edge of her abum's bed, one small hand resting on the crimson coverlet over his legs.

"He got a little better, Healer. Why wouldn't I trust you now?"

"Besides the fact that he has declined again?" *And the fact that my abum didn't heal your little brother after he fell, and you may think that his supposed incompetence runs in the family?*

She absently traced the pattern of the coverlet with her finger. "Kammani, I trust you. I know you're doing your best.

I still remember meeting you the first time, and even then, you knew exactly what to do to help your abum."

"He really was a good A-zu, despite what many think, and I am trying my best to be like him." I played with the edge of the lugal's coverlet, assessing his cheeks, looking for any signs of pinkening. Hoping my comment didn't offend.

She touched my shoulder. "I am sorry about what happened to your family. I felt wary at first, inviting your abum back to the Palace, but thinking back on it, I realize there was nothing he could have done for my brother, Ditanu."

Her words boiled and bubbled in my belly. "And yet we were cast out. My own brother taken."

She smiled sadly and shrugged a small shoulder. It touched the long, fringed gold earring dangling from her ear. "No reasoning could quench my abum's anger that Ditanu had passed. He was his favorite. At least your brother's life was spared and he is treated well."

I was supposed to feel grateful that they simply stole Kasha away instead of taking his life? As she straightened the coverlet over the bony chest of the lugal, I sighed. The irony that this man, who'd been so cruel to my family, now needed my help to heal him was not lost on me. But it didn't matter. The past was the past. What was done was done. The lugal had to be healed, or Nanaea would perish and meet my parents in the Netherworld without me.

She lovingly laid a hand on Lugal Marus's leg, then looked into my eyes. "I know you are doing your best for my abum despite everything, and I thank you for it. He's all I have left."

I sat up straighter on the stool. Took in her long black hair that fell like a sheet down her back almost to the floor while she was sitting. Her openness made me bold.

"Nin? What happened to the sarratum? Your mother?"

She looked down at her hands. "She died." Her eyes clouded over with some emotion I couldn't name. Sadness? Despair? Regret?

"How?" Different causes buzzed into my head like little bees. Birthing a child? But there were no other children other than the nin and her younger brother, who'd passed. A disease? A plague she'd brought over with her from her city-state? Had she been poisoned like her husband?

She shook her head. "I don't want to talk about it, if you don't mind." She smoothed her tunic and stood.

I nodded. "Of course, Nin Arwia. You're right. You're the nin, and I spoke out of turn."

"No. I want you to be my friend." She clasped my hands in her birdlike ones. They were so small, I could have crushed them if I'd wanted to. "I thank you for even thinking of me as a human with real feelings and not as just the lugal's daughter. I certainly think of you beyond your current station."

And what will you think if the antidote kills your abum? I swallowed audibly. "Nevertheless, I shouldn't pry."

"Let's forget about it, shall we?"

I smiled. "Yes, that's a wonderful idea."

She nodded, and the jewelry on her ears twinkled in the firelight. "I came to see how I could help. Do you need me to sit with him this evening?"

The lugal's cheeks seemed to be pinkening slightly, but that might have been my imagination. "Yes, that would be so helpful, if only while I catch a quick rest. But there's much to do before then, too."

"Where do we start?" she asked. I smiled at her eagerness. It reminded me of how I used to be at the behest of my own abum.

"Let's grab that water pot on the fire."

We bathed the lugal with warm, wet cloths and dripped water into his mouth, bit by bit. She helped me change his tunic and linens, stoke the fire, and exchange the rushes for fresh-smelling ones. While we worked, she chattered softly, but in the back of my mind, my head was spinning. Would the antidote help him? I kept checking his pulse, listening to his breathing, and studying his face for any positive effects.

I wondered as I worked who in his right mind would want to kill the lugal?

Despite what he'd done to our family, most would consider him fair. We were a prosperous city with very little war. He had solidified good trade agreements with neighboring cities and proposed a law that gave food to orphans and widows. Maybe a lowly man who'd been toiling for meager earnings? I realized that was *exactly* who would have wanted to do it—someone bitter over his lot in life. But how would such a man get access? Even if he wanted to bribe a rich man or a guardsman like Lamusa outside the door, he wouldn't have the funds to do it.

After several turns of the dial, she left to fetch some more bone broth from the kitchens, and I collapsed onto the stool again in exhaustion. Outside the window, the black sky glittered with millions of stars. It was well beyond the time for sleep. I yawned and dripped water from a sponge into his mouth for hydration, then tugged my hand away in fascination. His lips were a peachy pink! That was *so* much better than the gray they'd been when I'd first arrived!

Hope flickered to life. Could I actually do this? Save his and the Maidens' lives? My sister's laugh as she sat in the milk bath echoed in my ears.

Dear Enlil, please help me. I must save them! I could not bear it if I failed.

For a moment, I studied the lugal's face, the beard on his chin reminding me of my abum's. Tears welled in my eyes. My abum would have been proud of the job I was doing with the lugal, although he would have figured out it was poison long before I did.

And then a thought popped into my head that made my blood run cold through my veins. He *would* have figured it out earlier. Almost *immediately*. He'd certainly dealt with poisonings before, and if Shiptu had known right away, then my abum would have, too. My head began to swim as I allowed the question to creep into my mind: *Could he have been murdered to prevent anyone from finding out the truth?*

I sat up, the linen cloth falling from my hands, then stood and began to pace, gnawing on the nail of my thumb.

It made perfect sense. If the person intent on assassinating the lugal knew that the best healer in the city was on his way, then they'd *certainly* want to do something about that! My thoughts buzzed and flitted like bees in a flower field. My abum. My good, kind abum, slaughtered in the street because of his skill, yet despised by Lugal Marus because that skill hadn't been enough to save his son. And he never got the chance to redeem himself! I bit my lip so I didn't cry out with frustration. He could have lived a long, full, happy life. I could have cured him of the poisons in his brain and his sadness over my mother's death. I could have, but I'd never gotten the chance.

Stepping to the window, I allowed the cool night air to wash over me as I breathed and calmed myself down. The wide expanse of the city unfurled before me, crackling with low cookfires and torches, accompanied by the muted noise of loved ones settling in for the night. But unbidden, a thought crawled into my brain and would not shake loose: *Will someone try to kill me too, now that I've taken his place?*

Have they already tried?

I clapped my hand over my mouth. During the Maidens' Welcome festival, my lips had tingled strangely after drinking the sikaru, and I'd vomited all night. What had that servant said to me when she'd given me the flagon? *Compliments of the lugal?* I'd probably been poisoned, too, but someone hadn't provided a lethal dose. And then it hit me: Nanaea had sloshed nearly half the drink from my cup when she'd stumbled into me, and likely spilled half the poison! In a panic, I drew the blankets up around the lugal's chin. His breathing had evened out, and his color was improving by the moment. He was certain to vomit up the last of the poison, but for now, the antidote was doing its work. And there was work for me to do. I had to tell Nin Arwia what I'd discovered and find out who was trying to kill her abum. She'd be furious if she knew the truth!

I flung my healing satchel over my head to go fetch her from the kitchens, but the door opened, and I was stunned to discover a person who certainly had no business being outside the lugal's chambers in the middle of the night:

Dagan.

And he had a sicklesword to his throat.

The hair stood up on my head. Torches cast wavering light over Nasu's weapon, just a hairsbreadth from ending Dagan's life. Dagan clenched his jaw, his eyes flashing at Nasu, whose entire body quivered like an arrow set loose. Before, when Nasu had been upset that he couldn't read the tablet, I'd used deference to calm him. I lowered my voice and spoke quietly.

"Nasu, has Dagan done something wrong? He would never hurt anyone, least of all the lugal. Is that why you have him by the throat?"

Dagan held up his hands in surrender, but his muscles were tense. "I *had* to see you, Kammani." His eyes didn't leave Nasu's face.

Nasu clenched his jaw. "You've no business here."

"Didn't you hear him? He came to see *me*. Please let him

go. I'll escort him out to the Palace Libbu, and we can talk there."

Nasu's eyes squinted in indecision. "That doesn't excuse his presence. Why was he near the lugal's chambers?"

"There is no good answer to that, of course." I gave Dagan a hard look. Why cause such trouble at a time like this? "But for the lugal's sake, I beg you to forgive him. Please. He isn't a threat. I swear it on the lives of my ancestors. On my dead parents. Please! Release him!"

He narrowed his eyes.

I decided to make it easier for him. "Nasu. Nin Arwia is on her way and wouldn't want to see this right outside her abum's door. I will get Dagan to leave. I swear it." I placed a hand over my heart.

That seemed to satisfy him. He dropped the sicklesword, leaving barely enough room for Dagan to scoot out from under it. Dagan rubbed his throat where the sword had been as a thin line of blood bloomed against his bronze skin.

"You're lucky Lamusa has gone on rounds, or this may have ended differently." Nasu squeezed the hilt of his sword, his eyes glinting in the firelight from the torches.

Dagan lifted his chin, flexing his chest muscles, his own hand going for his dagger, but I pulled desperately at his solid arm. "Dagan, please! For my sake!" It would do no one any good for these two to come to blows. Nasu's sicklesword was as sharp as a blade could get, but Dagan was lethal with his dagger. I'd seen him fell a she-lion with one throw from more than a hundred handsbreadths away. "Come. We can use the back stairs."

Dagan nodded grimly to Nasu, then followed me.

As we walked past a window down a long corridor, I scowled at him, despite the moon's soft beams falling across his face, accentuating the angles of his cheekbones, the curve of his brow. The divot above his upper lip. "Dagan, you must leave here at once." We reached a landing and jogged lightly down the stairs. "You could have been whipped. You can't be inside the Palace on the lugal's floor at night!"

"Well, take me somewhere safe, then. We must speak."

"Have you taken leave of your senses, Farmer's Son? No! I only said that so I could escort you out. The guardsmen . . ."

"Oh, Kammani, shut your mouth, or I'll shut it for you." He quoted a favorite phrase of ours from when we were young. I reddened mightily, thinking of the way he'd closed my mouth earlier.

"Come on, then." Glancing over my shoulder, pinpricks going into my hairline, my thoughts focused on the grim reality that someone in this Palace was a murderer. "And quickly."

Racing, we took the rest of the stairs two at a time and landed, breathless, on the first tier of the Palace in a courtyard blooming with flowers.

"Kammani, slow down. We're out of the area where I'm not supposed to be. Why are we running?"

"Shhh!" I moved stealthily around a wall, past hanging vines, and reached the last flight of stairs, which led down into the Libbu.

"You are acting as if someone is *chasing*—"

"Who's there?" a deep voice rumbled from somewhere above.

"Quick!" I breathed. "Follow me!" I ran blindly, madly, down the remaining stairs, Dagan one step behind.

Flattening myself against the east wall, I peered around the corner, then darted into the booths of the Libbu, Dagan still at my heels. We wended around the stalls, sidestepping carts, until we came to the grower's tent, with its flaps down and secured for the evening. I slipped through a crack, untied the rope, and led Dagan inside and through potted rosettes, lotuses, shrubbery, and small tamarisk trees until we came to a little bench in the back. The flowers were all closed now in the evening's coolness, but their scent drifted in the air, as sweet as honey.

We collapsed onto the bench, breathing heavily, worry making my breath come out in gasps. "I don't think they saw where we went."

"Why were we sneaking? Nasu just asked me to leave the lugal's corridor. I'm a member of the noble class. It's not like I can't be elsewhere in the Palace—"

"Dagan, shhh." I held up a hand, listening. Straining for any sounds indicating that someone had followed us. The notion that I'd been poisoned was not something I'd take lightly from now on.

"Kammani, what is going on?"

When I heard no movement outside the stall, I dropped my hand and allowed myself to relax. "It's been a rough night."

He wiped the sweat from his forehead with his arm, his eyes growing serious. "Is your safety in jeopardy because of administering the antidote? Did he not take it well?"

Of course Shiptu had mentioned it. That was why Dagan had come to the Palace.

"No, that's not it." I dropped my voice even lower. "The antidote is working, which means someone has been poisoning him. And they may have killed my father, too." I swallowed the lump in my throat. "To prevent him from finding out about it."

"Sweet Enlil," he whispered.

I nodded. "And I think someone even . . ." I closed my eyes and shook out my hands, which I'd clenched into fists again.

"What?"

"Someone even tried to poison me. That must be what happened after the Maidens' Welcome festival."

Dagan's jaw worked, tensing and releasing. "But you're all right?" He brought a rough hand to my cheek.

"Yes, I am. Just a little shaken." *Was* I all right? I'd been poisoned and had risked the lugal's life on an antidote I wasn't even sure would work. And although I believed it could cure him, it was much too soon to fan a spark of hope to a flame. I wiped sweat from my brow with the hem of my tunic.

Dagan looked around the grower's tent and found a stack of linen cloths lying next to a few earthen pots and a plant whose purple blooms had closed for the evening. He held a cloth out to me. "So you don't have to use those nice clothes."

I took it gratefully, then patted my forehead. "Thanks."

He fiddled with the hem of his own tunic, then grew serious. Beads of perspiration had formed above his perfect lips. Thick black lashes framed his intense eyes. I swallowed around a lump in my throat. I was suddenly very aware of his thigh pressed against mine. The scent of his skin.

"Look. I came here to find out about the lugal, but I also wanted to apologize for taking liberties with you earlier. I shouldn't have done it, especially when I know what you believe to be true."

"What do I believe to be true?"

He took my hand in his. Pressed warm lips to my knuckles. Heat enveloped my body. The fragrance of the jasmine in the air intensified. It wasn't fair that a man should be so expertly carved. It made me nervous.

"I know you don't want to love me, and you will never marry me."

My cheeks grew bright red, and I pulled my hand away from him. "Dagan, this isn't the time."

"I know it isn't, but I need to say it anyway. It's important to me that you know you don't have to worry about me hounding you, all right? You have enough to worry about right now. I respect your choice, Kammani. You don't want me, then that's so. It's done. I have been making a donkey's ass of myself, hanging all over you, kissing you. Hand on my heart, you don't have to worry about it anymore, okay?"

I fidgeted with the hem of my tunic, unraveling a thread. I'd kissed him back. "What do you mean?"

"I mean I understand. Well, at least enough to honor your wishes and leave you alone. I will always—*always*—be your friend, but if that's all you want, then that's enough for me. I don't want you pushing me away because you're nervous about marrying a man of wealth and humbling my station. That isn't acceptable to me."

"What? I'm not worried about marrying into wealth, Dagan."

"You aren't?" He sat back and scratched his beard. "Then what *is* it? Is it *me*?"

"Of course not. You should *know* better than that."

His amber eyes were confused, hurt hiding behind them, too. I wanted to soothe him but had no idea what to say. No idea how to put my complicated feelings into words, and little time to sort any of them out, either. "It's difficult to explain. I—I just—can't. Not right now. Please understand." Once the words left my mouth, everything in me felt like I'd betrayed him. My insides twisted in discomfort, but I pushed the feelings aside and stood. There was no time. "I must go, though." I peered furtively out the opening of the stall at the Libbu, which was vacant save for one or two guardsmen making their midnight rounds. "I need to find Nin Arwia."

He sighed. Looked at his hands. Then back at me, resigned. "So late?"

"Someone is trying to kill her father. She needs to know."

He rubbed his chin thoughtfully. "You didn't tell her about the poisoning yet?"

"No. She was gone when I figured everything out."

188

"Well, to be honest, I think telling her about it is a bad idea. Think about it, sweet. Who stands to benefit the most from a lugal's death? Some random person or the nin herself?"

He had a point.

But as I chewed on my lip, thinking of it, I dismissed his worry. That wasn't who she was. Or . . . at least not who she appeared to be. "She's distraught over the loss of her ummum. I don't think she'd poison the one person she has left in the city who loves her."

He shook his head. "She's to inherit the throne if he dies. She'd have a suitor in a moment's notice. Ensi Uruku may even try to force the match."

True. I gnawed on my lip. But could she be so duplicitous? He was right about her having a motive, but her character was very different from a skulking poisoner's. She was—sweet. And unmarked by the greed and flashiness I'd seen displayed so easily here in the Palace. The girl I'd spoken to in the lugal's chambers moments ago and the girl with whom I'd interacted when I was younger didn't appear to be like that. She didn't seem like someone who would murder a person for power.

But the more I thought about it, a creeping sense of surety crawled its way into my head. My memory flashed back to the look in her eyes as she'd waved to the crowd atop the Palace balcony the day of the Maidens' Welcome festival. She'd been eager. Hungry for more.

But that was probably just a fleeting moment. It couldn't possibly be who she was. *Could it?*

189

"She doesn't seem like a killer." My excuse sounded feeble, even to my own ears. I crossed my arms over my chest, shivering, the cool night air wafting over me from the crack in the stall's curtain.

Dagan blew air out of his mouth in annoyance and pushed his hair back from his face. "Not all killers *do*. I'm trying to protect you. If she finds out about this, you could be dead. She could be the one who tried to poison *you*!"

"Dagan. Listen. If it worries you so much, I will use extra caution around her, all right? And I can wait to tell her until I've sorted it out a bit more. But I'm probably right."

Am I, though?

"I'm worried for you," he said as I backed away from him, standing framed by two potted plants in the grower's stall. He looked strong, and completely capable. But I couldn't let his worry distract me from my duty.

"I have to get back to the lugal."

"Kammani, for the love of Enlil, at least let me escort you. Someone could be trying to *kill* you."

"Dagan, do you want another sicklesword to the throat? I will stick to the shadows, and I will hurry. I'll send Kasha to update you as soon as I hear more."

"Kammani."

"Good evening, Dagan." And I was gone. I let the curtains close behind me and ventured off into the chilly evening to tend to the lugal, then head to my chamber, listening for any step behind me, trying to sense a change in the air. But as I traveled, and weariness from the lost sleep of the past moon settled heavily into my bones, a sense of unease filled me to the core.

Is he right? Could the nin be behind her own abum's poisoning? I swallowed thickly, remembering the way she'd avoided talking about her ummum's death. *Is she so artful at trickery and lies?*

Perhaps. My thoughts kept flitting back to the shine in her eyes as she took in the crowds. In fact, the closer I got to the stairs leading to the lugal's chambers, the more it made sense, and my hair prickled strangely. Caution was key here. I'd simply peek in on the lugal, then head to my chamber, *lock the door*, get some sleep, and wait to act until I'd had some time to think it through.

Rubbing my eyes as I looked over my shoulder to see if anyone trailed behind, I darted up the long flight of stairs, the moon a stark beacon shining a path for me. I, however, stuck to the shadows of the ivy hanging along the wall, the memory of my poisoned drink a reminder that someone out there believed I was a problem.

CHAPTER 13

NIN ARWIA'S CHAMBER was, in a word, extravagant.

A pallet of unbelievable height and width was blanketed in luxurious, downy-soft linens. Bright-pink hyacinths seemed to grow from the bottom of the coverlet to the top. Several pillows graced the top of the bed, one still indented from Nin Arwia's sleeping head. A platter of partially eaten grapes and dates, along with an assortment of fresh breads, sat on a table next to her pallet. A cask made entirely of silver glistened with droplets of water in the early-morning warmth.

Heavy white draperies tied back with golden ropes adorned the windows on both sides of the room. A mural depicting a magnificent Enlil with shimmering wings surrounded by dancers, musicians, and smaller gods splashed across the ceiling where, I was certain, Nin Arwia fell asleep looking every night.

It was what I'd do.

But it wasn't why I was there. As I'd lain on my own pallet in the wee hours of the morning, one ear listening for sounds at the door (someone coming to finish the job the poison hadn't?), the other pressed into the softness of my pillow, I'd tossed and turned, thinking about what Dagan had said. Nin Arwia *did* stand to gain the most by the lugal's death. And it only made sense that I check out her chambers to see if there was anything remotely incriminating before deciding what to do.

After another night with no sleep, I'd competed for space around the washbasin with Nanaea, who washed so thoroughly with the aleppo soap, I was sure she'd take her skin right off. We'd moved with such familiarity around each other that I was handing her a linen to dry herself at the same time she was handing me a tunic. After she'd braided my hair and I'd kissed her heavily made-up cheek—she was preparing to go hand out coins to our old neighbors as an act of love from the Maidens—I'd ventured off to see the lugal, albeit cautiously. I'd almost asked Nanaea to come with me, thinking that there would be safety in numbers. But remembering how much it would hurt her to know that the lugal was healing, even though she had asked about whether my trip to Dagan's farm had led to any clues, I'd refrained.

As I'd crept to the lugal's chambers, however, the slightest noise in the passages had made me leap like a cat. When I'd found him, he'd been sleeping peacefully, a small bed of blankets by his side a sign that Nin Arwia had been there. I'd sent for my brother and, after arguing with his Palace watcher that the lugal's life was at stake, had instructed Kasha to stay by the lugal's side and feed him broth until he could hold no more. He'd nodded dutifully, saluted to the guardsmen standing to attention outside the door, and stepped inside. I'd watched my brother's calm, efficient demeanor and wondered when he'd gotten so incredibly big.

Then I'd slipped into an alcove outside Nin Arwia's chamber to wait for her to vacate to break her fast. Once the door squeaked open, releasing the scent of jasmine and juniper blossoms, and the rustle of Nin Arwia and Gudanna's garments faded away down the hallway, I stealthily entered her chamber.

Looking for what? I didn't know. But the previous evening, as I'd lain working out whether or not to trust her, reviewing the conversations we'd had, something she'd said struck me as odd: *"He is all I have left. My whole family is dead. All of them—are dead."*

All of *whom?* As far as I knew, there had just been the four of them: Lugal Marus, the sarratum, Nin Arwia, and Malku Ditanu. You didn't refer to two people—her mother and brother—as "all of them." So who else had died? When I'd asked about her family, she'd changed the subject.

I'd seen the beautiful sarratum years ago. She'd been small, like Nin Arwia, and had stood behind her husband, Lugal Marus, during a match in the Pit, which was reserved exclusively for the vilest criminals. One man, a mass murderer, had squared off against a guardsman. The criminal had been thoroughly bested and had bled out, dying in shrieks from his wounds. I'd looked up to the lugal, afraid of the nature of the punishment, and seen the pixie face of his wife crumpled in grief.

But I had no other memories of the queen. When did she die? And if she had conceived again, there were no other little ones running around, so how did *they* die? I was now suspicious of *anything* that seemed odd, and Nin Arwia's statement seemed like a good enough spot to start.

Though the thought of being caught in her chamber left me breathless with terror.

My breath coming quickly, I stepped across the rugs and rummaged through the contents of the tiny cabinets and baskets about her room. One basket contained piles of sandals, cut from leathers of all different types and stains. My eyes practically fell out of my head at the sight. One could only hope to have even *one* pair of leather sandals of this quality in a lifetime! But to have so many sitting in a basket not being worn? People had been murdered for less. I carefully placed the basket exactly as it was and moved on.

Another basket was filled to the brim with scarves of every shade—violet, azure blue, lemony yellow. A large cabinet on the right side of her bed contained small trinkets carved of precious jewels, along with rings, earbobs, bracelets, and necklaces shimmering and twinkling in the sunshine coming in from the window. She didn't even have the good sense to lock up such treasures!

I opened bins, looked under chair cushions, and ran my fingers over every single surface of the room. Nothing. I didn't know *what* exactly I was searching for—anything that would show her to be less true than she appeared to be—but I figured I'd know it when I found it.

And then my eyes fell on a small leather-bound chest tucked away in an alcove at the far end of her chamber. My eyes lit up. *This.* This is where she'd keep a secret. If she left such precious jewels lying out in the open, anything she'd hide would be for her eyes alone.

I stooped in front of the chest and lifted the lid. The leather was worn away from many hands over many years opening and closing it. Inside lay an assortment of tablets chipped and scratched. I scanned quickly through them. They seemed to be love letters from one person to another, but since no names were inscribed, I couldn't tell who'd written them. I had to assume they were to Nin Arwia, or why else would she have them? Did this support Dagan's theory that she had a secret lover who wanted the throne? The thought raised the hairs on the back of my neck.

Rummaging some more, I found a little linen bag, tied with a leather strap. The contents were heavy. Using my teeth, I untied the knot, and a bronze amulet carved with the lugal's emblem fell into my hand. I sucked in my breath. It was the little malku's necklace. He'd worn it everywhere he went, and after he'd died, he'd been carried around the city on a pallet, the necklace settled in the middle of his concave chest. How had it come into the nin's possession? He should have been buried with it to use in the Netherworld for bartering, especially if he was going alone as a child! I stuffed it back into the bag, tucked it where I'd found it, and then quickly lifted the last tablet. I found *another* small linen bag, and my hands shook as I lifted it out. This one was as light as air. I tugged open the tiny drawstring at the top and peeked inside.

It was hair.

I dumped the contents of the bag into the palm of my hand. A single snippet of deep brown hair tied with a silk ribbon lay there in my palm. Nin Arwia's curls? No, her hair was as straight as a pin! It wasn't the malku's, either; his hair was the same as the nin's.

Suddenly, I heard voices from outside the door. Panicked, I shoved the curls into the bag, tucked the bag back into the chest, and stacked the tablets as I'd found them on top. I closed the lid quietly, but it didn't shut all the way. I didn't, however, have time to do anything about it. The door was opening.

I propelled myself over to the bed and stood near it, trying my best to appear as if I'd been waiting for the nin. My thoughts scurried from one idea to another in an effort to excuse my trespass into her chambers.

Gudanna walked in first, but her indignation at seeing me in the nin's private quarters evident in her flashing eyes. "What in the name of Enlil?"

"I'm here to see the nin," I said in what I hoped was a pleasant-sounding, perfectly innocent voice. "Where is she?"

"I'm here!" Nin Arwia breezed cheerfully into the room, her unimaginably long hair trailing after her like a sheet.

She walked to my side and pulled me into a quick, tight

hug with her tiny, birdlike arms. Her upturned face was so sweet and innocent, I had a difficult time believing that the love letters inside that chest belonged to her. But who else could they belong to?

"What brings you to me?" Nin Arwia unwound a scarf from about her shoulders. The day was already getting warm, and the sun had barely broken free from the horizon. "I'm sorry I wasn't here when you arrived. I hope you didn't have to wait long?" she asked, tossing the silken wrap into the basket with the others.

"No, Nin. Not long. I knocked several times, but you didn't answer. So I came back and knocked again, and then I tried the handle and it was open."

"Why in Enlil's name would you presume to walk in the door?" Gudanna asked, standing tersely against the wall, hands clasped tightly.

"I, well, I—" Enlil save me, I could think of nothing plausible. "Well, you see ..."

"Because she is my friend, Gudanna," Nin Arwia answered coolly, picking up a fine-bristled brush and smoothing her hair. "And since I've asked her to consider me a friend, I'd never suggest that she couldn't come into my chamber." She winced, working at a knot near the base of her head. "Kammani, will you come help me with this?" She proffered the brush.

Grateful for something to do with my quivering fingers, I obliged, quickly.

As I worked at the knot, we chatted about the day to come.

Well, mostly she chatted as my thoughts centered on whether I should bring up the poison or not. The partially open chest with its mysterious contents loomed from the corner, so my mouth remained closed for the time being.

After a quarter turn of the dial, she turned to me. "So, what did you want, my friend?" she asked brightly. "You certainly didn't come in here to listen to me prattle on and on." She laughed, but I sensed something behind her tone. An edge of some sort. And although she was smiling and talking nicely, she didn't offer me a seat at her table.

"I wanted to say that your ministrations to your abum last night helped. I looked in on him this morning. He's eating soup and his color has improved, although he is not speaking. Not yet."

She stood, her eyes lit up with what I wanted to believe was hope. "They did?"

"Yes, Nin. He is doing slightly better. It's still too early to say what that means, but for now, he's perked up a bit."

She squealed and enveloped me in a hug, practically knocking me over. "Thank you, thank you, thank you!"

I awkwardly patted her back. Over her shoulder, Gudanna's eyes were roving the room. I prayed to the gods she wouldn't notice that the chest was open a quarter of a handsbreadth.

Nin Arwia pulled back from me, a wide smile splitting her face almost in two. "That's the best news I've heard in a moon, although I realize that if he truly *is* on the mend, then it'll be difficult to tell your sister. But don't worry. If he gets well, then we'll have a Maidens' Release festival, and they will be honored with coins and jewels when they return to their old lives." She squeezed me again, and then turned to Gudanna. "Come, Gudanna. You and I have to inform the kitchen to roast a goat in celebration."

Gudanna tipped her head obligingly. "Of course." Together, they walked back toward the door.

"And you must go and get some rest. You must be quite exhausted from tending my abum with such great care. I know I am, and I left his room shortly after you did. Nasu told me you'd had to run out."

I nodded. "I am a bit tired, Nin." I knew a dismissal when I heard one.

Nin Arwia and Gudanna walked through the door, and I followed. Two guardsmen stood at the ready on either side of her doorway. Behind me, Nin Arwia pulled a key from her pocket and locked the door securely. "Silly me. I always forget to do that." She tucked the key away, then walked quickly down the corridor, her dignified, retreating back used to the fact that Gudanna would follow without question. The guardsmen certainly did.

But Gudanna tarried a moment.

"Did you find what you were looking for?" she whispered softly.

I blushed instantly. "I—I wasn't—"

She reached a clawlike hand out and squeezed my arm. Hard. "Liar."

I blanched.

"Remember," she hissed, "I am from the huts along the wall. I know what you're made of."

What in Enlil's name is that supposed to mean?

"It's my duty to protect Nin Arwia, and I will do anything it takes—anything—to ensure she is not disturbed."

"Gudanna, you are quite mistaken. I mean no harm. I was—"

From around the corner down the hall, I heard a muffled, "Gudanna?"

Gudanna looked over her shoulder, then dropped my arm. "Leave her be," she growled. Then she drifted on down the hallway after her charge, her hips swaying casually as if she hadn't just threatened me. "You have no idea what she's capable of," she called quietly over her shoulder.

I sank against the doorjamb in relief, calming my breath, but I could not calm my mind.

What is she capable of?

Love letters in a strange hand. A dead malku's amulet. Curls that could be a token of remembrance for good or ill.

The nin was hiding *something*.

I just needed to figure out what it was.

CHAPTER 14

I NEEDED SPACE to think, and the solace of my chambers would work perfectly with the girls gone to deliver coins to my neighbors. Looking over my shoulder to ensure no one had followed, I opened the door.

But no quiet was to be had. The room was filled with laughter and the scent of perfumed oils. Nanaea stood, combing through her long curls, while Simti sat on Nanaea's downy pallet, nibbling cherries.

"There's our lovely A-zu." Simti picked up a few more cherries from an oval platter on the bed, overflowing with cucumbers, dried apricots, melons, cherries, and cheeses, and popped two into her mouth. She held the platter out to me as I walked in and dropped my healing satchel on my pallet. "Want some?"

"What in the name of Enlil are you doing back here so soon?"

"Oh, hello. Nice to see you, too." Simti popped her eyes out at me.

"Sorry. That's not what I meant." I softly nudged her in the foot, and she smiled, her teeth stained with cherry juice.

Nanaea piped up: "We were finished early. The coffers weren't as full as we'd thought they'd be, so it didn't take long to distribute." She took a cask from one of the tables arrayed with pots of face paint and beauty tonics and drizzled some rose-scented oil onto the palm of her hand. Setting the cask down, she rubbed her hands together and then smoothed them down her curls. "But the exciting news is that they are setting up for a Sacred Maidens bazaar on the morrow."

Huna, rosy and damp from a bath, lay swathed in linens on her pallet, popping grapes into her open mouth. She snorted. "You mean visiting the dirty huts of your neighbors wasn't exciting enough?"

"Oh, Huna, why don't you just silence yourself?" Nanaea pursed her lips in disgust.

Huna rolled her eyes so far into the back of her head, only the whites were visible.

Ignoring Huna, I turned to Nanaea. "What's this about a bazaar?" Sinking down onto my pallet, I bent to loosen my sandals, my joints aching, my head fuzzy. Likely being sleepless and nearly poisoned to death meant my body needed time to recover. Time I didn't have.

"Vendors are coming from all over the city to showcase their wares. I heard that the weaver will be selling tunics with our likenesses, and there will be jewelry makers and face painters and different foods and special brew from the Palace. I'm so excited!"

"That sounds wonderful, Nanaea. And I *am* glad to see you. But I came here to think. I have a problem I need to solve." I sank back into my pillows, then sprang to my feet when the last part of Nanaea's sentence settled into my brain.

Special brew from the Palace.

Poison.

And Simti is eating the food.

I leaped across my pallet and smacked the cherries from her hand.

"What in the name of Alani do you think you're doing?" Simti cried, her mouth stuffed.

"Spit them out!" I demanded. "Spit all of them out!"

She spat all the cherries onto the floor, then wiped her mouth with the back of her hand. "What is wrong with you? Are they rotten?"

I snatched the platter from her, sending fruit and cheese flying. I raced to the window with the tankards and dumped the drink and the food out the window. A moment later, far below, I heard someone squeal.

Huna paused when I eyeballed her bowl of grapes. "You can't have mine." She pulled them close to her body.

Nanaea and Simti stared at me openmouthed.

"They're not rotten," I said, breathing heavily, setting the platter and the tankards down and wiping my hands on my tunic. "Someone tried to *poison* me. And it was through the food or the sikaru coming from this Palace."

Nanaea frowned. "You're as crazy as Zuzu down by the well. Why would they do that?" She tugged my ummum's shawl from underneath Simti, folded it gently, and placed it on a shelf with exquisite care.

I frowned at her use of the word "crazy." Zuzu was sick in her mind, as my abum used to tell me. Something that could have been helped with his remedies if she'd ever let anyone near her.

"They would poison me, Nanaea, because they were trying to prevent me from figuring out—" But I snapped my mouth shut. They all liked to gossip. What if one of them said the wrong thing to the wrong person? It was too risky to explain.

"Figuring out what?" Simti said.

"Never mind. Just trust me, okay?"

Nanaea sighed. "Kammani, I think you need some sleep. You're imagining things. You were tossing in your pallet last night, mumbling about the Boatman, and haven't slept much since. But we are getting ready to see some of the wares to be sold in the bazaar, so you'll have to sleep with us getting dressed around you." Nanaea pulled an amber tunic from a hook, draped it over her body, then tossed it aside and selected one the shade of a summer sky.

They were going about as if it were business as usual. "Fine, Nanaea. Just be wary of what you put in your mouth. Try to get your food from the Libbu instead of the platters the servants bring in."

Nanaea snorted. "That's one of the perks of being a

Sacred Maiden, Sister. Not having to scrounge for every meal."

Simti stared longingly at the cherries on the floor.

"I realize that, but—you shouldn't get used to it." I dropped my satchel next to my pallet and lay back against the softness of my pillows.

"Kammani. I *will* get used to this finery. What do you think we will be getting when we cross over? We'll be queens in the Netherworld!" She tossed a soft green tunic to Simti. "Here, try this one on. It suits your coloring."

This would not go well.

"Well, I don't want to say for certain, Sister, but I think the lugal is on the mend." Wincing, I crossed my arms behind my head and waited for the fury.

Nanaea, Huna, and Simti, with the green tunic halfway up her hips, froze. "What did you say?" Nanaea's black eyes flashed, her hand poised to select yet another tunic off one of the hooks.

"You heard correctly, my sweet. I'm—I'm sorry." And a part of me *was* sorry. She thought she was losing. That I had somehow gained the upper hand. But she didn't realize she was the one who gained the most by this news.

"How do you know that?" Anger brought her eyebrows almost together.

"Please, Sister." I closed my eyes. "I don't *know* for sure. I *suspect* that he's healing. That's all. And as soon as I can take a nap, as you suggested, I'll go check on him and report back to you straight away." I lay down on my side, yawning widely, my back to the girls. I tried desperately to ignore my sister's pain. I could do nothing else for her.

As I sank deeply into my pallet, someone whacked me in the back with something.

"Hey!" I bolted upright. Nanaea, her face flushed with wrath, clutched one of her overstuffed pillows. "Listen. I know you're upset." I pushed my hair out of my face. "But this really is for the best. Can't you see that?"

"You have no idea what this appointment means to me. *No idea.*"

And then I could not control my irritation. "Oh, I think I do. You want to be the queen you think you've always deserved to be. You hate that we had all our wealth stripped away from us and lost our status, so becoming a Sacred Maiden means you have the privilege you think you deserve. I *have* figured it out."

"That's not fair!" She flung the pillow at my head. I deftly dodged it, but the pillow shattered a clay pot, sending shards exploding across the floor.

I narrowed my eyes. "Clean that up!"

Huna sat up, her mouth open with shock. Apparently, she'd never met any sisters.

"I don't have to. As you've said before, you're not my ummum." Nanaea stormed back to her pallet, tears in her eyes, selected a tunic, and slipped it angrily over her head.

My shoulders drooped, her words weighing on me, but I turned away. Nanaea wasn't going to listen to me, and I had no way of making her. It was almost as if she really believed she was still nobility. It occurred to me then that since Huna *was* an actual noble girl who'd never lost her place, she might know more about the family life of the lugal. Perhaps I could pry without revealing too much of what I'd found.

I turned to her. "Huna?"

"What?" She drew her legs under her body and wrapped her arms around her waist. "I didn't do anything."

"I know that. Listen. Did the sarratum ever have any more children besides the nin and Malku Ditanu?"

"Why? Who cares?" She picked at a hangnail on her middle finger.

"I obviously care." But honestly, why did I care? What would it prove? Arwia had told me that her family had died. I guess I wanted to see how. Or why. Or to see if she was covering something up that no one else knew.

"She might have," Huna conceded, studying the beds of her fingernails. "I remember hearing about a second malku or something. But why does it matter? The sarratum is dead."

"Yes, why do you want to know, Kammani?" Simti sat near Nanaea, rubbing her back. My heart sank at her closeness to my sister. It used to be that *I* was the only one who could comfort her.

I bit my lip and turned back to Huna. "When I was in the nin's chamber with her, I saw what appeared to be a lock of curls on her dressing table. With her oils and things." No sense telling them *how* I found it. "Maybe they were from a baby? If so, I wondered why she would have them."

Simti gathered Nanaea's hair into sections and began

braiding them into long plaits. "They probably are from a little brother or sister. My ummum snipped a piece of hair from her first baby, who died, and kept it in a little box in her room. She said it was to remember the boy."

"Wouldn't the lugal have had a big funeral for a baby if one had died? I mean, wouldn't they be buried in the royal burial grounds?" I asked Huna.

Typically, the dead were buried right next to or under the homes of those who loved them so they could tend to the graves. My mother and baby sister were buried in between the farmers' fields and our little hut. It took me thirty-seven paces to reach their headstones. But those in the Palace buried their dead in a specific place. Hmmm. A visit to the burial grounds might be in order, to see if there happened to be another little grave.

"Probably, but it would be strange to just keep a bunch of baby hair." Huna jammed the last handful of grapes into her mouth and wiped her hands on the linens around her body. "You know, guardsmen keep body parts, too, not just sad mothers."

"They do what?" Simti asked.

"Oh, that's right. You're not nobility. You wouldn't know." Huna snorted in disgust. "Guardsmen keep trophies of their kills—bones or hair or a cutting from the tunic of a victim. Something they can hold to remember how good it felt to slit someone's throat." She drew a line across her neck with her finger.

I flashed back to the day the four guardsmen had come to

fetch me and Nanaea. Two of them had finger bones around their necks.

Was that a remote possibility? Was the nin that sick in her head?

You have no idea what she's capable of.

Perhaps, if the nin was a killer who wanted the throne, she *would* have smothered a little brother to ensure that she got it. Everyone knew that the first living baby boy—the highest of the malkus—would inherit, despite an older sister. Could I have misjudged her so completely? Who could do something like that?

But my abum always told me that power changed people. He'd watched a poor woman gain a wealthy husband through bribery and begin to treat those she'd lived with her entire fifteen years as if they were beneath her. And I'd seen the way people had treated us as soon as our wealth had been stripped away. As if we were nothing. Power was destructive like that.

Maybe Huna wasn't so far off.

But the whole idea was making my head ache. I needed to think. I needed sleep.

I yawned widely. "Thank you for the enlightenment. But now I am afraid I must take your suggestion and lie down, Nanaea. Are you all leaving soon?" I lay down on my side and exhaled deeply.

"We were in here first and can stay all night if we want to," Nanaea sniped behind my back. Huna chortled from her pallet.

I did my best to ignore the jab but found myself gritting my teeth.

"Hey, Simti, that color is amazing on you," Nanaea said loud enough to wake the Boatman.

"Nanaea!" I snapped, sitting up. "Please!"

She laughed, but there was little mirth in her eyes. "You should see your hair."

I threw my pillow at her head, but she deftly dodged it. With a humph, I lay back down, burying myself in the covers, trying my best to ignore her and the others, but she sat down hard on my pallet and poked me in the leg. "Did you see Dagan when you went over to the farm last night? Is that why you got back so late?"

My cheeks grew warm, and I squirmed away from her prying eyes. "Leave me alone. I'm asleep. Don't you hear me snoring? See? I'm snoring."

"Ha!" she shrieked. "You *did* see him!"

At this point, it felt as if my entire body was baking in a brick oven. "Nanaea, get away from me! Seriously!" I pulled my head under the covers.

"No!" She yanked the coverlet off me, a terrible smile on her face. "Well, obviously Shiptu gave you whatever medicine it was you needed, because the lugal is healing." Her chin quivered, tears glistening in her eyes. "But what did *Dagan* give you that has your cheeks so rosy? Huh?" She poked me in the leg again. "Huh? Huh?"

From across the room, Simti laughed, not understanding how angry Nanaea was. Not understanding any of this.

"Stop it, please," I said. "I'm trying to save you."

"He kissed you, didn't he? Didn't he?"

"Nanaea, you are acting like a child."

Simti's eyes landed on me from across the room. "Dagan, Farmer's Son, kissed you? You're serious?"

"I may not be the beauty that my sister is, Simti, but I'm not entirely repulsive, for Enlil's sake." I stood, pushing my hair away from my face, then searched for a ribbon to tie it back. "And I'm not answering any of these questions." My cheeks flaming, I found a ribbon next to my bed and whipped it around my head.

"*He did!*" Simti screamed, clasping her hands together.

I knotted the ribbon under my hair. "Fine. Yes. He kissed me. And I told him it was inappropriate, and he apologized for it. So it's done."

Simti shrieked. "Dagan kissed you, and you made him *apologize?*" Her mouth hung open. She wrapped herself in a hug and danced around in a circle, her eyes bright with merriment, but Nanaea's mouth was turned down.

"How did it feel, Sister? How did it feel to have everything you want all in one night? A remedy *and* a kiss?" Her fists were clenched at her sides.

"You know what, Nanaea? I am done here. I will get no time to rest or think at all. The healer who is trying to keep all of you miserable wretches alive will get none of it. Thanks. Thanks for that." I yanked my healing satchel off the floor and threw it around my neck. "Thanks for being the sister I need during this time. You think you know pain?" I jabbed my finger at her heaving chest. "Try having the noose of everyone's lives in this room wrapped around your throat. Strangling you."

At that, her chin lifted. "I'm a burden, huh? Well, sorry I was ever born."

I held my hands up, my anger ready to burst through my chest. "I love you, but if I don't get some room to breathe, I will suffocate." I stalked out into the corridor and slammed the door shut. From behind it, a muffled shout of "Good! Stay out!" resonated in Nanaea's shrill soprano. I gritted my teeth and tugged my satchel into place. If I couldn't get any rest, I would go to the burial grounds to see if I could find a little grave that nobody knew about.

At least there, in the land of the dead, I would have the silence I needed to think clearly, without the interminable chatter of the living filling my ears.

CHAPTER 15

THE CROWDS WERE sparse along the winding path back to the royal burial grounds, but I constantly checked my back, watching for someone—anyone—who didn't seem to belong. I wished for Iltani at my side. Her wit would calm my anger, soothe my spirits. Plus, she always seemed to know what to do. If she didn't? She'd improvise, like the time our families were both starving and she'd knocked at a wealthy woman's door and offered our childcare services for food. We'd spent the day wiping hands and building play palaces but walked back to our homes at dusk, stuffing ourselves with smoked trout.

And I readily admitted that having a friend like her near would at least reduce the possibility that someone with ill intent would act.

I picked up my pace.

Occasionally a woman walked by, head held high, a servant trailing behind with a woven basket atop her head and children wrapped against her back. In my neighborhood, the women carried their own baskets and their own children. They were their own servants. But truthfully, I wouldn't want it any other way, now that I'd lived on both sides. It was certainly nice to have someone bring me my food every morning and provide me with these sturdy leather sandals. But I knew, as everyone who lived in the hovels did, that you had to eventually rely on yourself. If you got too used to the help of others and suddenly it was gone, you'd be completely destitute. At least I could carry my own.

Ahead of me, the dusty path shimmered in the morning sunlight, then disappeared into an enclosure barricaded on three sides by mudbrick fencing. Thickets of date palms, olive trees, and golden-flowering shrubbery shaded its borders. A blackbird, squawking its displeasure at my presence, stood sentry to the burial grounds and was my only companion as I crossed through the gate into the graveyard.

I walked around the headstones, chiseled with likenesses and names of women, men, and children. Some of the graves were pretty basic. A stone with a name. A small hand clutching a little scepter. Others were more elaborate, with a bigger stone and the deceased's relationship to the lugal.

As I moved back toward the far edge of the burial grounds, walking along the paths, reading the names of ghosts, the graves became bigger, giving way to the tombs for the lugals of the past. Those along the back wall of the graveyard were crumbling with age. But the tombs stretching along the sides were fresher. Newer. I recognized the name of the lugal who'd died fifteen years past, inscribed above a doorway. Beyond it was the tomb reserved for Lugal Marus.

I shivered as I walked over to the sandstone structure, my sandals filling with grit. *Remnants of the dead?* I stood shakily in front of the cold tomb. Dread filled my belly. My sister, my Nanaea, would be buried here if the lugal wasn't doing as well as I thought he was. My hands found the cool stones of the doorway and traced the outline of his name, and I uttered a quick prayer to Enlil to help me continue to heal the lugal so I didn't have to watch my sister be placed inside these stones.

To the right, underneath an olive tree, was a cluster of graves. Walking quickly to the circle of headstones, I knelt down on the ground and cleared some sand from the largest stone. On it, chiseled neatly, were the words: HUMUSA, WIFE OF LUGAL MARUS, SARRATUM OF ALU. This was her! This was the queen who'd died. She'd been placed near where her husband would eventually lie. My breath coming fast, I wiped the sand from the small headstones near her. There was one just slightly shorter than I was tall, and as I scrubbed the grit from the inscription, Malku Ditanu's name appeared.

The days of his funerary rites were fresh in my mind. He'd been climbing along the Palace balconies and had fallen several stories to his death after lying in agony for three days. My abum had cursed the Palace healer's remedies and had stepped in to try to save the boy, resetting broken bones and even performing a surgery to try to inflate the boy's collapsed lung, but the malku had perished. And my abum had been blamed.

How sorrowful he'd been that night. He'd clung to Kasha, begged Lugal Marus not to take his son, pleaded with my ummum to do something, but we'd watched, in anguish, as they'd led Kasha away. I pushed the heels of my hands into my eyes to quell any tears, remembering my ummum's low moan as they'd tugged him from her arms.

Next to the malku's grave, partially concealed under a flowering bush, was another. A smaller one. Maybe half the size.

A grave for a baby.

A strange sort of excitement welled in my chest. A bird was carved into the stone, instead of a name. My breath lodged in my throat. Tradition held that it was foolhardy to name a child before he was six moons old. My suspicions rising like bubbles in a cask, I bent down to the grave. There appeared to be stones on the little dirt mound. But after squatting and brushing away the sand, I realized they were bone talismans, not stones. A bird, a statue of Enlil, an ox, and a woman cradling a child.

All the hair stood up on my head. *The talismans at the lugal's bedside.*

My stomach twisted with nausea. Another little grave next to Malku Ditanu. A swatch of hair in Nin Arwia's chest of secrets. Talismans meant to ward off illness or bad humors.

Or *guilt.*

You have no idea what she's capable of.

The talismans were meant to be a remedy for someone's *guilt!* My hand flew to my throat. There was a dead little baby boy—likely another heir, if Huna had heard correctly—and no one was talking about him. That didn't make sense, unless there was some foul play involved. The birth should have been cause for joy, especially considering the original heir had died. Why had he been kept out of sight? I didn't even remember seeing the sarratum heavy with child, unless, of course, she'd kept her pregnancy a secret. Or hadn't known. I'd once known a girl who didn't even realize she was with child until the babe showed up between her legs after a particularly long bout with a stomach ailment, or so she thought. She'd run to our hut in shock.

Why doesn't anyone know?

Appalled, I walked quickly back the way I'd come, winding around the final homes of the dead, between ragged shrubs, and through small wildflowers that had sprung up from the nourishment of the bodies. I was shivering, so I quickened my pace to a jog, then yelped as one of the ragged branches snagged my tunic. Bursting into a run, stumbling around headstones, crashing around potted plants, and upsetting startled crows who took flight at the sound of my panic, I lurched out from the burial grounds and directly into a middle-aged serving woman with a basket of clean laundering on her head.

"Oof!" she cried as I ran smack into her, upending the basket all over the dusty ground. "Watch where you're going!"

Angry eyes met mine as she sat in the dirt, surveying the damage around her.

"I'm so sorry." Of their own accord, my hands reached out and grabbed at the clean linens, cloaks, tunics, and underthings, trying to shake off the dust.

"Leave them be," she ordered, righting herself. But then she must have noticed my beautiful white tunic. My wonderfully soft woven sandals. The cleanliness of my nails. And she corrected herself.

"My apologies, my lady." She thought I was a woman of means. A woman who could, with a word, have her whipped. That was no longer my life.

"No, please. I apologize." I handed her the linens, which would now need to be scrubbed in the river, dried, and folded yet again. I closed my eyes. This poor woman. An entire morning's worth of work—gone.

Ahead of us, a bright-eyed young noblewoman turned back, hands on her full hips. "What's wrong?" The headdress she wore gleamed with agate and amber stones.

"Nothing," the servant next to me answered, her eyes filling with frustrated tears. "I'm sorry." She dropped her eyes to the ground, then scrambled to her feet. I followed, smoothing my skirts and dusting myself off.

"No. I ran into *her*. The fault is mine. I was here offering my respects in the burial grounds, and in my haste to leave, I knocked into her and all your laundering."

The noblewoman's eyes softened. "Are you quite all right?

Were you visiting someone you cared for?" She nodded to the burial grounds.

I didn't know how to answer. "I was visiting a grave. Yes. But no one I knew," I answered bleakly.

"Aren't you the young healer from along the wall?"

I took in her face. Her gleaming headdress. This was the young woman who had tried to pull me along to the festival for the Maidens the first morning I awoke in the Palace.

"I am, in fact."

"Oh!" She brightened. "What are you doing here?" Her eyes grew round. "Nothing's happened to the lugal, I pray?"

"Oh no! He is doing nicely. Healing."

She put a bejeweled hand to her cheek. "Enlil be praised. I was so worried for him. He's been a just lugal." She lowered her voice. "The man who would replace him is less forgiving."

"What do you mean?" I asked. "Nin Arwia would take the throne."

She cast her heavily drawn eyes around and shooed her serving woman away. The woman nodded once, put the basket of dirty linens atop her ahead, and strolled casually down the path, humming absently to herself. She knew when she wasn't wanted. I almost reached out to her. She was probably a mother, having to bend to this younger noblewoman to feed her family.

The wealthy woman stared at me in silence, her brow furrowed. "You may not understand this as someone living along the wall," she whispered, "but some may not want the nin to rule alone. They may believe her to be too inexperienced, so they'd push for an advisor who is older and wiser to help her make the best decisions."

Impatience rose in my belly. I wasn't stupid because I lived a lowly life. She must have sensed my aggravation, because she retreated.

"I think you take me wrong. The lowly are not privy to everything that happens in this realm. I mean to convey that a young woman isn't as influential as a man, especially a man with a taste for power."

She was being careful not to say too much, and to shade her meaning to appear to be praising Uruku. But her eyes were full of another import.

"Yes, my lady. I understand."

Her eyes lit on mine. "Yes," she whispered. "And powerful but gracious rulers like Lugal Marus are few and far between. We can only hope that the delegate who assists our own Nin Arwia exercises the same courteousness."

But I knew *that* was an impossibility for Ensi Uruku. I'd helped to heal the mouth of the woman he'd maimed.

I stepped closer to her and dropped my voice to a whisper, looking over her shoulder to see if anyone was close enough to overhear. "But he can't completely take charge of the city unless he marries the nin, right? No one in Alu would allow it. This family has ruled for at least three generations."

She reached up her hands, pretending to adjust the pins in my hair. She smiled as though we were talking about something else. "The nin has survived, so she'll take the throne. But he may rule anyway, albeit from the sides. Or he may try to force a marriage. Or, if she dies, the role goes officially to the first man who can take it."

"What do you mean, 'the nin has survived'? Has survived what?"

"She's survived being a lugal's daughter. It can't have been easy, since everyone knows the lugal carries a curse in his seed."

At that, I smiled. "As a healer, I can tell you that there is no curse that would affect a son or daughter."

She rested her hands on my shoulders. "Then why have both his sons died?"

I searched her face. It was open. Earnest. Questioning. My blood thrummed in my veins. *The grave.* "So there *was* another malku."

"Yes, although not many people knew. But both his sons have perished now. One after birth, within a few hours, I'm told, and another in his eighth year. They say the baby sickened and died, but the nursemaid who found him dead in his cradle said he didn't look right. He looked . . . swollen. An effect of the curse!" Her eyes grew wide as she told the tale, and she wrapped her carefully groomed hands around her arms for warmth. "That's what we've heard."

I swallowed.

Poison could make a body swell.

"Well, why wouldn't anyone have a funeral for the little malku, then? Or a celebration for his birth? There was never any word. Not an announcement or anything. Those of us along the wall had no idea." We were usually in the know about the comings and goings in the Palace. Word spread. Things got out. But this—*this*—no one knew.

"Some say it was her shame. She kept him—the birth and his quick death—silent because she knew she'd borne a child not meant for life. Still others say she kept it silent because she was protecting someone who may have caused his death. But either way, it is of no importance anymore. After the baby died, she was found dead the next morning."

My head was spinning. Two dead boys who would be heir to the throne. An eager ensi determined to have the throne for himself. A young nin who would inherit only if there were no malkus to take her place. The dull ache that had begun this morning spread throughout my neck and shoulders. Could Nin Arwia have had anything to do with the deaths of her little brothers? Would her lust for the throne compel her to kill the only siblings she would ever have—one shoved from a balcony, the other poisoned or smothered? Did her ummum keep the boy's life quiet to protect her young daughter? And what of the trinkets! Were the necklace and the lock of hair—*trophies?*

And the *love tablets* in her chest. I shuddered.

They couldn't have been from a suitor looking to marry her to gain power himself. Ensi Uruku? I blanched. There was no way. I could not have completely misjudged a person in such a way.

Yet—I remembered her smile as she blithely but purposefully locked me out of her room. The way she asked me to help the poor woman with her mouth while Lugal Marus was nigh unto death, and then insisted, again and again, that I join her in attending various events instead of tending to him. Was it so she could finally have the throne to herself? I had a difficult time believing it, but the facts—the facts were pointing me in her direction. The woman was studying me curiously now, waiting for a response.

"Yes, extreme grief can kill a person," I mumbled, thinking of my own father. How he'd nearly drunk himself to death in his own misery. And been murdered to prevent him from finding out the facts I was discovering now. I glanced around the burial grounds. A thought occurred to me: my father had a grave somewhere.

"Thank you for your time. May I ask one more question?" I asked.

"Of course." She graciously dipped her head.

"Do you know where one might bury a pauper? Say, one who died under the lugal's care? A servant?"

"The servants' grounds are that way." She pointed toward a small dip in the path, past a group of fig trees clustered together like guardsmen. "There's a big stone, a hedge of shrubs, and beyond that, the graves." She walked ahead a few paces, then turned back. "But I must warn you, Healer. None of the graves are marked. If you were looking for someone in particular, you wouldn't be able to find him." She smiled softly, turned, and walked away.

But I still had to look. Because if someone had murdered

my abum and the Palace had found him alongside a road, they probably would have dumped him in a pauper's grave with no markings. I swallowed the lump in my throat at the thought and headed past the fig trees.

The burial ground was no more than a plot with mounds and a scattered headstone or two outlined by scraggly bushes and weeds. It was no place to lay a great A-zu of unsurpassable talents and skill. No place.

Tentatively, glancing over my shoulder all the while, I made my way around the mounds, looking for a fresh pile of dirt. There was barely a path between them. Some were fresher than others. The sandy dirt piles were darker and more rounded. The older mounds had settled a bit. But the woman was right. There were barely any headstones, and those that existed were inscribed with illegible scrawls.

The field of the dead would keep its secrets buried.

The thought crawled into my head and took hold. My abum could never be properly put to rest. I closed my eyes, fighting the sadness that wrapped itself around my shoulders, then sank down to my knees in front of a fresh mound.

This, I supposed, was as good as any. Perhaps my father lay beneath me, his hands, once so warm and tender, crossed over his chest. His eyes, once filled with concern when he was caring for a small child, closed in eternal sleep. His mouth, once filled with laughter as he swung me up high, high, high to the tippy-top of our home, still agape at the horror he'd felt as his blood drained away.

Tears threatened, and I shoved them away. He was gone now and not of an illness or an accident. Not of old age. He'd been slaughtered like an animal.

"Oh, Abum." My whispered voice strangled in my throat. Given more time, I could have healed him. I could have saved him. I put my hands over my face and willed myself not to cry.

Just then, there was a rustling behind me. Two quick footsteps and a whoosh of air.

A crack landed on the back of my skull, and I suddenly knew more pain than I had ever felt. Stars burst across my vision, and I pitched forward onto my abum's makeshift grave. Instinctively, I curled into a ball, clutching the back of my head. Waves of searing heat enveloped my entire body. I was instantly, violently ill. I retched down my face and turned, so I wouldn't choke. I tried to scream, but only a strangled cry exited my mouth. There was a muffled shout from someone, and then footsteps quickly retreated. I was engulfed in wave after wave of excruciating pain.

And then I felt—nothing. I turned onto my back and let my arms and legs flop down to the sides. Above me, the sky swam as my eyes faded in and out of blackness. And as suddenly as I'd found myself face-first in the dirt, a dizzying darkness spiraled me quickly into the blessed relief of those who sleep.

CHAPTER 16

I WOKE TO the noonday sun beating directly into my eyes and the distinct feeling that the back of my head was going to fall off. Gingerly, I touched my hair and pulled shaking fingers away. I held them over my face and tried to focus. They were blurry, and they were crimson.

Blood.

As I shoved myself to my feet, the ground tilted dangerously beneath me. Every object in sight—the scraggly bushes at the field's edges, the Palace in the distance, a few travelers—was fuzzy. Blinking, I tried to gauge what had happened. I'd been hit with something by someone who'd made a hasty exit. There'd been a shout from nearby—maybe someone scaring him away—but no one had bothered to stay to see if I would live. I was almost certain the person who'd hit me was a man, but only the gods knew for sure, as my memory of the incident seemed far away. My hair fell into my eyes as I took a tentative step forward, away from the graves concealing their dead.

As I walked, swaying, inwardly screaming in pain, toward the confines of the Palace walls, I mentally reviewed my priorities. Go to my chamber. Find a looking glass so I could stitch and bind my wound properly. And take a pain tincture. Definitely a pain tincture. My head throbbed in rhythm to my heartbeat, and every step was torture. It was as if I could feel the hardness of the packed-sand path directly through my feet and up into my skull. Sweat dripped down the back of my neck as I walked under the hot sun, and when I wiped it away, my hand was coated in fresh, bright blood. The wound was bleeding freely.

At long last, a side entrance to the Palace appeared as if by Enlil's hand. As I stepped inside the cool interior, I was nearly run over by Nasu, who looked in a hurry to get somewhere, his tan skin flushed red. His eyes immediately widened when he saw my face.

"Kammani. What is wrong with you?" he asked brusquely, placing a hand on my elbow and pulling me to the side. "You look a fright. Is that . . . blood? Are you bleeding?"

"It's nothing." I stumbled, then braced myself against the wall.

He put a hand against my back. "It doesn't look like nothing."

"I'm quite fine, thank you for asking. I'll need to know the direction of my quarters. I'm turned around."

As I spoke, my knees tried to give way. I commanded them

to straighten and support me, but they were paying me no mind. After I wobbled and nearly fell against the wall, Nasu slung his arm around me, draping my arm over his neck. "You're hurt—or something. I'll help you to your chamber."

"I'm fine. Please."

But struggling was futile. Sinking into the warmth of his side, I stumbled along toward my chamber. Perhaps he could sew me up. I conjured up the image of Nasu's big hands trying to force a thread through the eye of a needle, then giggled in the delirium of my torment.

"Healer. Relax. Let's get there."

My snicker turned into a groan as we climbed a set of stairs, his weaponry jangling with each step, pausing every few moments so I could catch my breath. After I stumbled several times, Nasu asked to carry me. Looking up at the flights we still had to climb, then whimpering at the prospect, I nodded, and he scooped me up as if I were a child.

To his credit, he was barely even breathing hard from such an arduous climb with the dead weight of my body in his arms. Finally, we approached my chamber. He knocked softly and, upon hearing no response, opened the door. Mercifully, all praises be to Enlil, the chamber was empty. He set me down on my feet, and I immediately swayed, grasping onto his arm to steady myself.

"Easy, now. Let's get you settled on your pallet."

I let him lead me to my bed, then felt the hot flush of embarrassment climbing up my cheeks at having him so close to all my things. Where I slept. My old sandals were kicked off near the pallet, years of dirty toe prints pressed into the leather, and a sweat-stained tunic lay in a heap on the floor.

"I'm fine, Nasu."

"Healer?" He showed me his arm. Blood from my wound covered the leather greave from wrist to elbow.

"It's nothing." I was fairly convinced I wasn't convincing anyone.

"You're bleeding quite a lot." He set his smooth-shaved chin. "You need to get that stitched. I'm going to fetch someone." He turned toward the door.

But he didn't know what *I* knew. Someone was poisoning the lugal and wanted me dead, too. I couldn't let him leave me alone. Not yet.

"Nasu, don't. Please. I can handle it. I'll tell you why after I've done my work."

He stood, grim-faced, but nodded, crossing his arms over his armored chest.

Immediately, I fumbled open my healing satchel and pulled out a standard pain salve. I dabbed it under my tongue until I sensed a softening around the edges of the room. A calming of my humors. A dulling of the ache. Outside the window, life streamed on. Vendors called out their wares, and merchants found new buyers for their goods.

Kammani, hand me my needle.

My father's voice echoed in my head as I rummaged through my healing satchel for the needle and thread. I'd assisted him so many times, it was as if he were standing there with me.

Clean it, Arammu. My little love.

I obeyed the voice of my dead father, as I had many years before, and held the needle over the open flame of a candle on a nearby table to kill any disease.

Thread the needle.

I pulled a boiled thread through the eye of the needle and knotted it neatly at the end.

Now clean the wound. Carefully, child.

I found an old linen cloth and the deep waterbasin. I dunked my head repeatedly to loosen any dirt, yelping with the sting. Behind me, Nasu murmured something about Nanaea helping me, but I ignored him and scrubbed the dirt and blood from my head with the Aleppo soap until my knees were faint with weakness. But I soldiered on, drying my hair with a linen cloth, then felt along the back at the wound. Holding a binding to it to stop the blood, I searched among the Sacred Maidens' things for a pair of handheld looking glasses. Simti had looked into one earlier as she painted the kohl around her eyes and ruby red on her cheeks.

"Healer, let me see if Nanaea or *someone*—" Nasu started.

"It's fine, thank you." I *had to* just keep moving. If I didn't, the pain would be too much. The looking glass was nestled among the necklaces and scarves and headdresses atop Simti's dressing table. I set it up against the windowsill. Now for another. There was a large copper looking glass stuffed into one of Huna's baskets with an array of wildly colored tunics and etched sandals. Perfect.

I positioned myself in front of the first looking glass and

held the other one in front of me, then shook my head dismally. There was no way these stitches could be sewn with one hand occupied. But . . . there was always cauterization. Nasu had a knife, and if we heated it until it was blood-red, I could press it against the wound, melt the skin, and seal it tight. The only problem with that, as my father had explained it many years ago, was that it was more prone to infection that way. Stitching was usually better.

"It appears I'll need your assistance."

"What is it?" Nasu quickly came to my side, tucking his black curls behind his ears.

"I need someone to hold this looking glass."

Nasu looked doubtfully at the elaborate looking glass. "How long will it take?"

"Less than a quarter turn of the dial. I'm a fast stitcher."

He nodded with a calloused hand outstretched. "Give it to me. Where should I stand?"

"Here." I nodded to a spot that afforded me a perfect view, positioned myself appropriately, and detached myself enough to push aside my hair to assess the damage. There was a red jagged zigzag across my skull, one that oozed blood, but I could stitch the wound and apply poultices for the swelling if I shaved a bit of my hair.

"I'll need your sharpest dagger."

Without questioning me, Nasu pulled it from the scabbard at his belt. I held it to the fire to cleanse it and then deftly shaved the hair around the wound.

"Are you certain you can do this? Surely, there's someone else who could help?" he asked as he saw the depth of the slash.

I set my mouth grimly. There were no other options, as nobody seemed to be all that trustworthy and time was not on my side. I'd lose too much blood and be in much worse shape than I was now.

Plus, I could do it.

"I'm positive." I took the needle and began my work with a clenched jaw but a resolute mind. Sewing a flesh wound was easy, even one that belonged to me. What was more difficult? Stitching closed a lacerated spirit, one that had been torn asunder, repeatedly.

❖ ❖ ❖ ❖ ❖

A short while later, I was sipping cool water and nibbling tinnuru bread on my pallet, when Nasu's thick black eyebrows shot so far up his forehead in disbelief, I was concerned they'd fly right off his skull.

"So someone bashed you on the back of the head?"

I grimaced as a fresh wave of pain overtook me. "Yes. I was in the burial grounds, looking for my abum's grave."

The pain tincture was working . . . slightly. I'd have to tinker with the proportion of arnica to hemp.

His warm brown eyes flickered to mine. Serious, but with a trace of compassion. "He was a good man."

"You knew him?" I tore off a piece of the bread and offered it. He swiped his black curls away from his face, took it, shoved it in his mouth, and chewed.

"I broke my leg in training two summers ago. He was kind when he healed me, even though he disapproved of our training methods. Said they were horrible." The ghost of a smile appeared on his face, but it left as quickly as it came.

My heart tugged. Abum *would have* said that. "Yes. He *was* a good man. And someone is trying to send me to join him in the Netherworld, I think. Because they hit me hard. With a board or a brick or something."

He rubbed his clean-shaven chin. "Why in Enlil's name would someone do that?"

His eyes were full of concern and confusion. Well, it clearly wasn't *him*, not that I suspected him, since he'd just helped me as I'd sewn my wound closed. But should I tell him? It might be helpful to have someone watching over my safety. And if that someone happened to be handy with a sicklesword, then . . . even better. Besides, I was nearly incoherent with exhaustion, and minding my tongue seemed like too much of a bother.

"They likely hit me because of the facts behind the lugal's illness."

His jaw flexed, and he clenched his hand into a fist as his eyes searched mine. "Tell me."

I had to tread carefully. "You must swear to keep this between us, Nasu. No one else can know."

He pressed his lips together impatiently. "I'll swear to nothing unless I know what it is."

Can I trust him? I studied his face, searching for a clue to his trustworthiness. But at this point, I didn't really have a better option.

"The lugal is being *poisoned*," I whispered, glancing at the door. He leaned in closer. "The little tonic I gave him last evening proves it. If he hadn't been poisoned, he would have died from the antidote."

His angular face went from disbelief to angst to anger in a matter of moments. "That tincture with the X on it could have killed him?"

"Don't trouble yourself. He's doing well. Healing, even, if I may be so bold."

His big hands flexed as he weighed my words, regarding me thoughtfully. But eventually, he realized I was right. "*Something* is certainly working. I saw him earlier with your brother at his side. So, either from the boy's ministrations or from your tonic, the lugal looks . . . better."

His eyes were sincere, but his mouth was grim. He stood, took two paces to the door, looked out in the hallway, then closed the door softly behind him and turned the lock.

Immediately, I was afraid. Had I guessed incorrectly? Was *he* the person who'd hit me and was poisoning the lugal? I leaped to my feet, the room tilting. "Nasu, please." I held my hands up in front of me. "Whatever you're going to do to me, don't. I'll scream!"

I opened my mouth to do so, but he rushed to me in three quick strides and held a hand over my mouth. I struggled against his firm grasp to no avail. His breastplate was cool against my skin as he regarded me intensely. "Kammani. Stop. Stop it at once! You've misunderstood my actions."

I ceased struggling but watched his every move.

"I'm going to remove my hand. Do not scream. I would never hurt you, but it appears there are those who would."

I nodded, and when he released me, my body sagged against the wall and to the floor, my head reeling. This was too much. All of it. The Palace. My sister. The crack against my skull. Stuffing my hands between my knees, I willed them to stop shaking. But then a thought occurred to me. *Nasu* was outside the lugal's door all the time.

"Nasu, has anyone come or gone from the lugal's chambers who seems out of the ordinary? Who has been in there?"

"Honestly, I cannot say. I'm not the only one who guards him. It could be anyone." He gripped the hilt of his sickle-sword. "But if what you're saying is correct, and the lugal has been poisoned, then that crack on the back of your head means someone suspects you have figured it out. So if I were you, I'd leave here. Late tonight. Get away to where no one can find you."

The thought made me dizzy. Crimson droplets were spattered on the floor from my laceration, and my head was throbbing so badly I wanted to vomit, but he thought I should flee.

"How can I go away? The lugal is healing, but he's not out of the Boatman's skiff just yet. In fact, I should be tending to him *now*. The only way to make sure he's healed for certain and Uruku does not get the throne is for me to stay here and make it so! Do you want to serve that terrible man?"

He lifted thoughtful eyes to mine. "Watch your tongue. You never know who could be listening."

The words chilled me to the bone.

He stood stiffly, arms hanging loose at his sides. Prepared for whatever might come. "Do *you* have thoughts as to who would want him dead? You can be honest, although it *does* puzzle me that you'd be fighting so hard to save the lugal when your sister benefits so greatly from his death."

There was no time to explain my feelings about dying *not* being a privilege, since he obviously felt like everyone else did about it. "Although she'd be given *such* an incredible honor, our city would lose a great ruler if he died. So that's why I am trying to determine who is poisoning him." I shrugged. "But I don't know who it could be."

Of course I had my suspicions about Nin Arwia, but his loyalty to the family might not allow him to believe that. There was no way I could tell him. Not now. I brought a shaky hand up to my stitches. It came away tinged with red, and I thought of the smear of blue on the linen. "Have you seen anyone bringing in a bouquet of flowers to the lugal?"

He shook his head. "Not that I can remember. Why?"

"The poison is from the monkshood flower. It's blue."

He furrowed his brow thoughtfully, then shook his head. "I will think on it. But for now, I must go and *you* must think of yourself. Flee tonight. I can keep the lugal safe while you're gone. He is my first duty, after all." He took a breath and put one hand on the door, his brown eyes firm and resolute once more. "Having you here could complicate the matter. Your abum was kind to me once, and I owe him, but while the lugal is in a perilous situation, I don't want to have to repay the favor by saving his daughter. Do you understand?"

"Yes, I do."

But like it or not, repayment of a favor or not, I had no intention of fleeing. Nasu, despite his confidence, would never be able to keep the lugal safe if he couldn't prevent Nin Arwia from visiting her abum.

"Good. Then it's settled." He turned abruptly and exited.

As soon as the door closed, I raced to lock it, then lay carefully on my pallet. Tonight, I'd give myself a chance to rest.

But tomorrow? I'd find out who in the name of Enlil was determined to keep me from saving my sister.

❖ ❖ ❖ ❖ ❖

I threw myself onto my belly into a patch of ragged weeds. Above me, an olive tree loomed, its gnarled branches reaching into the brilliant blue sky. Sweat dripped from my forehead into the sand, and my tongue flicked out to lick the saltiness from my lips. Every beat of my heart, every pulse in my veins, repeated the same refrain:

Hide or die.

After apparently sleeping from the late afternoon straight through till morning, I'd awoken, my head wound throbbing, to an empty room. I'd panicked at Nanaea's empty pallet. Had she left this chamber of her own accord, or had someone pulled her away because bashing my head in hadn't killed me? Still fuzzy from the arnica pain tincture, I'd quickly washed and redressed my wound so I could find her and check on the lugal, but life had become startlingly clear the moment I'd crept out the door and heard whispered threats from down the hallway.

"Yes, kill her. We've been given the instruction. We must."

"But—"

"Today. This very day. Or everything falls apart."

The voices had been unfamiliar to me, but their armor clinking in the echoey passageway certainly had not. They were guardsmen. And their proximity to my chamber had been enough to set me in motion. I'd glided around a corner, crept down the hallway the other way, and heard, from two corridors away, their gasps of surprise when they found my chamber empty.

I'd been dodging them for the last quarter turn of the dial, hoping, racking my brains, to come up with a plan. Nasu had been right to warn me to flee, but I couldn't leave Nanaea and Kasha behind.

Sixty handsbreadths behind me, a mighty wall hewn of solid baked bricks protected the Palace from bands of raiders. But who would protect me from the threat inside the walls?

There was a clattering at a side door to the Palace, the same place I'd exited moments earlier. Hunkering down low, the hair on my head standing on end, I watched as two guardsmen I'd never seen before, clad in the telltale silver breastplates and leather greaves, emerged. At their waists, gleaming sickleswords and maces hung like unspoken threats.

A lump formed in my throat, and I pressed myself lower into the brambles and weeds, cursing my white tunic. It was sure to give me away—my old, drab tunic would have blended in perfectly with the dirt. *Dear Enlil, make me invisible!* One of the guards stooped to study the sand. He saw my tracks and stood, narrowing his eyes at the olive tree. His right hand moved to his sicklesword.

And I was off the ground and bolting for the dazzling colors of the Sacred Maidens bazaar before they could act.

"Stop! *Healer!*"

But I ran, plunging into the commotion of bright booths piled high with food fit for queens: roasted peppers, succulent stuffed fish, honeyed dates strung together like decorations. Thick legs of lamb roasting on spits hissed, while golden and crimson tapestries bearing the lion and blooms of the lugal's emblem whipped in the wind. I shoved past a man hefting a huge barrel of Assata's brew and three young girls arrayed like Sacred Maidens with crowns of red blossoms. Then I grabbed a stitched scarf from an artist's stall, hand-painted with my sister's likeness. The artist screeched, but it was already wrapped around my head as I dipped low, weaving in and out among the throngs of people shouting out their wares and collecting their coins.

Behind me, there were screams.

They drew closer.

I pushed past the grower's stall, overflowing with greenery, the one I'd sat in with Dagan, but tripped on a long trail of ivy and sprawled into the sand.

"Girl! Are you all right?" A merchant, his gray beard streaked with white, pulled me up by my elbow. He held on tight.

"Please!" I strained against his grip. "Let me be!"

His brow furrowed, but he released me. Dashing into the crowd—*hurry! hurry!*—I ran smack into a fisherwoman with a basket of eels on her hip. She stumbled, and the basket toppled. Writhing eels exploded over us both and onto the ground.

Screeching, I yanked their wriggling bodies off me.

"*Healer!*" one of the guardsmen bellowed, and my throat tightened in panic.

The woman scrambled out of my way as I raced behind her stall, shaking the last squirming body off my leg. Another side entrance to the Palace loomed dimly on my left. On my right, a dusty street led into Alu. Blood pumped wildly under my skin. *Go! Get lost in the crowds of the city!* But the road was exposed, and it meant leaving my brother and sister. A woman shrieked too close for my ease, and my decision was made: lose them inside the Palace and figure it out later.

Sprinting at full speed, I ducked inside the cool, dim interior and tore down a hall, my sandals slapping against the bricks. A quick left brought me to a steep flight of stairs.

I climbed. And climbed.

Sweat dripped down my temples and my head wound

throbbed as my legs carried me farther and farther away from certain death.

Breathing hard, I stopped at a small landing with a window and looked outside at the Libbu, searching desperately for the guardsmen. Had they gone into the city? Had they followed me? My ears strained for any chink of armor or squeak of leather greaves shifting against a strong forearm. Nothing but the muted chaos of the bazaar. Below the window, a few upturned baskets littered the common area where the guardsmen had pursued me, but tradespeople milled about, shouting at others to buy and sell, the chase already long gone from their minds.

There'd be no help for me from down there, and the guardsmen could be *anywhere*.

I leaned far out the window to look for an escape and spotted the one person who would race to my aid if necessary: Dagan. He was talking to a raven-haired noblewoman. Even from this distance, her beauty was apparent. Costumed as a Sacred Maiden, she smiled into his face, then touched his arm. He leaned back and laughed. His name was on my lips, ready to be shouted, but I bit it back. He wouldn't hear me, and even if he did, he wouldn't reach me in time.

Below me, there was scuffling on the stairs. The sound shot my blood faster through my veins, and my legs bolted up another flight. And another.

Gasping for breath, I reached a landing with a large window facing the courtyard. Two small, potted date palms stood on either side. Outside, Dagan still chatted with the lovely noblewoman, and the ache to call his name welled in my chest, but it would only alert my pursuers to my position. Turning away in a panic, I moved to bolt up another flight but was roughly yanked backward into the hard breastplate of a guardsman's chest. A beefy, calloused hand pressed against my lips, silencing me with suffocating force.

Panic tore through my body. I kicked backward against leather-clad shins but received only delighted yaps of surprise.

"Send her over the ledge," a female's soft whisper echoed from above me.

Stilling in the guardsman's hold, chills ran up my arms. A woman. Nin Arwia? It was impossible to tell. She spoke so low. But who else could command this man to kill me, and who else had the motive? The guardsman pressed me tighter, solid arms chaining me against him. I sank my teeth into the fleshy part of his hand. He grunted but didn't let go. He pressed his other forearm against my throat, and I gagged.

I could not breathe.

"No." The woman's voice was quiet. "An accident. Send her over."

"It'll be easier this way—" the guardsman started.

"You have heard my command."

He dragged me toward the window. I clawed at his forearm, his cheeks, anything I could reach. He pressed me against the sill. Below, Dagan stood with his back to me, his attention riveted on the noblewoman.

Dagan! I didn't want this to be my last memory. Him, standing there talking to someone who could love him and would happily give him the life he wanted. This couldn't be how it ended.

As the guardsman pushed me closer, trying to send me to the Netherworld and leave Nanaea and Kasha orphaned and sisterless, I thrashed against him wildly, my eyes blurring, my lungs bursting with the need for air. But he did not relent. I elbowed him in the side, and he bellowed, pressing my throat even tighter.

A scream tore from my throat, guttural and raging, as stars burst in my eyes. I grabbed the guardsman's hair. Scratched at his eyes in terror. Braced my shaking legs up against the windowsill as he pushed closer. Closer.

But the guardsman was stronger than my fear. I tried to wrench away, twisting frantically, grasping at the windowsill, but before the disaster of it even took root in my brain, he growled and shoved me out the window.

"*Dagan!*" I screamed.

But there was nothing he or anyone else could do. In the moment he startled and looked my way, I found myself hurtling end over end toward the shimmering sand like a white bird shot from the sky.

CHAPTER 17

SEARING FIRE. STARS. Blood in my mouth. Lightning up my leg. My eyes opened and closed, then opened, closed again.

I sank beneath the surface of the sea. Then spluttered awake.

Please. A drink!

Maybe I said the words, but I didn't think so. I was so thirsty. I couldn't breathe. My ribs had to be cracked. My leg throbbed with a thousand fires. And my shoulder. Out of its socket?

No no no no no no.

I sobbed. Someone's cool hand pressed against my face.

I'm going to die!

Nobody heard my cry. The Boatman's long bony fingers caressed my cheek from the other side of the river. Behind him, his face a blur, my abum sang, "She is fair, she is fair, she is lovely and fair."

Please, Enlil. Release me to the night. Make me forget.

But no. Writhing, agonizing pain washed over me in wave after wave after teeth-chattering wave.

Abum! Save me. Ummum? Where are you?

Her voice murmured soothing words, and then it was Nanaea's scent and Dagan's prayer, his lips on my forehead. Moisture landed on my tongue. Trickled down my throat.

More!

Then the crushing coldness. Bone-shattering frigidity of unrelenting torment.

And finally, blackness swallowed me whole.

※ ※ ※ ※ ※

My mother's high-pitched keening raises all the hairs on the back of my neck.

It is her second full day of labor. She should have delivered the baby by now.

I try to squash the hysteria rising in my throat as I rub my aching eyes. I've been by my mother's side for two full days, with barely enough to eat and no sleep. Shaking fingers push back the sweaty tendrils hanging in my face, then dip into the small pot on my abum's healing table to check the level of the almond oil. I take a panicked look around the common room to see if there is anything else that will get this baby out. Now.

A cracked cistern full of water stands by the doorway. My mother's potter's wheel sits next to that, with a half-thrown pitcher atop. Next to it, a basket of mending. My sister's sandals. Six withered dates, which would have to do for the evening meal.

Touching my father's healing table for luck, I prepare to reenter the birthing room. On the table lie a mortar and pestle. A hollow, dried reed for suction. A copper lance, the tip burned black from repeated cleansing. Stacks of boiled linens. The reed goes into the healing satchel at my waist.

A deep, throaty groan exits the sleeping chamber as I push back the frayed gray curtain. The room, muggy and dim, reeks of blood and vomit. Rose and golden light from the setting sun filters through the room's small window. Dusk will come soon, and with it, hopefully, my abum.

Another groan, followed by a series of whispered curses, draws my eyes to the pallet in the center of the room, where my pale, sweating mother strains against the birth pangs of the life inside her.

"The baby is coming, Ummum," I say with more firmness than I feel. "You'll be delivered soon. I've helped Abum many times in deliveries, so it can be done. You can birth this baby—"

"Kammani!" Iltani hisses. "Your mother is in a terrible state. Stop droning." She sits next to the pallet, cooling my mother's forehead with a damp rag. Even after a day cooped up in this room, she still has enough fortitude for us both.

For all three of us.

Nanaea is huddled in the corner, her eyes round.

I asked Iltani here because there is no one else who can help me. Nanaea is so terrified, she's almost useless at this point. She's tried her best, but healing isn't for her. The midwife left yesterday to attend to her own daughter's delivery. My father went to aid a dying rich man whose family promised to speak to the lugal about returning Kasha to us if my abum manages to heal him. I sent word with a friend from the neighborhood to fetch him this morning, but he hasn't yet returned. Dagan's mother is ill in her own bed.

There is only me, my best friend, and my sister. That is it. It is up to us to get the baby out. Bile rises in my throat at the thought.

My mother flings an arm over her face and weeps weakly.

"The babe will kill me," she whispers. "It will. I cannot go on any longer." She raises glassy eyes from the pallet. Her face is a sickly shade of amber, her black hair matted. The setting sun casts her entire body in an ethereal glow.

"Ummum, I have more of the almond oil. Just let me give it to you. Please," I beg. It is the only remedy I knew that can bring about more pulses to get the baby to move down.

Dipping into the bedside basin for another wet cloth, I wring the excess water from a linen rag and lay it delicately across her forehead. "Stay strong, Ummum. The oil cramps, but it can help you birth this child."

"Kammani," my mother pants, her tired eyes boring into mine, "the child won't come. I don't feel him moving anymore."

"Ummum, you know that they stop moving as much in birth. You've birthed three of us before. Let me give you the oil."

She gasps, clutching her abdomen as another pulse seizes her in its grip. Her scream makes me want to run into the streets.

I nod to Iltani, and she holds my mother's head still while I lean over and drizzle a bit more of the oil inside her mouth. My mother spits the liquid down her chin.

"Ummum!"

I sink to my knees next to the pallet. If she won't take it, what can I do? Think, Kammani! Think! What can help her? Poppy? It will make her too sleepy. Walking? She is too weak to get up. I've already made her change her position dozens of times. I chew on my thumbnail.

"What should we do?" Iltani asks, taking in my mother's sweat-soaked bedding. Her limp hands. Her deathly pallor. The life drains from her with every moment that passes.

"I don't know. I don't. She should have delivered by now. The babe was turned sideways this morning, but I thought that shifting her to her knees had turned it."

"So maybe the babe didn't turn all the way?"

"I'm positive it didn't. Or it could have moved back."

"Can't you smoosh it to the right spot?"

"I don't know how to do that!" It isn't as simple as that.

Now, my abum knows how to turn a babe in the womb. I've seen him do it several times. One time, he massaged along the mother's belly until the rump moved up and the head moved down. The woman had wailed in anguish but delivered the babe whole and healthy.

If only he were here!

I know in my soul that this baby might not see the light. And that the child may take my mother along to see the Boatman if I don't do something about it. A cold wave of dread washes over me.

Can I turn this child myself?

I ease next to my mother, who lies panting, bathed in sweat, awash in the delirium of pain gone too long.

My left hand pushes deep along the side of her protruding belly, searching for the baby's rump, and I feel it straining against the skin exactly where I know it will be. I reach my other hand to the right side, where the baby's head bulges.

My mother's eyes flutter, as I feel along her neck for her pulse. It's weaker than the last time I checked.

And I make up my mind.

I have to try. There is nothing else to do.

"All right. We're doing this. Iltani? You'll need to hold her. It hurts terribly. Nanaea? I need you to comfort her. Please."

Iltani takes a deep breath and nods once. Nanaea, tears coursing down her face, comes and squats next to my ummum's head. Iltani stands, grasps my mother's limp arms firmly, and grits her teeth. "Do it."

I swallow the wad of phlegm that's practically choking me and shake my hands as I stand, summoning all my nerve.

"Gods of the skies, help me."

With a deep breath and every scrap of strength in my being, I push down on the baby's head on the right and massage my mother's belly upward on the left side the way I've seen my father do, urging the baby to turn.

"Don't touch me!" my mother groans, wild-eyed.

"Ummum!" Nanaea whispers, her voice cracking. "Kammani is trying to help you. You're fading."

I keep pushing.

A scream tears from my mother's throat, and my hands falter.

250

"Stop it!" Nanaea cries, covering her ears.

"Don't listen to her! Keep at it!" Iltani screeches, holding my mother's shoulders down as she writhes.

I feel faint, but I keep on. I climb onto the pallet, straddle her legs, and put all my weight behind my push against the baby's head. My mother groans, kicking weakly. I keep on, grunting with the effort. My left hand massages the rump upward while my right hand guides the baby's head down. I strain, sweating and cursing, as my mother squirms beneath me, bleating like a sacrificial lamb.

With a final sweep of my left hand, the baby's rump moves up as the head turns downward into the recesses of her womb.

At once, my mother sits up and bellows. Horrified, I leap backward off her legs and crash to the hard-packed floor.

"Kammani! I think it worked," Iltani whispers, stepping away from my mother's pallet, her hands over her mouth.

"My baby!" my mother screeches, clasping her abdomen with clawlike fingers.

I jump up and feel along my mother's abdomen. "The baby has turned. It's turned."

"I have to push!" my mother screeches. Red-faced, she pulls her knees to her ears and strains with terrifying force.

Iltani looks at me like she's seen the Boatman. "The child is coming!"

"Yes. Help me! Nanaea! Get those linens over there."

My mother groans loudly as she strains, holding her legs with both hands. I can see the baby's head bulging from between her legs.

"Again, Ummum. Push again!"

My mother strains once more, bellowing like an ox. Even more of the baby's head appears.

Nanaea runs up behind me. "It's the baby's head," she announces softly.

"I know. Give me that." I grab a clean linen and hold it below the birthing canal. She is bleeding heavily.

"Again! Once more, Ummum! Push again!"

My mother screams, and the baby's head, glistening with birth, eases past the opening.

"It's here, Ummum. It's arrived." I place the reed in my mouth, then lean down to suction out the baby's mucus. Iltani holds a cistern for me while I spit.

"One more big push now, and you'll have your child, Ummum. Just one. You can do it."

With a swollen face and bulging eyes, my mother draws her knees up, cursing the gods, and pushes the rest of the baby out with a great cry.

A small, slimy set of blue arms and legs appears at the end of the pallet. The long white pulsing cord of life stretches from the baby's navel into my mother. I peer down. A little girl!

"You've done it, Ku-aya!" Iltani shouts as my mother sinks back against the bedding, as pale as death. Iltani rushes to fluff the pillows, and Nanaea collapses onto the floor near my ummum's head in tears.

I rub my baby sister vigorously, waiting for that first cry.

Completely spent, my mother lies almost motionless against the bedding. "What is it?" she pants.

"It's a girl, Ummum. A beautiful baby girl," I say as I rub the child.

But something is wrong.

She isn't pinkening up. Her arms are flaccid.

My breath seizes.

"Kammani?"

"Iltani, get my mother some water." I hold the child over my left arm, rubbing her back vigorously.

Shaking my head, I try to force the panic from my chest. Out of my veins. The babe is blue. Limp. I cut the cord with the knife and rush her over to my own pallet.

"Kammani, what's wrong?" Nanaea asks.

"Nothing! Please, tend to Ummum."

I sit down with my little sister, pull her close, and suction her mouth once more, clearing out every last bit of mucus, then glance to the window. The sun is near setting.

Where is my father? He'd know what to do!

My mother groans loudly again. She is lying flat on her back, pushing limply. Iltani sits on the stool between her legs.

"Kammani?!" Iltani questions. "The afterbirth is emerging! What do I do?"

"Sit there and catch it in the cistern. Pull it out by the cord if you have to once you see it. But not before."

Come on, baby girl. Take a breath!

Slapping the baby's backside, I hold my breath, waiting for a twitch. An inhalation. Anything. But she lies still. I suction her again, knowing she is clear, but trying to do something, then remember my father's strong thumbs pushing repeatedly on the chest of a child who'd drowned, then revived. I position two fingers on her breastbone and push again and again and again the way my abum did. Placing my mouth over her rosebud lips, I breathe life into her limp little body.

"Kammani?" Iltani says.

"What?!" I breathe again into the baby's mouth. Sweat drips from my temples.

"She's bleeding. A lot."

Next to my ummum's head, Nanaea moans.

My teeth grit in panic. A red river is pouring from my mother's body.

I rub the babe's back with force. Come on! Breathe!

"Kammani, what do I do? The afterbirth already came out!"

My brain roves frantically from one idea to the next as the babe in my hands lies limp. As if of their own accord, my hands continue to rub her back. What can help my mother stop bleeding? And then I remember.

"Push linens tight between her legs."

Iltani rushes to follow my orders. My mother lies slack, like a wrung-out rag. I look from the tiny life in my hands to my mother. One is blue, the other nearly gone.

I stifle a cry.

Dear Enlil, help me!

"Kammani, your mother is fading fast. We have to do something!" Iltani whispers harshly in my direction as she shoves linen after linen between my mother's legs. They grow dusky red immediately.

My little sister's sweet face is still as I breathe again into her mouth. She already has a thatch of soft curls on her head. They are as light as feathers.

"Kammani! Help me!" Iltani pleads. "I don't know what to do!" She stands, hands pressing against her cheeks, tears streaming from her eyes in fright. Nanaea is sitting on the floor, legs splayed, openly sobbing.

Laying the babe gently on my pallet, I feel along her soft neck for the pulse of lifeblood. Nothing. My hands on her chest feel no heartbeat. There's no movement. No breath. She is cold. Blue.

Gone.

A sob rises in my throat.

"Kammani!" Iltani screeches, but her eyes must read my distress. "The babe is dead?"

Mutely, I nod, tears falling from my eyes.

"Well, then get over here and help me. I'm serious. I cannot do this." Her strangled voice brings me to my senses.

I may not have saved my sister, but I may be able to save my mother.

With a surge of hope, I jump up, but I know there are only moments to spare. Not even that. I run to my mother's side. "Ummum? Can you hear me?" I pat her cheek.

Her eyes flutter open.

"Kammani. Take care of—Kasha—Nanaea." Her eyes drift to the corner of the room. A chill races up my spine. Her eyes have taken on a faraway look. One that sees past me to a world I know nothing of.

The Boatman must be here to collect her. My heart seizes as my eyes fill and tears spill down my cheeks. "No, Ummum. No.

Do not go with him. Stay with me. Please. Stay here. I need you. We all need you so much," I sob, clutching her slack hand tightly.

Her eyes close.

"Promise me you will be strong," she whispers. "Promise me, no more tears—just strength. You're the only one who can help."

"I promise, Ummum. I promise."

Of course I promise. What else can you do when your mother is standing at the precipice between this life and the next?

At that moment, the little vial of agrimony sitting atop my abum's healing table calls to me. I slap myself mentally and grab it to stop the bleeding—but I know, as any good Healer's apprentice would, it is already too late. Snatching it from the table, I dump a glob onto a rag and shove it against her womb, knowing it will not be enough to heal her bleeding or make up for the blood she's already lost. But I try anyway. Because despite the knowledge that she will pass at any moment, that the Boatman is likely approaching from the other side of the room, she is, after all, my ummum. So I try. I dump more onto the rag and more and more until the bottle is empty and Iltani is pulling me away and Nanaea is clutching at my hands and my sobs are loud enough to be heard throughout the city.

Then I drop to the floor, my head in my hands, my eyes squeezed shut, and scream until I'm empty.

Later, when the sun has set and darkness has enveloped the chamber, I raise my head and pull myself off the floor. I know then, with every fiber of my being, that my ummum and sister are gone, and I am left with Iltani, the responsibility of my siblings, and the awareness that it was up to me to heal my ummum and save my sister this day.

And I have completely, miserably failed.

But I resolve, deep in my heart, as I stare at their lifeless bodies on the pallet, the babe tucked in my ummum's arms as if asleep, that though I may have failed my family today, for the rest of my life, I will not fail them again.

CHAPTER 18

I CRACKED OPEN swollen eyes into the harsh, blinding sunlight reflecting off a looking glass in my chambers. The weight of my dead baby sister still filled my arms. My um-mum's words—*Promise me, no more tears—just strength*—rang in my ears. My heart filled with anguish, living for a moment in that misery; then I shook off the assault of the memory, distracted by the more prevalent assault of the pain in my entire body.

My slightly addled brain tried to make sense of the scene in front of me. Lush rugs and a quilt as silky as a duck's feathers. Sunlight streaming through an open window where white draperies blew in a breeze. This was the Palace. Some-one's chamber but not mine. My mouth was as barren as a cask left out in the sun, and sweat covered my limbs. My lips were cracked, my tongue was swollen, and my head pounded with a deep ache. My mind felt like it had been stuffed with linen rags. I tried to stand to go for water but suddenly remembered a breastplate pressed against my back. A woman's whisper.

I'd been pushed out a window.

I cried out then, recalling my panic as the sand had rushed closer and closer. The cloth roof of a pavilion tearing off as I grabbed it before thudding to the ground. The pain of impact.

"Kammani!" Dagan was at my side in an instant.

"Dagan?" My voice was a cracking whisper. The fire in my right leg was intense, and the edges of my vision blurred with the sensation. "I need pain tonic. And water." I gestured to my healing satchel, and he brought it over to me.

His worried amber eyes searched my face. "How do you feel?"

I tried to sit up but was instantly incapacitated by nauseating, shooting pain from my leg. It had to be broken. "Terrible," I admitted, panting a little. "Where's Nanaea? Kasha?"

I took a dash of the pain tonic and drank deeply from the flagon of water he handed me.

"Shhh, my sweetest one. They're fine. Safe. They were both just here. Kasha left to run an errand for the scribe, and Nanaea went to the Temple with Simti to pray." I breathed a sigh of relief. As I sat, sipping, Dagan smoothing the blankets and murmuring gently, the pain began to ebb, as did my immediate anxiety about my siblings. Soon my body relaxed.

"You hungry?" He smiled gently, reaching across me to pull a platter of food close to my pallet. Instantly, my mouth watered.

"Starved." My voice was hoarse. Like two bricks scraping together.

I dined on a bowl of lentil soup with fresh watercress on top while he anxiously watched me spoon every bite from the bowl to my mouth.

"Why are you staring at me?" I asked, wiping my chin, then pushing the bowl away. The soup suddenly felt too heavy in my stomach.

"I'm worried for you. You almost died. I've been sitting here for four days." Dagan took the bowl and set it on the table next to me.

"I've been out for four days?" *Gods of the skies, I must stink to high heaven.*

He nodded solemnly. "Yes, and everyone has been in to see you. Your sister and brother, of course. Iltani. Simti. Even Nasu, the guardsman. He told me he'd warned you of the danger and how you'd been hit on the head and sewn your own wound closed, which was *not* a great decision."

I smiled weakly. "What else was there to do?"

"I don't know. Come to the farm and find my mother to stitch it closed for you?"

"Yes. While I was bleeding everywhere."

"He said he helped you the night you were hit on the back of the head. Is that true?" Dagan's face clouded over. "He's stationed himself by the door, too. He's out there now, as if you need more protection than me."

I took a peek under my coverlet at my leg. It was bandaged and braced from ankle to mid-thigh. "He helped me,

260

yes. And because of that, and knowing he is repaying a debt to my abum, he is trustworthy. He judged my abum a good man when others obviously did not." I winced, shifting on the pallet, my leg trembling from the effort. Moving the other way left me in a sweat as pain shot through my body. "But if he's here, who's guarding the lugal?"

"That other big guardsman. And my mother has been hand-feeding the lugal for four days straight. I told Nin Arwia my ummum could handle his care while you recovered, and the nin looked grateful." He shrugged. "She's a masterful liar."

Carefully, I scooted up, testing the workings of my body, moving arms, hands, fingers, legs, and neck. Ache wrapped around my body like a snake from head to toe, but everything was working except for my leg.

"Is the lugal speaking yet? Has he said anything or accused anyone? Does he even know he's been poisoned?"

He shook his head. "He's taking broth, but my ummum says he hasn't said anything. Neither has she. She was afraid you'd be accused, especially with the rumor going around that you'd tried to kill yourself."

"What did you just say?" Maybe my hearing had been damaged in the fall, too.

He paused and blinked rapidly, his jaw working. When he spoke again, his voice was hoarse. "Everyone in the Palace is saying you tried to take your own life."

"What? That's—that's—" I couldn't even come up with a word. "That's absolutely untrue, Dagan. Why would anyone ever believe that?"

He cracked his knuckles. "Well, a couple of reasons. Some are saying you were distraught because your sister got the honor of Sacred Maidenhood and not you."

I snorted.

"I know." He shook his head. "That's ridiculous. But others are saying—" He paused, looking down at his hands. Fiddled with a callous on his palm.

"What is it?"

He swallowed roughly. "When you fell, you yelled my name. And at that exact moment, I was talking to a young woman. So some who know me are saying you saw us together and were jealous because we never had a formal betrothal, so you—" He looked at his hands, heat creeping up his neck.

I blanched. He *had* been talking to a woman before I fell, and the sight of them together had been a shock. *Jealous?* Maybe. But under no circumstances would I ever even think to do something like that. "I would *never*—"

A muscle worked in his jaw. "I never believed it of you. Never. Not once. I know how you feel about me, so I knew that wasn't the case."

"Dagan—" I started, but didn't know how to finish.

He looked out the window, biting his lower lip. "I carried you inside the Palace, but you were knocked out. You were limp. Your head was—" He swallowed and looked out the window. "I thought you were dead."

"I'm sorry," I said, although I wasn't sure what for.

"Don't apologize. Please. I simply want to know what happened."

I relayed the story of waking to the muttered threat, the chase through the Libbu, and my eventual push. "And it was Nin Arwia. I know it. She ordered the guardsman to act."

"And I let her in to see you."

"You did?" My mouth went dry at the idea of her even *looking* at me lying there, helpless. I sagged against my pillows and replayed the nin's voice as she told the guardsman to push me to my death.

He reached across and rubbed my fingers. "It's okay. I stayed here while she visited. I didn't know what had happened to you, but realized she likely had something to do with it. It's hard to imagine someone could be so cunning." He pursed his lips. "Clearly, I'm naïve."

"And I," I whispered. "I thought she was my friend, but it seems she wants the throne more."

"She must be desperate to get it too, if she's willing to do this." He gestured to my body. "That desperation scares me. It's why we're getting you out of here."

"I can't leave the Palace."

"Oh no?" His left eyebrow cocked. His voice was a question, but his face said he already knew the answer.

"No. I have to make sure the lugal fully recovers."

"Kammani, be reasonable. Someone tried to murder you. Twice."

"Nasu can be my guardsman. I trust him. He saved me

before; he'd do it again. He seems like the kind of man who always repays his debts."

Dagan's face went black with some emotion I couldn't read. Jealousy, most likely, if I was being honest with myself.

"I have no feelings for Nasu."

He rubbed the back of his neck with a sigh. "I just want you safe. And the safest place is at the farm. With me."

"But if the lugal dies because he wasn't properly ministered to, then my Nanaea goes to the grave anyway, and this was all for nothing. For nothing!" My teeth grit in agony at the thought.

"And that's where you're wrong. Nanaea *isn't* in any danger anymore. The Sacred Maidens are being released, now that the lugal is healing. They're going to have a big celebration for them on the morrow, and then she can join us." He leaned forward, clasping my hands in his. The earnestness in his warm eyes was unnerving. "Don't you see? You've done it. You've *saved* her. You've done what you wanted to do."

"They're—releasing her? From the Sacred Maiden duties? The lugal really has healed?" I shifted in the bed, suppressing a wince as fire raced up my leg to my hip.

"Yes, my sweet! Yes, they are." He gently took one of my hands in his and kissed my injured palm. "You saved her. It's all going to be okay."

Staring at my hand in his, I swallowed profusely as my heart swelled. I'd *done* it. She was going to be released! I pictured us back along the wall, me building up my own healing practice and Nanaea caring for Kasha and tending to our home. We could make it work. We *could*, as sisters. It would take some time for her to forgive me for robbing her of her joy, but the coins and jewels the nin had promised would help.

But right when the thought of getting back to some semblance of normalcy hit me, the vision was replaced with this cold realization: Nin Arwia was still free.

"But what if the nin tries to kill the lugal again? She has full access to him. If she succeeds in killing him any time before Nanaea is married, they'd call her back as a Sacred Maiden!" I felt rage welling up at the prospect. I'd have to prove Nin Arwia had done it, somehow. Find the monkshood or go through those love tablets to see if they were from a lover intent on the throne or *something*.

"Nasu can keep him safe."

"The only thing that will keep him safe is his knowing that his daughter is a murderer. I have to find the proof and show it to him."

He released my hands and crossed his bronze arms over his thick chest. Set his jaw. His eyes were flinty. There would be no convincing him.

So I'd have to be clever to buy myself some more time in the Palace, outside his watchful eyes. I scooted my legs over the side of the bed and nearly fainted from the pain. I hissed through my teeth.

"All right, Dagan. You do make some valid points. Getting out of here is probably the best idea, although your mother would have to be willing to tend to the lugal in my stead."

"Yes." He nodded. "She has been doing so, and I know she'd continue." My head felt woozy, and he stretched out a hand to steady me on the edge of the bed. "No one would dare mess with her."

"But," I panted, "it will be a while before I can travel, as you can plainly see."

He nodded. "Then I won't leave your side until you can."

"But, Dagan, don't you realize I'm in a predicament here?" It was low, but I used what I knew I could. He was, above all else, a gentleman.

"What predicament is that?"

"I need a bath." Meeting his earnest eyes, I smiled as sweetly as I could around the pain. I must've looked wretched, but he didn't seem to notice, because his face flushed a brilliant vermilion all the way to his ears. "Would you mind getting someone to help me? Nanaea, maybe?"

"Yes, er—of course. Ummm. Yes. Let me go and get her right now." He stood too quickly and knocked over the stool by my pallet. "I'll be back. I mean, I won't be back. But I'll keep watch. I mean—not watching *you* while you bathe or something—" His face bloomed even brighter. "Just watching at the door. Behind the door. The closed door. With Nasu."

We heard voices outside the room. A woman's high laughter, followed by Nasu's grim response.

I stifled the urge to groan. My leg was throbbing, I desperately needed to relieve myself, and I wanted to sneak out of here soon. "Right. Since Nasu's already out there, why don't

266

you go and get some rest?" He started to shake his head, despite the dark bags under his eyes. He was stubborn, and I realized he'd ignore his own well-being for me, so I hurried on. "Or you could go get a cart to fetch me. It's not like I'll be able to walk all the way to the farm, right?" I gestured to the splint on my leg.

He thought about it, his eyes squinting speculatively. Probably wondering what I was up to. But he finally conceded. "Well, maybe I'll head to the farm for a bit. I can get things ready for you, check on the planting, and have a solid meal. I've been living on scraps at the Palace. I don't think they're used to feeding an appetite as solid as mine!" He patted his stomach.

"That sounds great. When you return, I'll be refreshed and ready to go."

He brightened. "Then I'll send Nanaea in to you." He winked, squeezed my hand, and was out the door. In the hall, his deep, rumbling voice indicated he was speaking to Nasu, and then his heavy footfalls echoed down the hallway.

A moment later, Iltani breezed into my room, scented like lavender and looking like a bright summer day.

"You're awake, but you smell like the Boatman."

Panting slightly, I set my chin, refusing to be baited. "Yes. I do. But you're not Nanaea."

"No, indeed I am not. I was just outside." She nodded to the door, her hands on her hips. "And me being me is a very good thing, because Nanaea is about to roast you like a goat over an open flame."

"For healing the lugal?"

"What else? Gone is her glory. Gone is her fame. She will likely have to settle for falling in love with a devastatingly handsome man and living out her days with barrels of children to make her happy, the poor dear."

Stifling a groan, I shifted on my one good leg. "Well, she'll have to wait a little longer to kill me, because immediately after I bathe, I'm headed out."

"Is that so? And how do you think you'll manage that all by yourself? I know you don't need *my* help for anything. You can do it all on your own. Despite the fact that the last time I saw you, you were vomiting into a pot so violently, I feared you would choke to death."

"Oh—yes. That. I thank you for your help that day. I'm sorry. As it turns out, I was poisoned. I haven't even had a chance to catch you up on what's been going on."

"Dagan told me some, but I'd like to hear it from the horse's behind. I mean, horse's mouth."

Despite my pain, I laughed. As I filled her in, her shock turned into righteous indignation.

"Let's flog Nin Arwia. Wait! Tie her to a stake and throw those ugly headdresses she wears at her."

"Ooh. We could just serve up the Palace's punishment and bash out her teeth with a brick."

"Or wait! Let's *burn her alive*! And I get to light the fire."

"That's getting a little gruesome."

"And I'll roast a duck leg while she writhes in agony!"

"Heavens, Iltani."

She snorted. "I know. Too much. I'm always too much."

I reached out a hand. "Yes. You're too much, and I love that about you." Tears pricked my eyes at my words. It was true. I'd missed my friend while I'd been here at the Palace.

I shifted to stand up, and fire shot through my body. I tried to act nonchalant, even though a cry lodged in my throat. A pair of rough-hewn crutches stood against the wall—my means of escape. "It looks as though someone has been thoughtful enough to provide me a way to get around."

"Yes, Nasu brought those in here two days ago."

"He did?"

She nodded. "He said he'd broken his leg when he was younger and your father had patched him up. He still had these from when your abum gave them to him."

"That's right. He told me about that. Well, perfect. They're just what I need." I grimaced and pushed myself up to stand. The room immediately spun. Gripping the window ledge for support, I hopped tentatively toward the soap. "I will still need your help in getting some fresh water in the room, though. Would you mind?"

"Not at all. It's my honor to serve, oh, great A-zu of Alu." She bowed dramatically, then headed toward the door. "Do you need anything else?"

"A clean tunic. And sandals . . . er . . . sandal. Just one, apparently. That's all." Beads of sweat broke out on my forehead as I concentrated on acting like I wasn't about to die.

"Great. I'll be back soon." She slipped out the door.

I let out the gasp I'd been holding in and hopped over to the stand with the soap and clean linens.

First, I had to take care of my body. Wash the filth away. Check my head wound, which was still throbbing and likely crusted with blood. Do a thorough inventory of every limb to ensure that nothing else was amiss.

Then I had to find the evidence to send Nin Arwia to the dungeons for trying to kill the lugal and punish her soundly for murdering my abum. And while I was at it? I must ensure the safety of my little sister and *all of us* in Alu.

It was the only thing that mattered anymore.

CHAPTER 19

WE CRINGED EVERY time the crutches creaked as we trekked as quietly as possible to Nin Arwia's chambers. My nerves, at this point, were rubbed raw from three attempts on my life, as were my hands from snagging the booth cover on my way to the ground. Grabbing it, however, had apparently saved me, because it had broken my fall.

Nasu was by my side, his face sternly set. He didn't like my plan. Not one bit. Iltani was at my other side, yammering like a crow in a voice that was entirely too loud that I was an idiot for even venturing out of my chambers. But if I didn't take the risk of searching Nin Arwia's room to at least try to find some evidence against her, I'd never get the means to make my accusation. Uruku had said to the woman who'd had her teeth bashed in that a woman could not accuse a man of a crime.

. . . unless she had *proof of wrongdoing.*

So proof I would find.

Taking a quick break, I wiped the sweat from my temples and tried, for the six hundredth time, to silence Iltani and force myself to think of something other than the ache. Shoving my healing satchel behind me, I adjusted my grip on the crutches and continued.

Nasu jogged lightly ahead, then expertly checked the cross path.

"We're clear." He waved me on.

"You know," Iltani muttered in my ear, "if this whole you-and-Dagan thing doesn't work out, that guardsman would make an excellent substitute."

I shot her a look. My satchel was banging against my lower back with every movement, and my wounds were throbbing, but she was thinking of love.

"I'm just saying." She held up her hands.

Nasu walked quickly back to my side, his mouth downturned. "Remind me why I'm helping you find the means to accuse the nin. Although I owe a debt to your abum, I'm not sure this is the best repayment. Nin Arwia is a perfectly sweet young woman," he said quietly.

"Ahh, but don't let that little bird's lovely song distract you, Nasu," Iltani whispered when I held my finger to my lips to quiet her. "Kammani *heard* her give the order to the guardsman to shove her out the window."

He looked around furtively, stepping closer so as not to be heard. "I know you said that, but there's no way you could have been mistaken?"

"It was a *woman*. She is about to take the throne. Of course it was her."

He bit his lip thoughtfully, his eyes clouding over with confusion. "It doesn't make sense."

"Nasu, I know you're loyal to the family. And I honestly wish my theory was wrong. But Nin Arwia has the means, the motive, and the opportunity. No one would deny her access to the lugal." I reached out and tentatively placed a hand on the greave about his forearm. "She gave the command to have me killed. I *heard* her."

He looked at my hand, then up into my eyes. "You're certain, Healer?"

"Unfortunately so."

"Well, then it's my duty to warn you against this." His right hand rested lightly on his sicklesword. "If you're found by someone less inclined to believe you . . ." He let the words hang ominously in the corridor.

"I know," I said softly.

We commenced moving forward, although every step was beginning to feel torturous. "But we have to find the proof, Nasu. Or she could try again." And my abum needed vengeance, but that was a secret just for me.

I paused, panting. "Which brings me to my next point." I'd thought about it during my entire bath, while assessing my wounds and finding, to my delight, that nothing was infected. "I'm going to need you to come into Nin Arwia's room with me and help me search."

He angled his face to me, his voice raised. "Now you're asking too much, Healer. I'll guard the door. Outside. As a favor to you, because you've healed the lugal and determined what was ailing him. But aiding in accusing the nin?" He lowered his stately voice to a whisper. "That would be treason!"

"But you have to be a witness, Nasu, or the lugal will never believe me, a cast-out who was sneaking around in his daughter's room. But you? He'd surely believe the most beloved guardsman."

Nasu held out a hand, pausing like a dog whose ears have picked up something no one else can hear. And then the quick two-step of guardsmen making their rounds echoed through the corridors. He calmly glanced around the hallway. There were no doors for us to slip into, and my broken body was in no condition to run.

"Do you trust me?" he whispered.

"No," Iltani answered.

"But you must." He drew his sicklesword and pushed me against the wall, grabbing a handful of my hair. I cried out as fire shot from my right knee to my hip. Immediately, sweat covered my body. His face took on the mask of an angry man.

"You dare defy me!" he growled, pushing his sword against my throat.

"Let her go!" Iltani screeched, pulling against his arm. And then I realized the part I was to act in this farce. I twisted my features into fright. It wasn't difficult, considering the blade was nearly touching my exposed throat.

Lamusa and another guardsman turned the corner and

slowed when they saw us against the wall, Nasu clutching my hair and his sicklesword, and I gripping his arm. They both drew their weapons.

"Nasu?" Lamusa called, rotating his sicklesword in his hand. "What is this?"

Nasu spat on the floor in disgust. "This healer tried to defy me."

"These lowly rats get bolder and bolder every single day."

"I know. It's disgusting."

Lamusa squinted his eyes under his bushy brows and rubbed a hand across his full black beard. Beneath his armor, his muscles bulged. I felt the press of the guardsman's breastplate against my back as I was being pushed over the ledge. It could have been this man who'd done it. His arms were about the same thickness. And that voice. I shuddered. It could have been he.

"Need some help?" he asked, his eyes lasciviously glancing back and forth between me and Iltani.

Nasu licked his lips. It was a gamble to answer, and I could see the indecision in his eyes. If Lamusa had been instructed to kill me, then he certainly would want to finish the task and fulfill his duty. If Nasu didn't let him, then Lamusa might retaliate. I decided to intervene.

"Please! Please don't hurt me!" I scratched and clawed at Nasu's face.

Iltani took her cue and tried to silence me. "Kammani, stop it! You'll get yourself killed!" She yanked on my hands, and I pretended to lose my footing and drop my crutches.

"Help!" I fell to the ground, but the act cost me. Stars swam in front of my vision, and I almost burst into tears from the shock. With determination, I held them in.

"For the sake of Enlil," Nasu intoned, "get up."

"I can't!" I flailed desperately toward my crutches.

Lamusa and the other guardsman broke into laughter. "Looks like you got your hands full there." Lamusa sheathed his sicklesword and saluted. "And since I don't feel like getting my eyes scratched out, good luck wrangling these two yowling cats."

"Go ahead and leave me to it. You're both worthless anyway. I'll do my duty, as I always have done," Nasu growled, reaching down and hauling me to my feet in one swift move. I braced myself against the wall as he scooped up my crutches and handed them to me. "Now *move!*" he shouted a mere handsbreadth from my face.

Instinctively, I shrank away.

The guardsmen waved and headed down the hall. Nasu continued the farce for far longer than he needed to. His eyes were hooded. His mouth was tight. I wondered how much helping me was costing him personally. He was the most loyal of the guardsmen, it was true. He believed in Lugal Marus. In Nin Arwia. He'd do anything for them. Yet he was helping *me.*

In short order, we approached Nin Arwia's door. No one guarded it. I scooted close and planted my ear against the surface. "It's clear. Now, Iltani, be gone. I don't want you getting into trouble for my sake."

"Too late for that, I'd think. I'll stand watch and knock if anyone happens by. Now hurry!"

I didn't need to be told twice. I pulled the door handle, but it was locked. Nin Arwia had learned from her last mistake with me.

"Nasu," I cried. "Do you have a key?"

"No." He mumbled something under his breath.

"What was that?"

He brought a stormy face up to mine. "I said if one of you had a hairpin, I could get inside."

"You can pick the lock?"

"It's necessary sometimes."

Interesting. He wasn't quite as much of a rule follower as I'd believed.

Iltani smoothly reached back to the bun knotted at the base of her head and pulled a pin free. She handed it to Nasu. He quickly set to work on the door, putting one end of the pin in the lock and rattling the handle with the other. Within moments, it was open.

"Now hurry!"

I scooted into Nin Arwia's chambers, then glanced behind me. Nasu stood stoically next to Iltani, his lips pressed in indecision.

"Nasu! Please!"

He looked right and left, frowning in displeasure, but followed me inside.

"Thank you," I whispered. "We must move quickly!" Propping the crutches against the doorframe, I hopped as fast as I could toward the chest where I'd found the baby's hair. Walking my hands down the wall, I lowered myself to my left knee and tugged at the lid.

Nothing happened.

I tugged again. But it did not move. Desperately, I scrabbled my fingers along the sides. The back. The bottom. I knelt and looked down along the corners and found, to my dismay, that the chest had been sealed. A thin layer of mud fastened the lid to the chest, and hot wax sealed it tight. I refused to lose hope. The answer could still be here—just somewhere else.

"Kammani, make haste!"

"I'm trying!" My brain was a frenzy of nerves. I looked over my shoulder at the door, listening for Iltani's signal that someone was interested in our doings. Behind me, Nasu used his sicklesword to poke around a basket of her scarves. Finding nothing, he eyeballed the nin's pallet warily, as if approaching it might be too intimate a gesture.

Grimacing, I struggled onto my left foot and hopped crazily to the pallet, then reached under and around the pillows, stripping the soft coverlets from the ticking. Nothing. Her tunics were next, followed by her shawls, her shoes, and a basket filled to capacity with underthings. No poison. No makings of poison. No vials. *Vials!* Her dressing table.

"Kammani!"

I yelped. "What?"

Iltani's face loomed in the crack of the doorway. "There is chatter one floor down!"

Enlil help me. "Nasu! Please, help me search!"

"I have no idea what we're looking for, Healer, and I don't want to disturb her . . . things."

"Just look for anything out of the ordinary."

He walked to the table with all her jewelry and bottles of beauty oils and grabbed a cask of talc. He shook it, and a little puff exploded from the top.

"Never mind. Just—stand there. Watch me."

Struggling and out of breath, knowing our time was running out, I pulled the little pots to me one by one and sniffed. Lavender. Jasmine. Evening primrose. Nothing but scented oils in those. Willing my hands to stop shaking, I opened a small painted cask filled with tiny linen squares for removing face paint and a woven basket of tyets for absorbing the blood of the moon. As my fingers rifled through her jewels and headdresses, my eyes searching under and around all the glittering pieces, a lapis lazuli pin caught my eye.

It seemed crooked, for some reason, as if the stone was set oddly against the gold.

Glancing frantically toward the door with Iltani's face pressed in the crack, I picked it up and felt along the four small prongs. There was something in there! Between the stone and the gold!

"Nasu! Look!" My fingers trembling, I wedged my nail between the backing and the jewel and pried one of the prongs away from the stone. A small linen packet was stuffed inside. Using the tips of my fingernails, I eased the packet out. It was knotted with a silken string.

"Kammani! I hear footsteps!" Iltani hissed. "Move!"

"Hurry, Healer. Hurry!" Nasu growled.

"Okay! Okay!" I squeezed the packet and slipped it out from the strings completely without untying it and anxiously drew the four corners away from the center. Five bluish petals from the monkshood plant lay inside.

"Oh, Enlil. Look at this." Gooseflesh rose on my arms. "It's the poison!"

"Indeed, it is." His lips were taut. "Put it in your satchel so we may leave."

"You *saw* me take it out of here, right? I have your word you'll swear you witnessed me finding this?"

"Yes, Healer. Now come! We must go!"

Just then, the door slammed shut and I heard raised voices outside the room. Iltani's and a man's.

Enlil save us.

Quickly, I folded the corners together, stuffed the packet back into the string, then tucked it into my healing satchel. After pressing the prongs of the pin back down, I thought again, then grabbed one of the linen squares from the painted cask, folded it neatly into the same shape, and replaced the monkshood packet with it should anyone go looking.

Nasu handed me my crutches, and as he reached for the handle on the door, it flew open and I came face to face with an angry pair of eyebrows.

"Get out here!" Dagan whispered harshly, pulling me out the door. "How dare you put your life in jeopardy? We have to flee!" He jerked his thumb at Kasha. "I sent him to clear your room, so you can leave."

Kasha held up my belongings. "Everything's here. Nanaea filled the sack for you."

"And now"—Nasu gripped the hilt of his sicklesword—"you should go. Speak elsewhere, for I swear, it could mean your lives. And mine, too."

Dagan looked into my eyes. "Do you hear that? You could *die* here. Please." He rubbed his hand down my arm. "Let's get to the farm."

"But, Dagan, I have to get in to see the lugal right this moment!" Leaning in, I lowered my voice. "The proof of Nin Arwia's treachery is in my bag. Here." I patted the outside pocket.

"You found it?" Iltani's hand covered her mouth.

"Yes!" Excitement filled me to bursting. "And Nasu was there to witness it. I need to show the lugal so Nin Arwia can be thrown into the dungeon and we can finally get everyone out of this mess!"

"Kammani." Dagan shook his head, his hands on his hips. "Right now, we need to save *your* life. As I was walking into the Palace, a group of guardsmen with Nin Arwia at their head had just come from the corridor outside the Sacred Maidens' chamber. They're *looking* for you. We have to get you out."

"No. I have the proof, and I'm taking it to him, *now*!" I shoved my satchel aside and made a move for the lugal's chamber. Dagan moved in front of me like a living, breathing wall.

He crossed his arms over his chest. "Think! Kammani! You're no good to anyone if you're dead! Besides, if you've taken the monkshood, she can't keep poisoning the lugal, can she?"

"What if she has more? This is just a small amount. Who knows if she has another stash?"

"Well, then Nasu will keep the lugal safe until you can show him." Dagan nodded to Nasu. "Can't you?"

"I always do my duty, Farmer's Son." He stood up straighter, lifting his chin. "No one will hurt him again."

"And my ummum has already agreed to stay at the lugal's side to ensure that he continues to heal, and no one would dare harm her. I'd cut off the food supply." Dagan's voice rose in earnestness. "So let's get *out of here*. We'll come watch Nanaea perform tomorrow to end her Sacred Maiden duties, then collect her and go back home and figure everything else out from there." He turned to Kasha. "You're coming with us, too."

Kasha's eyes grew round. "You can't *steal* me! I have to check in every night with my watcher, or I'll be whipped!"

Dagan's eyes glittered. "There's a lot you don't understand about the power of hunger, Kasha. People like your watcher, who live at the very edge of their means, do. If I stop supplying grain from the farm, his family will starve." His jaw flexed. "I've spoken with him. He will do as I've asked and report that you've checked in each night. I'm not leaving you here to be harmed."

"What about Nanaea, though?" Iltani gnawed the inside of her cheek.

"They wouldn't touch the lugal's Maidens, not until they're released, anyway, I said. "They're too valuable."

"But after they're released, she's in danger, which is why we'll be collecting her immediately after the ceremony," Dagan said.

At this point, I knew he'd carry me out of here despite my objections. I'd have to find another time to expose Nin Arwia to Lugal Marus.

I nodded slowly. "Okay. Let's leave. It's the only thing that makes sense."

Nasu directed us down a hallway toward a back staircase, and Dagan quickly scooped me up in his arms.

"Don't even protest. This will be faster."

And we scuttled away.

But despite my acquiescence, as they helped me down six flights of stairs, in and out of rooms to dodge guardsmen, through the kitchens, past the colorful booths of the Libbu, and into a creaking wagon bound for Dagan's farm, I couldn't help but brood on that little linen square in my satchel with the blue petals of monkshood. My father's grave. My little sister's glee when she thought she'd be honored in the Netherworld. Nin Arwia's face when she declared that she wanted to be my friend.

All memories that burned beneath my breastbone, stoking a flame that was threatening to roar to an inferno.

Because the nin had taken everything away from me. Had she never poisoned the Lugal and killed her brothers, *my* abum and ummum would still be alive. My sister would never have been selected as a Sacred Maiden. Kasha would still have his rightful place in our home.

She'd better be glad I was leaving the Palace tonight. Because for every crime she'd committed against my family, I'd repay her twofold—and soon.

CHAPTER 20

❧

THE PLAN FLOATED to me as if sent from Enlil himself as I sat next to Dagan on the cart, my bones rattling, lightning strikes of pain zinging up my leg. My left thigh pressed against Dagan's right, and when he looked at me, a certain tightening along his jawline sent heat all the way down into my toes. I did my best to ignore his proximity and instead focused on my daydream: I was standing tall, overlooking a crowd of my fellow Alu citizens, denouncing Nin Arwia, explaining how she'd killed my father and attempted to kill hers in order to steal the crown. The ceremony for the Maidens that took place on the morrow would be a perfect venue. With an entire city witnessing as I held up the proof I'd found in Nin Arwia's brooch and Nasu standing beside me to back my claim, the lugal would *be forced* to take me seriously.

Now I only had to convince Dagan to let me out of his sight so I could sneak away from the farm to get back to the

Palace. I'd need some time before the morrow to figure out how best to insert myself into the production. And that would take some strategy. And probably some of Iltani's nerve.

Dinner at the farm was a noisy affair. We entered the raucous courtyard just as it began, and I commenced pretending to enjoy the meal while I worked out the details in my head and thought of a way to dodge Dagan. Cutlery click-clacked against earthenware bowls and plates. From one low table, the farmer's sons' voices boomed with guffaws, loud smacks, and grunts as they dove elbows-deep into the feast. The meal Shiptu must have prepared before leaving—roasted mutton with mint, coriander, and marjoram; stewed chickpeas with roasted leeks and beets; and the finest honeycake topped with apricot sauce—sat heavy in my belly as I yawned loudly, resting my chin in my hands. I needed to make my excuses and head to our room with Iltani and Kasha to tell them of my plan, but I knew that the evening wouldn't come to a close anytime soon.

Dagan saw my yawn, as I expected he would.

"Kammani?" he asked, concern in his amber eyes. "Do you need to retire to your chamber?"

I rubbed my eyes. I actually *was* worn down—a symptom of my injury—but I would not be able to rest yet. "I hate to be ungrateful for your hospitality—" I ventured.

"Say nothing more about it. I'll escort you," he offered around a mouthful of food. He laid a half-finished leg of mutton on his plate.

"No." I raised my hand. "You're not finished. Iltani and

Kasha can come with me to help me settle in." I rested my hand on his shoulder to soothe my remarks. "Perhaps you'll stop by to say goodnight before you retire for the evening?"

At the other table, Kasha and Dagan's brothers made kissing sounds, hooting and hollering as boys do. I cleared my throat loudly.

Dagan laughed at their antics. "I'd be happy to stop by." He winked, and I smiled benignly. When he came, I'd be conveniently "asleep."

Across the table from me, Iltani squinted at me as she chewed. She knew I was up to something. I gave her a subtle nudge with my good foot, and like the best friend she was, she immediately knew her role.

"I'd be glad to assist her to her room." She wiped her mouth on a clean linen and stood. "Kasha!" she yelled. Kasha looked around Dagan's youngest brother, Rish. Kasha's face was covered in grease. "Take two more bites, then come with us right now."

"Awww, but it'll be cold when I return—"

"Please join us." My voice was sweet, but my eyes held the hidden threat an older sister can wield.

He stood, grumbling.

After a careful walk down a short hallway, I smiled to myself as we settled into a guest room. Dagan had taken great pains to make it comfortable. A soft lilac quilt lay over the pallet. Fluffy pillows were propped at the head, and a warm handwoven multicolor blanket lay at the foot. Twin wall sconces held squat candles, while a small wooden table near the pallet held a bowl full of cracked walnuts, a washbasin, a cask of bubbling sikaru with flagons for drinking, and even a looking glass. From my position at the foot of the bed, my gaunt, wavy reflection stared back at me from an oval frame.

Kasha flopped onto a bright green rug, and Iltani sat cross-legged nearby, unbraiding her hair as I explained my plan to lay bare Nin Arwia's deeds in detail.

After several moments, Kasha held up a hand.

"Wait. So you want to take Huna's place in the Sacred Maiden ceremony tomorrow and then accuse Nin Arwia on the spot? In front of Lugal Marus and the whole city?" he asked, reaching to grab the bowl of walnuts from the bedside table.

"Yes, Kasha. It sounds ludicrous, and that realization isn't lost on me. But honestly, is there another way, with Nin Arwia and the guardsmen after me? Under the Sacred Maiden veil, I'll be protected. And with Nasu's support, the people will believe me." The evening surrounded by hordes of young boys was getting to me, and the throbbing from my leg being jostled along the dusty roads was intense. I winced as I reached over and poured myself a flagon of the sikaru.

"How do you know Lugal Marus will be well enough to even be there?"

"Well, Shiptu had said he was sitting up, if a little confused, but he can surely sit in a performance for a while. In fact, the fresh air would do him some good." The brew tasted sweet and cool. Refreshing. "And ensuring that he's sitting there to hear my accusation is where *you* come in, Kasha. Nasu doesn't know my plan. So when we sneak out of here tonight, you're going to go through the Palace to the lugal's chamber and tell Nasu to escort Lugal Marus to the ceremony tomorrow. Then he'll be present to hear my accusation and see the guilt all over Nin Arwia's face."

"Why can't we do that tomorrow?" he whined. "I've barely left the Palace, and now you want me to go back?"

"We have to go at night, silly. When no one is watching. They'll see us leave in the daytime." I leaned over and ruffled his hair. "But don't worry. Once Nin Arwia is accused, Lugal Marus will be so grateful to me for healing him and presenting him with the murderer that he will release you from your stay at the Palace. I'm sure of it."

Iltani spoke up. "I'm with you—you know that for a fact—but if I'm being honest, I don't particularly want to see you run through with a sicklesword when you miraculously appear on the platform in Huna's stead and accuse the nin." She set the brush down she was using to untangle her soft brown hair, and reached for a small cask of olive oil to rub onto her feet.

"No one knows when they will die, Iltani. But letting my abum's murderer go free means I've failed everyone . . . again. I have to at least try and pray to Enlil that the Palace doesn't retaliate."

"But how will you even get ready for the ceremony? You know the Maidens will be adorned in their finest splendor! If you sneak out tonight, you'll have to sleep somewhere on the sly and then somehow get all the way to the Palace and dressed before tomorrow's festivities." Iltani massaged her feet with the olive oil. "Also, you can't walk." She nodded to the cast on my leg.

"Well, that's where *you'll* come in. The plan involves a petty theft and maybe a little bit of misdirection."

She smiled devilishly. "I was hoping I'd have something illegal to do."

I snickered. Of course she did.

"Wait a minute," Kasha interrupted. "How are we going to sneak out of here? Everyone will see us in these." He gestured to his brilliant white tunic, then pointed to me. "We'll look like shining torches walking around."

"With these." I crawled over to the chest near the pallet and pulled out several black capes. As children, Dagan and I had worn them on occasion, pretending to be the Boatman for the express purpose of terrifying his brothers. "They will help us stay out of sight."

"Plus, we have this." Iltani pulled from a band about her thigh a jagged, razor-sharp blade.

"What in the name of Enlil is that for?"

"Insurance." She stuck it smartly in the belt of her tunic. "Now, Kasha? Shut up, get your scrawny hindquarters off that floor, put on the black cape, and let's get out of here. We're going to send Nin Arwia to the *dungeons*."

❋ ❋ ❋ ❋ ❋

We crept out the farm's south gate, Kasha making more noise than a mare birthing a stuck colt. I squatted awkwardly, my broken leg in front of me, my left knee pressed into the sand. I carried one crutch. The other was stashed in a cart already, with a change of clothing and some food.

"Shhh!" I hissed as my brother slunk around beside me. Ahead of us, the fields lay in straight green lines, with tributaries for water in between. Beyond them the outbuilding with the cart Dagan had driven inside stood illuminated by pale moonlight. The cart was the only way I could get back to the Palace with my broken leg, but it would be noisy.

I looked Iltani, then Kasha in the eye. "You remember what we need to do? Kasha, you'll run ahead and hook the donkey to the cart. Iltani, stand guard. Act drunk if anyone comes upon you, and get them to go back to the house. I'll take off on my own to get a head start, and then you'll join me and Kasha."

"Yes, but I still think I should run with you," Iltani whispered. "I can help you, and you'd move faster."

"No." I was adamant. "Because if Dagan discovers we've gone and comes out here looking for me or something, you'll need to lead him elsewhere so he doesn't discover what we're doing. You can meet up with us later."

"Okay, Nin." She bowed graciously. "Whatever Your Grace desires."

Smirking, I nudged her. "All right. Then let's go!"

She helped me up, I threw the cape over my head, and

Kasha and I were off, he racing hunchbacked toward the outbuilding, me hobbling along, hunching as best I could manage with one crutch.

I tripped over a stone with an "Oof!" loud enough to wake the Boatman but righted myself and hopped frantically to a haystack. I cursed my broken leg. Without it, I could have run to the Palace in much less time.

"Quickly! Before they come!" Iltani whispered.

"I'm going as fast as I can!"

"Gods of the skies, someone's here!" Iltani hissed. "Get down!"

I immediately dropped to my belly, then peered around the haystack, trying to see who'd run into her. It was a field hand, eyeballing her warily. At least it wasn't Dagan.

Iltani, work your magic! I pressed my lips together so hard, they hurt. But Iltani *was* magic. She smiled lazily, laughing about something the man had said. He propped his hip against the fence and grinned, taking in Iltani's figure.

Go away! Go away!

If he didn't leave, he'd hear Kasha rolling up with the cart.

Iltani moved her hands behind her back, pointed at me, then pointed toward the cart. She did it again. She wanted me to get my head start, but the field was wide open between the haystack and the outbuilding. I bit my lip and stayed low.

She laughed, then fell into the man, pretending to be in her cups. "Oh, how I'd *love* to join you in your room." She giggled after he whispered something in her ear. "Why don't you go back and get things ready for me?"

Her cheek pressed to his shoulder, she shot a furious look in my general direction and inclined her head toward Kasha. In the distance, the donkey brayed. Kasha was on his way.

There was no more time. I had to move. On my stomach and dragging my crutch, I crawled toward the sounds of the approaching cart. Iltani leaned in close to the field hand, her lashes lowered, her eyes full of promise. She shoved him softly with a smile, and he took his leave, waving as he walked away, a smirk on his face. Apparently, he thought this was going to be his lucky night.

Frantically, putting as much distance between myself and the house as possible, I crawled, my leg throbbing with each movement.

"Go on!" Iltani called softly to the man. "I'll be along soon. I need to wash up." She waggled her fingers as he traipsed farther and farther away, whistling. As soon as he was out of sight, she turned and raced toward the haystack I'd been hiding behind.

What in Enlil's name was she doing?

She disappeared from my line of sight, and I continued struggling—elbow, knee, crutch—toward the cart as Kasha, his white clothing neatly obscured by the cape, drew near.

Behind me, the whoosh of a full blaze coming to life tore a yelp from my mouth in horror. I crawled faster until I reached a stand of trees. There, I pulled myself up and turned to see Iltani loping like a jackrabbit away from a roaring fire, a bit of flint in her hand and a wicked smile on her face.

"What have you done?" I hissed as she caught up to me.

"Kammani, we needed a distraction. There were still about eight field hands outside, and the man I was flirting with did not believe my story for one moment. He was going to get Dagan!" She turned back to the blaze, bouncing on the balls of her feet.

Just then, Kasha rattled up with the cart. His mouth was a perfect O. I looked into his eyes—so much like our father's—and saw the reflection of the fire.

Iltani grabbed my shoulders. "You can yell at me later, but for now, I've done what you asked."

"I didn't ask you to set the entire farm on *fire*!"

"Just . . . let's go! Don't waste this distraction!"

I bit my lip, agony tearing me apart as the haystack roared into an inferno and the field hands ran in panic. We threw back the cover on the back of the cart and jumped in as it began to roll.

"Go, Kasha! Get out of here!" Iltani whispered harshly.

Frenzied, Iltani and I lay down and pulled the cover over our heads. I could hear Kasha's "Hiyah!" and the slap of the reins on the donkey, which increased its gait from barely walking to an agitated amble.

I looked fiercely at Iltani. "That was a stupid thing to do."

She sat up on her elbow, excitement dancing in her eyes. "But it worked!"

"Iltani, you cannot go around doing whatever works in the moment. You have to plan ahead a little bit, or you can cause even more trouble! What if you set the whole farm ablaze? And think how angry Dagan is going to be when he discovers that his farm is on fire and we are missing!" I bit my thumb-nail, thinking of one of his little brothers being caught in the fire. The burns that the men might have to treat alone be-cause both Shiptu and I were gone. It was maddening.

She stuck her tongue out at me. "It was a calculated risk, my friend. There were eight field hands and row after row of tributaries. If those men can't put the fire out, then they should all be taken outside the city and run through with spears."

I closed my eyes in exasperation. "You put too much faith in the good sense of others."

"And you don't put enough."

I remained silent on that point.

We rolled farther and farther from Iltani's deed, the cart lurching and heaving down side roads and back alleys toward the Palace. I lay there breathless next to my senseless friend, clattering down a road that would lead to justice for my abum and safety for us all. Hopefully, the farm didn't burn to the ground to accomplish it.

After several moments of silence thick with words unsaid, Iltani nudged me. "Where is Kasha going to park the cart?"

There would be no apology from her. She didn't think she was wrong. I only had to pray her calculations were correct and the field hands would put out the fire. Fast. "I'll tell him to park in the burial grounds. No one will look for us there. He can find a shady area in a grove of trees and cover the cart with branches. You can go out tomorrow to scavenge water and some food, and when the festival begins, I'll make my move. It'll be easy." It wouldn't be easy, but I had to try to believe it so I didn't back out.

Then Kasha spoke up, his voice muffled through the cover over Iltani and me. "What if there are guardsmen around the perimeter near the burial grounds?" he asked quietly.

"I'll *distract* them." Iltani arched an eyebrow. "Men are happy to have the mere promise of a kiss. Imagine what a real kiss could do."

"You know that makes you a pleasure-woman," Kasha whispered forcefully.

"So? I'm a woman and I want pleasure. No harm in that."

"You have no shame," Kasha replied. "Good luck finding a husband who will take you with those morals."

"Oh, hush, Kasha. You'd be my husband one day, wouldn't you?"

He fell silent, and I imagined the blush that covered his face all the way to his ears.

She nudged me with her elbow. "Well, that shut him up."

"And few things do."

We lurched along in silence, both of us settling into our thoughts. After a beat, I spoke. "Iltani, you know what's going to be the most fun?"

"What's that?" she asked as she turned to me, resting her head on her arm, her breath warm and close.

"Taking Nin Arwia down. I can't wait to see the look on her face when I hold up the packet of monkshood. Her true nature will surface for the entire city to see. Finally."

She reached over and found my hand, giving it a squeeze that was a bit too tight, a bit too much. I didn't mind, though, as it was Iltani's way.

"Yes, and let's hope saving the city doesn't cost you more than we bargained for."

CHAPTER 21

THE SUN WAS beginning its descent to the horizon by the time I immersed myself in the crowd milling about near the outskirts of the Palace Libbu. Enlil had granted me a fortunate sky—pale pink as soft as a newborn baby's cheek, swirled with peach, lavender, and gold. Wispy clouds drifted placidly past the disk of amber as it slowly melted into the distance, but I couldn't take solace in the peaceful heavens, because the task that lay before me could very well get me killed.

I was going to accuse the nin, the lugal's daughter, of murdering my father while attempting to kill her own.

Shivering, I pulled the cape more closely around my face and focused on blending in until we found the Sacred Maidens. *Nanaea.*

She was likely to be overcome with anger at me. I'd secured her safety but stripped her of the honor of being the lugal's bride.

Enlil, please let her forgive me for it. And let Dagan forgive me for my betrayal of his trust.

After a night of restless sleep and a day making stealthy preparations, the dark circles under my eyes only added to my disguise, so no one was paying me any mind as I chewed my thumbnail, looking past the platform to the Libbu, transformed into a paradise for the Maidens' Release festival.

Wild purple irises clustered around the Libbu walls, which were draped in white linen and adorned with shimmering sapphire ribbons. White linen also covered the large block benches for the wealthy crowd, and yellow chamomile pulled from all over the city blanketed every aisle and pathway around the square. Torches glowed around the edge of the stage where my sister, Simti, and Huna were supposed to perform, creating an aura of nearness in the flickering light. The illuminated faces of those just beginning to find seats were expectant as they waited for the girls to entertain them. Waited to fasten their hopes for brighter futures on the health of the lugal. I hoped I wouldn't disappoint them too much with what I was about to do.

I searched everywhere for Dagan, who was certain to be furious with me, but didn't see him or any members of his family. Enlil forgive Iltani if she'd done too much damage. The fear that she had, plagued me.

A large platform sat to the right of the one my sister would ascend. There, Ensi Uruku, the nin, and an entourage of guardsmen and nobles assembled, some gleaming in all manner of jewels, gold, and silk. Even Uruku had banished his traditional attire for a clean but drab cape and a beige tunic. He wore the look of having eaten something distasteful as he looked down his nose at the crowd clamoring at his feet. Next to him, seated slightly above him on an ornate chair, was the nin. Her long black hair was braided in loops about her head. Gold necklaces shimmered above a long, tufted tunic as green as an emerald and almost as luminous. I gasped when I saw the lapis lazuli pin fastened to her shoulder. She would dare wear the brooch that she thought still contained the poison around others! She had no soul. She flicked a delicate wrist at a serving woman, who knelt down to hear her; then she smiled sweetly and sent the servant away. Lies. All of it. Gudanna stood three handsbreadths behind her, dressed in royal blue, her eyes unreadable.

Servants circulated platters of figs, dates, grapes, and apples, flagons of wine and sikaru, haunches of roasted lamb and goat, and bowls of steaming lentils and beans. The rich all ate, laughing boisterously and licking their fingers.

The lugal was nowhere to be seen yet, but Kasha had told me his mission was successful—he'd gotten word to Nasu. They'd be here soon.

I looked back at the crowd, my stomach flipping over. "You ready?" a voice whispered in my ear. Nervously, I jumped. But I nodded as Iltani put a hand on my back and stealthily propelled me through the crowd, all pressing in toward the row of benches and booths piled high with food for the event.

"I've secured us passage to the Maidens' tent with some misdirection," she whispered, the hint of a smile in her tone.

"A kiss? A real one this time?"

"No. The guardsman looked like the backside of a donkey. I don't kiss everyone, for Enlil's sake."

"You would make out with a fish. Don't lie."

She laughed. "Ah, but luckily, my lips were saved today. All it took was the notion that there was a battle in the Palace courtyard with a petty thief and a distressed noblewoman, and he leapt at the chance to play the hero." She stopped and perused a table full of beaded necklaces the merchant said had been strung with the Sacred Maidens' hair. "Men are so predictable that way."

She thought she had *everyone* figured out. "My thanks for your quick thinking, Iltani. But, please, will you lead the way there?" It was warm in the press of the crowd, and my healing satchel kept getting tangled on the crutches.

Finally, we reached the white tent where the Sacred Maidens were being made up as the sarratums they would no longer become. As promised, the entrance stood unguarded, and we stepped inside to glory. Flowers of ruby red and the palest pink dangled from the tent's points in clusters, while soft candles flickered in golden dishes on gleaming mahogany tables. At one end, several lounging pillows in various colors lay about, while a table in the center was filled with pots of face paint in pinks, reds, and blues as brilliant as a summer sky.

Nanaea was the first to see me.

"Kammani!" she cried, running up as if to hug me, then stopped short. She wrapped her arms around her own body instead. "Where were you? You disappeared like a thief in the night. I had to hear it from Palace gossip that you'd left your chamber." She reached up a hand to adjust her wobbling headpiece.

"Stop fussing with it." Simti held out a hand painted with delicate red vines to steady it. "I told you it would fall if you didn't pin it tightly enough!"

The headpiece was of hammered gold inlaid with garnets, sapphires, and lapis lazuli. Nanaea's eyes were outlined with black kohl; her lids were bronze. On her cheeks were swirled bouquets of violet wildflowers dotted with yellow and white. Lush grapevines encircled the bouquets, then rose to trail past her temples into her hairline. Her lips were a deeper shade of bronze than her lids, and her lashes had been blackened. The whole effect picked up the flecks of honey in her eyes. The bloom on her cheeks.

"Nanaea." I held one hand out to her. "I had to leave the Palace. There is much you don't know, but as soon as the Maidens' Release ceremony is over, I will tell you everything." I let my hand fall to my side when she didn't take it. "But I am relieved to see you. And you look beautiful tonight. Stunning."

It was true. Never had she been more radiant. Her womanly form was ensconced in a feathered white tunic and a sapphire capelet that tied about her throat and reached to her elbows. Around her waist hung a shimmering copper belt with little coins; when she twirled, the coins chinked and twinkled in the flickering light.

"Thank you, Kammani. I *feel* beautiful, but I am very . . ." Her voice trailed off and her eyes turned liquid. "Disappointed."

And there it is.

Her lower lip quivered. "This was all for nothing." She held her hands out to the splendor around us and blinked back tears. "We aren't going to the Netherworld after all."

I reached for her hand again, awkwardly balancing on my crutches, but she moved away. Exhaling out my nose helped tamp down the flare of annoyance that crept up my spine. "Nanaea. I know you think you've been robbed of a lovely future as a queen, but you get to live! You don't have to go with the Boatman! That's nothing to be upset about, for the gods' sake. You should be rejoicing!" Why did she persist in this line of thinking? Why?

She jerked away from me. "This is not a day to rejoice."

And then my annoyance bubbled to the surface. I'd been pushed out a window because I wouldn't abandon her, and she was *angry at me*? I didn't tell her my suspicions about the nin, or that our abum had been murdered to inoculate her against the resulting pain, and she felt like she could be *mad*?

"Nanaea, please. For the sake of Enlil, silence yourself."

303

"Stop telling me to be quiet." The words spilled from her mouth in a torrent. "You have no idea what this whole thing has meant to me. *No idea!*" Her cheeks bloomed red with anger.

"But I do, Nanaea. You won't get to be queen now that the lugal lives. You won't get the riches of our old lives back. You won't get all the splendor and glory in the Netherworld."

"And I won't get to see Ummum!" she cried, her voice strangled in her throat.

Her words stopped me cold. I took in her trembling lip and flared nostrils. Her tightly clasped fists. Then I looked past her and saw our ummum's shawl folded atop her other things on the table nearby. The memories floated to the surface. How hard she'd fought to take it to the Palace with her, and how she'd kept it with her ever since. Bunched on the pallet in the Sacred Maidens' chamber, as if she'd been sleeping with it. Tucked around her elbows in the library.

It was a punch to the gut. So *that* was what this was about? "Oh, Nanaea." My voice broke on her name. She didn't want to be a queen—she wanted to be with *Ummum*. She missed her terribly. How had I not seen this? She'd been my mother's pet. She'd followed her everywhere, learning everything Ummum could teach her. How to barter and trade in the Libbu. How to sew and cook and take care of Kasha. How to spin clay into a pot on her wheel. While I'd been with my abum, learning his craft, she'd been with Ummum, learning hers.

Of course she missed her; I knew just how she felt.

She backed away from me, shaking her head, tears coursing down her cheeks. "You don't know everything. You think you do, but you don't."

"I'm so sorry." I reached bleakly for her hand, my chest heavy with the weight of what she bore, but she shrugged me off.

"No. I don't need your hugs. Please go on and do what you need to do. Because you think this is all about me, but it's mostly about you."

I stepped back as if slapped. "What are you talking about? I've done all this to *save you!*"

"Are you sure about that? No part of you wanted to show everyone what you could do? How great you could be? Don't lie to yourself. You want nothing more than to be the best healer in Alu. It's all you care about. You study and learn and take care of all the sick people around you, but you don't even realize that the person who needs your help the most is right under your nose. I am broken," she whispered, tears falling down her face. "I act like I am happy, but nothing *really* makes me feel better. And after Ummum died, you abandoned me for everyone else."

"Oh, Nanaea." I choked back my own tears. She was right. I'd been so focused on healing the lugal to save her, I couldn't see how badly she needed me *now*. "Come here." I held out my arms. But her chin quivered and she turned away, falling into Simti's arms.

I stood, grasping my crutches until my knuckles were

white. There was no remedy for this kind of pain. No tincture that would dull it, no herbs to reduce its severity. It was a red-hot wound lacerating her spirit, and there was little that could heal her right now, especially if she didn't want me near.

Twenty handsbreadths away, Iltani caught my eye. She gave me a sort of half smile, understanding the emotional turmoil in which both Nanaea and I were so heavily embroiled. "Come on over here." She shook out a gleaming white feathered tunic with scarlet stitching along the hem. "We need to get you suited up."

I took in Nanaea's slumped shoulders one more time, squared my own, then turned toward Iltani. Huna sauntered up just then, her hands on her hips.

"I heard you'd left."

Gods of the skies, now I had to deal with this wretch. "Well, I'm back."

"You look like a vagabond."

"And you look like a partially decayed toad," Iltani quipped, one eyebrow cocked. "Now come here and eat your honeycake, or I will." She winked at me behind Huna's back.

We'd laced Huna's treat with a sleeping tonic. Everyone expected three Sacred Maidens to perform, and they'd get what they wanted—except I'd take Huna's spot. No one would know the difference, since we'd be under heavy veils before our turn. But instead of dancing or whatever it was Huna had planned, I would speak when it was my turn to perform. The performances were the Sacred Maidens' way of saying goodbye and showing the Palace their gratitude for such an esteemed honor.

I would use my performance to accuse the nin.

Huna obediently sat and ate the honeycake that had been provided for her, although she eyeballed us speculatively while Iltani scrubbed me clean, fastened my curls into a ring around my head, and painted my face like Nanaea's and Simti's.

"What are you doing?"

"She's preparing herself for her big performance, don't you know?"

"What big performance?" Huna asked, yawning broadly.

"You'll see," Iltani snickered while her hands busily added the finishing touches to my face. When she was done, I almost didn't recognize myself in the looking glass. Golden chamomile wound its way up from my cheeks to my temples and into my hairline. My eyes shone a brilliant golden brown under the jade color she'd painted my lids. My lips were the color of blood.

"Iltani," I whispered in wonder. "What magic is in your hands?"

She smiled. "I made you look like a Maiden, which you're destined to remain until the end of time if you don't take a husband."

I rolled my eyes. She always knew how to ruin a moment. Across the room, Simti put the finishing touches on Nanaea's face, erasing the evidence of her distress, then walked up to us, fastening a bouquet of wildflowers on the shoulder of her tunic.

"Umm, Kammani? What happened to Huna?"

Next to us, Huna lay on a lounger, mouth wide open in slumber.

Iltani looked at me and I looked at her, and together we burst into peals of laughter.

⊠ ⊠ ⊠ ⊠ ⊠

I pushed a small slit in the crimson draperies to peek at the bustling Palace Libbu before I was thrust into it. We'd stopped in our procession with an unsteady jolt, and outside the cocoon of my sedan chair, the murmurs of the crowd rose.

A little girl on a man's shoulders tried to look through the crack in the silks, and I quickly closed the drapes, leaning back against the woven pillow behind me. Although the sights of the Libbu were momentarily out of sight, the smells—seared meat, cinnamon, smoke, a crowd's worth of bodies and working animals—made their way past the fabric. Next to me, Nanaea sat stiffly, her long brown legs stretched in front of her, ankles crossed.

"Everyone is here, Nanaea." Simti fussed with her crown, tucking in stray curls. "They will all see us shining like the stars in the heavens."

Nanaea shrugged a smooth shoulder and looked the other way. "I'd just like it to be over." As she sat back heavily against the pillows, we pitched to the left. The men holding our chair shifted to accommodate the sudden movement, but we wobbled anyway.

"Be careful!" Simti yelled to the men as she clutched the side of the chair in terror.

"They aren't going to drop us," Nanaea said. "Besides, I think we've arrived." And sure enough, the sedan chair came to a stop behind the platform.

She tossed her veil over her head and swung her legs over the side of the chair. As she was revealed through the gap in the draperies, the crowd gasped in awe. She leaned over, placing fingers bedecked with gold rings on the guardsmen's shoulders as they reached up to assist her descent.

My abum's face flashed in front of my eyes with an encouraging smile, and I flung open the draperies, ready to face the crowds in the Libbu and Lugal Marus's judgment. I hopped down onto my good leg and, with Simti's assistance, made my way up the stairs leading to the platform. A lump formed in my throat. My ummum would have loved to see me give a speech in front of a crowd. My abum. They would be proud that I wanted to stand up to the nin. Tucking my crutches under my arms, I hopped up another step. Then another. The platform grew nearer. My breath moved the veil over the top of my head with each exhalation.

As soon as I reached the top stair, a tug on the bottom of my tunic brought my head closer to Iltani's anxious voice. "Kammani, do what you must. Kasha and I will be waiting for you near the front, should you have to run away."

Without making a peep or turning around, I nodded my understanding. I forced my hands still.

I would not—could not—lose faith. "Did you see Lugal Marus? Is he here with Nasu?"

She hesitated, then said with a note of insincerity in her voice, "He is, and he's looking great!"

Iltani took two steps up and handed me my mother's blue shawl. "I took this from Nanaea's parcel, because she said she didn't want to wear it and end up crying. So . . . you must wear it tonight in her honor." My throat closed. I gripped her hand in thanks, not trusting myself to speak. "Compose yourself. Tonight will change everything. Be brave," she whispered.

I tried to swallow, but my mouth was completely dry. I wiped sweaty palms on the sides of my tunic.

"I don't need bravery. I need a miracle from the heavens above."

※ ※ ※ ※ ※

After I followed Nanaea and Simti onto the platform—moving shakily on my crutches, my ummum's shawl tucked securely into my waistband—we took our seats on a bench near the town crier, who reviewed a tablet perched on his knees. From the platform with the royalty, Nasu stood tall and stoic, studying my veiled head as if trying to determine who I was. I longed to give him a signal that all was going as planned, but I dared not bring more attention to myself than my crutches were already bringing before it was my turn.

Nanaea sat at my side, her nervous breath coming rapidly under her veil. Offering a mute apology, I reached out my hand. She looked down, and just as I was about to withdraw it before someone noticed, she quickly reached out and clasped it in hers. I squeezed once.

We are in this together, Sister. I have not forgotten you.

The town crier stood, shuffled to center stage, and made opening remarks on the healing of our great lugal, gesturing toward him with a grand sweep of his arm. The crowd screamed and sang Enlil's praises, celebrating Lugal Marus's return to good health. I dropped my eyes to the lugal, who sat next to Ensi Uruku.

But the town crier was *wrong*.

Lugal Marus *was not* in good health. He looked like the Boatman was coming for him at any moment! His skin was gray, his breathing shallow. Nin Arwia must have had more poison hidden away! Beneath my veil, I lifted a thumbnail to my mouth and chewed a ragged edge off. I had to speak up as soon as possible, or Lugal Marus could miss my accusation altogether.

How could Nin Arwia have gotten to him? Where was Shiptu? Maybe she'd left when she'd found out the farm had caught fire! But why hadn't Nasu protected him? Could I have mistaken his honor? Could *he* be the one sending love tablets to Nin Arwia?

The town crier announced Simti's name, and she shakily stood and dropped the veil from her head. The crowd gasped in surprise. I was certain that never before had they seen a lowly woman arrayed so beautifully. She smiled, walked to center stage, then closed her eyes and sang a sweet, simple version of one of Enlil's worship songs, accompanied by harp and lyre. The audience cheered, and after she curtseyed, she returned to her seat.

"Your turn, Nanaea!" she said brightly.

I breathed deeply to quell my nerves as Nanaea was announced, then stood, dropped her veil, and walked confidently toward the center of the platform. She nodded to the musicians, and the music drifted from their instruments. Then she began to dance. As she whirled around the stage with practiced ease, I went over in my mind what I'd say, wringing my hands in my lap and casting furtive glances at Lugal Marus's declining figure. His eyes were barely open; not even Nanaea's performance could keep his attention.

I turned back to the crowd as Nanaea twirled, then gasped as I found Dagan's face. He was seated near the front of the nobles' section, an unreadable expression buried within his amber eyes. But he wasn't looking at my sister.

He was looking at *me*.

A lump formed in my throat. Did he hate me for the fire at his farm? Would he still support me, even though I'd betrayed his trust?

But before I could contemplate any of it, Nanaea's dance was done. With a final leap, her hair flowing in wave after wave of shining ebony, Nanaea finished in a low crouch. She paused, her back rising and falling with her breath. For a moment, the crowd was silent.

And then it exploded.

After a few moments of taking it in, she stood, beaming and curtseying, then floated back to her seat next to me. This time, my sister reached out for me. I squeezed her hand with all my might. She was blooming after her successful performance, but her rich brown eyes were serious as she crouched in front of me.

"Kammani, I don't understand why you're doing what you are," she whispered, "but I ask you to be careful."

And with that, it was my turn. My abdomen quaked and my teeth chattered. I was sure even my bones were rattling.

The town crier blew his trumpet to quiet the crowd once more. "And now, the last Sacred Maiden, Huna, Merchant's Daughter, will dance." He nodded to me.

I stood, balancing on one leg, quivering under the anonymity of the veil, then reached up to its hem.

Could I do it? Pull it from my face? Running away was still an option.

I searched for Dagan in the crowd, then found him. He shook his head at me, his eyes pleading. *Don't do this*, he was asking. *Please.* My purpose was instantly reborn with a surprising ferocity. He loved me, that was certain. And he'd always want to protect me. But I needed to have justice. For the sake of my abum and the continued safety of the lugal—for all of us—Nin Arwia *must* pay for her crimes.

In one swift move, I tugged the veil from my head and was greeted by the shocked stares of hundreds of pairs of eyes.

CHAPTER 22

WHEN I PICKED up my crutches and hobbled to the middle of the platform, the town crier's eyes bulged out of their sockets, and Nin Arwia's mouth fell open in amazement. Behind her, Gudanna stiffened, her eyes frigid. Ensi Uruku sank in his chair, his mouth turned down. And though Nasu lifted his chin to me in recognition, beneath him, Lugal Marus looked almost asleep. I nodded to Nasu, and he gently tapped the lugal's shoulders.

The enormity of what I had to do hit me like a fist in my gut.

I heard, reverberating from the Netherworld, the voices of my abum. My ummum. Urging me to stand strong. To use my voice. My healing. A great surge of power filled me to the core, and I stood as tall as a mountain and addressed the crowd without a shadow of hesitation or a flicker of doubt.

"People of Alu. I am not Huna, Merchant's Daughter, as

you can plainly see. I am Kammani, Healer's Daughter, and I was brought to the Palace to heal Lugal Marus because my abum was—" I cleared my throat, working up my nerve to utter the words aloud. Dagan's eyes were full of misery. He shook his head as the wavering torchlight danced across his face.

"—murdered on the road to the Palace."

The crowd began to murmur feverishly, and I turned to look at Nanaea. Her face was pale. She shook her head, her face crumpling in sorrow, and leaned into Simti's embrace. But I could not help her now. The anger coming from the platform where Nin Arwia sat was alive and pulsing. Trying to suck me in.

"I could stand here and try to say these things happen— people are killed for nothing more than the sandals they are wearing or a fistful of shekels in their pockets. But I cannot say that today, because my abum was killed to protect the murderer's own misdeeds, of which I have proof." With trembling fingers, I pulled the packet of monkshood from the belt at my waist.

The crowd's murmuring swelled to outraged chatter.

I held the packet up in my fist, plunging into the cold waters of the truth. "The person who killed my abum on the road to the Palace"—my eyes filled with tears, but I shoved them back where they belonged—"did so to keep his attempt to murder our lugal a secret. My father, the greatest A-zu this city has ever seen, would have known a poisoning when he saw one."

The crowd gasped collectively. Confused voices, raised in alarm. Uruku stood slowly to attention, his mouth screwed into a frown. Nin Arwia quivered, and Nasu readied his sicklesword for whatever might come.

Lugal Marus stared blankly into the middle distance. I grew panicked. I needed to attend to him but *had* to prove my case first!

"Lugal Marus, I found this packet of monkshood in the murderer's chamber, and Nasu, your trusted, loyal guardsman, was with me when I did." I opened the monkshood packet and sent the blue flowers floating to the platform. Nasu stood stoically and nodded to confirm my story. Ensi Uruku's face grew angry.

"Who is it?" a woman called from the audience.

I lifted my shaking arm and pointed to the platform. "Guardsmen, please, I beg you, take Nin Arwia into custody. *She* is the murderer."

At once, a press of guardsmen and other noblemen stood to their feet on the platform around Nin Arwia.

Uruku turned to Nin Arwia. "Is this true?" He tugged her to her feet. The guardsmen circled her like dogs going in for a kill. Nasu knelt in front of Lugal Marus, his sicklesword drawn, one arm around the lugal's shoulders.

"Certainly not!" she cried. "Let me go!"

Cries of alarm rippled across the surface of the crowd like waves on the river. Many were staring in openmouthed horror at me, whether out of fright for my own fate or because of the knowledge I had shared. Several women ushered their children away from the benches toward the gates. Palace guardsmen from the corners of the Libbu grasped their spears and sicklesswords.

I raised my voice to be heard above the increasing movement. "Please, arrest her!"

"Get your hands off of me!" Nin Arwia cried, tears running down her face, batting a guardsman's hand away from her arm. "It isn't true! It isn't!"

I looked around the crowd on the platform, searching for Lugal Marus and Nasu, but I couldn't see them in the press of moving bodies. "I found your poison, Nin! It was in your brooch. And Nasu saw me!" Behind her, Gudanna took two steps back, her scarred hand over her mouth. She closed her eyes in what appeared to be anguish.

"Guardsmen! Nasu!" Nin Arwia shrieked. "Arrest her, not me! She's lying!" She pointed in my direction, but the guardsmen paid her no mind. They converged around her, their faces grim, sicklesswords and daggers drawn.

"Take her," Ensi Uruku growled.

Uncertainty bubbled in my stomach for the briefest of moments as the scene unfolded in front of me: Nin Arwia's panicked cries. Ensi Uruku's firm command of the platform. The guardsmen rushing to take her into custody.

Have I been manipulated into believing the nin is a murderer?

But as people broke into frantic movement, with shrieks of panic and cries for Nin Arwia's imprisonment, I could do nothing more than help Lugal Marus live. I searched again for him and Nasu, but their seats were empty.

317

I took my crutches up under my arms and began moving around the crowd who had leapt onto the platform, trying to get to Lugal Marus.

"Kammani!" someone cried, but I kept going. I *had* to see to the lugal. He was dying and needed me immediately! It was all for naught if he passed to the Netherworld!

"Excuse me! Please, let me through!" I shouted, pushing around the press of bodies.

When the royal platform came into view, I saw Ensi Uruku ordering two guardsmen to take a sobbing Nin Arwia to the dungeons. But my eyes were drawn to an area of the platform where there was no movement at all.

To Nasu and Lugal Marus.

Nasu sat on the floor of the platform, holding Lugal Marus's head in his lap. He lifted an ashen face to mine. Amid the clamor and the raging cries, his eyes met mine.

"It's the lugal." His plaintive voice stood out from the angry cacophony of the crowd.

Dread filled my belly. I dropped my crutches and quickly hobbled over to where Nasu sat, then knelt in front of them, reaching out to the lugal's throat.

Nasu's hand reached up and seized mine. I yelped in surprise.

His face was grave. "Don't touch him," he whispered.

"Nasu! I need to see if the blood is pulsing in his veins so I can heal him. I need to check!" I shouted.

He shook his head. "They'll accuse you."

318

"Let me at least check him!"

"Kammani, it's no use."

And as I dropped my gaze to the lugal's face, taking in the colorless skin, the vacant stare, and the limp hands, my eyes allowed my brain to accept what I had known was going to happen.

"The lugal is dead," I whispered.

"And now you must run," Nasu answered.

My stomach dropped to my knees. I had to escape. I had to get Nanaea out of there before they found her and buried the Sacred Maidens with the lugal. We had to flee!

"Guardsman, what is wrong?"

Thick calves encased in greaves moved into my line of sight. I lifted my eyes to their owner: Ensi Uruku.

I shakily got my crutches underneath me, stood, and turned to go. I tried to make myself small. To go unnoticed.

"Kammani!" To my left, Dagan weaved frantically through the crowd, trying to get to me.

I ducked, trying to sneak away from the platform. But a strong hand latched on to my elbow. Bile rose to my throat.

"Healer. What is it?" Ensi Uruku squeezed with unrelenting strength.

My hands began to shake. "It's the lugal, sir."

Just then, Nin Arwia wailed, "Abum!" Her face twisted in anguish, her arms hung limp at her sides. "Is he dead?" Her tears flowed freely, the kohl from her eyes bleeding down her cheeks.

A murderer she might be, but delivering this news was never easy. It gave me no pleasure to utter the words "Yes, Nin. He is."

Her chin bunched and her small shoulders shook as sobs overtook her body. The bubble of uncertainty in my belly grew.

"Kammani!" Dagan shoved a guardsman aside, brandishing his dagger. "Come with me!" He leaped atop the platform, holding out a hand, but was knocked down by Lamusa. The burly guardsman held his sicklesword menacingly over Dagan's face when he tried to move.

"Well." Nin Arwia's voice sounded strangled in her throat, but after a moment, she calmed it. "Then I must make my first command as the Sarratum of Alu." She pointed at me, her hand shaking like a branch in the breeze. "Kammani, Healer's Daughter, you have been found guilty of treason for speaking lies against the sarratum. Guardsmen, take her to the dungeon, and call back the Sacred Maidens."

And that bubble of uncertainty popped.

With torches blazing over their heads and sickleswords drawn, guardsmen released the nin and turned to me. I screamed as they seized my arms and hauled me toward the stairs, my crutches falling away. Nasu laid the lugal's head carefully on the platform and unsheathed his sword.

"Kammani!" Nanaea's scream tore from the crowd.

A guardsman was roughly trying to pull Nanaea and Simti back toward the Palace, but they resisted his force, looking confused. Iltani jumped on the guardsman's back and landed several roundhouses to his temple before he knocked her to the ground with one massive paw.

"Nanaea!" I screamed, desperately trying to yank myself free from the guardsmen's chainlike hold. *"Nanaea!"*

The only thing my struggles earned me was a blow to the face that filled my mouth with blood.

I spat, reeling, as Iltani jumped up and tried to wrench Nanaea away from the guardsman's hold, but he swatted her back.

"Nanaea!" *My sister. No, no, no, no, no, no. Not again. Not after everything.*

My cry earned me another blow, but this time, the stars exploding in my vision prevented further speech.

A group of those who lived near me along the wall attacked, shouting my name. I was knocked to the ground in the struggle as the guardsmen's lustrous sickleswords clashed against their makeshift weapons. I struggled to gain my freedom from the fray, crawling, scrabbling in the dirt as sand and debris dug into my knees. A poor man pulled me to my feet, and his arm was immediately hacked off by a guardsman. I shrieked and dropped his hand as blood spurted across my face. The guardsman yanked me up and threw me like a sack of grain over his shoulder. He ran, my head banging against his back as we headed toward a large cart.

"Dagan!" I searched desperately for his massive frame. He was embroiled in a battle with Lamusa.

My hair had loosed itself from its braids and fell across my eyes. I couldn't see! Where was my family?

We reached the cart, and several other Palace guardsmen loped up, shouting:

"*Load her!*"

"Bind her first!"

One guard grabbed a rope sturdy enough to fell a full-grown tree and roughly, with no regard for my cries, tied me up like a pig on its way to slaughter. He tossed me in the back of the cart and sat near my head as the others scurried aboard.

"*Go!*"

One slapped the flanks of the horses, and we careened out of the Libbu, toward the back of the Palace, people scurrying out of our way as we plowed through their midst. I yelled as a lowly mother and her three small children were nearly trampled.

"Shut your mouth, Healer!"

"She's gonna need to heal something after Ensi Uruku gets ahold of her tonight, that's for certain!" another snickered.

The guardsmen laughed, their intentions clear on their faces. I realized with sick dread that they meant to turn me over to Ensi Uruku.

Anything these men could do to me would be a fraction of what he was capable of.

As we rumbled toward the Palace, the guardsmen bet that Nin Arwia would have Ensi Uruku execute me at sunrise, although they wagered shekels over his method. One bet on the tigers, another on the dogs. The last emptied his pockets on a bet that I'd be stoned, but thought they should bash my teeth out and be done with it. They all hoped I'd be given to them before any of it happened, though, to while away the evening.

My head banged against the side of the cart as we rattled away, my fear intensifying with every jolt. As the final smear of daylight melted into the blackness of the night, I wondered, vaguely, which of the guards would win his wager.

CHAPTER 23

MY WRISTS WERE raw from the rope chafing against my skin. My throat was ablaze, as I'd not had even a drip of water in several turns of the dial. My mouth felt full of ashes. My broken leg ached mercilessly, as my crutches were gone, lost in the fray of the festival. My ummum's shawl had fallen to my feet long ago, and I'd toed it over as far as I could reach with my broken leg so I wouldn't continue to step on it.

The guardsmen had left me like this, promising to return "in due time" with Nin Arwia and Ensi Uruku, who wanted to ask me a few questions. Two people who were probably working together to rule the city-state, although it didn't seem possible that Nin Arwia could be so naïve as to think marrying Uruku would be good for her in any way. But then again, nothing truly made sense anymore. And those love tablets in her chest told the story that someone was courting her. Why wouldn't it be the man who would rule at her side?

Footsteps echoed down the hallway leading to my cell, and I prayed to Enlil for anyone other than Ensi Uruku to appear at the entranceway.

Enlil didn't hear my prayer.

"Ready to talk, Healer? Nin Arwia is on her way." His words were soft as he leaned casually against the doorframe, but the look in his eyes was anything but.

I closed my eyes against his unrelenting stare, preparing myself for the worst.

"I'll take your silence as agreement."

He entered my cell with a long, sharp dagger unsheathed.

"No! Ensi, I beg you, no!" My voice was hoarse. Desperate, I thrashed against my restraints as he stalked closer.

He smiled lazily, a hand gripping the ropes above me, then sliced down the front of me in one swift motion. I gasped, expecting pain.

Instead, I felt the sudden chill of icy air on exposed flesh.

I opened my eyes to see that my body was unharmed but completely unclothed. My white tunic lay in a shimmering heap at my feet.

"Please, no . . . ," I whispered, trying to cover myself with crossed legs. My shame lay upon me like a yoke.

He took a step back, staring hard at my body, then, before I could brace myself, slapped me hard across the face. Once. Twice. Thrice. My ears rang with the force of the blows. My stomach churned and heaved.

"Please, have mercy. . . ." My raw voice reached my ears, but it barely registered in my brain that I'd spoken. Blood dripped from my nose. My lip. Its coppery warmth sat thickly on my tongue.

Uruku stepped forward then and groped every inch of my body, his hot, rotten breath filling my nostrils. I screamed at his rough pawing. When he laid wet lips on my neck, I bellowed like a felled ox and kicked at him with my good leg. I'd rip his throat out with my teeth if I had to. I knew just where to bite.

"*Unhand her!*" Nasu growled, appearing at Uruku's elbow like a cat and holding a sicklesword under his chin.

"Ensi Uruku, that'll be all." Nin Arwia stood framed in the cell's entrance. Her chin was up. Defiant. But her hands shook at her sides.

"You said—" Uruku blurted, breathing heavily.

"I said I needed your assistance, but this was not what I had in mind. You may go."

Instead of listening, Uruku shoved Nasu back against the cavern wall, took my hair in one fist, and crammed his mouth against mine. I sunk my teeth into his lip until I tasted blood. He jerked away with a yell.

"Enough!" Nasu shoved Ensi Uruku, brandishing his sicklesword in a tight fist. I collapsed against my restraints in shock. Rage. I screamed at him with everything in me. Uruku stood against the cavern wall, staring at Nin Arwia, chest heaving. Eyes bulging in contempt. He was unhinged.

Nin Arwia crossed her arms over her chest casually, but her lips trembled. She pressed them together. "Thank you for your services, noble Ensi. But it appears you've overstepped your bounds." She drew herself up as tall as she could, and a bit of confidence crept into her voice. "Either vacate this cell at once, or I will have Nasu decorate the city walls with your deconstructed body. Am I clear?"

Nasu turned toward her, shock registering in his eyes. My eyes must've looked the same. She had been acting alone this whole time? Surely she wouldn't say such things to a co-conspirator.

Uruku stared hard at her with eyes narrowed almost to slits.

"I have the whole of the guardsmen behind me, Uruku." She nodded to Nasu, who stood with legs hip-width apart, hands at the ready. Ensi Uruku would not win a fight against him.

Something sparked in Uruku's eyes but was quickly diminished. He glared at me, one hand on his hip, for several moments. He dragged the other hand through his hair, cursed, and then slapped me again. Hard. Stars burst in my eyes on impact. Nasu cursed him, then deftly slashed a laceration across Uruku's throat, just under his jaw.

"The next one kills," Nasu said quietly.

Ensi Uruku stilled, then looked at Nasu with an almost calm reserve. "You'll pay for that, guardsman. You'll pay, and good. Mark my words." He held a hand to his neck, then pulled it away. It dripped with blood.

"Excellent. Then it's settled. Out you go." Nin Arwia clasped her hands in front of her, knuckles white.

Uruku straightened his tunic, then walked calmly past

Nin Arwia with a muttered "My lady," his heavy footsteps echoing madly off the walls.

Nin Arwia entered the cell. "Nasu, you're dismissed. Please find a tunic for our healer and return."

He nodded once, looked pointedly at my face, then left as quietly as he'd come.

Nin Arwia took a dagger out of a sheath at her waist and sliced the ropes that held me prisoner. I sank to the ground in relief once I was free.

"Why did you do it?" she asked quietly as I scooted away from her, grabbing my ummum's shawl, and huddled against the dungeon's wall. I wrapped the cloth around me to cover my nakedness.

Her eyes were shining with tears as she tucked the dagger back into its sheath.

"Why did I do *what*?" I wiped blood from my lip with the back of my hand. My ears were still ringing from Uruku's blows, my body buzzing with unfettered rage at his rough pawing.

"Why did you accuse me of killing my abum?" She drew herself up to her full unimpressive height. From where I sat, she towered.

Wasn't my being in a dungeon proof that she'd done just that? "Didn't you?" I winced when I spoke and reached into my mouth. A tooth in the back had been knocked loose.

"Of course not! How in the name of Enlil did you come to *that* conclusion?"

"I found the evidence in your brooch, Nin Arwia. I found

the monkshood." I dried my hand on a scrap of my tunic. "And, trust me, that was a good hiding spot. But I figured it out, like I figured out everything you've done."

She laughed, a trace of bitterness in her voice, and waved her hand as if conjuring spirits. "Yes, please enlighten me on everything I've done."

I plunged in with the only theory that made sense. "You killed your competition for the throne." I shrugged. "Maybe you hated that you could never have it if your brothers were alive. So you either pushed Ditanu from a window or had someone push him, or you just capitalized on his death and poisoned your baby brother to guarantee that you were the heir." Though the more the theory unraveled, the less likely it seemed. But I kept on. There was no going back. I'd traveled too far down this road. "Why else wouldn't your ummum announce the child's birth? She probably knew you had done it and wanted to protect you!"

"You are daft," she snorted. "I'm only sixteen. I was twelve years old when Ditanu died, and thirteen when the little one came along, but I've been plotting my abum's death and murdering my siblings for *years?*" She waved me away as if shooing a fly. "Hold your tongue. You know not of what you speak."

Swallowing around the terror that I was wrong—had *failed* to bring my abum's murderer to justice—I steeled myself and forged ahead. "No, I *know* the truth. After you killed your siblings and your mother died, you decided to poison your father so you could rule. You waited until the Palace healer was 'conveniently' gone from the city so nobody would suspect that your father's illness wasn't natural." I spoke so fast, spittle flew from my mouth. "Except you didn't count on Dagan recommending my father to you. So you had to bring *him* to the Palace, for appearance's sake. But since you *knew* that my abum would catch on to the poisoning quickly, you had him killed to keep your filthy secret."

"This is completely absurd."

I wiped my chin with the back of my hand but kept on. "No, Nin, your actions weren't absurd. They were carefully planned. Masterful, almost." *I have to be right. If not, it means a killer remains unchecked, and I am even more of a failure.* "You brought me to the Palace to make it seem like you'd get through *any* obstacle to heal your father, *hoping* that an apprentice like me wouldn't be able to figure it out." I laughed, half-crazed with the blows I'd received. The situation I was in. The idea that perhaps—just perhaps—my theory wasn't everything I thought it was.

Nin Arwia snorted. "I asked you to come because you actually *were* my best hope when your abum died. Dagan reminded me of the girl I'd once met, who was so smart and could rattle off tinctures like she'd been healing for years, and despite my hesitation, I bid you and your abum come. You have no idea what you're saying. Grief has addled your mind. I would never have killed my little brothers! They died. Ditanu fell to his death—no one knows how. And the little one died in his sleep! Do you think you're the only one who has ever lost someone? That pain you feel"—she jabbed a finger at my chest—"belongs to me, too!"

"Oh. Is that so? But you kept the amulet and the baby's hair to glory in your misdeeds, for Enlil's sake. I found them in your chest."

Her voice cracked. "Out of sadness. I loved them! I was so grateful for my brothers. When Ditanu died, I took his necklace to remember him. And then, when the baby left in the Boatman's arms, I snipped one of his little curls and treasured it. That's why I put it in the box with all my most precious belongings." Tears sprang to her eyes and ran down her angry face. "You don't know anything!"

I shook my head violently, beginning to shiver in the cold, pushing away the word that had begun to echo in my head: *Failure. Failure. Failure.* "No! Liar! I know everything. *Everything!* I found the evidence. I cannot be wrong! Not now!"

She crossed her arms over her chest, crying. She was lying. She *had to be.* So I hit her where I knew it would hurt the most: "Yes, and I have *friends*, real friends, who help me, unlike you, who have only Gudanna following you around. I am not alone. I have friends who stay with me no matter what happens. No matter how many times I refuse them." The thought set my head spinning. My friends had been helping me, supporting me, and holding me close this entire time, despite their misgivings. I hadn't wanted their assistance, had done *everything* to push them away, but they'd been there, regardless.

She blanched, stifling a sob with the back of her hand. "You're being cruel."

My heart squeezed at the pain I was inflicting, but she deserved it. Every bit of it.

And I deserved the misery of watching her cry. I'd shoved Dagan away. Pushed Iltani aside. Ignored Nanaea. Failed everyone, though I'd said I would not.

And they'd stuck by me, regardless of my mistakes. They'd loved me, helped me anyway. My heart wrenched inside, and the hurt was too great. Too much to bear. The raw agony of their love and the pain of everything I'd lost were warring in my chest and threatening to break loose. So I gave all my pain to the nin. "I'm not cruel; I'm honest. I have *real* friends, Nin Arwia. Something you will *never* have. Something you don't deserve!" *Something I don't deserve.*

Nin Arwia leaned back against the wall, her shoulders beginning to shake. "Stop it," she whispered.

But I couldn't. My words tumbled out of my mouth in a rush. "I won't. I want you to feel sad, Nin. That's how my whole family felt when Kasha was taken. It's how I've felt, knowing I was left all alone by a mother and a father I could not save. A father *you* murdered. It's how I felt when Nanaea was chosen. Like I was gutted. Go ahead. Feel that hurt. Feel angry. Your abum stole my brother and took my sister and left me brokenhearted, trying to save everyone. It's a terrible feeling. A merciless one. It will rip you into shreds and make you want to die. But you won't be able to, because you have responsibilities to those around you, you stupid girl. You won't be able to grieve, because if you don't help your abum, your family won't be able to eat. And if you don't care for them and heal the lugal, your sister will die and you'll be all alone. A miserable *failure* ... of a person ... who ... who ..."

I couldn't continue. My throat burned, and a terrible ache welled up in my chest, like water backing up behind a dam, and suddenly, without being able to fight it off, the dam burst and my words turned liquid. Sobs of grief burst from inside me, and I cried for what I'd lost and what I was going to lose. My abum, with his scruffy beard and deft thinking. My ummum, with her firm smile and soft hands. My sister, who was going to be killed on the morrow to go with the lugal.

And myself. The little girl I'd once been and the woman I'd been forced to become before I was entirely ready. The woman who had failed everyone, including herself, yet again.

I raged and I cried and I wailed, and somewhere in the middle of all that, Nasu brought a tunic and Nin Arwia helped me into it and I lay on the floor grappling with my loss until all the tears left my body and the only sound I could hear was quiet crying from this nin next to me, stroking my hair, who probably felt a little bit like I did.

❖ ❖ ❖ ❖ ❖

After what seemed like an entire moon, Nin Arwia spoke. "It isn't true." She'd sat somewhere in the midst of my grief. I pushed myself up to sit, wiping my leaking nose and blotchy face with the hem of the tunic.

"Nin Arwia, I—"

"No, listen. I would never"—she swallowed, then continued hoarsely—"never have killed anyone, let alone my family. I *loved* Ditanu. I even loved that baby boy. They were my little brothers, and now they're gone. They're *all* gone. My abum, too. So, yes, I am getting the throne, but it will be bleak."

Her words held a note of unmistakable truth, but it didn't answer all the questions in my mind.

"But what about the poison in your brooch? And why would my abum have been murdered right before coming to the Palace if you didn't want him dead?"

She furrowed her brow in concentration. "That *is* a mystery. A troubling one." She drew her knees up to her chest as if she were cold. "But it must be that someone wants to make it look like I did it. Don't you think there's anyone else who wants to rule the land? Ensi Uruku comes to mind, for instance."

"But he doesn't have access to your rooms. He doesn't have access to you like that."

She lifted a shoulder, then fiddled with the hem of her white tunic, which was now stained with the sand of the cavern. "He probably paid someone off. He could get it done if he wanted to. After all, you made it into my chamber. Why couldn't he?"

It made sense. Far more than that *she* had done everything I'd accused her of. "Well, what about those love tablets in your chest? Do you have a secret lover who wants the throne through you?"

She shook her head. "The only one who wants the throne

through me is Ensi Uruku. He asked for my hand a moon ago, but I refused him. Those tablets in my chest were from my ummum to my abum. I kept them because they were etched in her hand. That is all. I wanted a memory of her, too." She paused. "Look at me, Healer."

I obliged.

"I felt sorry for your family, you know. When my abum cast you out and took your brother. Deep down, I knew it wasn't your abum's fault and that what was happening wasn't fair. That's why I chose Nanaea as a Sacred Maiden. To try to restore some of your family's status. I thought if she could die with honor, then maybe you'd be able to live a happier life. I'm no monster."

"You *what?*" I whispered, shock sending tingles into my hairline. I looked her straight in her eyes. "You chose Nanaea to *honor our family?*"

She blinked rapidly, her lashes like little moths in the darkness of the dungeon. "It was the least I could do."

I sagged against the wall, trying to work out that the nin beside me had been the cause of all this pain and death because she'd been trying to *help* my family.

She looked at me, her eyes filled with despondency. "But now I am sarratum." She stood then and wiped the grime from her legs. "And although I don't want to do this, I must. Or I will never be taken seriously as a leader. You committed treason by accusing me, and I can't let that go."

My stomach dropped. "You'll have me whipped, won't you? In the stocks. To prove your strength!"

Her hands fidgeted with her tunic. "No," she whispered. "I will not. As I said, I am not a monster."

"What, then? Battling in the Pit with the dogs? Tigers? Please, don't say that. I'd have no chance." My stomach twisted and churned, as if I'd swallowed live eels.

"I'm going to be merciful to you. As merciful as a newly appointed sarratum can be." Her eyes filled with tears, but she quickly dashed them away. "This is especially difficult for me, because I truly did think we could be good friends, despite how cruel you've been to me. Now I'll miss the opportunity to find out."

"Merciful? What do you mean? Please, tell me my punishment."

"It's actually not a punishment, Kammani. I'm being merciful because I'm bestowing on you the honor of tradition." She looked right at me, her black eyes almost glowing in the torchlight of the dank cavern. "I'm granting you Sacred Maiden status, so you'll join your sister tomorrow evening at sunset."

I opened and closed my mouth like a fish. I couldn't speak. Tears fell from my eyes in abject disbelief. "In the tomb? You'll bury me with my sister?"

"You'll be sent to the Netherworld tomorrow, draped like a queen. It's an honor, Kammani. You should be grateful."

My gut flipped over, and my eyes filled. "Grateful?" My words came out as a whisper.

"Yes, my friend. When I cross over one day, we'll be united as family for all eternity." She nodded once, then exited through the cavern door. She squared her small shoulders and, without turning back, left me alone in the gloom. I could have sworn I heard her crying as her footsteps echoed down the hall.

A guardsman closed the door behind her, then stood outside it, his lanky form stiff and formal.

Nasu.

Immediately, quelling my panic and dashing away my tears, I called, "Nasu?" I had a newfound skill: I could ask for *help*.

"Yes, Healer," he answered, his voice muffled but stoic. Reserved.

"This might sound strange coming from me, but—I wondered if I could get some assistance." I struggled to stand, then hopped on my good leg over to the door. I peeked between the rough slats.

When he turned, the sliver of his face I could see was grim. "You quite clearly need it."

"Can you let me out?"

His eyes fell. "I can't, Kammani. As much as I'd like to. I was happy to aid you before in service to the lugal, but now? I don't know what to believe. And Ensi Uruku threatened my life and the lives of my family should you escape this room. I must do my duty to them."

"But, Nasu," I pleaded. "Nin Arwia is going to kill me, Nanaea, and the other Maidens. I need to get out—" My voice cracked, and I allowed my tears to come. They refreshed me. Bathed me in sorrow.

He shifted outside the door. "I'm sorry, Kammani. I cannot risk opening this door."

I bit my thumb and stopped to think. What could I possibly do to help myself while sitting inside a cell? I sank against the wall of the cavern, gnawing at my nail. I came up with sixty different implausible situations.

But then—the white light of inspiration.

"Nasu?" I called, and banged on the doorframe.

"Yes?"

"Can you get Dagan for me?"

Silence. Then: "That's one thing I *can* do."

His steps echoed down the corridor a moment later, and I was left sitting in a cold, dank cell, nearly delirious with fatigue but feverish with the possibility that I might have figured out a way to get myself, my sister, and the other Sacred Maidens out of this whole mess.

I just couldn't do it alone.

CHAPTER 24

THE SETTING SUN winked off Nasu's silver breast-plate as he walked down a line of archers with his torch, face drawn in concentration, lighting all eight pitch-coated arrows.

We stood in a dusty field surrounded by olive trees and date palms, their branches casting craggy shadows across the sand like an army of ghosts coming to take us away.

The graveyard lay just over the rise.

"Nock!" Nasu raised the torch high above his head.

The archers fit their arrows on the strings.

A steady *dum, dah-dah-dah, dum, dah-dah-dah, dum* of four large goatskin drums started a rhythm. Tambourines joined in. The crowd, drawn from the far corners of the city to the event, picked up on the beat, chanting and clapping and dancing along. And why wouldn't they? Today marked the last day of what was possibly the grandest event of their lifetimes.

"Draw!" Nasu called again, and the archers stretched back their strings, arms quivering with tense restraint.

The drums dropped to a roll, and the crowd followed along, tapping the rhythm on their thighs. Each other. The tables outside the gravesite were full of wares people were selling for the occasion: locks of our hair, a golden replica of the lugal's crown, cloth cut from the same bolt as the grave tunics we were wearing. The drums went faster and faster and louder and louder, until all at once, Nasu gave the final command:

"Loose!"

And the eight flaming arrows soared. They thunked into the pitch-coated center of a monstrous target painted with the names of the lugal and all his Sacred Maidens. Immediately it was engulfed in roaring flames.

The crowd screamed with delight for the spectacle. The splendor. The horror. And for the occasion that was on the verge of reaching its conclusion.

Lugal Marus's funeral.

A Sacred Maiden quivering next to the other three, I watched as my name twisted, shriveled, and melted off the center of the target in the raging, blood-red roar of the inferno.

❖ ❖ ❖ ❖ ❖

"I'm going to vomit."

"Stop, Simti," Nanaea said.

"But I am honestly going to vomit." Simti gulped a great lungful of air, as if she couldn't get enough.

"Well, please let us go to the Netherworld with dignity. Please. It's all I ask of you." Nanaea's lips, painted as red as cherries, pressed together as if she were holding down her last meal.

Each of us Maidens wore a white silk ceremonial tunic with special embroidery. Yellow chamomile crested the bodice of my tunic from shoulder to hip. Simti's tunic was covered in brilliant orange hyacinths. Nanaea's swirled with golden ribbons that matched the bracelets encircling her arms from wrist to elbow. Vivid blue birds encircled Huna's. Each of us also wore a glittering headdress for the occasion. Mine sparkled with topaz, while amber, jade, emerald, carnelian, and lapis lazuli gems winked in the headdresses of the girls next to me. Our lips were various shades of crimson, gold, and blush, and our cheeks and eyes were encircled with painted flowers, vines, birds, and even stars.

I didn't understand why they'd bothered, considering that, for all they knew, we were marching to our deaths. I knew better. For the ninth time, I touched the clasp of my healing satchel at my waist. After I'd apologized to Dagan again and again for Iltani's setting the farm ablaze, he'd granted me his forgiveness and handed me my satchel, which Kasha had managed to secure in the frenzy of the ruined Maidens'

Release ceremony. I'd asked Dagan to have his mother stuff as many types of remedies into it as she could and bring it back. He did, and secured me a new set of crutches, too.

I knew that we'd be drinking poison, but I didn't know what I'd need besides an antidote. Rhizome root to bring about vomiting, in case the antidote wasn't enough? Poppy to calm someone? Arnica for pain? So I had it all. The guardsman who'd accompany us into the tomb and give us all "safe passage" to the Netherworld would force us to drink the poison, so there was no getting around it. Our only hope was that the antidote worked.

Ensi Uruku and the nin had almost made me take my satchel off, but I'd convinced them to let me keep it, saying I'd need the tinctures and tonics to keep the lugal healthy in the Netherworld. They'd relented. I don't know what I would have done if they'd taken it from me.

The *ting* of the bells belonging to the town crier and the dozens of priests and priestesses surrounding him brought my eyes from my feet up to the center of the field. Guardsmen moved to encircle us, each holding flaming torches that crackled high above our heads. The priests swung copper jars of incense on chains, which emitted a warm cinnamon and sage smoke, filling the dusty field with the scent of the burial. It didn't mask the stench of the lugal's corpse, which had already begun to turn. It was swathed in burial wraps—save for his head, which was left bare—and lay on a mat that was held overhead by six guardsmen more stoic than I about the stink.

Nin Arwia wavered on her feet like a reed in a hard wind.

Her face was pale—even a little green. I was less worried about Simti vomiting than about the nin doing so. Beside her stood Ensi Uruku, his hands clasped in front of him as if in prayer, and Gudanna stood to Nin Arwia's left, her eyes respectfully on her toes. My guts burned as I looked at Uruku's face.

The town crier carried a large burial tablet and began chanting a repetitive prayer to Enlil. The clergy danced as he prayed, holding their hands to the heavens. A priest approached the Sacred Maidens to give us a blessing. He laid his rough hand gently on my head, then moved on to my sister, who was, for the first time, shaking. Her face was bathed in firelight. Her lower lip trembled as the priest laid his hand on her head. Teardrops sparkled on her long black lashes. Her forehead was knotted in worry. For the briefest moment, I allowed myself the satisfaction of feeling smug. It wasn't so glorious. It wasn't so beautiful. But because she was my sister and I knew the cause of her distress, I rubbed her back, silenced myself, and turned back to the town crier. He concluded his prayer, then motioned for us to follow him to the burial grounds.

The guardsmen carrying the lugal's body led the way, with the drummers following, hitting a steady *thump thump thump* as we marched.

The footfalls of those in front of me led me over the rise. I took the deepest of breaths as tears flooded my eyes. This time, I allowed them free rein. I had every right to be scared. But as I wiped them away, I acknowledged that my duty was to Nanaea and the rest of the Maidens. I *had* to protect them. To keep them safe. I might not have done it before, but now was the time for me to use my healing abilities and save them—for good. Nanaea offered me a small, terrified smile as we crested the rise and saw the graveyard, so I wrapped my arm around her shoulders. Kasha appeared at my elbow, and I pulled him under my other arm and kissed the top of his curly head as we walked the pathway to the tombs.

"Don't forget, okay? Don't forget how much I love you and always will."

He squeezed his arms tightly about my waist. "It's going to work. I've prayed to Enlil for his guidance."

"In case it doesn't, Kasha, I want you to know."

He brought big brown eyes up to meet mine. "Then I won't forget. Just in case."

One of the priests rang a silver bell, and the town crier stopped at the archway that led into the royal burial grounds. He turned back to the crowd and raised his arms to ask for silence. A priest whose eyes had been removed to show his blindness to worldly possessions lifted his face to the dusky skies. With a toothless mouth, he begged Enlil to accept Lugal Marus and us Maidens into the Netherworld, where we might live in peace, and to spare us from the evil of Alani. He prayed for prosperity in our new lives across the river and pleaded for mercy for the people we were leaving behind.

Sinking to his knees, he pressed his forehead to the sand, imploring Enlil to give the Boatman a sound boat. Steady winds. Smooth seas. And he ended his prayer by beseeching any other gods to follow Nin Arwia the rest of her life and grant her health and happiness.

Then he stood and nodded to the town crier.

"Kammani!"

I turned, squinting into the distance. *Dagan?*

There! Two figures strode steadily forward, pushing their way through the horde. It was! It was Dagan! A sob rose from my breast. His face was grim. Determined. But who was that trailing behind him? Iltani? My eyes blurred with tears, and I could not stop the sobs from escaping my mouth.

They were supposed to stay behind—to remain unnoticed. But now I was glad they hadn't listened to that part of my plan. Their presence would give me strength for what I needed to do next.

Dagan approached with fierceness in his eyes, and when he reached me, he engulfed me in a bear hug, picking me up from the ground. I squeezed him around his neck, burying my face in the scent of him.

Lamusa was immediately on him. "Unhand her, Farmer's Son. She is a Sacred Maiden meant for the lugal's embrace only."

Dagan's eyes flashed as he set me carefully on the ground, pushing me behind him. I gripped his arms to stay steady on my one good leg.

"Back away," he said. His hand went to his belt, where a long dagger lay sheathed. Lamusa went to pull his sickle-sword, but Nasu appeared at his elbow.

"Stand down, Lamusa. We can allow them this last exchange."

"But she's spoken for—" Lamusa began.

"And one embrace will not change that. Go back to your duties."

Lamusa's hand hovered over his sicklesword briefly, but after one last menacing look, he dropped his arm and disappeared into the crowd.

Nasu nodded to us, then followed him. Dagan turned back to me, wrapping me in a hug once more. "I had to see you. How can I let this go on?" He buried his face in my hair.

My eyes filled with tears again. "What go on? The burial?"

"Yes. I can't let you do this."

"Dagan, it's not up to you." I wiped tears from my face with the back of my hand, smearing the paint. I didn't care. "I've told you the plan, and it is going to work. It *has* to." I gently pushed away. Iltani handed me my crutches.

"Kammani, what if we run away right now?" she whispered. "I could distract everyone, and Dagan could carry you out of here. We could hide out for a few days and then bolt out of Alu!"

"What? And leave my sister to this?" I jutted a hand at the site. "They'd kill her and Kasha the moment we ran. No. If we follow the plan, all of us—together—can do this." I pulled her into a quick hug, then placed my hands on Dagan's massive chest and looked into his eyes.

"I'm nervous for you, my sweet."

346

"Dagan, I know I am a mess, but I promise you—I swear it—this will work."

And before he could say anything else, I wrapped my arms around his neck and pulled him down to me. His mouth covered mine. With passion. Fiercely. Wildly. Tears streaming from my eyes with abandon, my hands in his hair. His arms enclosing me in comfort, the horror of the day diluting within his strong arms. And though I'd kissed him before, it was nothing like kissing him this time.

He broke from my lips, breathing raggedly.

"Kammani, I love you." His voice was low but intense. "I will be here for you when it's finished. I can't do anything about it, and it makes me furious, but I swear I will follow your instructions to get you out. I swear on my life." He put his hand over his heart.

I nodded, not trusting myself to speak. I pushed Kasha to him and Iltani as our procession moved toward the tomb, leaving them standing outside.

"Kasha is yours, Iltani. Dagan. Just in case." My voice cracked on my words.

They nodded solemnly, Dagan's face darkened with grief and Iltani's chest heaving with unshed tears. I tore my eyes from them with more strength than I knew I possessed.

And as swiftly as that, our train was moving through the archway of the burial grounds toward Lugal Marus's tomb. Simti and Nanaea clutched each other in fright, both crying softly, while Huna had a glazed look about her face, indicating that someone, somewhere had given her some poppy to quell her fear.

When we stopped, Nin Arwia, Ensi Uruku, and Gudanna, covered in black cloaks of mourning, lined up to the far right of the tomb, the mouth of which gaped widely, like a sea monster's craw. The clergy shook the incense around the doorway; then one priestess moved over to Nin Arwia and handed her a gold flagon filled with poison. Her hand shook as she took it. Then the priestess nodded to the guardsmen, who, grunting and sweating profusely at this point, descended into the tomb with the lugal's body.

As the guardsmen moved past Nin Arwia and she turned her head to follow the descent of her abum into the tomb, Ensi Uruku reached behind the nin's back and flicked Gudanna gently in the right arm. It was a small movement, really. A tiny gesture. But I remembered Dagan doing the same thing when I was a child after we'd been plotting against his little brothers. His mother had questioned us, but I'd known to maintain my innocence when Dagan had flicked me during our interrogation. The gesture meant "I'm in this with you." It showed camaraderie. A commonality.

And even after the memory flooded over me, I might not have ascribed anything to Ensi Uruku's gesture had I not seen Gudanna's resulting flicker of a smile after he touched her.

But I did. And my belly dropped.

It was *both of them.*

You have no idea what she is capable of.

Her words hadn't been a warning; they'd been a nudge.

A gentle push to make me suspect the nin more than I already did.

They were behind it all. Gudanna and Ensi Uruku. The lugal's death. The hidden poison. My push out the window. It had been *Gudanna's* voice in the hallway instructing the guardsman to push me over. She'd been acting on *Ensi Uruku's* authority. Who else had the proximity to the nin but a woman who was with her every single day?

But before I could do anything or say anything about it, I watched in horror as Nin Arwia handed a nearby guardsman the flagon of poison, dropped her heavy headdress to her feet, removed the black cloak about her shoulders, and followed her father's body into the tomb. Her face was almost as blank as Huna's. The people around me murmured in shock. Several of the women called out for her to stop. To come back out. But she didn't exit the tomb. I began to shake. Uruku and Gudanna clasped hands briefly, the glee in their bodies barely contained.

"Wait. This isn't right!" But the drums began rolling again, and then Nasu was behind us Sacred Maidens, prodding us forward like lambs to the slaughter.

"Move, Healer. You'll want to walk to your death in dignity." He held a torch overhead, and for once, he wasn't perfectly clean-shaven. A growth of stubble covered his jaw. His face, on further inspection, looked haggard. Drawn. Not composed and in control, as it usually did.

"Nasu!" I cried, my teeth chattering as I stumbled along in the uneven growth, around graves, toward the yawning, putrid mouth of the tomb. "It was never Nin Arwia! It was never her."

"It doesn't matter. It appears as though she's preparing to leave with her abum to join the rest of her family in the Netherworld. Now please keep walking."

"What do you mean, it doesn't matter? It matters! We could stop this whole thing!"

"No. It's too late." He nudged me forward, and before I could even comprehend it, I was entering the torchlit tomb, which reeked of rot, and easing my crutches down the three steps that led to the beds. Nin Arwia stood inside it as if she were already a ghost, blankly staring at her father's dead body on his bier. The cavernous tomb was filled end to end with riches for the lugal in the Netherworld. Mina-filled chests. Lyres inlaid with carnelians and topazes. Headdresses and beaded necklaces and gold rings and silken clothing.

Nanaea, Simti, and Huna followed closely behind me, wailing in their fright, and Nasu, a torch held high overhead, followed us in with sicklesword drawn. The guardsman holding the poison given to him by the nin handed it off to Nasu.

I was immediately confused.

Because behind him, a heavy stone was being pushed over the doorway.

"Nasu—the stone. You have to leave."

But he said nothing.

"Nasu! Get out! The stone is being rolled over the doorway! Where's the other guardsman?"

As I spoke, the stone inched even farther over the opening,

eventually closing off the faces of Ensi Uruku, who was no longer hiding a smile, Gudanna, who'd moved right next to him, and the horrified crowd who'd come along for the show.

"Nasu!" Terrified, I yanked at his arm. "Get out! They're closing the tomb!"

But when he turned a grim face to me and I saw the hopelessness in his eyes, the dawn of realization hit me: *He* was the guardsman who'd accompany us to the Netherworld.

He was the one who would kill us all.

CHAPTER 25

NASU, HIS JAW flexing, turned back to stare as the heavy stone settled into place with an echoing *whump*, bits of sandstone raining to the floor as it sealed us off from the outside world. Nanaea howled at the top of her lungs, and all the hair on my arms stood up. Save for one torch, all was blackness. We'd choke to death from the smoke if I didn't act quickly.

Nanaea wailed softly into the bleak tomb, her voice echoing off the walls.

"It's you? You're the guardsman who will escort us?"

"He was given the honor, Kammani." Nin Arwia's voice was strange. Off-kilter. "There's no one else I'd rather accompany us."

I nodded at the dagger in his belt. "Will you slit our throats if we don't take the poison?" I coughed. The smoke was already beginning to thicken.

"If I must." He pressed his lips into a line. "And it's not that I want to. But the lugal must be accompanied to the Netherworld." He stood to his full height. "And since I am an Alu guardsman, I will do my duty. My own family's life is at stake if I don't fulfill it." He looked at Lugal Marus's body, lying on a bier and tucked into a niche in the wall, then turned his nose away in distaste, his eyes watering. "Ensi Uruku made that completely clear."

"You are noble and brave." Nin Arwia coughed into her hand.

"Yes, but he also has a weak stomach." I noted the tinge of green about Nasu's nostrils.

His eyes flashed at my words, but he didn't deny it. I turned and searched Nin Arwia's blank face.

"Nin, it was Gudanna who killed your abum! She and Ensi Uruku. They smiled when you walked into the tomb." I grabbed one of her hands in mine. "Why would she do something like that? I thought she loved you like one of her children." I turned my head and coughed, the smoke thickening. Nanaea crouched against me, quivering in fright.

As she answered, Nin Arwia stared at her abum's shrouded body and bare face now mottled in the first stages of decay. "She never loved me, Kammani. I was a poor substitute for her children, and I knew how she felt, because she was a poor substitute for my ummum. She was filled with bitterness when she arrived at the Palace, did you know that? She blamed your abum. He'd failed her and her children when they died in the fire. She spoke of it often."

"He tried everything, just as he tried with your brother. Sometimes people die and there's nothing anyone can do!"

"But that is logical, and logic doesn't matter when you're in misery." She traced her fingers over one of the paintings of Enlil on the wall near her abum's head, which was obscured in shadows. "Although I don't understand why she'd suggest Nanaea to me as a Maiden. But since I remembered how terrible I felt after your family was cast out, I agreed that she would be a perfect choice. I thought it would help restore your family's honor."

So Nanaea's selection fulfilled two women's desires: Gudanna's for revenge and Nin Arwia's for atonement. Nin Arwia might not have understood the woman's motives, but I certainly did. Apparently, Gudanna, like me, realized that death was no honor. And either she was running things, with Ensi Uruku as a pawn, or he was molding her bitterness for his own uses.

Then Nin Arwia shook her head gloomily. "But it doesn't matter anymore."

"It doesn't matter that they killed your abum? And now you? Why did you come in here?" I blinked, tearing up against the stinging of the smoke.

She wrapped her arms around her thin shoulders. "It was the only way to see my family again. It was the only thing that made sense." She coughed again into her hand. Beside me, Nanaea sobbed forlornly into my shoulder. I pulled her into my embrace and kissed her head as the nin continued. "I want to go with my abum to a place where no one can ever die again," she whispered, her eyes glistening. "I don't even care about the throne. Is that wrong to say?"

My heart sank at her words. "No, Nin." I pulled her in for a hug. "I know you're sad. I know the feeling. Losing my parents is the hardest thing I've ever experienced." I swallowed around the lump in my throat. "Still, although I'd love to see my family again, I don't want to give up my life to do so."

At that, she grimaced. "It's my fault you're here. I sent you to your death."

My throat tightened at her words. "Yes, Nin. On your command, I am here. But"—I looked pointedly at Nasu, who had plugged his nose—"if Nasu releases us from taking the poison, we could leave. And"—I coughed—"if we leave, we don't have to die in this smoke."

Nasu held a dagger to my heart with one hand and covered his mouth and nose with the other. "Lugal Marus's needs must be met in the next life. The Sacred Maidens will attend him, and I will as well. Now, your method of dying is up to you. So choose. The poison or the blade." He glanced at Lugal Marus's body again, then turned away and gagged.

Suddenly, I had an idea. "Here, Nasu." I rummaged around in my healing satchel and pulled out a sleeping tonic. My abum had painted the word "poppy" on the side of the bottle after Nanaea had dipped into it as a child and fallen into a sleep so deep, we were terrified she'd never wake, but Nasu couldn't read it. "This is an anti-nausea tincture of peppermint and fennel. It will help settle your stomach."

He eyed my hand speculatively, squinting at the words on the bottle, then looked away. "I don't need it."

Behind me, Nanaea fell into a fit of coughing. Tears coursed down her cheeks, smearing the paint that had been so carefully applied. "Sister," she moaned, "I cannot breathe." She sat down heavily on a chest, and shekels and minas spilled from the lid.

"Nasu, please." Tightness welled in my chest at her words. At the loss of air. "Take it. You'll feel better."

Around his head, black plumes billowed from the torch. My eyes stung, and my lungs seared with shortened breath.

"Stop it. Put it away. I don't need it." He coughed, gagging and choking on the smoke.

Frustrated and growing more and more desperate, I chewed my thumbnail, searching my brain for another solution to our predicament. *Think, Kammani! Think!*

My lungs were tight, and I did my best not to succumb to panic. Huna sank to the floor and stared at a wall that was covered with motifs of the Boatman ferrying Maidens across the Garadun, which would be our grim fate if I didn't do something—right then—to save us.

I decided to stick to my original plan. We would swallow the poison, I'd administer the antidote afterward, and I would convince Nasu not to kill himself and let us out. If Nasu slit my throat, then he slit my throat. I had to try. But then, in a fit of coughing, Nasu did something for which I hadn't prepared.

He extinguished the torch's flame, and we were plunged into blackness.

"Nasu!"

"I can't breathe, Kammani!" he hissed.

Panicked, I opened my satchel and tried to see inside. Nothing but darkness. I wouldn't be able to find the antidote!

Behind me, Nanaea wailed in earnest. I pulled her off the chest into a fierce hug. "Be brave for me, Nanaea," I whispered in her ear. She clung to me, sobbing against my shoulder, but I pushed her gently away, dropped my crutches, and sat on the floor. I rummaged around in my satchel, trying to *feel* the bottle that contained the antidote. I touched cask after cask, running my fingers over the hard edges and ridges, trying to urge my fingers to do my eyes' work, but my method wasn't working well, because the little vials felt so similar.

"Nanaea?" Nasu fumbled toward us in the gloom.

"Be quiet!" I murmured to Nanaea, who cowered against me in fear, her fingers clutching my tunic.

Then I thought to smell the vials. One by one, I pulled the tops from the bottles and sniffed. No, that was the anti-nausea. I set it aside. And this one was babchi for curing skin ailments. I tried another, but it was difficult to determine which was which in the suffocating smoke. I cursed myself for wanting as many remedies as possible on hand. I found another bottle, which was the white peony root, for women's moon cycle cramps. Annoyed, I set it aside, my hands starting to shake. Then I smelled another. That one was clearly the poppy for sedation. I slipped it into my belt in case I should have to ease someone into her death.

The thought made my hands tremble violently. *Move faster!*

Nanaea continued to sob against my shoulder, and I heard the fumblings of Nasu in the dark as he approached her.

"Nanaea, you will be first."

She screeched as she held on to me. "No!" she cried, pulling at my arms.

As she fought, weeping, and Nasu tugged her away, I bit my lip so I could focus on not collapsing in sobs.

"No, Nasu. Stop it!" she cried, but the glug of a flagon being tipped up and the muffled protests of it being pressed against her mouth made my skin grow cold.

"Drink, Maiden. Drink it," Nasu whispered, his voice wobbling with a modicum of control.

My hands frantically pawed through my tonics. I began to dip my finger in to taste them, consequences be damned. Hemp oil. Violet leaf. Goldenseal.

"No!" said Nanaea, muffled and choking. Gagging. And Nasu was moving on to someone else.

"Here, Simti. Simti. Where are you?"

Simti was quiet.

Good, Simti! Stay silent so he can't find you!

But eventually, he fumbled through the darkness and found her.

"Here, Simti, drink it, for Enlil's sake. I don't want to do it!" he said feverishly. But again, the flagon tipped up against a struggling girl's mouth. She coughed, swallowing, and a sob escaped him as she dropped to the floor, gagging and gasping.

"Huna? Where are you?" he yelled, openly crying then, determined to do his duty but struggling against his heart, which was pulling him in another direction.

Tears streamed from my eyes, and I struggled to tell which tincture was which. I was getting confused as to which bottles I'd already checked and which I hadn't. I pulled corks and stoppers from one after another, sniffing and tasting, and then nearly dropped one in my excitement when I realized what I held. The rhizome root! It wasn't the antidote that I'd given the lugal, but it could make them retch up the poison, which was almost as good. Frantically, I crawled toward the girls.

While Nasu poured the poison into the mouths of Huna and Nin Arwia, I followed behind in the blackness, finding gagging faces and chasing the poison with the rhizome root. Nanaea. Then Simti. Then Huna. Then Nin Arwia, who tried to spit it out. I poured more and pinched her mouth and nose shut so she'd have to swallow. Immediately, they all began to retch, and the tomb was filled with smoke, the stench of death, and the sounds of vomiting.

I crawled to a far wall, waiting for Nasu to find me, and shook the little life-saving bottle in my hand. I stilled, my blood running cold in my veins. There was no sound of the dried powder inside. I shook it again, more violently this time, then dipped my finger in to check. It came out as dry as a dead man's bones.

There was none left.

The rhizome root was gone, I couldn't find the real antidote, and Nasu was out there in the darkness, softly calling my name.

CHAPTER 26

I BEGAN TO shake. There would be no cure for me.

"Kammani?" Nasu said, his voice ragged, his sense of duty taxed to the limit. "Come here and let's be done. Everyone is already dying."

But they weren't. They were getting rid of the poison, as I would not be able to do. He didn't realize it. And by the time he did, the tomb would be cracked open by Dagan, but I would be dead. I had to find the antidote. I crawled crazily away from Nasu's voice.

I pawed blindly in my healing satchel, pulling tops off of bottles and spilling half their contents onto my hands. Then I licked at the tinctures, tasting fennel, frankincense, tea tree oil, but no antidote. Nothing. It wasn't in my satchel. Someone must have sneaked into it and taken it out.

Tears filled my eyes, washing some of the burning sensation away as they rolled down my cheeks. I had to *think*.

What else could I do? I couldn't overpower him. I couldn't talk my way out of there. His sense of duty was too great.

But what if I could sedate him? I reached for the bottle at my waist. I still had the poppy. I had enough to sedate him for an entire day. But how could I get it into his mouth?

And then I had it. I'd have to exchange it for the poison. I'd have to dump the poison onto the floor, pour in the poppy, and pray to Enlil for the best.

"Nasu? I'm over here. I'm tired of fighting this."

He sniffled, then stumbled in my direction, tripping over and around chests of riches with chings and clinks as he clambered in the dark. His hand came to rest on the top of my head, and I sensed that he'd sat down in front of me, though I could see nothing. I reached through the blackness and felt the muscles of his wiry arms. His shoulders. I followed them to his neck and rubbed my hands up the stubble at his jawline to his cheeks. They were wet. "You're crying."

"Yes," he whispered, choking on a sob.

"Then let's be finished."

"All right." He sniffled. "No tricks?"

"What trick could I possibly have at this point? I'm scared. I want . . . to be with my family." A sob escaped my mouth, and I had the distinct thought that maybe I was on the verge of insanity. That maybe, if I got out of this, I'd be sitting next to Zuzu at the well while people made fun of me as they passed by.

"Well"—he cleared his throat—"then open your mouth.

Drink. Don't make me force you. I can't do that anymore. I cannot."

"Okay. Okay, Nasu. I will." I felt through the shadows and took the flagon from his hands.

"No. You'll pour it out." The flagon left my grasp.

Sweat formed on my lip. In my armpits. "No, I won't. I swear it on the life of Kasha. I swear it. I won't pour it out."

"I can't do it." He sounded miserable. "I don't trust you. You sound as if you're lying. And then I'd have to kill you with my blade, which would be terrible. Please, let me pour it in your mouth."

I couldn't allow him to do that! I had to get the poppy into *his* mouth! What would my abum have done? He'd calm him with his words and his soft hands. He always did that. He'd speak baby words into the ear of a small child, smoothing back their hair while he set the broken bone, and the child was often so pacified they didn't even feel the hurt. But here, I didn't know how well soft hands would work. Well, what would *Iltani* do? She'd teased the farmhand with the promise of a kiss. And then I remembered Dagan's kiss. His tongue had moved against my lips.

As if emerging from a shadowy corridor into the sunshine, an idea came to light: I'd have to *kiss* him and push the sedative into his mouth from *mine*.

"Open your mouth, please." He reached across for my face. His fingers brushed my cheek.

"Wait." My heart beat wildly.

"What? Please don't make me force you."

"I won't."

"Then what do you want?"

I licked my lips. "I want you to kiss me."

"What?"

"I want you to kiss me, Nasu. If we're both going to die, and nothing else in this world matters, then kiss me. I don't want my last memories to be of these girls dying and me choking on poison. Please. Let me leave for the Netherworld with the taste of your lips on mine." I scooted closer and reached, feeling for his hair. I pushed it back from his forehead. Felt the tears on his cheeks and wiped them away.

"What? I can't do that."

"Please. Have mercy on me. It's my last wish in this life."

"That's. Absurd. I'm going to kiss you and then kill you?"

"Everything in here is absurd! What does it matter, since we're both going to die anyway?" Sitting across from him, our knees touching, the heat from his body radiating toward mine, I could feel his indecision.

"Please?" I reached up with my right hand and stroked the side of his face. With my left, I pulled the bottle from my waistband and uncorked it.

"All right," he whispered after a moment. Then he moved. He was shifting toward me. Leaning in. Before he reached me with his lips, I poured enough of the poppy into my mouth to sedate him. And then his lips found mine. And we kissed. I got to my knees and wrapped my arms around his shoulders and kissed him with desperation. I was saving my life.

I was saving the Sacred Maidens' lives. I pushed as much of the poppy into his mouth as I could, but after a moment, he jerked away from me.

"What did you give me?"

As he spoke, I became aware of a warm, peculiar sensation against my neck. I reached my hand up to investigate, and when I pulled it away, it was wet. I held the wetness up to my nose.

It was blood. *My blood.* He'd been trying to slit my throat as we kissed.

The horror of it knocked me backward.

"Kammani?" His speech was already slurred. "What did you give me? I'm seeing things, Healer."

Terrified, I hurriedly backed away from him, my sense of up and down getting confused, "Nothing, Nasu. What do you mean?" I asked innocently.

"I feel strange." His voice rose in panic, his words heavy as a brick. "I feel so strange. I can see something. What is it? What is that *light?*"

As he spoke, the center of the tomb began to glow.

"Do you . . . have a torch?" He stumbled over his words. I'd given him enough poppy to incapacitate him, but hadn't expected it to work so quickly. As the glow in the center of the tomb swelled, he was illuminated, and I watched as his eyes grew round in fright, his jaw slack, and he fell sideways, his dagger clattering to the floor, the poppy taking full effect.

But when I turned to the center of the tomb, a strangled cry wrenched from my throat.

For glowing in the center of the tomb was *not* just a light. It was the cloaked, skeletal figure of the Boatman.

His eyes were hollow like caves, his teeth fixed in an awful, ghastly smile.

His glow shed light on the retching figures of the girls, Nasu's limp body, and the dead hand of the lugal, which had somehow gotten loose from its wrap. I lunged for the dagger, which lay near Nasu, falling on it like a starving woman on food, and as I did, the Boatman raised his bony arms, opened his cavernous mouth, and shrieked with the power of every wraith he'd ever taken from Alu.

I pulled myself up, clutching the dagger in my fist, quivering in my bones.

"STAY AWAY!" I screamed, pointing the dagger at his chest.

Shaking, I flattened myself against the wall as my thoughts ran wild. He was here for us. For me! I'd failed. We were all going to die, and he was going to scoop us up and take us across the river in those skeletal arms of his. Sobbing, I desperately tried to cling to sanity despite his figure hazy in front of my eyes. But as the poppy made a spinning top of my senses, I watched, dumbfounded, as the Boatman moved clickety-clack toward Lugal Marus. He reached under his body, picked him up, then, after tipping his head as if saying goodbye, cradled the lugal to his chest and turned his back.

At the last moment, right before they disappeared into the Netherworld like a wisp of smoke, the lugal opened his dark eyes over the Boatman's shoulder and looked at me, blinking in resignation. And before I could even comprehend it, they faded away, leaving behind an ethereal glow, which softened, then dissolved into blackness.

Suddenly, my whole world was whirling, and nothing could stop it. It was as if I were a child on a swing going round and round and round. I tried to walk toward Nanaea but crashed against the wall and stumbled over a retching girl. I fell on the sandstone tiles of the tomb's floor within arm's reach of Nasu, and the dagger fell out of my grasp and skidded away into the dark. As I held my hand over his mouth to check for breath, I felt myself plunging into a black hole. My head dropped onto something warm and solid—maybe a shoulder or an arm—and when I looked up, the shining white face of the Boatman hovered over my body.

CHAPTER 27

THE RAIN MARCHES in over the ridge on clouds as black as night. I am standing in a field bursting with yellow chamomile flowers, their golden, dancing brightness contrasting sharply with the dark clouds hovering overhead. They bend and dance and bob in the winds pushing the rainstorm in my direction. Behind me, the sunshine is warm on my back, while in front of me, the wind blows cold.

My whole family is here.

Abum, his bristly beard streaked with white, bounces a baby girl on his shoulders. Her hair is brunette and curly like Kasha's, and when she smiles, two teeth peek out at me from pink rosebud lips. Her name is Belessa.

Kasha runs by, chasing a black and white pup I've seen running around the city, its ribs sticking out, its tail tucked between spindly legs. Today, the pup runs freely, rich in body and bright in eyes. Kasha throws a stick, and the dog races to fetch it. Coming up from the ridge, her head encircled by wildflowers, Nanaea plucks sprigs of chamomile, bending and twisting them into a crown. She walks up to me tentatively, then places it on my head when it is finished. I utter a thank-you, hardly believing she's forgiven me for ignoring her this past moon, when she grips me fiercely in a hug, then races off, beaming.

From behind, warm hands caress my face, and a sweet, familiar scent wafts around me. I turn, and my ummum appears, her skin glowing. Radiant. Her blue shawl is tucked around her shoulders. She takes my face in her hands, rests her forehead against mine, and kisses me on both cheeks, the honeyed scent of her filling me to the brim. I pull her into my arms.

After a moment, she steps back.

"You forgot something." She pulls a beating heart from her pocket. She lets it go, and it hovers in the air between us like a bird, filled with life and blood, its thumps louder than everyone and everything else in the field. Shocked, I look down at my chest and notice, for the first time, a gaping hole where my heart should be.

"You'll need to heal that," my abum calls as he dips and spins my little sister.

"Yes, Abum." I reach out and take a firm hold of my warm heart. It pulses steadily in my palm as I watch in wonder. Then, carefully, oh so carefully, I tuck it back into my chest, behind my breastbone. My wound closes, and all at once, blood surges through my veins. It flows, sending warmth to my fingers, a spring to my feet, a bubbling glow to my cheeks.

And then the rainstorm is upon us.

My ummum grabs Nanaea's hand, and they shriek with laughter, dancing around in the shower while my abum takes Belessa from his shoulders and covers her with his cloak. Kasha and the pup run in circles, their mouths open to the rain, drinking as much as they can.

And I?

I lift my face to the rain, too, and feel it cleansing me, inside and out, like a new baby being washed after birth.

✿ ✿ ✿ ✿ ✿

"She's coming around."

The statement came from underwater. I reached blindly toward the source.

"She is! She's coming around!" Chilled raindrops plipped softly against my face. A cool breeze washed over me from head to toe. I struggled to open eyes that felt sealed with wax.

"Get another flagon of water!" someone whispered. "Quickly!"

My hands searched for whoever was speaking. They brushed against warm, broad shoulders. Moved upward to the wiry scratchiness of a beard. With all the strength in me, I managed to pry open one of my eyes. Dagan's face swam in front of mine. I blinked, trying to clear my foggy vision.

"Kammani's awake," he said to someone over my shoulder. "She's awake!"

And then the face of my little brother appeared. My hands

buried themselves in his soft curls. "Where's your dog?" I asked, not certain where that thing had gone. I pushed myself up on my elbows. "Where's Abum?" I asked. "Ummum?" Stars glowed in the black night sky. I was in one of the farmer's fields. Green foliage blanketed us on every side, reaching, it seemed, all the way up to the heavens. "Why are we here?" I shivered as the wind picked up.

"Thank Enlil above." The words came from over my shoulder. Iltani squatted into my field of vision, the full moon shining brightly behind her. "Kammani, you're safe. It's okay." She wrapped me in a warm, scratchy blanket that smelled of smoke.

And with the scent, everything came rushing back to me all at once. "Nanaea!" I screamed.

A warm hand caressed my cheek. Dagan shook his head cautiously. "Be quiet, love. We are in hiding. Your sister is safe." He nodded in the direction of a small tent that had been erected over the top of a pushcart. "She's over there. My ummum is with them. They're all fine. All of them."

But I didn't believe it. I pushed myself up to my feet. "I want to see her." I realized my mistake as I was falling: My cast. My leg was broken. Dagan caught me before I fell and carried me over to the tent, with Iltani and Kasha trailing after us. I leaned into his chest, light-headed, not quite believing that any of this was real. Shiptu's murmurs grew in volume as we approached.

Dagan set me gently on the cart, and I pulled aside a black

drape to see all four girls lying enshrouded in blankets from the farm. Shiptu smoothed my cheek with a cool hand when she saw me, then kissed me on my forehead. "You're all right. I was worried when you weren't coming around."

The girls moaned on their cots. "They're alive?" I pulled the scratchy coverlet tighter around my shoulders.

She nodded.

My eyes closed; my tears fell, and I let them come. I'd tried so hard to keep my sister safe. And, somehow, I'd managed. "The plan worked?" I asked her after a few moments.

She nodded to Dagan, who stood behind me, one hand resting on my back. "Two of my closest field hands and I took a mattock to the back of the tomb." He rubbed my back as I shifted to better see him. "We made a hole big enough to fit through and then carried all of you out. I paid them to patch it back up. So—yes, sweet. Your plan worked."

"What did you do about the guardsmen in front of the tomb?" I asked, wiping the tears from my cheeks with the blanket.

Iltani spoke. "Well, guardsmen can be bought off."

Next to her, Kasha rolled his eyes. "Don't even tell me you kissed them."

She smirked. "Actually, I didn't, but I should have. The one on the left was devastatingly handsome."

Shiptu chuckled as she bent over Nanaea.

"We hid when everyone left the burial grounds, then Dagan and I snuck back in. Two guardsmen were standing there, and for a handful of minas, they looked the other way." She nudged Kasha with her elbow. "Not everyone is as honorable as that Nasu."

"Nasu!" Frantically, I turned this way and that. "Where is he? Did he—" My hands flew to my mouth. If Dagan had left him in the tomb, he would have suffocated by now. I wasn't certain how I felt about that. Part of me would be relieved. He'd tried to kill me! But another part of me would feel awful. He *had* helped me again and again, and he'd only wanted to save his family. He simply valued his honor more than he valued me. My gut tensed. I reached to my throat where he'd been trying to slit it. A clay poultice had been applied.

Dagan stared into my eyes, his jaw flexing. "Nasu is alive, but I've tied him in an outbuilding at the farm until I can figure out what to do with him. He was, um— When we found you two, you were—" He shook his head and looked at his ummum. She sent him a reproachful look.

"What? What happened?"

"You were in Nasu's arms when we found you." Iltani nonchalantly inspected the beds of her nails. Kasha looked from me to Iltani to Dagan and back to me.

"I was?" My hand flew to my collarbone. I nearly choked when I remembered the kiss. "Look, not only was I about to die, but he was going to slit my throat. I kissed him to try to give him the poppy."

Dagan leaned closer to me. "You owe no one an explanation for anything. Please, don't feel as if you do."

I swallowed the lump in my throat. "I don't care for him."

"I am just happy you're alive." He kissed my forehead, then nudged me forward. "Nanaea's been asking for you."

I turned to Shiptu. "Can I talk to her?"

"Of course. They're all going to be fine."

I scooted farther onto the cart and bent over Nanaea's curly hair. She reeked of vomit, but her eyes were clear, if pained. She reached a shaky hand up to my face. "Shiptu says I will live, but I don't feel like I will. It hurts so much. So very much."

Immediately, I began to cry. "Nanaea, my sister. My family. I was terrified for you," I whispered. "I didn't know if you would live." I took her hand and held it in my own. Kissed it and let my tears fall. "I'm so sorry. I can care for you now. I will make the hurt go away. Let me get my healing satchel. . . ." I looked around the cart to see if it was there. It was propped in the corner, open, the contents a mess. I reached for it, but Nanaea grabbed me fervently.

"Kammani. You *saved* me. What you did in that tomb was"—she searched for the right word—"incredible. I always laughed at you, following Abum around like a duckling, thinking you were some great A-zu, but I didn't realize how great an A-zu you actually are. You saved us *all*." She winced and turned her head.

I leaned down and kissed the top of her head, tears coursing down my face. "Ahh, my sweet, I couldn't let you go. It would have killed me to see you cross over."

"In the end, I didn't want to die, even to see Ummum. I was afraid."

"I know, Nanaea." I pulled her to me and rocked her like a babe. My sister. My lovely, infuriating, amazing sister. "I am so sorry for the way I treated you this past moon. I didn't understand why you wanted to be a Sacred Maiden. I know how much you loved Ummum, and I"—I choked on my words—"I'm so sorry she's gone."

A smile flickered across her face. "And I like pretty things," she whispered.

I laughed then, a belly laugh that was full of tears and relief and joy and the miracle of having her in my life. "Yes, you do."

I kissed her cheek, and laid her gently back down on her side so she could rest. "Shiptu, would you hand me my satchel? I want to give her a tincture."

"Yes, of course." Shiptu lifted my bag and leaned over to hand it to me. "I went through it, but I didn't know everything you'd mixed, and many of the vials were empty, so I was careful when I gave things to the girls."

"Thank you so much. We are all so lucky you were here to help us. It's almost like having my abum with me." I took my bag from her.

"No, not like your abum, although I did learn from him." Shiptu helped Huna sit up to take a sip of water from a flagon. "I learned so much from him."

"You did?"

"Yes." Shiptu wiped a drop of water from Huna's chin, then set the flagon down as Huna groaned, then fell, panting, onto her side.

"You studied under my abum? I never knew that."

"I didn't study *under* him, I studied *with* him under his father, for a while. Then life happened, and later I married Dagan's abum, and here we are." Her face flushed, and she folded a linen cloth and set it aside.

"You loved my father, didn't you?" Nanaea's voice was muffled by the blanket.

I looked in incomprehension at Shiptu. "Nanaea, don't be silly—"

But Shiptu nodded slowly. "I did. I certainly did."

My mouth fell open. "You *loved* him? As . . . as . . . as a woman?"

"Yes." She nodded, smiling softly, her eyes lost in reminiscence. "A long time ago."

"But you didn't marry him."

She leaned over to grab a tincture—it smelled like peppermint—and pinched a bit into Huna's mouth. "I never told him. I kept quiet. Then one day, my oldest friend, my truest love—your father, Shalim—told me he had arranged to marry Ku-aya, your mother, and that was the end of that."

Somehow, I thought that wasn't all there was to it, but I let it go. "But you married afterward and found happiness, did you not?"

She smiled. "Eventually. My abum arranged a marriage with Dagan's father, and I grew to love him, and continued to love him after he passed. But there is something special about your first love. There is." She smiled at me, then bent to care for Nin Arwia.

I looked behind me at Dagan, who had left to fetch a flagon of water and was now returning across the field. His amber eyes caught mine. His smile was sure, and as I studied his easy stride, radiating confidence and strength, I felt Shiptu's message resonating deep within my bones.

"Yes, Shiptu. I believe you are right. There *is* something special about your first love."

CHAPTER 28

꧁❀꧂

DAGAN WALKED MUTELY beside me, the dagger at his waist gleaming in the morning sunlight. He wasn't happy about any of this, but I was not about to be deterred for another day. Barley fields that reached all the way to the Garadun waved softly in the breeze. My good foot, wet from the dew-soaked grasses, slid in my sandal as we neared the outbuilding. He'd wanted to carry me, but I'd insisted on using the crutches. Now I was regretting the decision, although I didn't care to admit it. I paused to catch my breath.

"Will you please leave the door open so I can see in there, at least?"

I wiped the sweat from my lip with the back of my hand. "I will—and I have this anyway." I patted the dagger he'd placed in my belt.

"Are you certain you're fine?"

I exhaled heavily. "Yes, of course. He's tied up, thanks to you. What could he possibly do?"

"You never know with him. Slit your throat? Kiss you? It's difficult to tell."

I sent him a reproachful look, and he grinned back at me, the mischievous boy with whom I used to play in the fields still present in his eyes.

"I just need to speak with him. Alone. That's all." I searched his handsome face.

He nodded. "I know. I'm sure you have *many* things you need to discuss."

"Dagan, please."

He held up his hands. "I said I wouldn't listen in, and I won't. But I will be watching. Your safety is my only concern."

"Your *only* concern?"

He grimaced, crossing his arms casually. "I don't want to think about anything else."

"You don't have to *worry* about anything else, okay?" I reached out a hand and took his in mine.

He squeezed it. "I'm just relieved to have you here on this side of the Netherworld. That's all." He winked at me, and my throat tightened at the impossibility of his good looks. How had I ever been immune to him?

"Well, I am glad to be here, too, breathing in this air and basking in this glorious sunshine." I held my hands up to the sky and breathed in the heady scent of the turned earth in the fields beyond. "And when I am through chatting with Nasu, you can tell me all about how relieved you are." I winked back at him, and he grinned so wide, his face nearly split in two. He strolled to the shade of a nearby olive grove and took his dagger from his sheath. The sun filtered through the branches, sending dappled morning light onto his bare shoulders. His hair, still wet from a wash, was slicked black in a knot. I tore my eyes from his and walked away.

Toward Nasu.

I creaked open the door into the outbuilding to see that Dagan had Nasu strung up like a side of meat. His face was blotchy, shadowed by the makings of a full beard. He squinted into the light of the open doorway, the sunshine of the morning chasing away the shadows.

I'd never seen him so unkempt.

His tunic was filthy, his hair a mess. His eyes were hollow, as if he'd experienced a tragedy. I supposed, in a way, he had. He'd lost some of the reserve he'd kept so carefully tended, and as someone who'd recently had a little bit of an awakening herself, I knew how unhinged it could make you feel.

"Nasu?" My crutches rubbed against the insides of my arms. I'd have to apply more salve to soothe the rawness. Probably the same salve I would have to put on Nasu's wrists, since Dagan had tied him so tightly. It had been two days since we'd arrived at the farm, and this was the first opportunity I'd been afforded to see Nasu. Dagan wouldn't even tell me which outbuilding he was in before, because he knew I'd seek him out, but I'd pestered him repeatedly until he finally relented.

"Hello, Kammani."

"Oh!" I startled as Nin Arwia emerged from the shadows, holding a cask of chilled water and a platter of diced apples and smoked trout. Her hair trailed behind her in a braid as long as a rope, and her dress was a simple homespun tunic made with goat-hair threads. The only thing fine about her was her sandals. Otherwise, she looked like an ordinary girl.

"Well, isn't this an honor. Nasu, a humble servant of the throne, being served by the Sarratum of Alu."

She smiled. "I got here right before you. I've brought him food and water, since it appears Dagan intends to starve him." As she picked up a slice of apple, she shook her head. "And no, I am not the sarratum." She nodded to Nasu. "This one has been trying to convince me of the same. But what you both fail to remember is that Ensi Uruku thinks we're dead. I am in no position to make a claim to the throne. He'd kill us all if he knew we escaped."

I thought of the missing antidote. I hoped Uruku believed that by stealing it—or dispatching someone else to do so— he had sealed our fates in that tomb.

"But you're the nin," Nasu interjected with a groan. "The throne is rightfully yours." He hung his head, exasperated. It appeared they'd been speaking on the subject at length already.

"I know." She placed a slice of apple in Nasu's open mouth. "And one day, perhaps I will make a claim."

"When? After Ensi Uruku and Gudanna start bashing in the teeth of even more poor women?" I asked. It unnerved me that she could so willingly abandon her people. I'd done everything in my power to save mine. And would do it again.

Her eyes flashed dangerously. "I never wanted that to happen."

"Inaction can be just as bad as the wrong action, Nin."

"Well, for now, I'm concerned about staying alive." She paused, slicing off a piece of the smoked trout. Beside her, Nasu eyed it brazenly, like a dog panting after a bone. "I realize that it's important now."

"So you're not angry with me?" I asked tentatively. We hadn't talked much since we'd been freed. She'd only just yesterday gotten to her feet.

She turned to me. "For what? For saving my life though I tried to take yours?"

"Yes!" I exclaimed, hobbling over the threshold and lowering myself gently onto a stool. "You wanted to go with your abum to the Netherworld. I guess you and Nanaea both thought that was an excellent plan."

She pursed her lips ruefully. "I did, but I no longer do. I was distraught and overwhelmed. Everyone who truly loved me was gone, and I was supposed to run this great city alone." She lifted the bite to Nasu's mouth, and he eagerly took it, chewing and swallowing quickly.

"More," he demanded softly.

"Has Dagan been starving you?" I demanded. I looked out at a stoic Dagan, who stood with hands on hips. He shrugged his big shoulders.

Nasu laughed bleakly around another bite of smoked fish Nin Arwia stuffed into his mouth. "Well, I tried to kill you, so I imagine he's not so happy with me." Nin Arwia held the cup of water to his lips, and he drank greedily, gulping until it ran down his chin. "I guess both Nin Arwia and I tried to send you to the Netherworld."

"You did." They'd tried, and even though it probably meant I was half out of my wits, I didn't hold it against them. I was simply grateful they hadn't succeeded.

Nin Arwia dropped her eyes, guilt all over her face. "I'll fetch some more water."

"Wait, Nin," I said.

She paused, her small hands clasped around the empty flagon.

"I want you to know I forgive you for sending me to the tomb, and I offer you my apologies for being cruel while I was in there. I wasn't . . . quite myself."

"You don't have to apologize. Honestly."

I grabbed the cup from her and set it aside, then took her hands in mine.

"Yes, I do. Your directive allowed me to save all of you in that tomb. And maybe I'm not even offering forgiveness or asking for yours to please you. Maybe part of it is for me. I let myself wallow in my heartache before, and it festered like a boil. As any good healer knows, it's better to lance it cleanly before it has time to set in and kill you. So let's forgive one another. I believe that what you said to me in the Palace could be true—we really could be great friends."

She nodded, tears filling her eyes. "I've never had a good friend before. Ever."

I grinned. "Well, you do now."

"I believe that with everything in me, Kammani. And I thank you." She released my hands and took up the cask. "I'll be right back."

She left, her face lifted to the morning sun, and I turned to Nasu, whose eyes held some inner distress.

"Your neck looks terrible."

"Thanks." I reached up a hand and rubbed a knuckle against the stitches. This time, I'd let Shiptu sew me up. "*Someone* tried to slit my throat."

His eyes fell. "I don't even know what to say to that, Kammani. 'I'm sorry' doesn't suffice."

"You're forgiven, too." I waved my hand. "I know why you did it."

I'd meant what I'd said to Nin Arwia. Letting go of anguish meant forgiving those who'd caused it in the first place. "That doesn't mean I'm not wary around you, because I now understand that your family is first, your duty is second, and the rest of us come after, but I realize you acted out of love. Not for me, but for your parents and siblings. I do understand that."

His face clouded over. "How will you ever trust me again?"

"It's a choice, I suppose. One I want to make."

"Well, how will I trust *you*? You poisoned me in the tomb." He lifted his brown eyes to mine accusingly.

"I did no such thing!"

"You gave me *some* sort of tincture. I saw"—his eyebrows furrowed in confusion—"a light."

And then I remembered. *The Boatman.* I'd seen the Boatman in the tomb! He'd taken the lugal to the Netherworld right in front of my eyes. My heart hammered as I thought of it, but I put the fear of that moment away. I wasn't in the grave anymore. I was safe. I didn't need to worry about that *ever* again. "It was poppy, Nasu. It can make you see strange things. Things that don't make sense." Easing his mind might help ease mine, too.

His face visibly relaxed, his shoulders sagging. "I felt as if I was dreaming."

"And maybe you were." *Maybe we both were.* "But the only thing that should concern you now is fleeing the city with us. We can't live undercover on the farm forever."

He shook his hands in the ropes binding him. "I may try my luck in hiding, but either option would best be accomplished by Dagan setting me free." He cast worried eyes at Dagan, who was staring into the outbuilding.

Leaning my crutches against the side wall, I pulled the blade from my belt.

"What are you doing, Healer?" He followed the blade with his eyes. Widened his stance.

Hopping closer to him, I reached up with my dagger. "Not every decision is Dagan's to make. I want you to remember that this is from *me*." I brought the blade up, and he flinched away from me, his eyes wary. "I thought you forgave me—" he started.

Then I sawed cleanly through the ropes binding his wrists.

He laughed in relief as he pulled his hands down to his waist, wincing as he rubbed his biceps. His shoulders.

"Kammani! What in Enlil's name are you doing?" Dagan jogged lightly toward me, his hand on his dagger.

I turned toward him. "I've handled worse situations than this, Dagan. I've got it."

Dagan stilled in his tracks, cautiously observing.

I turned back around and took hold of Nasu's hands, lowering my voice. "Thank you for helping me in the Palace before. I couldn't have escaped without you. And I never would have been able to stitch my head wound or search Nin Arwia's room without your help."

He smiled simply. "You're quite welcome, Healer."

"But this"—I reeled back and slapped him across the face as hard as I could, putting every bit of the terror I'd spent in the tomb at his behest behind it—"*this* is for kissing me and then cutting my throat, because *that* was a dirty trick."

Nasu reeled back, shocked. His hand flew to his face. "I... I... didn't..." he spluttered, his eyes bulging. I'd bet on the Boatman's bones he didn't see that one coming.

"Now." I smoothed my tunic over my hips. "Your wrists are chafed raw. But like any good healer, I have a remedy for that."

CHAPTER 29

One Moon Later.

"JUST FOLLOW THE river, Kammani."

"But how will we—"

"Let the great river guide you."

I looked into Shiptu's amber eyes, so much like Dagan's, fear gripping my innards with long, sharp talons. She'd been my healer, and a sort of mother this past moon while my leg had finished mending. I turned to scan the road behind me.

Where were Dagan and Iltani? Around me, hordes of huts massed against the wall. The long road I'd traveled to bring me to the gate lay like a tawny ribbon unfurled, with threads reaching out to various parts of the city.

I chewed on my thumbnail, squinting against the glare of the sun, then checked to be sure my healing satchel was still at my waist. It was. We stood at the north gate of Alu, possessions and provisions packed in bags and crates atop two donkeys. Our horses nibbled on the weeds along the wall. Kasha tossed a small sack of grain in the air alongside Nin Arwia and Simti. Nanaea, who wouldn't leave my side for the past moon, would not leave it again today.

"It's two hours past our meeting time. Where *are* they?" she asked.

"They'll be here." I pulled her hand into the crook of my arm and patted it with more reassurance than I felt. If Dagan or Iltani had been detained, I didn't know what I'd do.

Shiptu, brushing down one of our horses, caught my eye. "Stop worrying, you two."

She read me so easily. "I will try." I looked down the road again, then back to Shiptu. "You're certain you'll not come with us?"

"No, child." She took a long breath and expelled it in one heavy sigh. "I have far more sons to care for and many mouths to feed in this city." She tucked the brush in a saddlebag, then pulled me into her motherly arms and squeezed. When she pulled away from me, tears glistened in her eyes.

"Besides, this city is in turmoil. Lugal Uruku has been in the Palace executing the poor for small injustices. I need to help those around me when I can."

The thought that he lived, persecuted the poor, and even ruled this city, while my abum lay buried in an unmarked grave set my blood boiling. A murderer walked free, and right now, there was nothing to be done about it.

Perhaps someday I would get the chance.

"Kammani! We must go! We'll be caught by the guardsmen if we don't leave now." It was still strange to see Arwia in plain garb, her long hair tied back in braids, looking less like a queen and more like a girl I'd known every day of my life. She glanced behind me down the road.

An excited light had come into my little brother's eyes the moment I'd told him we'd have to leave the city. Uruku couldn't know we'd escaped the tomb, or he'd execute us all, so our only choice in a city as small as ours was to leave its walled protection and venture somewhere new. We couldn't stay holed up at the farm forever, and the watcher who was supposed to be caring for Kasha could be trusted to keep his mouth closed about his absence for only so long, as could the guardsmen who'd been watching the tomb.

I could see that the possibilities of excitement and freedom would barely keep Kasha seated on his mount as we journeyed. Simti, who'd alighted onto one of the horses, looked anxious. She fussed with her packs, adjusted the bridle, and looked over her shoulder idly, casting longing looks at the road that stretched in the early-morning haze beyond the gate. Huna sat, arrayed like a sarratum, on a fine white stallion her parents had given her, with packs of foodstuffs and casks of brew trailing behind on two donkeys. She hadn't stopped grumbling that we'd ruined her life since the second we'd pulled her out of the Boatman's arms, and I wished, for the hundredth time that day, that she would shut up.

"I know, Arwia. I know." It was still strange to address her by her name without the "Nin" attached. To me, she was, and always would be, royalty. But she'd insisted. "We'll leave as soon as they get here."

"They will come," said Shiptu. She stuffed an array of smoked meats, walnuts, and dried fruits into a saddlebag. "They are securing more mounts or provisions. Be as patient for my son as he has been for you."

I was patient but *nervous*. If Dagan and Iltani had been killed or hurt, it might break me. I needed them. More than ever. I had no idea what sort of mischief they were pulling, but it probably wasn't worth the risk. Before me, the city of Alu lay like a cat basking in the sunshine. The Palace stood to my right, shining in all its splendor. A thin line of smoke trailed from one of the Temple windows, and I said a prayer to Enlil for a safe journey.

Shielding my eyes from the sun, I squinted into the distance. A disturbance on the road captured my attention. There it was! Dust kicking up!

"Shiptu! Look!"

She looked at the commotion, her hands on her thin hips.

"I told you. Never doubt the trueness of my son. He will never disappoint you."

From the direction of the Palace, the frantic forms of three riders galloping on horseback appeared like a mirage.

"Three? Who is the third rider?" Arwia asked, shading her eyes with her hand, too.

"I guess we'll see," I murmured.

As the trio galloped to us, growing larger and larger, I recognized the lanky frame and noble set of a particular guardsman. They rode up to the gate, their faces glistening with sweat, the highborn face of Nasu greeting me with a nod of his head.

"Thank Enlil above." I took in each of their faces.

Breathless, Iltani slid down from her horse and wrapped me and Nanaea in a hug that was entirely too tight. "My friends, you've no idea what pains we've taken to secure these additional mounts. But now we have them, thanks to some misdirection"—she waggled her eyebrows—"and some muscle."

"And Nasu finally agreed to come, when I convinced him his family would be killed if they knew he was alive and kept it from the lugal," said Dagan. "Uruku is showing very little mercy these days." He dismounted gracefully, the perfect specimen of ease and fearlessness. Nasu stayed on his horse, a line of worry between his black brows.

"Did you hear what happened to Lamusa?" said Iltani. "Uruku hung him up by his feet for not bowing low enough during the coronation parade!" She tucked several tattered bags into the donkeys' packs.

"I hadn't heard, but I'm not surprised," I said as Dagan walked over to me, wiping his hands on his midnight-blue tunic. He greeted me with a kiss on my cheek and an extra one on my forehead. As it had been doing of late, my heart flipped over, and I very nearly swooned on my feet.

"So . . . is there a wedding coming soon?" Nanaea whispered into my ear, her deep brown eyes luminous with mirth.

"We shall see, Nanaea. We shall see." I bumped her in the shoulder, my heart flipping over at the thought.

"You ready?" Dagan asked, tucking a coin purse near the dagger at his waist. His eyes met mine.

"I am now. You're all here." I looked at each of them. Nasu, sitting tall and proud. Iltani, in her oversized blue tunic. Dagan, looking for all the world as if he could handle *anything* we met on the road beyond this city. "And that's all I really need."

"Assata has sent some more provisions, too. And sikaru." Dagan hoisted a large barrel of the drink like it was a feather-stuffed pillow and secured it to one of the donkeys' backs. "She, Irra, and Warad, her son, bid us a safe trip to our destination, wherever that may be."

"And when you arrive"—Shiptu swallowed with some difficulty—"you will send word to me so I won't worry myself sick."

Dagan nodded, then bent and kissed her cheek. "Ummum, I swear it. Now we better get on, while the dawn is breaking."

"Yes, it's time." With the ease of many years of practice, Arwia mounted her horse and dug her heels into its sides. And she was gone, out the gate and on the road before we could stop her. Huna followed, the donkeys trailing balefully behind. Nasu took off after them both, riding easily, his sicklesword gleaming in the sun. I supposed his instinct to protect the royal family wouldn't be shed so easily. Maybe that was a good thing.

I mounted my own horse with the help of Dagan's sure hands, my leg still aching after weeks of disuse, then he handed Nanaea up behind me. He alighted next to me on his own chestnut mare, pulled Kasha up behind him, then warily checked the horizon. He nodded for me to go ahead of him, dug in his heels, and we took off after Nasu and Arwia. Iltani and Simti followed closely behind, chatting across the backs of their mounts.

As we passed through the gate and crossed the heavy wooden bridge that would lead us from the city, I turned for one last look at the only place I'd ever known as home, allowing Dagan to pull ahead. I sent a kiss back toward Shiptu. To the little hovels along the wall, remembering my ummum. My abum. My sister named Belessa.

Mounted on a frisky white stallion with a heather-gray tail, Iltani rode up next to us, the reins firm in her hand, laughing her head off about something or other.

"What's so funny?" I called to her. The tight feeling under my rib cage at the memories I was leaving behind released as I caught her dimpled smirk. I couldn't stop myself from grinning back.

"Simti and I were talking, Healer's Daughter." She shook her hair out of her face as her eyes twinkled. "Since you've kissed two grown men now, will you be adding to that number in our adventures outside these walls?"

"Iltani!" I shrieked.

Behind me, Nanaea laughed and squeezed me tight, my mother's blue shawl wrapped around her shoulders.

"Iltani, one day that mouth will be the end of you." I smiled so hard, my cheeks hurt.

She snickered, smacked the horse's flanks with a loud "Get up!" and took off, kicking up dust.

As she rode away toward the river, I bubbled over with joy. My family and friends were safe, and my healing satchel was at my waist, restocked with tried-and-true tinctures and a few I'd never used, those that had sat long on a shelf in Shiptu's outbuilding. And although I didn't know all their medicinal properties, in the new city—wherever that was—I was going to find an A-zu who could teach me. I was going to drink my fill from their cup, so never again would I have to say goodbye because of something I didn't know. Ahead of me, Nasu and Dagan rode easily next to each other, pointing down the road, gesturing to a map.

"You ready?" I closed my satchel and looked over my shoulder at Nanaea.

"For whatever is ahead, Sister!"

At that, I dug my heels into the sides of the mount as I'd watched Arwia do. My horse leapt forward eagerly into a gallop, pulling ahead of the group. The wind whipped my hair into a fury as Nanaea and I raced, laughing, breathless, toward the road stretched beyond.

ACKNOWLEDGMENTS

In middle school, I used to read eleven books a week—lounging on my bed, ankle over my knee—losing myself in the wonder of words. Although I dreamed about being an author one day, only after many people lent me their brainpower did that hope solidify into the rectangle you hold in your hands right now.

It's with humility and tearful astonishment (I'm actually crying as I type this) that I offer my heartfelt thanks to every person who assisted that middle-school girl achieve her wildest dream.

Kari Sutherland, the first member of the #magnificentKs, the most magical unicorn of all agents, thank you for taking a chance on a writer who'd been rejected too many times to count. Your brilliant guidance gave Kammani a heart, and as I reshaped her into someone a little less direct (heh), I found myself admiring the compassion you breathed into her almost as much as I admire you.

Kelsey M. Horton, the esteemed leader of the #magnificentKs, who cut me zero slack, called me out, and cheered me on, thank you for inspiring me to take a closer look at the details. Your guidance directed me beyond my self-inflicted borders, and your savvy intuition and heartfelt praise were *just* what this story, and this author, needed.

To the entire Delacorte Press team, I'm honored to be counted as one of your authors. Special thanks to copy editors Colleen Fellingham and Candice Gianetti; to Sammy Yuen and Alison Impey in design; to Cayla Rasi, Elizabeth Ward, Kate Keating, and Amanda Smith in digital; to Janine Perez in marketing; to Elena Meuse in publicity; to Kim Lauber in sales for loving the book; and of course, to Beverly Horowitz and Barbara Marcus.

Writing used to be a solitary expedition for me, but I'm eternally grateful I'm not slogging along that lonely path anymore. To Heather Christie, my original ride-or-die critique partner and friend, thank you for your incredible insight in helping me shape this story and all the rest to come. To Calvin Dillon, your creative genius and absolute loyalty mean the entire alien universe to me. To Lillian Clark, I will forever be inspired by your dazzling mind and our petty texts.

Erin Hahn, Jennifer Dugan, Gita Trelease, Heather Kassner, and Gabrielle Byrne, we'll always have the beach and DMs for the rough days. Thank you for your constant kindness and jokes and shoulders when I need them. My Tiny

Peas—L. D. Crichton, Victoria Lee, RuthAnne Snow, Keena Roberts, Nikki Barthelmess, Kara McDowell, Claire Eliza Bartlett, and Jennifer Camiccia—our little pod means more to me than you know. To Kell's Skeleton Crew, I'm #blessed you're on this ride with me and pleasantly shocked you decided to jump on board.

To the Class2K19 authors I haven't already mentioned— Sarah Lyu, Erin Stewart, Alexandra Villasante, Tiana Smith, Quinn Sosna-Spear, Naomi Milliner, Gail Shepherd, Katy Loutzenhiser, Sara Faring, and J. Kasper Kramer—I'm proud you even let me be on your team. My sensitivity readers, Delacorte Mavens, and fellow Novel19s, you inspire me to try harder and write better, and I so appreciate your generous spirits and love.

Betty and Hez, you already know what your support means to me, but in case I don't say it enough, it's here. Rose, my MTC moms, and Moms Gone WOD, your inquisitiveness about my writing process and encouragement when I'm blabbing on and on has gotten me through more rough days than you know. Emily Hussin, I couldn't have written this book without you.

Mike and Tony, thanks for shutting down my bad ideas and endlessly brainstorming with me. (Why are titles so hard?) Mom, thank you for feeding my insatiable reading addiction and buying me Pulitzer winners to keep me inspired. Dad, thank you for teaching me the discipline I needed to sit my butt in a chair and keep working until the job is done. Lacey and Kimmy, Nanaea exists because of you.

My Matt, I'm lucky you decided to kiss me. And keep kissing me. There will never be a day when I'm not grateful I'm the recipient of your love. To Brady, Kaden, and Brennan, I'm a better person because you exist. Thank you for teaching your momma patience and for bringing me so much joy.

And finally, to my readers, you made the dreams of a little twelve-year-old girl who sat in her room, read books, and daydreamed about this very moment come true. You can't know just how much that means to me. Truly, I will be forever grateful.

ABOUT THE AUTHOR

Kelly Coon is an editor for Blue Ocean Brain, a former high school English teacher, and a wicked karaoke singer in training. She adores giving female characters the chance to flex their muscles and use their brains. She lives near Tampa with her three sons, her brilliant husband, and a rescue pup who will steal your sandwich. *Gravemaidens* is her debut novel.

kellycoon.com
@kellycoon106